A

Abby Green spen[...] romances. She then [...] Film and TV indus[...] day while standing [...] she thought: there has to be more than this. So, she sent off a partial to Mills & Boon. After many rewrites, they accepted her first book and an author was born. She lives in Dublin, Ireland and you can find out more here: abby-green.com

Maisey Yates is a *New York Times* bestselling author of over one hundred romance novels. Whether she's writing strong, hardworking cowboys, dissolute princes or multigenerational family stories, she loves getting lost in fictional worlds. An avid knitter with a dangerous yarn addiction and an aversion to housework, Maisey lives with her husband and three kids in rural Oregon. Check out her website, maiseyyates.com or find her on Facebook.

USA TODAY bestselling author **Joanne Rock** credits her decision to write romance to a book she picked up during a flight delay that engrossed her so thoroughly, she didn't mind at all when her flight was delayed two more times. Giving her readers the chance to escape into another world has motivated her to write over one hundred books for a variety of Mills & Boon series.

One Night...

One Night...
for Revenge

ABBY GREEN

MAISEY YATES

JOANNE ROCK

MILLS & BOON

First Published in Great Britain 2022
By Mills & Boon, an imprint of HarperCollins*Publishers*, Ltd
1 London Bridge Street, London, SE1 9GF

www.harpercollins.co.uk

HarperCollins*Publishers*
1st Floor, Watermarque Building,
Ringsend Road, Dublin 4, Ireland

ISBN: 978-0-263-30579-1

This book is produced from independently certified FSC™ paper
to ensure responsible forest management.

For more information visit: www.harpercollins.co.uk/green

Printed and Bound in Spain using 100% Renewable electricity at
CPI Black Print, Barcelona

ONE NIGHT WITH THE ENEMY

ABBY GREEN

CHAPTER ONE

MADDIE Vasquez stood in the shadows like a fugitive. Just yards away the plushest hotel in Mendoza rose in all its majestic colonial glory to face the imposing Plaza Indepencia. She reassured herself that she wasn't actually a fugitive. She was just collecting herself... She could see the calibre of the crowd going into the foyer: monied and exclusive. The elite of Mendoza society.

The evening was melting into night and lights twinkled in bushes and trees nearby, lending the scene a fairy-tale air. Maddie's soft mouth firmed and she tried to quell her staccato heartbeat. It had been a long time since she'd believed in fairy tales—if ever. She'd never harboured illusions about the dreamier side of life. A mother who saw you only as an accessory to be dressed up and paraded like a doll and a father who resented you for not being the son he'd lost would do that to a child.

Maddie shook her head, as if that could shake free the sudden melancholy assailing her, and at the same time her eye was caught by the almost silent arrival of a low-slung silver vehicle at the bottom of the main steps leading up to the hotel. Instinctively she drew back more. The car was clearly vintage and astronomically expensive. Her mouth dried and her palms grew sweaty—would it be...?

The door was opened by a uniformed hotel doorman and a tall shape uncurled from the driving seat.

It was him.

Her heart stopped beating for a long moment.

Nicolás Cristobal de Rojas. The most successful vintner in Mendoza—and probably all of Argentina by now. Not to mention his expansion into French Bordeaux country, which ensured he had two vintages a year. In the notoriously fickle world of winemaking the de Rojas estate profits had tripled and quadrupled in recent years, and success oozed from every inch of his six-foot-four, broad-shouldered frame.

He was dressed in a black tuxedo, and Maddie could see his gorgeous yet stern and arrogant features as he cast a bored-looking glance around him. It skipped over where she was hiding like a thief, and when he looked away her heart stuttered back to life.

She dragged in a breath. She'd forgotten how startling his blue eyes were. He looked leaner. Darker. Sexier. His distinctive dark blond hair had always made it easy to mark him out from the crowd—not that his sheer charisma and good looks wouldn't have marked him out anyway. He'd always been more than his looks…he'd always carried a tangible aura of power and sexual energy.

Another flash of movement made her drag her eyes away, and she saw a tall blonde beauty emerging from the other side of the car, helped by the conscientious doorman. As Maddie watched, the woman walked around to his side, her long fall of blonde hair shining almost as much as the floor-length silver lamé dress which outlined every slim curve of her body with a loving touch.

The woman linked her arm through his. Maddie couldn't see the look they shared, but from the smile on the woman's face she didn't doubt it was *hot*. A sudden shaft of physical pain lanced her and Maddie put a hand to her belly in reaction. *No,* she begged mentally. She didn't want him to affect her like this. She didn't want him to affect her at all.

She'd wasted long teenage years dreaming about him, lusting after him, building daydreams around him. And that foolish dreaming had culminated in catastrophe and a fresh deepening of the generations-old hostility between their families. It had caused the rift to end all rifts. It had broken her own family apart. She'd realised all of her most fervent fantasies—but had also been thrown into a nightmare of horrific revelations.

The last time she'd seen Nicolás Cristobal de Rojas had been a few years ago, in a club in London. Their eyes had clashed across the thronged room, and she'd never forget the look of pure loathing on his face before he'd turned away and disappeared.

Sucking in deep breaths and praying for control, Maddie squared her shoulders. She couldn't lurk in the shadows all night. She'd come to tell Nicolás Cristobal de Rojas that she was home and had no intention of selling out to him. Not now or ever. She held the long legacy of her family in her hands and it would not die with her. He had to know that—or he might put the same pressure on her as he'd done to her father, taking advantage of his physical and emotional weakness to encourage him to sell to his vastly more successful neighbour.

As much as she'd have loved to hide behind solicitors' letters, she couldn't afford to pay the legal fees. And she didn't want de Rojas to think she was too scared to confront him herself. She tried to block out the last cataclysmic meeting they'd had—if she went down that road now she'd turn around for sure. She had to focus on the present. And the future.

She knew better than anyone just how ruthless the de Rojas family could be, but even she had blanched at the pressure Nicolás de Rojas had put on an ailing man. It was the kind of thing she'd have expected of his father, but somehow, despite everything, not of Nicolás...*more fool her.* She of all people should have known what to expect.

With a shaking hand she smoothed down the glittery black dress she wore. Maddie's meagre budget since she'd left Argentina hadn't run to buying party dresses. Tonight was the prestigious annual Mendoza Vintners' Dinner, and she wouldn't have been able to get close to the place if she didn't look the part. Luckily she'd found some of her mother's dresses that her father hadn't destroyed in his rage eight years before...

At first it had looked modest enough—high-necked at the front. It was only when she'd had it on, aware that if she didn't leave soon she'd miss her window of opportunity, that she'd realised it was backless—to just above her buttocks. All her mother's other dresses needed serious dry-cleaning. This one had somehow miraculously been protected in a plastic covering. So it was this dress or nothing.

Maddie just wished that her mother had been less flamboyant—and taller. Maddie was five foot nine and the dress ended around her mid-thigh, showing lots of pale leg. Her unusual colouring of black hair, green eyes and pale skin was courtesy of a great-great-grandmother who had come to Argentina with a wave of Irish immigrants and subsequently married into the Vasquez family.

So now, as she finally stepped from the shadows outside the hotel and the gentle breeze whistled over her bare flesh, she felt ridiculously exposed. Mustering all the courage she would need for this encounter, she valiantly ignored the double-take glances of recognition she drew, and strode into the luxurious marbled lobby.

Nicolás Cristobal de Rojas stifled a yawn. He'd been working around the clock to ensure this year's grapes would be ready to pick soon. After a mercurial summer, they would either have one of the best vintages on their hands or the worst. He grimaced slightly. He knew bringing in his vintage wasn't the only excuse for driving himself like a demon. That work ethic was buried deep in his fraught childhood.

'Really, darling,' came a dry voice to his right, 'am I that boring?'

Nic forced his attention back into the room and looked down at his date. He quirked a mocking smile. 'Never.'

His blonde companion squeezed his arm playfully, 'I think the ennui is getting to you, Nic. You need to go to Buenos Aires and have some fun—I don't know how you stand it in this backwater.' She shuddered theatrically, then said something about going to the powder room and disappeared with a sexy sway to her walk.

Nic was relieved to be immune to this very feminine display, and watched as male heads swivelled to watch her progress. He shook his head ruefully and thanked his lucky stars that Estella's presence tonight might at least temporarily stave off the more determined of the Mendoza man-eaters. He was in no mood to humour the mercenary women he attracted in droves. His last lover had screamed hysterically at him for an hour and accused him of having no heart or soul. He had no desire to head down *that* path again any time soon.

He could do without sex if that was going to be the outcome. If truth be told, his last sexual encounters had all felt curiously…empty. Satisfying on one level only. And as for a more long-term relationship? He certainly had no intention of even thinking about that. The toxic relationship of his parents had cautioned him from an early age. He was going to choose a long-term partner with extreme care and diligence. Naturally there *would* be a long-term partner at some point in the future; he had a valuable legacy to pass on to the next generation, and he had no intention of breaking the precious cycle of inheritance.

Just then he saw a figure appear in the doorway to the ballroom. Inexplicably his skin tightened over his bones and the back of his neck prickled—the same way it had just now outside the hotel, when he'd felt as if he was being watched.

He couldn't make out the woman's features. He could only make out long, long shapely pale legs and a glittering short black dress which outlined a slender figure. But something about her was instantly *familiar*. In his gut. Midnight-black wavy hair was swept over one shoulder—and then he saw her head turn. Even from where he stood he could see a stillness enter her frame, and then she started to walk…directly towards him.

Ridiculously Nic felt the need to turn and leave. But he stood his ground. As she came closer and closer, weaving through the crowd, suspicion grew and formed in his head. *It couldn't be,* he told himself. *It's been years…she was in London.*

He was barely aware of the hushed murmurs surrounding him, growing louder as the woman finally came to a stop just a few feet away. Recognition and incredulity warred in his head. Along with the realisation that she was *stunning*. She had always been beautiful—slightly ethereal—but she'd matured into a true beauty since he'd seen her last. She was statuesque and slender and curvaceous all at once. An intoxicating package.

Nic hadn't even realised that he'd given her such a thorough examination until his eyes met hers and he saw the pink flush in her pale cheeks. It had a direct effect on his body, causing a hot throb of desire in his groin.

The ennui he'd just been teased about was long gone. Too many emotions and sensations were starting to fizz in his gut—the dominant ones being acrid betrayal and humiliation. *Still*, after all these years. He retreated behind a cold wall of anger. Anything to douse this very unwelcome stabbing of desire. His eyes narrowed and clashed with eyes so green they looked like jewels. He had to exert every ounce of his iron control not to be flung back into time and remember what it had felt like almost to drown in those eyes. The problem was he *had* drowned.

'Madalena Vasquez,' he drawled, not a hint of his loss of composure in his voice, 'what the hell are *you* doing here?'

Maddie winced inwardly and fought to retain her composure. She could remember a time when he'd called her Maddie. The walk from the door to here had felt as if it had taken years, not seconds, and hadn't been helped by the fact that her mother's shoes were a size too big. She was aware of the hush surrounding them, and the whispers—none of which she could imagine were complimentary after the very public way her father had thrown her and her mother out eight years before.

Nicolás de Rojas's mouth became a flat parody of a smile. 'Please accept my condolences on the death of your father.'

Fire flashed up Maddie's spine. 'Let's not pretend you care one iota,' she hissed, mindful of the eavesdroppers. Nicolás de Rojas didn't seem to be fazed by their audience at all, but the grief and futile anger she felt over her father's death nearly choked her.

The man in front of her folded his arms across his formidable chest, making him look even more intimidating. Maddie's skin itched uncomfortably where the dress revealed her back. Her hands were clenched to fists at her sides.

He shrugged negligently. 'No, I can't say I did care. But I can be polite at least.'

Maddie flushed at that. She'd seen in the papers that his father had died some years before. They were both products of generations who would have merrily danced on each other's graves, yet it wasn't in her to glory in someone's death—even an enemy's.

Awkwardly but sincerely, she said now, 'I'm sorry about your father too.'

He arched a brow and his face tightened. 'Are you going to extend that to my mother? She killed herself when she found out your mother and my father had had an affair for years...after your father told her.'

Maddie blanched to hear that Nicolás was aware of the affair. She saw in that instant how much anger his apparent civility was masking as his eyes flashed dangerously and white lines of tension bracketed his sensual mouth.

Her brain felt fuzzy. She shook her head. She'd had no idea her father had told his mother about the affair, or that she had taken her own life. 'I didn't know any of this...'

He dismissed her words with a slashing hand. 'You wouldn't, would you? You were so quick to leave and spend your family fortune running around Europe with your wastrel of a mother.'

Maddie felt sick. This was so much worse than she'd feared. She'd somehow naively imagined that she would say her few words to Nicolás de Rojas, he would respond with something at least civil, and that would be it. But the ancient feud between their families was alive and well and crackling between them—along with something else Maddie didn't want to acknowledge.

Suddenly Nicolás de Rojas cast a quick glance around them and emitted a guttural curse. He took Maddie's arm in one big hand. She was being summarily dragged to the other side of the room before she knew what was happening. He whirled her around to face him again in a quiet corner. This time all civility was stripped away, and his face was lean and stark with displeasure and anger.

Maddie yanked herself free and rubbed her tingling arm, determined not to let him see how shaken she was. 'How dare you treat me like some recalcitrant child!'

'I've asked you once already—what are you doing here, Vasquez? You're not welcome.'

Maddie felt anger surge up at his sheer arrogance and remembered why she was there and what was at stake: her entire livelihood. She stepped forward, dropping her hand. 'For your information I am just as welcome here as you, and I've come to tell you that my father didn't give in to your pressure to sell and neither will I.'

Nicolás de Rojas sneered. 'The only thing you own now is a piece of useless land full of gnarly vines. It's an eyesore. Your estate hasn't produced any wine of note for years.'

Maddie disguised the pain of knowing that her father had let it all go so spectacularly and spat back. 'You and your father systematically pushed and squeezed him out of the market until he couldn't possibly compete any more.'

His jaw clenched at that, and he bit out savagely, 'It's nothing more than was done to us time and time again. I'd love to tell you we spent all our time concocting ways to sabotage your business, but the Vasquez wines stopped selling because they were inferior—pure and simple. You did it to yourselves with no help from us.'

His words hit home with a dismaying ring of truth and Maddie took a hasty step back at his ferocity. She saw his eyes flash indignantly. Her reaction had more to do with his proximity and its effect on her body, and more disturbingly on her memories, than with his anger. She couldn't halt a vivid flashback to when she'd pressed herself so close against him she could feel every taut sinew and muscle. And the evidence of his arousal for her. It had been intoxicating, thrilling. She'd wanted him so badly she'd been begging him to—

'Here you are!'

Nic growled at the woman who had just appeared by their sides, 'Not now, Estella.'

Maddie sent up silent thanks for the interruption and cast a quick glance to see the gorgeous blonde who had been with Nicolás outside the hotel. She backed away but Nicolás grabbed her arm again.

'Estella, wait for me at the table,' he bit out.

The young woman looked from him to Maddie with wide eyes, and then whistled softly before walking away, shaking her head. Maddie dimly thought that she seemed very easy-going for a lover, but then Nicolás was clamping his hands on her arms. Angrily she pulled herself free again, feeling very raw after that too-vivid memory. She was vaguely aware of her dress slipping down over one shoulder as she pulled away, and saw Nicolás's eyes go there for a split second before something hot flashed in the blue depths.

Maddie spoke in a rush to stop herself responding to that look—which she *must* have imagined. This man felt nothing for her except hatred, pure and simple. 'I came to tell you that I'm back and I won't be selling the Vasquez estate. Even if I was do you really think I'd sell to a de Rojas after all we've been through? I'd burn it to the ground first. I intend to restore the Vasquez estate to its full glory.'

Nicolás stood tall, and then he barked out an incredulous laugh, head thrown back, revealing the strong column of his throat. When he looked down again Maddie felt a weakness invading her lower body—and a disturbing heat.

He shook his head. 'You must have done quite the number on your father before he died to get him to leave it to *you*. After you and your mother left and people heard of the affair, no one expected to see either of you back again. I think people would have expected him to leave it to a dog on the street rather than either one of you.'

Maddie's hands clenched. Pain bloomed inside her to think of that awful time and how angry her father had been—justifiably so. She gritted out, 'You have no idea what you're talking about.'

It was as if he didn't even hear her, though. He continued easily. 'It was common knowledge your father didn't have a *peso* to his name by the time he died. Is your mother's Swiss financier husband financing this whim?' His jaw tightened. 'Or perhaps you've bagged yourself a rich husband? Did you find one in London? You were frequenting the right clubs the last time I saw you.'

Maddie's insides burned with indignation. Her hands clenched even harder. 'No, my mother is *not* financing anything. And I don't have a rich husband, or boyfriend or lover. Not that it's any concern of yours.'

Mock shock and disbelief crossed Nicolás's face. 'You mean to tell me that the spoiled Vasquez princess thinks she can waltz back home and turn a bankrupt wine estate around with no help or expertise? Is this your new hobby because the Cannes yacht parties were becoming boring?'

Maddie felt the red tide of rage rise within her. He had no idea how badly she'd fought to prove herself to her fa-

ther—to prove that she could be as good as any man...
as good as her poor dead brother. She'd never have that
chance now, because he was dead too. And she would *not*
let the legacy she'd been bequeathed die with her. She had
to prove that she could do this. She would not let another
man stand in her way as her father had.

Passion resonated in her voice. 'That's exactly what I'm
saying, de Rojas. Stay out of my way and don't expect a
"For Sale" sign to go up—*ever*.'

Just as Maddie was backing away, wishing she wouldn't
have to present him with her naked back, he said chillingly,
'I'll give you two weeks until you run screaming out the
door. You have no idea what it takes to run a successful
wine business. You never worked a day in the vineyard
while you were growing up. It's been years since Vasquez
produced a wine worth mentioning, and your father got
carried away with his overpriced wines. You're in over
your head, Vasquez, and when you realise that it won't matter what price tag you put on that sign because I'll match
it. Purely because I would relish knowing that your family is gone from here for good.'

Maddie hid the dart of hurt; he knew that she'd never
worked a day in the vineyard because she'd told him once.
It had been intimate information which would now be
used against her.

He took a step closer and said chillingly, 'So you see,
eventually that estate will become part of the de Rojas
brand...and by denying it you're merely prolonging your
own misery. Just think—within a week you could be back
in London, sitting in the front row of a fashion show, with
enough money to keep you satisfied for a long time. I'll
personally see to it that you have no cause to return here
ever again.'

Maddie shook her head and tried to swallow the terrifying feeling of stepping off a ledge into the great unknown. She was hurt at the extent of this man's hostility. It hurt more than it should, and that scared her to death.

She couldn't help the emotional huskiness of her voice. 'This is my *home*—just as much as it's yours—and you will have to carry my dead body out before you get me to leave.'

Maddie was bitterly aware, despite her little assertion, that everything he said was right. Apart from his perception of what her life was like. Of that he had no idea, and she wasn't about to enlighten him.

She backed away further and said, 'Don't come near my property, de Rojas…you or any of your people. You're not welcome.'

He smiled mockingly. 'I admire the act, Vasquez, and I look forward to seeing how long you can play the part.'

Maddie finally wrenched her gaze away from his and stalked off—but not before she almost stumbled in the too-big shoes. Gritting her teeth, she prayed silently all the way to the door that she would at least retain the dignity of not losing a shoe in front of the insufferably arrogant de Rojas and the gobsmacked crowd.

Maddie held her head high, and it was only when she finally reached her father's battered Jeep in the car park and locked herself inside that shock hit her and she shook uncontrollably for long minutes.

The awful reality was that he was right—she was on a hiding to nothing, trying to make their estate work again. But she'd be damned if she wasn't going to try. Her father had made long-overdue amends with Maddie, and even though it had come so late, Maddie had always clung to the hope that she would hear from her father. She would have returned here years ago if he'd welcomed her back.

For as long as she could remember she'd wanted nothing more than to work on the estate.

When she'd received the heartfelt letter from her ill father, with his outpouring of regret for his actions, Maddie hadn't been able to help but respond to his plea to come home to try to save their estate from oblivion.

Maddie's relationship with her father had never been close. He'd always made it clear he wanted sons, not a daughter, and had firmly believed that a woman's place was in the home and *not* in the business of winemaking. But he'd made up for a lifetime of dismissiveness while on his deathbed, when he'd realised he might lose everything.

Maddie had been hoping and praying she'd make it home in time to see him, but he'd passed away while she was in the air on her initial flight to Buenos Aires. His solicitor had met her with the news, and she'd gone straight from the airport in Mendoza to his private and lonely funeral in the small family graveyard in the grounds of their estate.

She hadn't even been able to get in touch with her mother, who was on a cruise somewhere with her fourth husband, who was some ten years her junior. She felt very alone now, when faced with the tangible animosity of Nicolás de Rojas and the seemingly insurmountable task of taking on the Vasquez estate.

Legend had it that Maddie's and Nicolás de Rojas's ancestors had been two Spanish friends, immigrants who'd made the long journey to Argentina to make new lives for themselves. They'd committed to setting up a vineyard together but something had happened—a woman had been involved: a love affair gone wrong and a bitter betrayal. As revenge Maddie's forefather had vowed to ruin the de Rojas name. So he'd founded Vasquez wines in direct competition and built it up right next door.

Vasquez wines had become ridiculously successful, decimating the de Rojas name, thus ensuring that the feud thrived and deepened as each generation fought for dominance and revenge. Violence between the families had been habitual, and once a member of the de Rojas family had even been murdered—although it had never been proved that the culprit had been a Vasquez.

Reversals in fortune had happened through the years, but by the time Maddie had been born the two estates had been almost neck and neck in terms of success. The generations-old dark cloud of hostility between the families seemed to have settled into an uneasy truce. In spite of the relative peace, though, Maddie had grown up knowing that she would be punished if she was caught even looking in the direction of the de Rojas vineyard.

Her cheeks stung with colour now when she recalled Nicolás's jeering *'princess'*. He'd only ever really seen her on the few social occasions when their families had been forced to mix, when hosts had nervously ensured that they didn't actually mingle.

Her mother had used those opportunities to parade Maddie in the latest fashions, forcing her naturally tomboyish and bookish daughter into the mould of the fashionable daughter she'd really wanted. Maddie's beautiful mother had wanted a confidante, not a child.

Maddie had been so mortified and uncomfortable in those situations that she'd done her best to fade into the background, while at the same time being aware of the very taboo fascination she felt for Nicolás Cristobal de Rojas, six years her senior, who even as a teenager had exuded unmistakable arrogance and virility. The tension and distance between their families had only made him more fascinating and alluring.

Then, as soon as she'd turned twelve, she'd been sent to

boarding school in England and had only returned home for the holidays. She'd lived for those few months, and had endured her mother's determination to parade her as if she was a doll just because it meant she could catch illicit glimpses of Nicolás de Rojas at the annual polo matches or the few social occasions their families shared. She'd look out of her bedroom window and sometimes would see him far in the distance on his horse as he inspected the neighbouring vineyard. To her, he'd looked like a golden-haired god. Strong and proud.

Whenever she'd seen him socially he'd always been surrounded by girls. Her mouth twisted when she thought of the beautiful blonde he'd so casually dismissed just now. Evidently nothing had changed there…

Eight years ago the uneasy truce between their families had exploded into bitterly fresh enmity and had shown Maddie the real depth of hatred between them. The fact that she'd actually challenged Nicolás's perception of her for a few days in time was something she had to forget. Because it had been undone as quickly as it had been done. What would someone like him be more likely to believe? A lifetime of propaganda and erroneous impressions? Or the briefest of moments fuelled by lust which had quickly been soured for ever?

Maddie shook her head and forced her trembling hand to start up the engine. She had just enough diesel to take her back to the small town of Villarosa, about thirty minutes outside Mendoza. No doubt someone of Nicolás's standing had a suite in the palatial hotel tonight, where he would be accompanied by his long-legged golden companion, but Maddie had nowhere to go except a crumbling homestead where the electricity had been cut off months ago and where she and a loyal skeleton staff depended on an ancient generator for power.

Maddie swung out of the hotel car park and reflected miserably that there must be plenty of de Rojas ancestors laughing down at her predicament right now.

CHAPTER TWO

Nic was stuck in a trance. All he could see in his mind's eye was the bared expanse of pale, slim back and the tumble of jet-black hair against her skin as Madalena Vasquez walked away. She'd stumbled slightly in her shoes, and it had made her look achingly vulnerable for a moment—before she'd recovered and swept out of the ballroom with all the hauteur of a queen. She'd had no right to look affronted at his taunting *'princess'*, for that was what she had always been.

When she'd been much younger she'd reminded him of a fragile porcelain doll, and he hated to admit it now but she'd always fascinated him with her unusually pale colouring and green eyes. There had been moments—the memory of which burned him now for his naivety—when he'd believed she'd been uncomfortable in their social milieu, when she'd looked almost sick as her mother pushed her to the fore. He'd sensed that beneath the delicate exterior lurked something much more solid.

Nic's mouth firmed. Well, he had first-hand experience of exactly how solid she was beneath that ethereal beauty. As if he needed to be reminded of the kind of person she was. Once she'd challenged his preconceptions of her, but it had all been an act.

She'd shared her mother's temptress nature—an earthy

sensuality that could ensnare the strongest of men. His heart thumped hard. It had ensnared his father before him, and then, a generation later, *him*. She'd only been seventeen. Humiliation burned Nic at recalling it, and he couldn't halt the flood of memories—not so soon after seeing her close up and in the flesh for the first time in years.

One evening he'd been inspecting the vines which were closest to the Vasquez estate; they always had to be ever vigilant in case of sabotage. That particular evening Nic had been weary and frustrated...weary of his mother's constant melancholy—never properly diagnosed as the depression it had been—and his father's caustic cruelty and habitual violence. At the dinner table his father had been drunkenly ranting about how the Vasquez run of success was threatening their sales. Nic had always firmly believed you made your own success, but, constrained by his authoritarian father, he hadn't been able to implement his own ideas.

Something had made Nic look up to the small hill which acted as a natural boundary between the two estates, and he'd seen a feminine figure with long black hair astride a huge stallion. *Madalena Vasquez*. Looking right at him.

His weariness had morphed instantly into burning irrational anger—at her for making him think about her, wonder about her, when she was forbidden. She also represented the dark and tangled feud which he had never really understood.

The supercilious image she presented on her horse had only galvanised him further and, giving in to an urge stronger than he'd been able to resist, Nic had spurred his horse to a canter and headed straight for her—only to see her whirl around and disappear.

He could still taste the urgency thrumming in his blood eight years later—to catch her and see her up close. Never once in their lives had they been allowed to speak to one another. Although he'd seen the way she would look at him from a distance and then glance away with artful shyness.

Finally he'd caught another glimpse of her, low down over her horse, hair streaming in the wind. She'd been cutting through the landscape like a bullet. With increasing urgency he'd thundered after her. It had been on the very edge of both their estates that he'd eventually seen her riderless horse, tied to a tree. She'd come to a remote part of their land where orchards had been planted. And then he'd seen her standing in a clearing of trees, as if she'd known he'd follow her.

More mesmerised by her flushed cheeks and that glossy fall of hair than he'd cared to admit, Nic had swung off his horse and come to stand in front of her. His anger had dissolved like snow on a hot stone. The very forbidden nature of what they were doing had infused the air around them.

'Why did you follow me?' she'd asked suddenly, her voice low and husky.

Nic had spoken on an unthinking reflex. 'Perhaps I just wanted to see the Vasquez princess up close.'

In that instant she went white as a ghost, her eyes like two huge wounded emeralds.

She backed away and Nic put out his hands, instantly contrite. 'Wait. Stop. I don't know why I said that… I'm sorry.' He took a breath. 'I followed you because I wanted to…and because I think you wanted me to.'

She'd flushed pink then, the colour rushing into her cheeks dramatically. Without even being aware of it Nic reached out a hand and touched her cheek, fascinated by the way her emotions showed so clearly, feeling its satiny texture beneath his callused palm. A shudder of pure longing went through him—so strong he nearly shook.

She stepped back, biting her lip, looking tortured. 'We shouldn't be here... If anyone sees us...'

Nic saw a tremor go through her slender frame, the way her young breasts pushed against the material of her shirt. Jodhpurs encased long, slim thighs.

He struggled with his control, waves of heat building inside him. She'd speared him with a defiant look then, which confirmed his suspicions that she wasn't as delicate as she had always appeared—as if her little gallop through the wilderness of their lands hadn't already told him that.

'I'm not a princess. I'm not like that. I hate being paraded in public like some kind of mannequin. It's my mother...she wishes I was more like her. They won't even let me go out riding unsupervised. I have to sneak out when they're busy...'

Nic saw her gaze fall to his mouth and her cheeks pinken again. Power and testosterone flooded his body, and he smiled wryly. 'I spend practically every waking hour on a horse...working in the vineyard.'

She looked back up at him, but not before torturing him with an innocently hungry look at his mouth.

'That's all I ever wanted. But when my brother died my father found me helping to pick the grapes one day and sent me inside. He told me that if he ever caught me in the vineyard again he'd take his belt to me.'

Nic winced and his stomach clenched. He knew only too well what the wrath of a father felt like. Gruffly he said, 'Your brother died a few years ago, didn't he?'

Madalena looked away, swallowing visibly before saying, 'He died in an accident when they were crushing the grapes. He was only thirteen.'

'I'm sorry.' And then he asked, a little wistfully, 'You were close?'

She looked back, her eyes suspiciously bright. 'I adored him. Our father was…*is*…prone to rages. One day I angered him, and he would have hit me but Alvaro stepped in and took it. My father wouldn't stop hitting him, enraged at being shown up by his own son. He was only eight at the time…'

Her eyes were swimming with tears. Nic had been the recipient of many a beating in his own time. Acting on an instinct too powerful to resist, he reached out and pulled her to him, enfolding her slim body in his, wrapping his arms around her. The need to comfort her was overwhelming, and completely alien for someone like him who generally held people at arm's length.

She was a complete stranger to him in so many ways, but in that moment he felt a deep kinship. After long moments she pulled back, and with the utmost reluctance Nic let her go.

She said shakily, 'I should go…they'll be looking for me…'

She turned and Nic reached out, gripping her arm with a desperate feeling in his belly. She looked back and he said, 'Wait…meet me here again tomorrow?'

The world seemed to stop turning for an infinitesimal moment, and Nic braced himself for a mocking laugh— some indication that he'd completely misread those few moments.

But Madalena's cheeks flushed red and she said huskily, 'I'd like that.'

They met every day for a week—stolen moments in that secret place where time seemed to be suspended in a bubble and where inhibitions fell away. Nic spoke to her of things he'd never told another soul as easily as if he hadn't experienced years of emotional isolation. Each day he became more and more consumed by Madalena

Vasquez. More and more entranced with her delicate beauty, which he'd discovered hid an earthy sensuality, driving him senseless with growing desire. Yet he managed not to touch her after that first day, when he'd pulled her into his arms to comfort her.

The depth of his need scared him, and the sensual and sexual tension building between them tipped over on that last day. When Nic arrived to find Maddie waiting, he didn't speak and nor did she. The air quivered and vibrated with awareness around them, and then she was in his arms before he'd stretched them out to pull her into them.

His mouth was on hers, and she was clutching him as if she were drowning. He sank a hand into her hair. It felt like liquid silk. He felt her legs shaking against his and slowly they lay down on the downy grass under the shade of the trees, oblivious to their idyllic surroundings. Heat consumed Nic so much that his hand trembled as he fumbled with the buttons on her blouse.

He was no callow, inexperienced youth, but he felt like one as she lay back and looked at him from under long, dark lashes, her cheeks stained red. When he'd opened her shirt and undid her bra to uncover pale breasts tipped with tight pink nipples, he nearly lost it completely.

He was drunk on her by then—drunk on the taste of those sweet breasts, and her soft mewling sounds of response and rolling hips—so he didn't hear anything until she tensed in his arms.

They both looked up at the same moment to see grim figures on horseback, staring down at them. It all became a blur as Nic scrambled to cover Maddie and she stood up behind him. Then they were both hauled unceremoniously out of the clearing by their respective estate employees and brought home...

'Hello? Earth to Nicolás?'

Nic flinched now, as if stung, and looked down to see Estella staring up at him.

She was holding two glasses of champagne. She handed one to him and said, 'Here. Looks like you could do with this.'

He was feeling incredibly raw and exposed, but he schooled his features and took the drink, restraining himself from downing it in one go.

'So, was that woman really one of the Vasquez family? I thought I might have to get a hose to cool things down between you.'

'She's the last Vasquez. She's come back to take over the family business,' Nic bit out tautly, wanting to rid himself of the potent images.

'That's interesting…' Estella mused in a far too innocent voice. 'You're the last in your line too…'

Nic glowered at Estella. 'The only thing interesting about it is that she'll be forced to sell that estate to me and we'll finally be rid of the Vasquez family for good.'

With tension radiating from his tall form he strode away from her and the speculative look on her face. The last thing Nic needed was someone analysing his encounter with Madalena Vasquez. And the last thing the de Rojas estate needed was for its name to be dragged back down into the mire of rumour and innuendo and a resumption of ancient hostilities. The sooner Madalena Vasquez realised the futility of her position and how unwelcome she was, the better for everyone.

'What the hell is he up to?' Maddie muttered to herself, and turned the silver embossed invitation over and back again, as if it might contain a booby trap.

The message was written on one side and simple.

You are cordially invited to a private tasting of
this year's finest wines from the world-renowned
de Rojas Estate.
  Saturday, 7p.m., Casa de Rojas, Villarosa, Mendoza.
  Black Tie.

The invitation had arrived with that day's post, interrupting Maddie as she waded through her father's papers.

She heard a noise and looked up from where she was
sitting at her father's study desk to see Hernan come in.
He was their oldest and most loyal employee, her father's
viticulturist, and his own father had been the viticulturist
before him. He and his wife, Maria, who was the housekeeper, were both working for board alone, even though
Maddie had told them she couldn't be sure when they
might get paid again.

Her father's head winemaker had long since gone, and
Maddie knew that she might have to take over that role
until she could afford to hire someone new. Fresh from a
degree in Oenology and Viticulture, she was lacking in
practical experience but had a burning love for the industry and craved the opportunity. Even if it was a poisoned
chalice.

She swallowed the emotion she felt at the evidence of
Hernan's loyalty now and handed the card to him. He read
it silently and handed it back with an inscrutable look on
his face.

Maddie just arched a questioning brow.

After a long moment the old man said, 'You do know
that if you accept the invitation you will be the first
Vasquez to be invited onto de Rojas land since as far back
as I can remember?'

Maddie nodded slowly. This was huge. And she had no

idea what he was playing at, but she had to admit she was intrigued to see the famed estate.

To her shock and surprise Hernan shrugged lightly. 'Perhaps you should go. Times have changed, and things can't go on as they always have. He's up to something. Of that I have no doubt. Nic de Rojas is infinitely more intelligent than his father, or even his father before him, so he is a dangerous enemy to have…but perhaps an enemy you know…?' He trailed off.

Maddie looked at the card thoughtfully. It had been two weeks exactly since her tumultuous meeting with Nicolás de Rojas, and she still felt shaky when she thought of it. Going through her father's papers since then had shown her the true ugly extent of how far Nicolás de Rojas was willing to go to to get his hands on their estate.

Her father had been bombarded with letter after letter advising him to sell up. Some had been cajoling, almost friendly in tone, and others had been downright threatening. They'd all been issued by the de Rojas solicitor but signed off with the arrogant Nicolás de Rojas scrawl. There'd even been a threatening letter dated the day her father had died.

As much as Maddie wanted to rip up the invitation and send it back in pieces to Nicolás, she knew she couldn't afford to isolate herself now. She needed to see what she was up against.

The party was the next evening.

She put the invitation in a drawer and stood up resolutely, clamping the gaucho hat she'd been wearing back on her head. 'I'll think about it. In the meantime we need to check the eastern vineyard again. It looks like our best prospect of a harvest this year.'

'You mean our *only* prospect,' Hernan said darkly as they walked out to the battered vineyard Jeep.

Maddie tried not to let the sensation of sheer panic overwhelm her. It was far too frequent for her liking, and not helped one bit by the realisation that the monumental task of harvesting their one chance of a wine that year was going to fall to her and Hernan and whatever friends and relations he could persuade to help with picking the grapes.

Her father had been a staunch old-school-style wine-maker, eschewing wholesale modern methods. That was all very well when you were producing top-of-the-line expensive wines in tandem with more affordable table wines, but in later years her father had all but stopped producing for the more accessible market.

Their one tiny glimmer of hope was in the grapes which had somehow survived the neglect of her father to flourish and ripen on the eastern slopes of the vineyard. These were the Sauvignon grapes which made the distinctive white wine which had put the Vasquez name on the map—particularly because red wines were more common in Argentina.

If they could harvest them, and assure investors of the quality and quantity, then perhaps someone would give them the money they needed to get back on track—or at the very least to be able to pay the basic bills again.

Nic was tense as he stood in the open-air courtyard in the middle of his *hacienda*. His focus was on the imposing entrance doorway, which was still admitting a long line of glittering guests who had travelled from all over the world for this tasting. Hundreds of candles flickered in huge lanterns, and waiters dressed immaculately in black and white moved among the guests offering wine and canapés. But all Nic could think was…*would she come? And why had he asked her, really?*

Nic told himself it was because he wanted her *gone*. His belly clenched. It went much deeper than that, and he knew it. Really, what he'd wanted since eight years ago, and since he'd had that electric glimpse of her in that club in London, was to see her broken and contrite. To see that pale perfection undone. To see her as humiliated as he'd felt. To see her as exposed. She'd lured him to expose himself and he'd stupidly believed the act she'd put on.

Her words resounded in his head. *'I was bored. OK? I wanted to seduce you because you were forbidden to me. It was exciting...'*

A smug voice came from his left. 'It'll only be a matter of time now before you can buy out the Vasquez estate.'

Nic took his eye off the door for a moment and looked at his solicitor, who had been a good friend of his parents. His mother's friend more than his father's. He was a small, overweight man, with mean, calculating eyes. Nic had never especially liked him, but it had been easier to retain him than to let him go after his father's death. He made a mental note to instruct his assistant to seek out new legal represention. He'd do his duty and give Señor Fiero a generous retirement package.

A movement at the door caught the corner of Nic's eye, and he looked back to see Madalena Vasquez entering. The instantaneous effect was almost laughable. His whole body tautened, and an urgent need to see her up close again rushed through him, shocking him with its force. He'd never felt that for another woman. Not even a lover.

From here she looked even more stunning than she had two weeks ago. Her hair was up and she was wearing a long midnight-blue sheath. Strapless, it showed off the delicate lines of her collarbone and shoulders. The gently muscled strength of her arms. There was something slightly odd about the dress, though, that he couldn't put his finger on. Much like the dress she'd worn the other night in Mendoza, it was as if it didn't fit perfectly. As if it wasn't hers.

He was so used to seeing women immaculately turned out that he could spot the slight anomaly a mile away, and it didn't fit with what he would have expected of Madalena Vasquez.

'Who is that? She looks familiar.'

'That,' Nic said tightly, irrationally not liking the fact that his solicitor was looking at her too, 'is Madalena Vasquez. She's home and taking over the family estate.'

The solicitor laughed cruelly. 'That place is a mess. She'll be begging you to buy her out.'

Nic moved away from his solicitor and towards Madalena. He couldn't fathom the urge he felt to turn around and punch the older man. It was visceral and disturbing, and the remnants of it lingered as he drew closer and saw that wide green gaze settle on him. Pink flooded her cheeks and he could see the faintest bruised colour under her eyes—signs of fatigue. His chest constricted. Once he'd believed in that artifice, but it was a trick to incur sympathy learnt from her mother. To make a man believe that she was as innocent as she looked. When she was rotten to the core.

Nevertheless his rogue body could not be dictated to by his mind. Desire was hot and instantaneous.

He put a smooth smile on his face and tried to ignore the increasing heat in his body. 'Welcome to my home.'

Maddie tried not to let Nicolás de Rojas see how affected she was just by watching him walk towards her. She felt like snorting incredulously. *Home* was a woeful understatement for this seriously palatial house. Once, a long time ago, her home had been as grand, but now it was a crumbling shell.

She didn't trust his urbane charm for a second. His eyes were like shards of ice and she shivered imperceptibly. Forgetting her resolve to appear nothing but aloof, she blurted out, 'Why did you invite me here?'

Quick as a shot he answered, 'Why did you come?'

Maddie flushed, all of her reasons for coming feeling very flimsy and transparent now. She should have just sent the invitation back in tiny pieces as she'd intended. But she hadn't.

She squared her shoulders. 'I came because it's been two weeks and I want to let you know that I've still no intention of going anywhere.'

Nicolás tipped his head slightly. She barely saw him make the gesture, and then a man appeared at his side.

'Yes, sir?'

'Madalena Vasquez, I'd like to introduce you to my house manager, Geraldo. He will show you around and see that you have everything you need. If you wouldn't mind excusing me? I have some new guests to attend to.'

And just like that he had turned and was walking away. Maddie felt inexplicably bereft, dropped…

The intensity of emotion he aroused so effortlessly was still high. Maddie cursed herself for allowing any hint of vulnerability through. She had to be strong enough to withstand Nicolás de Rojas and his brand of arrogance or she'd never survive.

She turned to the man waiting by her side with a big forced smile. 'Thank you.'

Maddie's head was spinning by the time Geraldo, who had proved to be a charming host, showed her back into the main courtyard, which was now thronged with people. Men were in tuxedos and women glittered in long dresses and jewels.

The reality of the sheer opulence she'd just seen was

a little hard to take in. The home itself—the few main rooms she'd been shown—was exquisitely furnished but also comfortable. Accessible. It was a *home*. And that had affected her deeply. Her own home had always been more like a cold and austere show house, full of dusty antiques. Unfortunately all of them had long since been sold to fund her father's downward spiral.

'I'll leave you here now…if that's okay?'

Maddie swung her gaze back to the pleasant house manager and realised he was waiting for her answer. 'Of course. You must be busy. I'm sorry to have taken you away from your duties.'

He said urbanely, 'It was a pleasure, Señorita Vasquez. Eduardo, who is our head winemaker, will see to it that you taste from the best of our selection of wines tonight.'

Another equally pleasant man was waiting to escort Maddie over to where the wine-tasting tables had been set up. It was only when she looked up and caught the coolly sardonic expression on Nicolás's face, where he stood head and shoulders above the crowd across the room, that she understood she was being effectively herded in exactly the direction he wanted her to go. And being shown exactly what he wanted her to see.

The transparency of his actions and the way she'd almost forgotten what was happening here galled her. So she merely skated her own gaze past his and made Eduardo the focus of her attention as he explained the various wines to her.

After a few minutes Maddie managed to take advantage of someone coming up to ask Eduardo a question and escape, turning instinctively away from the direction where Nicolás de Rojas was holding court with a rapt crowd. She hated being so aware of where he was at any moment, as if some kind of invisible cord linked her to him. And yet, a small snide voice reminded her, as soon as puberty had hit she'd had that awareness of him as a man.

She walked through a silent, dimly lit room full of luxuriously stuffed couches and rosewood furniture and out onto a blissfully quiet decked area which hugged the outside of the house. Little pools of golden light spilled out onto the ground, and Maddie went and curled her hands over the wooden fence which acted as a perimeter.

The strains of a jazz band playing for the very select crowd wafted through on the breeze. She smiled cynically. Nicolás de Rojas could have stopped her at the front door and she would have already been in awe of his screaming success and wealth.

The wide gravelled drive, the rows upon rows of well-tended fertile vines and gleaming outbuildings had been enough of a display. That was what she wanted for her own estate—to see it flourishing as it had when she was a young girl, with rows of vines full of plump sun-ripened grapes…

She heard a noise and whirled around. Her heart thumped hard in her chest at the sight of Nicolás de Rojas in the doorway of the room behind her, shoulders blocking out the light, hands in pockets. He was so rakishly handsome that for a moment she forgot about everything and could only see him.

Maddie called up every shred of self-control and smiled. But it was brittle. Seeing Nicolás's house up close like this had affected her far more deeply than she liked to admit.

'Did you really think that showing off your success would make me scurry to the nearest airport with my tail between my legs?'

His jaw was gritted but he stepped out of the doorway, making Maddie's breath hitch in her throat when his scent reached out and wound around her. She couldn't back away. The wooden posts were already digging into her soft flesh.

'It must feel very dull here after the bright lights of London…not to mention the ski slopes of Gstaad. Aren't you missing the season?'

Maddie flushed deep red. She smiled even harder, hiding the hurt at that particular memory. 'I wouldn't have had you down as a *Celebrity Now!* reader, Mr de Rojas.'

Maddie had long since berated herself that she should have been suspicious when her flighty mother had expressed a desire to see her—even offering to fly her out to meet her in the wealthy ski resort for a holiday. This was the same mother who had refused to help Maddie out because she believed that she'd already sacrificed enough for her daughter.

As soon as she'd arrived at the ski resort it had become apparent that her mother needed her daughter to help foster an image of dutiful motherhood. She'd been intent on seducing her current husband, who was divorced, but a committed and devoted father. Maddie had been too disappointed and heartsore to fight with her mother, and had given in to a cloying magazine shoot in which for all the world they'd appeared the best of friends.

Nicolás answered easily, 'I happened to be on a plane on my way home from Europe. The air hostess handed me the wrong magazine, but when I saw who was gracing the cover I couldn't resist reading all about your *wonderful* relationship with your mother and how you've both moved on *so well* from the painful split with your father.'

Maddie felt sick. She'd read the article too, and couldn't believe she'd been so hungry for affection that she'd let her mother manipulate her so crassly. She pushed the painful reality of her mother's selfishness aside.

'This evening was a wasted exercise on your part, de

Rojas. You've merely made me even more determined to succeed.'

The fact that he thought he had her so neatly boxed up and judged made fresh anger surge up inside Maddie.

'I've just spent two weeks in a house with no electricity, and as you can see I'm not running screaming for the nearest luxury health spa. Now, if you don't mind, it's late and I've got to be up early in the morning.'

Maddie gathered up her dress to stalk off, but at that moment one of her oversized shoes came off and she stumbled. A strong hand closed around one bare arm to steady her and the sensation was electric.

Nicolás didn't let her go, though. She was whirled around to face him again, one shoe on, one shoe off.

He was frowning down at her. 'What do you mean no electricity?'

Maddie was used to being considered tall, but right now she felt positively petite. Bitterness laced her voice at being made to feel so vulnerable, when she had no doubt that was exactly what this man had intended all along. 'We've been using an ancient generator to get electricity in our house since they cut my father off months ago—when he stopped paying the bills.'

Nicolás shook his head. He looked shocked. 'I didn't know it was that bad.'

Maddie tried to pull her arm back but his grip was firm. Panic at her helpless physical reaction galvanised her to say, 'As if you care. You were too busy signing off on your solicitor's letters, doing your utmost to get a dying man to sell up. Do you know that he received the last letter the day he died?'

Now Nicolás looked confused. His hand tightened. 'What are you talking about? I never signed any letters. Any correspondence between my family and yours stopped when my father died. I was too busy rebuilding our own brand and renovating the estate and house.'

'You can spout all the lies you like, de Rojas. This evening was a mistake. I've let down every generation of my family and my father by coming here. It won't happen again.'

Nicolás's hand softened its grip on her arm and Maddie felt ridiculously disorientated, her anger dissipating like mist over a hill. His eyes were intense blue flames that communicated something base and carnal directly to her insides.

His voice was deep. 'But you did come here tonight, and there's something in the air…it brought us together before, and it's still there.'

Maddie felt the sense of disorientation increase. She finally yanked her arm free from his grip, but his words were hurtling her back in time to when he had stood in front of her and said, *'You're nothing but a tempting tease. I was curious to know what the Vasquez princess tasted like and now I know—poisonous.'*

The bitterness and anger of that exchange eight years ago was far too acute, eclipsing everything else. Maddie had not trusted herself with another man since then because of it. She'd held a part of herself private and aloof for fear of getting hurt again, or facing painful revelations. She had to push him back before he guessed how vulnerable she was.

She squared her shoulders and forced herself to look Nicolás dead in the eye. 'I seduced you once, de Rojas. Did you really think this evening would induce me to try and seduce you again? Eight years isn't enough time for you to get over your wounded ego?'

Nicolás stood tall, and she saw him pale beneath his tan. 'You little bitch.'

CHAPTER THREE

MADDIE didn't know where on earth she'd got the nerve to say those words when, if anything, they could be more legitimately levelled at her. She hadn't got over what had happened eight years ago—not by a long shot.

She heard a rushing in her ears, but she ignored it and tossed her head. 'Don't worry. You won't see me again. I think we can safely say this farce is over. I came tonight because I was curious to see what you were up to. You've seriously underestimated me.'

She was turning away again when she forgot that she still had one shoe off. She stumbled into thin air, and would have fallen if Nicolás hadn't caught her and hauled her back against him. One strong arm was wrapped around her ribcage, just under her breasts, and the other was across her shoulders. Adrenalin pumped through Maddie's veins. She immediately tried to remove his arms but they were like steel bands. And they were completely alone.

She had an urge to shout out, but a hand came over her mouth as if he'd read her mind. Panic gripped her—not at the threat of violence but at the threat of something much more potent. The evidence of Nicolás de Rojas's hardening body at her back was liquefying her insides. A silent scream sounded in Maddie's head: *No! Not this, please.* He would expose her vulnerability in seconds if he touched her.

She bit down on the fleshy part of his hand and heard him curse—but not before she'd tasted the salty tang of his skin. Her belly swooped and fire danced along her veins. He moved her effortlessly in his arms and now she was facing him, his arms manacling her to his body, her hands behind her back. She was completely powerless. And, to her absolute disgust, the predominant thing she was feeling was excitement.

'Let me *go.*'

He shook his head, eyes glittering down into hers. Maddie felt as if she'd completely lost her footing. Past and present, everything was mixing, and she felt seriously overwhelmed.

'I'm not finished with you, Maddie.'

Maddie's heart lurched painfully at hearing him use the diminutive of her name. She could remember with painful clarity telling him that she preferred Maddie to the more stuffy-sounding Madalena. He had touched her cheek and said, 'Maddie it is, then...'

He smiled, and it was the smile of a predator, forcing Maddie back to the present moment. 'One thing you should know is that if I've underestimated you, then you've *seriously* underestimated *me.* We have unfinished business—and ironically enough it's got nothing to do with business.'

Before Maddie had even properly taken in his words or read his intent he'd hauled her even closer. His head descended and his hard mouth pressed against hers. For a second Maddie had no reaction except numb shock. And then sensation exploded behind her eyes—hot and urgent.

Desperately she tried to cling onto reality and not let that hot urgency take over her need to stay immobile and unresponsive. But she might as well have been hoping that the sun wouldn't rise in the morning.

Being in this man's arms again was like seeing a beacon of light strobing across a choppy ocean and reacting to it with an unthinking instinct to seek harbour. Maddie felt the inexorable and overpowering urge to follow it, even as everything rational was screaming at her to stop, pull herself free, not to react. But a much bigger part of her was aching all over with the effort it took not to react.

As if sensing her turmoil, Nic freed her hands and lifted his own to her head, fingers caressing her skull, angling her head so that he could better plunder her mouth. His tongue flicked against the closed seam of her lips and at that touch Maddie felt her resistance falling away. Her free hands hovered for a long moment. She knew in some dim place that she should use them to push him away, but when she put them between their bodies and felt the taut musculature of his torso underneath his thin shirt they clung...didn't push.

He growled low in his throat at her capitulation and became bolder, his tongue prising open her soft lips to seek the hot interior of her mouth. The devastation of that simple intimacy made Maddie sway against him. She could feel her breasts crushed against the solid wall of his chest.

One of his hands was on her waist, digging into her flesh, anchoring her solidly against him. She could feel the bold thrust of his arousal against her belly, and between her legs she felt hot and moist.

The world was turning into a hot furnace of sensation and desperate wanting—and then suddenly a cool breeze was waking Maddie as if from a drugged trance and she was blinking up into Nic's impassive face. It looked as if it was carved from stone. Maddie felt like jelly. Her mouth was swollen, her heart beating like a piston. Her hair was tumbling down over sensitised skin.

'You…' She couldn't even formulate a word beyond that.

In a voice so cold it woke her up more effectively than anything else, Nic said, 'What do you want to say, Maddie? You want me to believe this act? That I've effectively rendered you speechless with passion?'

A look crossed his face that was so bitter it took Maddie aback. For a moment she was distracted from her growing humiliation.

'You forget that you already tried that once with me. I'm not stupid enough to fall for it again. You can't, however, deny that you want me. As much if not more than when you were hot and trembling in my arms eight years ago. I could have taken you that day and you would have been with me every step of the way. You might have seduced me out of boredom, but there was nothing bored about your response then—or just now. And you've never been able to handle that reality.'

The sheer arrogance of his tone and expression revived Maddie from the fugue she'd been in. She moved out of his embrace with a jerky movement and saw dark colour flash along his cheekbones.

'I am not interested in your hypotheses, or your take on the past. The past is in the past and that's where it'll stay. *This*…' she waved a hand to encompass what had just happened '…is nothing but evidence that physical chemistry can be dismayingly arbitrary. That's *all*.'

Nic smiled. 'If I hadn't stopped when I had I could be taking you right here, just feet away from one hundred guests, and I'd have had to put a hand over your mouth to stifle your screams of pleasure.'

The sheer carnality of his words made Maddie raise her hand—he'd pushed her too far.

Before it could connect to his smug face he'd caught it in a steel-fingered grip. Shock washed through Maddie in a wave. She'd never raised a hand to anyone in her life. The line of Nic's mouth was impossibly grim.

'I was merely proving that you're no more in control of your desire for me now than you were eight years ago, no matter how much you tried to convince me that you'd found what we had done so abhorrent it made you physically ill. You came here tonight to test me as much as I tested you. My bed is free at the moment...you're more than welcome to join me there and we can indulge this *arbitrary chemistry* until you've come to your senses and decided to sell the Vasquez estate to me.'

Maddie ripped her hand free of his grip and had to curb the urge to try and strike him again. His version of what had happened that cataclysmic afternoon was very different from hers. She knew she'd given him the impression that what they'd shared had disgusted her...and for a while she *had* found what they'd done abhorrent. But not for the reasons he obviously believed.

And she couldn't tell him. As much as she hated him right now, telling him the truth would only expose her even more. He would know that that week had meant everything to her, that she hadn't set out coldly to seduce him just for her amusement. There was no way she could disabuse him of that belief now. It was her only defence against him.

She stood very tall and said frostily, 'You seem to have forgotten that your bed was busy enough only two weeks ago. I think I'll pass, thanks.'

And then she turned and walked out.

To her intense relief he didn't stop her. It was only when she got outside to the main door that Maddie realised that she was barefoot. She certainly wasn't going to go back now for her shoes and risk seeing Nic again. She scrambled into the Jeep as soon as the valet brought it round, and as she saw the lights of the *hacienda* grow smaller in her rearview mirror she finally let out her breath.

She'd been a prize fool to think that Nic de Rojas wouldn't bring up what had happened in the past. He was a very virile and proud man. She knew she'd damaged his ego then...and she shuddered now when she recalled the bitter look she'd seen cross his face just a short while ago. She'd had no idea it would all feel so fresh and unresolved between them.

Even though the events of eight years before had sent out violent ripples, she would have imagined that the actual week which had led to those events had faded in his memory. That the intervening years and the countless affairs he seemed to have had with beautiful women would have made Maddie's innocent and gauche charms fade into insignificance...

The way he'd just kissed her, together with the memory of that week—those heady days when desire had tightened like a steel coil in her belly until she'd begged him to make love to her—made Maddie shake so much that she had to pull over on the hard shoulder or risk a crash. She put her head down on the steering wheel between her hands and tried to empty her mind, but it was impossible... the memories were too potent—especially after what had just happened.

She'd managed to evade her mother and father that day, and take a horse out riding on her own. She'd always instinctively hoped for a glimpse of Nic de Rojas on his own estate, and her heart had almost stopped when she'd seen him just metres away. The intensity on his face had scared her and she'd turned her horse to run, not even sure what she was running from. Perhaps it had been the delicious and illicit excitement thrumming through her blood.

She could remember looking back and seeing that he was following with that same intense expression—and her excitement had spiked to almost unbearable levels. Her whole body had gone on fire. The friction of the horse as it had surged powerfully between her legs had nearly made her cry out she was so oversensitised. By the time she'd reached the remote orchard which straddled both their estates her body had been as taut as a bowstring, humming for him.

That orchard was a favourite spot of hers. A secret place. And then he'd been there, swinging lithely off his horse, full of that taut energy. It had been overwhelming to see him up close at last—nothing could have prepared her for his sheer masculine perfection.

He'd touched her so gently. And they'd spoken. Really spoken. After years of feeling as if no one could possibly understand her Maddie had found a kinship with the most unlikely person: the son of her family's sworn enemies.

That first day when Maddie had tried to leave, her heart had felt heavier than a stone in her chest. Until Nic had asked to see her again the following day. And then the next and the next.

The week had taken on an unreal aspect…dreamy. Those illicit moments under the spreading branches of the orchard trees had become the only reality Maddie wanted. Nic had consumed her, filled her nights with vivid and carnal dreams. By the end of the week she'd been in such physical turmoil—craving him but scared of that craving—that she'd all but thrown herself at him.

He'd kissed her and touched her, and Maddie's face flamed even now to remember the wanton way she'd writhed beneath his hands, begging for more of something she could only guess at.

And then all hell had broken loose.

Huge looming figures on horseback had appeared and smashed apart the idyll. Evidently their regular absences had been noted by keen eyes. Nic had put Maddie behind him and she could remember doing up her shirt with numb hands, panic-stricken as she'd heard the shouts get louder. And then they'd both been hauled out of the trees and marched away. Maddie could remember looking back to see Nic being corralled onto his stallion, flinging his father's men off him, snarling at them.

She'd sobbed out loud when she'd seen one of the men land him a blow to stop him hitting out. But by then she'd been unceremoniously dumped onto her own horse and was being led away.

By the time she'd got home her mother had been waiting, white-faced and seethingly angry. She'd asked, 'Is it true? You were found with Nicolás de Rojas?'

For the first time in her life Maddie had felt the fire of rebellion stir within her, and she had lifted her chin and answered in a strong voice, 'Yes, it's true.'

She'd not been prepared when her mother slapped her so hard across the face that her teeth had rattled in her head. She'd felt blood on the inside of her mouth. In shock she'd lifted a hand to her cheek and stared in horror at this woman who, at the most, had only ever touched her in public, to give an impression of a closeness that didn't exist.

Then her mother had broken down into hysterical tears. Before Maddie had known it, with her face still stinging hotly, she'd been leading her mother into the drawing room and forcing her to take some brandy to calm her down.

Eventually her mother had looked at her and shuddered expressively. Completely bewildered, Maddie had said,

'Mother, is it really so bad that I was with Nicolás? We... like each other.'

That had set her mother off again, and when she'd finally calmed down once more she'd pulled Maddie down onto the couch beside her. 'You cannot see him again, Madalena. I forbid it. Think of what it would do to your father.'

That rebellion stirred in Maddie's breast again—she could no more deny that she wanted to see Nic again than deny her own name. She stood up, agitated. 'That's ridiculous. You can't stop me seeing him. We don't care about the stupid feud. It's gone on long enough.'

Her mother stood up too. 'Madalena, you will *not* disobey me in this.'

Her mother's constant use of her full name, *Madalena*, broke something apart inside Maddie. Years of frustration at having to tiptoe around her father's mercurial moods, brought on by his abject grief for his dead son and her mother's blatant self-interest, made Maddie explode. 'If I want to see Nic de Rojas again there is nothing you can do to stop me.'

An awful stillness came into the room, and Maddie watched as her mother seemed to wither in front of her.

The glass in her hand was shaking so much that Maddie reached out and took it from her, saying with exasperation, 'Mother, your dramatics won't work with me. They might work on Father, but—'

'I'll tell you why you can't see him again.'

Maddie stopped talking. Something about the low tone of her mother's voice had made a shiver go down her spine. 'What are you talking about?'

And then her mother spoke—and broke Maddie's world into tiny pieces for ever.

'Ever since I was a young girl, when our families used

to socialise in Mendoza, I was in love with Sebastian de Rojas...' Her mother's mouth twisted. 'I wasn't from here, so I knew only the vaguest details about the feud between this family and his own...'

Maddie tried to make sense of what her mother had said. 'You were in love with Nicolás's father? But what's that got to do with anything now?'

Maddie's mother sat down again heavily, wringing her hands in her lap. She avoided Maddie's eyes. 'The truth is, I wanted Sebastian to marry *me*. But I was too young, and his family forced him to marry his wife because she'd been picked by his parents... He married her, and they had their son, Nicolás, very quickly.' Maddie's mother's voice broke. 'I thought he was lost to me for ever...until I met your father.' She looked up at Maddie, her eyes anguished. 'Part of the reason I married him was so I could be closer to Sebastian. When he saw me again he couldn't resist taking me back into his bed. We met in hotels, whenever we could...' Her mouth took on a bitter aspect for a moment. 'I wasn't under any illusions. Sebastian got a thrill out of taking the wife of his enemy to bed, but he'd never have jeopardised his reputation by revealing it.'

Maddie was feeling increasingly distant from everything, as if her mother's voice was coming from far away.

'He went to Europe one winter, to see about extending the business, and when he came back I was pregnant with Alvaro—your brother. He cut off all contact, believing that I'd turned my back on him, choosing my marriage over him.'

Maddie's mother's eyes swam with tears—but Maddie couldn't drum up any sympathy. She felt sick at learning the lengths to which her mother had gone just to get her own way. She'd married a man she didn't love just to entice another married man away from his wife and son.

'I don't see what any of this has to do with me not see-ing Nic de Rojas again.' Maddie turned to leave the room and heard her mother standing behind her.

'It has *everything* to do with why you can't see him again.'

With the utmost reluctance Maddie stopped and turned around.

Her mother swallowed visibly. 'I didn't stop seeing Sebastian completely. There were a couple of times when I…I managed to persaude him to meet me.' Her mother took in a deep shuddery breath. 'After one of those times I fell pregnant…with you.' Maddie's mother's cheeks flared a deep and ugly red. 'But in that time I'd also slept with your father. The fact is that I can't be sure that Sebastian de Rojas isn't your father.'

Maddie looked at her mother. The words had hit an in-visible wall and fallen somewhere between them, where she couldn't take in their horrible meaning.

Her mother seemed to realise that, and said harshly, 'You can't see Nicolás de Rojas again because he could be your half-brother.'

The glass Maddie had taken out of her mother's hand dropped out of hers to the parquet floor, shattering to pieces. She didn't even notice. Numb shock was envel-oping her.

The only thing that broke through the shock and hor-ror of her mother's revelations was the inarticulate roar of rage that came from behind them. Maddie's father stood in the doorway, red-faced, apoplectic. His eyes were mad, and he said in a choked voice, 'I knew it. I always knew there was something between you. Was my son even *my* son, or was he also the son of that bastard?'

Maddie's memory after that was hazy. She remembered a lot of shouting and crying. And being dragged roughly up to her room by her father and shut inside. The following day, after a sleepless night, Maddie had snuck out of her first-floor window and gone to find a horse. She hadn't even cared about her father's wrath any more. She'd needed to get out.

To her horror, she'd found that she'd instinctively made for the orchard again. Too overcome with everything, she'd slithered off her horse before she'd spotted that she wasn't alone. Nic de Rojas had stepped out from the shadows of the trees, his face grim.

Her belly had clenched painfully with a mixture of dread and that awful, illicit excitement. Had she been hoping that he would be here, as he had been every other day, despite what had happened? But what had felt so pure and right the previous day now felt tainted and wrong.

'Why are you here?'

He smiled but it was tight. 'I wanted to know if you'd come back.'

Seeing him here like this—when she carried such awful knowledge—was too much. Choking on the words, she said, 'I came to be alone, actually. I didn't want to see you.'

His face tightened and Maddie spoke quickly to stop him saying anything, 'You should leave. *Now.*'

He came up to her, put his hands on her arms. 'I don't believe that you don't want to see me. Are you going to let them intimidate you?'

His touch was too much. Maddie wrenched herself free, hysteria clawing upwards. 'Get your hands off me. I can't bear it if you touch me.'

She'd whirled away from him, bile rising uncontrollably. She was sick all over the grass where they'd lain the day before. Trembling all over, and icy cold, she stood up again to see a white-faced Nic looking at her.

'Please…just go. I don't want to see you again.'

'You could have fooled me yesterday.'

Bile rose again, and Maddie swallowed it down, saying thickly, 'That was yesterday. This is today. And I don't want anything to do with you again.'

He wasn't moving, and Maddie was becoming desperate. She couldn't bear to look at Nic. Not when he aroused such feelings in her, and not when he could possibly be—

Her stomach cramped with horror and she blurted out the first thing she could think of. 'I was bored, okay? I was bored and I wanted to see if I could seduce you. You were forbidden. It was exciting. That's *all*...'

Maddie lifted her heavy head from the steering wheel of the Jeep. The bright lights of a passing car made her wince. Her head felt thick from the onslaught of memories. She cut them off. She didn't need to remember the next bit—the way Nic had become so cold and dismissive. The way he'd told her that she'd tasted like poison.

He'd come close and said, with chilling emphasis, 'I used to think the feud was irrelevant...well, it's just become relevant again.'

Maddie had just wanted him gone, and when he'd finally left she'd sat down and cried and cried until she'd fallen into an exhausted sleep.

When she'd returned to the house hours later she'd found her bags packed and her father waiting with her mother by the car. Without even a word of explanation he'd driven them silently to the airport and left them there. He'd just said, 'You are no longer my wife and daughter.'

Maddie and her mother had boarded a flight to Buenos Aires. When they'd reached her aunt's house in the suburbs she'd turned to her mother and said, 'I want to know for sure who my father is. I think I deserve that much at least.'

Her mother, tight-lipped, had finally agreed, but one of the conditions of getting the DNA sample from her soon-to-be ex-husband had meant that she'd had to sacrifice a generous divorce settlement—something she'd never forgiven Maddie for.

A month after they'd left Mendoza and her home Maddie had gone to a doctor's office in Buenos Aires with the DNA sample and submitted to the test. Two weeks after that she'd got the results and found out that she wasn't remotely related to Nicolás de Rojas, or his father. She was, without a shadow of a doubt, a Vasquez.

The knowledge was cold comfort when she knew that she would take her mother's sordid revelations to her grave, along with the even more painful revelation that Nic had felt nothing more than lust for her. She'd believed that he'd shared an intimate part of himself with her, but it had all been an act to lull her into a false sense of security. When she thought of how beautifully he'd manipulated her, so that she'd been aching for him after only a few days, she felt shamed.

Maddie eventually felt strong enough to start up the Jeep again and continue the journey home. She'd written to her father to tell him about the DNA result, but he still hadn't forgiven her for the sins of her mother...until he'd been on his deathbed. Maddie had to honour his wishes now and do everything in her power to forget about Nic de Rojas and get on with saving the Vasquez estate.

'You left these behind last night, Cinderella.'

Maddie's back tensed at the all-too-familiar deep and drawling voice. Her skin prickled all over. Slowly she looked up from where she'd been inspecting the vines to see a tall dark shape silhouetted against the sun, holding out a pair of shoes.

For a second Maddie blinked uncomprehendingly. She'd hardly slept a wink last night, as every time she'd closed her eyes lurid images and nightmares had beckoned. So perhaps now she was hallucinating from tiredness.

When the shoes and the shape didn't disappear, Maddie scowled and stood up. Reaching for the shoes, she said stiffly, 'You really didn't need to go to the trouble.'

She was feeling dusty in worn jeans, a plain T-shirt and an old pair of riding boots. Thankfully the gaucho hat she wore shielded her from the intense blue of Nic's eyes as well as from the sun. She could see very well from under the shaded brim that he too was dressed casually, in a dark polo shirt and faded jeans which clung to powerful thigh muscles.

'I'm intrigued to know why you're wearing shoes and dresses a size too large.'

Maddie flushed and glared up at him from under the hat, not wholly surprised that he would know her shoe size. Her breath was taken away by his dynamic magnetism and the sheer force of seeing him in the daylight. The blue of his eyes was stark against the olive tones of his skin.

Without even thinking Maddie muttered, 'They're my mother's.'

He arched a brow. 'Your luggage got lost?'

Maddie started to move away from the intensity of his presence and said caustically, 'Yes—all twenty-four of my personally monogrammed designer cases.'

It was only then that she realised what she was doing— and Maddie suddenly realised the magnitude of Nic de Rojas seeing the exent of their pathetic crop. She whirled around to face him again. 'How did you get in here? You need to get off this land immediately. It's private property.'

He made a tutting sound and folded his arms, drawing Maddie's eye effortlessly to his impressive muscles. She looked back up, angry with herself for being so weak.

'*So* rude! And when I went out of my way to show

you such hospitality last night… We're making history, Maddie. The first time anyone in our families has breached the divide.' Then his mouth flattened. 'Apart from your mother and my father's sordid affair, of course, and our own…*unsatisfactory* foray following in their footsteps.'

Maddie felt sick and avoided his eyes. 'That was a long time ago.' She lifted her chin, but something in Nic's face had hardened, and Maddie shivered slightly.

'You're quite the enigma, aren't you, Madalena Vasquez? Somehow I can't really see you as the studious type.'

Maddie went cold for a second, and then recalled her conversation with his head winemaker, Eduardo. Bitterly she remarked, 'You got your employees to report back on our conversations? Or did you bug them and listen in?'

Nic was even more incredulous. 'You're *really* claiming that you did a degree in Oenology and Vitculture in between your frantic socialising?'

Incensed, Maddie hit back, 'Your own hectic social life didn't seem to prevent *you* from becoming one of the youngest Masters of Wine in the world.'

His eyes flashed. 'Been keeping tabs on me, Maddie?'

Maddie flushed and looked down again, and then a deep inner pride made her look back up. She wouldn't let him cow her. She lifted her chin defiantly. 'It's true. I graduated last year with a first-class degree. You can check the University of Bordeaux's records if you don't believe me.'

'Who funded your studies, Maddie? A generous lover? Or perhaps you seduced your way to gaining a First?'

CHAPTER FOUR

MADDIE shook with impotent rage. 'That's right, Nic. I seduced my teachers and lecturers into giving me the degree. I'm *that* good in bed, and they're *that* corrupt.'

Nic flushed. He'd never normally goad a woman like this. But no other woman pushed his buttons like this one did. The problem was that this knowledge was turning everything on its head. If she had indeed graduated with a First from Bordeaux University, it was exploding most of his firmly entrenched opinions of Maddie Vasquez.

Uncomfortable now, he asked, 'Is that where all your money went?'

For a moment it looked as if she wouldn't answer, and on some level Nic couldn't blame her. But then she did. Her voice was stiff.

'I was working on a vineyard in Bordeaux, and the owner there sponsored me through the course.'

She was avoiding his eye. Nic longed to tip her chin up so he could see her eyes but he was afraid to touch her. Afraid that after losing control as he had last night he'd lose it again and have her on her back on the ground right here under the vines.

She looked at him then, and her eyes were spitting green sparks. 'And before you ask—no, I did not sleep with the owner to get him to sponsor me. He runs a scholarship program in tandem with the University of Bordeaux to educate his employees and I qualified for it. It's as simple as that.'

'Lucky you, indeed,' Nic drawled, but desire was an insistent beat inside him, distracting him from these revelations. Maddie's breasts pushed against the fabric of her T-shirt. He could see a sliver of pale skin at her waist, where her top had come untucked from her jeans. Her hair was in a long plait, with loose tendrils trailing over her shoulders and stuck to her hot cheeks. She was more beautiful than any woman he'd seen in a long time. If ever. Something inside his chest twisted painfully.

Last night when he'd held her against him he'd known a large part of giving in to his desire was to prove a point to himself. He'd needed to see her undone. And she had been—she'd been swaying like a drunk person after that kiss. It had taken all of his self-control to appear coherent when his own head had been scrambled to pieces and all he'd wanted was to tip her over his shoulder and carry her to his bedroom like some caveman.

And, while it had made a dark satisfaction go through him to know that she did desire him, it hadn't been half as satisfying as he'd expected. Because he wanted more. Much more. He wanted the ultimate fulfilment of knowing this woman intimately. He wanted to finish what had started that week eight years ago.

Why was he looking as her so assessingly? Maddie didn't like it at all—or the way he seemed perfectly comfortable in her territory.

She crossed her arms over her chest. 'I want you to leave—*now*. You're not welcome here.'

His eyes narrowed on her as if he'd just thought of something. His voice was grim. 'I want to see those letters. The ones you said were signed by me.'

Maddie hadn't expected that. She opened and closed her

mouth, and then realised that she had no reason to deny him this. And it would get him away from the vineyard. 'Fine,' she said stiffly. 'They're at the house.'

She turned and walked to the edge of the row of vines, very aware of Nic behind her. She could see Hernan in the distance, inspecting another row of vines. He made a face, but Maddie just sent him a signal that she was okay. She saw Nic's gleaming Jeep parked alongside her battered one. Naturally he opened the passenger door of his own Jeep, and after a brief internal struggle Maddie took off her hat and got in.

Nic sent an expressive glance to her Jeep and muttered, as he turned and drove away, 'That thing is a death trap.'

Maddie smiled sweetly at his profile. 'Of which you must thoroughly approve.'

He sent her a dark glance, his jaw clenched. 'I don't wish you *dead*, Maddie, just gone. There's a big difference.' He shifted gears expertly and then asked, 'So, how long were you in France?'

Maddie hesitated before answering, loath to reveal anything of her personal life. 'I went there when I was twenty-one, after spending a year in London.'

Nic's mouth tightened. 'That would have been when I saw you in that nightclub.'

Maddie almost flinched when she thought of the disgust on his face that night, as his scathing gaze had raked her up and down before he'd turned on his heel and walked out with a bevy of beauties in his wake. She longed to tell him that she'd only been there because she'd bumped into some old friends from her English school days and they'd insisted that she go with them to celebrate the birthday of a friend.

They'd even loaned her clothes—which was why she'd been wearing a silver lamé sheath which had not left much to the imagination. She had to concede now that she didn't seem to have much luck with clothes around Nic de Rojas.

All she said, though in a slightly defeated voice, was 'Yes.' And she looked out of the window, missing the quick speculative glance Nic sent her.

Nic studied her profile and had the strong suspicion that she was holding something back—but what? Evidently she'd partied hard for a year in London and then moved to France to work on a vineyard. Maybe her money had run out and she'd been forced to that decision? It didn't quite fit, but perhaps she'd decided the bigger prize would be to come home and take over the business.

And perhaps he had underestimated her ambition. He remembered how wistful she'd been when she'd told him that she'd always wanted to work in the vineyard. He'd dismissed it eight years ago as part of her act, but had to concede now that if she had indeed completed a degree in Oenology and Viticulture then she must be more dedicated than he'd given her credit for.

Certainly she was still here and not running for the hills, as she'd pointed out. And she'd been on hands and knees in the earth just now, unafraid to get dirty. He had to admit that he was shocked at the evidence of how run-down the Vasquez estate had become. He'd seen the faint purple bruises of fatigue under Maddie's eyes which her makeup had failed to hide completely last night. What he didn't like was the protective feeling that had struck him when he noticed them.

They were in front of the villa now. It was crumbling, but still held the faded grandeur of its heyday. The reversal of fortune between the two estates was stark now, but Nic ruthlessly pushed down that insidiously lingering protective feeling and got out. There was no sense of triumph at all, which surprised him slightly. He waited for Maddie to lead him into the house.

'Maria, would you mind bringing some coffee, please?'

Maddie sent up silent thanks that Maria was there to greet them. The older woman bustled off again, for all the world as if this were a usual occurrence and she still had her normal job as housekeeper and all that it entailed. It was important for Maddie not to let Nic see how bad things were. If she could maintain an impression of some kind of normality then he might not circle them like a vulture over a dead carcass. She'd given far too much away last night—in more ways than one.

Colour flared into her cheeks at the thought of that kiss, and Maddie showed Nic into the bright yet dusty study, hoping he wouldn't notice. She went straight to her father's ancient heavy oak desk, took out the letters and handed them to him silently, curious as to his reaction. Maria came back with the coffee and Maddie served. Nic had sat down, and was opening the letters and reading them.

Maddie sat down on the other side of the desk and only realised then how shaky her legs were. So far his face was impassive, but when he got to the last letter his nostrils flared and colour tinged his cheekbones. Maddie's stomach tensed. She could sense his anger already.

Finally he looked at her. 'That's not my signature.'

She frowned. 'It's your name on the bottom.'

'I know,' he said grimly. 'But it's not my signature.'

Before she knew what he was doing he'd reached across for a pen and paper. He stood up slightly and scrawled his name with his left hand, swung it round to her. 'I have a very distinctive signature because I'm left-handed.'

Maddie looked at it. It was completely different—and very much him. An arrogant scrawl. She knew deep down somewhere she didn't want to investigate that he wasn't lying. He was too proud, and he wouldn't hesitate to tell her that he had sent the letters if he had. Why would he lie? He hated her and wanted to see the back of her.

She forced down a disturbing emotion and looked at him. 'So, who sent them, then?'

'The early ones *are* from my father and his solicitor. But once he died someone started faking my signature. I think I know who it is but I'll confirm it for myself first, if you don't mind.'

Maddie nodded.

Nic reached out to take his cup, and swallowed the dark strong coffee in one gulp. 'I've taken up enough of your time.'

He stood up, and she rose to her feet as well. To her chagrin, her first response wasn't relief that he was going.

Maddie felt seriously unsettled and more than a little vulnerable as she acknowledged that he *hadn't* sent the letters. She followed him out and said carefully, 'So this means the pressure to force me to sell up will stop?'

Nic turned at the front door and smiled down at Maddie. But any hint of friendliness was gone. It was a cold and hard smile, and reminded her succintly of who she was dealing with. She took a step back.

'Nothing has changed really, Maddie. I still want you gone so I know we'll never have to deal with a Vasquez again. But there are other means of persuasion than letters. Much more pleasurable means.'

Maddie cursed her gullibility, and the way her belly had quivered when he'd said *pleasurable*. 'I said it once and I'll say it again. It'll be over my dead body, de Rojas. I'm not going anywhere.'

He shook his head. 'And we were doing so well—on first-name terms. Face the facts, Maddie. You need a massive injection of capital to make this vineyard lucrative again, and even then it would take years of good vintages to undo the damage that's been done. Your degree, while commendable, means nothing when you've got no wine or fertile vines to work with. You haven't even got electricity.'

Maddie smiled brilliantly, hiding her panic that she'd told him so much. 'We do have electricity, actually. I managed to pay some money into the account so we're not totally destitute. Now, if you're quite finished with your fact-finding mission, I'd appreciate it if you got lost.'

Maddie took great satisfaction in slamming the door in Nic's face, and only breathed out shakily when she heard his Jeep roaring away. She leant back against the front door and blew some hair out of her face.

Just then Maria appeared from the direction of the kitchen. 'We need more diesel for the generator. It's just died again.'

Maddie could have laughed if she wasn't afraid she'd start crying. She'd told a white lie about the electricity, determined not to let Nic de Rojas know she was so vulnerable. But the fact was that things were much, much worse than even he could ever know. She did need a massive injection of capital, and right now the only option open to her was to look for an investor.

She pushed herself off the front door. She knew exactly who she *wouldn't* be approaching for that help. She shivered slightly when she thought that his *other* methods of persuasion would have a lot to do with showing her just how much she hungered for him, and in the process gain some measure of vengeance for the way she'd rejected him eight years ago. And for the affair between her mother and his father which had wreaked such havoc.

Whatever his meaning, Maddie knew that if she allowed any kind of intimacy between them he would have the power to break her in two—and she could not allow him that satisfaction.

Nic's hands tightened on the steering wheel of his Jeep as he drove away. The knuckles showed white through his skin and he had to consciously relax. He didn't doubt that Maddie was lying about the electricity, and he didn't like the feeling that he was backing her into a corner where she felt she had to put up such a front.

Dammit. Nic slapped a hand on the steering wheel. It was only as he'd been walking out of her father's study that he'd realised the magnitude of what he was doing. He was the first in his family to come to the Vasquez estate and he had done it as unthinkingly as taking two steps forward...because he'd wanted to see her.

That need had transcended the paltry excuse to return her shoes, or to question her about her degree. As soon as he'd come within feet of her he'd wanted her so badly he'd been able to taste it on his tongue. He could remember her scent, and the way she'd tasted all those years before. Despite making sure his bed was a busy place in the meantime. Even if he was blindfolded he knew with grim certainty that he could pick Maddie out in a line-up. And he hadn't even slept with her. Yet.

Damn. He cursed her again. He'd seen the stubbornness in every line of her body. He knew it well because it was deeply embedded in him too. A fierce drive to succeed and prevail.

Nic had been a sickly baby and child. His mother had suffered complications during the birth and hadn't been able to get pregnant again. His father had gone slowly mad with grief because the entire legacy of his family's estate rested on the shoulders of this one surviving weedy child.

And, even though Nic had become strong and healthy, his father had never seemed to be able to trust in Nic's ability completely. Nic's mouth twisted—not even when he'd achieved the remarkable feat of becoming a Master of Wine at the age of twenty-eight, when there was only a seven per cent success rate in graduating first time around.

Nic knew now that his childhood frailty had most likely had more to do with his mother's overprotectiveness than anything else, but from as far back as he could remember he'd known that he had to overcome the lethargy and allergies that held him back. And he had done it, slowly but surely, with single-minded determination and a deep desire to see his father look at him without that awful disappointment in his eyes.

By the time he was twelve he'd been bigger than most of the other boys in his class at school. His asthma had disappeared and his constitution had been as strong as an ox's. The doctor who'd used to come and see him had shaken his head and said, 'I've never seen anything like it in my life…'

Nic knew it was no miracle. It had been sheer determination to succeed. No one had ever known about that very dark and personal struggle to be strong and prevail. Until he'd told Maddie one day at the orchard. The words had slipped out of him before he'd even realised it, and even now he could see those huge green eyes, limpid with empathy, causing an ache in his heart.

Nic's hands tightened on the steering wheel again, hot anger coursing through him because he'd once been so gullible. Fooled by a pretty face and a lithe young body. That feeling of kinship…had he been so desperate that he'd conjured it up? The thought had always stung him. As a consequence he'd never let any woman close again;

the minute any lover tried to explore more personal avenues he cut them off.

His avowal to Maddie that he wanted to see her gone for good had far more to do with getting rid of his growing obsession with her than any need to extend the de Rojas empire. She was trouble and he knew it. He wanted her, and yet he knew he had to resist her for his own sanity. But, conversely, he knew that the only way to regain any sense of sanity was to have her on her back, beneath him, bucking against him and screaming for release.

By the time Nic got back to his own home he was seriously irritated. He decided to make the most of his mood and act on his resolve of last night to have a chat with his soon-to-be *ex*-solicitor about the letters. Anger whipped through him again at the thought of what he'd done in Nic's name.

Two days later, Maddie was weary all over. She felt as if she was fighting a losing battle as she drove the Jeep home from Villarosa with a pathetic amount of groceries to feed herself, Maria and Hernan. The petrol gauge was nearly on empty.

For a brief moment she thought how easy it would be just to give in…to call Nic up and say, *Fine—you've won.* She would get enough money from the sale of the estate to keep Maria and Hernan in comfort for the rest of their lives.

Maddie saw the outline of the estate in the distance and her throat grew tight. Despite being shut out of the workings of the vineyard her whole life by her father because she was a girl, she loved it. Ever since she was tiny she'd been fascinated by the whole process. She could remember being carried on her brother's skinny shoulders and reaching out reverently to touch the grapes, in awe of how these plump and bitter-tasting fruits could be transformed into complex and delicious wines.

Her blood sang here. She felt attuned to the earth and the seasons. Its backdrop of the magnificent snow-topped Andes was an image she'd held in her head during the long years of exile from her home. And now that she was back she wouldn't allow Nic de Rojas to run her off again just because he wanted to extend his empire.

But she faced an uphill battle. She'd just left the bank in Villarosa, where the manager had spent half an hour pointing out how impossible it was for him even to think about a business loan in the current economic climate.

The bank had been her last option. Over the past few days she'd gone to other vintners in the area, and one by one they'd all told her they weren't interested in investing. One of them had at least had the honesty to say, 'We simply can't go up against de Rojas. If he sees us investing in you it'll be like waving a red flag. He's too successful and we can't afford to get drawn into your feud…'

So even without lifting a finger Maddie was damned by her poisoned association with de Rojas. For ever.

When she saw his gleaming Jeep and his tall rangy body leaning against the bonnet with arms folded as she drove up to the house, her blood boiled over. She swung out of her Jeep and took out the shopping bags, holding them in front of her like a shield.

He made a movement to help and Maddie grabbed them tighter to her. 'I thought I told you you weren't welcome here.'

He had the gall to smile. 'Are you always so prickly in the evening? I must remember that for future reference. Perhaps you're a morning person.'

Maddie sensed him following her inside. She put down the bags on the nearest table and whirled around, hands on hips. Adrenalin was washing away her recent weariness. 'De Rojas, you're not welcome here. In fact I've heard your name enough in the past few days to last me a lifetime. So please, just *go*.'

Maddie would have physically pushed him, but was too afraid to touch him. Too afraid of her reaction when she could already feel it building up inside her. The insatiable need to drink him in, taste him. He was smartly dressed today, in chinos and a white shirt. Every inch the relaxed, successful vintner. She'd dressed smartly too, for the bank. She'd even splashed out with her fast-dwindling money to buy something that would fit, conscious of Nic's recent criticism.

As if reading her thoughts, he let that blue gaze drop and took in the pencil skirt, court shoes and tailored blouse. And then lazily he returned it all the way to where her hair was in a chignon.

'I like the office look—very demure.'

Maddie's hands became fists. She didn't feel demure. She felt hot. All over.

Before she could say anything else he said, 'Apparently you've been looking for an investor. I can tell by your mood you're not having much luck.'

Maddie choked back a curse and said, as calmly as she could, 'Unsurprisingly the local wine community don't want to upset their vastly more successful neighbour. How does it feel to know you're the don of the area, Nic? Does it make you feel powerful to know that people are too scared to invest because they might incur your wrath? That's hardly going to encourage healthy competition, now, is it? It's very easy to be successful in a vacuum.'

He flushed at that. 'Your father would be able to tell you all about that if he were still alive.' He elaborated. 'Your family was the first to quash any local competition, preferring to keep things simple and just between ourselves. If you'd done your research you'd know that more vintners have sprung up since the demise of your estate than ever before—and I've actually invested in some of them.'

Now Maddie flushed. Once again he was doing—or saying—the opposite of what she'd expected. She didn't like the way he was constantly putting her on the back foot.

His continued coolly. 'I came to tell you that my father's solicitor was responsible for the letters. He was a close friend of my father for many years and, unbeknownst to me, made a promise to him on his deathbed that he would continue to wage a campaign to get your father to sell. I suspect he also had a long-standing crush on my mother, and when she committed suicide he vowed some kind of vengeance on your father for having told her of the affair.'

Maddie sat down on a chair behind her. A sense of futility washed over her. Would the tangled mess that lay between them ever stop sending out poisonous tendrils into the future?

'Thank you for letting me know.' She looked up at Nic and saw something suspiciously like concern on his face, but it was quickly gone so she must have imagined it.

'I've also taken the liberty of paying your electricity bill for the forseeable future.'

Now Maddie sprang up, incensed. 'What did you do that for? I told you we were fine.'

Casually Nic reached out to a nearby switch and flicked it. Nothing happened, and Maddie went puce.

Just as casually he said, 'I knew you were lying. I'm doing it because it's a serious health and safety issue. I can't very well stand by and let an accident happen when I could have helped prevent it. Full power will be restored any time now.'

Feeling impotent with anger, Maddie quivered all over.

She couldn't say anything because when Hernan had gone out to get the generator going again he'd almost tripped and done himself a serious injury in the dark. Nic had her in a bind. How could she jeopardise the safety of her employees so wantonly by refusing this? And yet how could she accept?

'Like I said, Maddie, I just want you gone. I don't want you dead.' He arched a brow. 'Is it so hard to say, *Thank you, Nic*?'

Maddie's voice was constricted with the feeling of impotence, but finally she got out, 'What do you want from me?'

Nic came close to where Maddie stood and she fought not to let him see how she trembled when he got close. His eyes were all too assessing, and she could almost hear his brain whirring.

His jaw clenched, and then he said in a hard, flat voice, 'Dinner with me tonight. At my house.'

Maddie swallowed and fought the urge to run. He wasn't finished with pointing out how far she had to go to catch up. She longed to be able to say no, to refuse. But he had her in a corner, with no room to manoeuvre. The safety of her loyal staff was too important.

Ungraciously, she finally gritted out, 'Fine.'

After an infinitesimal moment when the very air around them seemed to vibrate with awareness and tension, he turned and walked out, leaving Maddie feeling as limp as a dishrag. She sank back onto the chair, her mind churning painfully.

He'd just pulled the rug from under her feet by doing an amazingly generous thing—and now, by asking her for dinner, he was blurring the lines, reinforcing the fact that he threatened her on many more levels than just the professional one.

Perhaps this was Nic's plan? To chip away at all the places where he would show up her weaknesses until he had her exactly where he wanted her. Maddie shivered when an image popped into her head of her lying back on a huge bed, with Nic looming over her like a marauding pirate. She would have to tell him tonight in no uncertain terms that she would repulse any further gesture, and set up a payment plan to pay him back for the electricity.

As if proving a point, suddenly the dark hallway was flooded with light. Maddie looked up and blinked, and then Maria rushed out from the kitchen, her eyes suspiciously bright. She came and hugged Maddie and said emotionally, 'Oh, *niña*, now I know everything will be all right…'

Maddie didn't have the heart to tell her that the sword of Damocles swung over them as much as it ever had.

'Good evening, Señorita Vasquez. Please come in.'

Maddie swallowed her nerves and stepped onto the flag-stoned floor of Nic's palatial hallway. Soft lights sent out a golden glow, reminding Maddie of how seductive it had been here the first time around. She tried to steel herself against it but it was hard.

She followed Geraldo through the now-empty court-yard, with its burbling fountain and flowers blooming out of pots everywhere, and into the main drawing room. He led her to a drinks cabinet and said solicitously, 'Señor de Rojas will join you shortly. He's been held up with a phone call. Please, can I offer you a drink?'

Maddie smiled tightly. 'Sparkling water would be fine.' She fully intended to keep her wits about her tonight.

Geraldo gave her the drink, and then excused himself after telling her to make herself comfortable. Maddie caught a glimpse of her reflection in a framed picture and smoothed down her skirt. It was the same one she'd been wearing earlier, but she'd teamed it with a dark grey silk top that thankfully was her own, and fitted. It was loose, with a wide neck, and she adjusted it now so that it wasn't falling down over one shoulder. She'd dithered over her hair and finally tied it up, not wanting Nic to think for a second that she was trying to seduce him.

She wandered over to a wall that was full of framed photos. She became more and more intrigued as she inspected what was obviously a history of the de Rojas family.

'Please forgive me for keeping you.'

Maddie's grip tightened on her glass before she turned around. Nic was standing in the doorway dressed in black pants and a pale blue shirt, open at the neck. His thick dark blond hair shone in the dim light, and those blue eyes took her breath away even now.

Maddie suddenly felt inexplicably shy, and it unnerved her. She'd had to develop a thick skin to survive these past few years and she didn't like this new vulnerability that Nic de Rojas seemed to bring out in her with such effortless ease. 'It's fine. I wasn't waiting long.'

He came towards her then, and stopped near the photos. He gestured with his head and Maddie had to tear her eyes off him. 'My family—all the way back to the nineteenth century, before they left Spain to come here.'

Maddie found herself smiling slightly. 'We have a wall like this too. I always wonder why my ancestors looked so fierce in the pictures.'

'Times were hard then…they had to fight to survive.'

Maddie snuck a glance at Nic. Something about the way he'd said that caught at her insides. At that moment she had a vivid memory of him revealing to her once how sickly he'd been as a child, and how hard he'd struggled to overcome that physical frailty. He was so virile now, so *vital*, that it was almost impossible to believe.

Then he was stepping back and the moment was gone. He indicated with a hand for her to precede him. 'Let me show you into the dining room.'

Maddie moved forward jerkily. She cursed Nic for making her remember things and for putting on this chivalrous act. It was so much easier to deal with him when the lines of battle were clearly drawn.

Nic solicitously pulled out her chair for her, and waited till she'd sat down before taking his own seat opposite. It was a small, intimate table, with candles flickering and lending a far too seductive air for Maddie's liking.

'An aperitif to whet the palate?'

Maddie looked up and fought the urge to adjust her top and let some air get to her skin. She was suddenly boiling. He was weaving some sort of sensual spell over her. And she hated to admit it but she was curious to know about the wines Nic would choose. She was having dinner with a Master of Wine, after all. There were only a few hundred in the world—a very select group.

'Just a small amount. I'm driving.'

He inclined his head and dutifully poured a taster into her glass from a bottle whose label was obscured. It was a white wine. Maddie lifted it and let the clear liquid swirl for a moment before dipping her head and breathing deep. As soon as the bouquet registered she paled dramatically. Nic watched her carefully.

Maddie didn't taste the wine and put the glass down with a trembling hand. She looked at him, willing down an incredible surge of emotion. 'Is this some kind of a joke?'

CHAPTER FIVE

Nic was innocence personified. 'Why would it be a joke?'

Maddie was vibrating with tension now. 'You serve me a Vasquez wine—why? Are you expecting me not to recognise it? Is this a test?'

Maddie put down her napkin and stood up, a little bewildered at how emotional she was feeling, afraid that it was coming partly from that memory just moments ago.

Nic's hand snaked out and caught her wrist. 'Sit down. Please.' When she just looked at him and tried to pull her wrist out of his grip he smiled ruefully. 'I'll admit that I was curious as to whether or not you would know the wine.'

Maddie pulled her wrist free finally but didn't sit down. She looked down at Nic with her most haughty expression. 'Of course I recognise the wine. I grew up watching those very grapes ripen every year.'

Passion made her voice low and fervent. Maddie sat down abruptly—conflicted about how she was feeling. So Nic had served her a Vasquez wine? What was the big deal?

As if reading her mind, he frowned at her now. 'I didn't mean to anger you.'

'No,' snapped Maddie. 'You were just testing me, to

see if I really know my stuff or if I slept my way to getting my degree, is that it?'

Now Nic flushed dark red. 'I don't believe you manipulated your results.'

To Maddie's chagrin, hot tears burnt the back of her eyes and she blinked furiously, only vaguely satisfied when she saw Nic's horrorstruck face. She knew the emotion was coming from a complex mix of bittersweet grief for her father and the overwhelming pressure she was under—not to mention the passion Nic was able to evoke in her so effortlessly.

Exerting a valiant effort to bring herself under control, Maddie picked up the glass again and took a sip. She closed her eyes for a moment, letting the liquid rest in her mouth before slipping down her throat like smooth silk. She opened her eyes again and narrowed a fiery green gaze on Nic. 'If I'm not mistaken this is from the ninety-nine vintage. It won us the Prix de Vin for the best white in New World Wines that year.'

Nic inclined his head, his eyes focused on hers with unnerving intensity. 'You're right. My father bought a case of every vintage of Vasquez wines to analyse them. Exactly as your father did with our wines, I'm sure.'

Maddie nodded, and could feel some equilibrium returning. She looked away for a moment, and then back. 'I'm sorry…it just caught me unawares. That particular wine was always a favourite of mine.' Her voice was husky. 'It reminds me of home. *Here.*' Maddie's fingers pleated the napkin on the table. 'It always made me so homesick whenever I smelt it abroad. People used to order it in the restaurant where I worked, and I would pretend not to know that I should open it at the table just so I could open it first and smell it without anyone watching.'

She looked at Nic, and down again quickly when she saw that gaze, no less intense.

'It used to amaze me to think of this bottle coming all the way from our estate. It made me wonder about the year—had the seasons been kind to the grape? I could always tell just from the smell if it had been good or bad. I can't believe I never got fired for making such a *faux pas*, but the customers always seemed to forgive me.'

Nic watched as candlelight played over Maddie's pale skin, casting her features into mysterious shadows. Her cheekbones stood out. Her lips looked ripe and full. The grey silk of her top lay against her collarbone like the most decadent covering, and the swell of her breasts pushed enticingly against the slippery fabric. He could well imagine the customers forgiving her anything.

He'd never seen anything so sensuous as the way she was cradling her glass. He was transfixed by her natural beauty and her innate earthy sexiness, and all of a sudden he felt as if he was hurtling back in time and out of his depth. The terrain he'd been so sure of was shifting. She was articulating exactly how he felt about the wines he cultivated—each year the vintage *did have* a certain personality, a complexity.

Maddie was about to take another sip when she looked up to see Nic's mesmerised expression. She halted the glass before it got to her mouth. 'What is it?'

He shook his head and colour flared along his cheekbones, making Maddie feel off balance.

'Nothing. I shouldn't have tested you like that.' His mouth quirked in a wry smile. 'You seem to bring out the worst in me.'

Maddie had to fight down a burgeoning sense of lightness. 'I'll take that as a compliment.'

He lifted his glass to hers. *'Salud,'* he said, and then took a deep sip.

The sheer masculinity of his movements while doing something that was inherently delicate made Maddie's toes curl. He was such a *man.*

Much to her relief, their starter was served and eaten largely in silence, with Maddie berating herself for having come over all hysterical just because Nic had fancied giving her some sort of test. And for waxing lyrical about feeling homseick. As if Nic was at all interested in what she thought.

When the main course was served she focused on the meat with single-minded determination, savouring every succulent morsel.

Much to her surprise, they managed to conduct a civil conversation about neutral topics, and when Nic handed her a glass of red Maddie took it without a conscious awareness of how comfortable she'd become.

He said, 'Try this. It's a new blend I'm working on, and this is the first run of wine. I'm not marketing it yet.'

Maddie put down her fork. 'Are you sure you want to be sharing secrets with the enemy?'

Nic's mouth quirked. 'After seeing your vineyard I know I'm in no imminent danger.'

Maddie flushed at being reminded of the painful reality. She raised the glass to her mouth and forced herself to hold Nic's gaze, refusing to be the first to look away. But in the end she had to, because as she savoured the wine she closed her eyes instinctively to try and figure out the various components.

She opened them again and saw Nic watching her. It set a slow fire burning deep inside. Slowly she said, 'Well, it's a classic Malbec…but not like anything I've tasted before—it's got a strain of something else.'

Nic inclined his head. 'Very impressive.'

Maddie had to admit grudgingly, 'I like it. It's not as straightforward as the usual Malbecs—it's got more complexity...a dark side... Pinot?'

Nic smiled. 'I can see how you got your First.'

Maddie felt a ridiculous rush of pleasure go through her just as the attentive staff member came in and took their plates away.

Nic stood up and indicated for Maddie to precede him out of the open French doors to the patio outside. Her belly clenched for a moment—this was where he'd kissed her the other night. Then she saw that a smaller table for two had been set there, with more candles flickering in the breeze.

She almost wanted to back away and insist on leaving. But she was loath to give Nic the satisfaction of knowing that he was getting to her. She moved forward and sat down in the chair that Nic pulled out. Presently the waiter came back and served them both small dishes that held exqusite-looking lemon tart desserts. Nic opened a bottle of dessert wine and poured some for Maddie. Her mouth was already watering at the thought of the tart lemon soothed by the sweet wine.

Feeling churlish at how easily he was entrancing her, she said, 'You really don't have to do this, you know. It's not working.'

Nic smiled urbanely. 'What's not working? You've proved your point, Maddie. You're happier to live in squalor than to come running to me for home comforts. Clearly I underestimated your ability to put up with discomfort.'

Maddie's appetite disappeared and she said tightly, 'You underestimate a lot more than that, Nic. You don't know one thing about what happened when I left here. You seem to have this halcyon fantasy that I went to Europe and spent my time skiing and partying.'

Carefully he said, 'Why don't you tell me what you did?'

Maddie wanted to refuse, to tell him it was none of his business, but she had a desire to make him understand that she was made of sterner stuff, that she wouldn't just turn around and give up. And also a dangerous desire to see him regard her with something besides mockery or disbelief in his eyes...

'When my mother and I left here we left with nothing. My father threw us out and turned his back on us completely.' Her mouth tightened. 'We spent three years in Buenos Aires living with my aunt, who eventually threw us out. In the meantime Mother had been divorced and found herself a rich suitor. She gave me a one-way ticket to London to get me out of her hair.'

Maddie didn't want to elaborate and tell him that her mother had blamed Maddie for being left with nothing in the divorce. Her gaze remained resolutely forward, out into the darkness that encompassed his vast estate.

'I got to London and found work in a restaurant by night, and as a hotel chambermaid by day. The night you saw me in that club was pure chance. I'd never been in it before, or since then.' Maddie blushed when she thought of the picture she'd presented in the revealing dress. She rushed on. 'When I'd made enough money I moved to France and looked for work picking grapes for the summer. I ended up at the vineyard in Bordeaux, where Pierre Vacheron took me in.'

Maddie sent Nic a quick defensive look. 'He found out where I came from, that I had some knowledge of wine, and decided to give me one of the scholarships. I'd most likely still be there if my father hadn't written and asked me to come home. Pierre offered me a full-time job.'

Nic's face was expressionless. 'That magazine article painted a very different picture.'

Considering that since she had divulged so much already she might as well tell him the whole truth, Maddie laid out the bones of the painful reality of her relationship with her flighty and self-absorbed mother. The humiliation of the whole episode was vivid again.

When she'd finished she put down her dessert wine glass and stood up. The full enormity of her naivety was hitting her—to allow herself to think for a second that Nic de Rojas was as urbane and charming as he appeared this evening. With any other woman, yes. With her, *no*. He was just trying to unbalance her, and she was letting him.

'I want you to realise that I won't be easily dissuaded, or seduced by the trappings of wealth.'

Driven by the wave of ambiguous anger he was feeling, Nic said, 'Don't underestimate *my* determination to succeed in this matter, Maddie. I've proved how determined I can be over and over again.'

Maddie fought not to let Nic see how he was affecting her. 'So we're back where we started?'

Nic's gaze grew hot and moved to her mouth.

Maddie moved back, putting up a hand as if to ward him off. *'No...'*

He reached for her easily and pulled her into him. *'Yes. This is where we started—and where we've yet to finish.'*

And he bent his head and took her mouth in a kiss so incendiary and devastating that Maddie had no defence. Especially not after laying herself bare like that. Her hands clung onto his powerful biceps, her whole body arched into his—he was bending her back further and further with the sheer force of his kiss.

Lips ground into teeth which clashed and nipped at soft skin. Maddie tasted blood at one point and didn't know if it was hers or his. Their tongues duelled madly, in a hot swirl. She only wanted *this*. She would have given every-thing up in that moment to prolong it…

And then abruptly Nic put her away from him with both hands. 'Get out of here, Maddie.'

Maddie looked up, shocked, hurt and bewildered. Her chest was aching with the effort to draw breath. She saw the blood on his lip. She'd bitten him.

A need to claw back some control forced her to say shakily, 'With pleasure. I won't whore myself to you for my vineyard, Nic—the sooner you realise that the better.'

Nic stood in a haze of sexually frustrated agony for long moments. On one level he couldn't fathom how he'd just let Maddie go, but then he remembered the way she'd kissed him back, biting his lip in her ardour. And *that*—hot on the heels of her further revelations about her life these past few years—had made him feel unaccountably vulnerable.

He'd assumed Maddie and her mother had been given plenty of money. He'd had no idea that her father had turfed them out with no support, or that her mother had all but turned her back on her too. That she'd had to take two me-nial jobs just to survive.

Nic went over to the wooden perimeter on the decking which wrapped around this side of the house. His hands curled around it tightly and he took a deep breath, still struggling for control. Kissing Maddie just now had re-minded him too vividly of losing himself to her seductive wiles before.

She'd spent a week reeling him in, making him trust her with pathetic ease. Only to reveal in the end how she'd really felt about seducing him. It had made her physically ill. He'd watched the way she'd retched and coughed after he'd touched her. Nic's stomach clenched hard. She must have been very bored indeed to have pushed the limits of what she could endure for the sake of doing something exciting and illicit.

Something very private and vulnerable in him had been destroyed that day. He'd become hardened. Impenetrable. No woman since then had managed to crack his protective veneer, or challenge his cynicism. But the way Maddie had kissed him just now, and the way she'd kissed him the other night—as artlessly and yet as devastatingly as he remembered—was a threat for which he hadn't been prepared.

He'd thought he could handle kissing her, but tasting her again was dangerous—he felt himself slipping and sliding away from everything that held him rooted to reality and sanity.

Nic had developed a mild aversion to being touched after his mother's nervous and overprotective constant fussing, which had been in stark contrast to his father's habitual rages, when he'd used his fists freely. But when Maddie touched him, he couldn't get enough. It galled him now that he found every woman's touch invariably cloying or too possessive, but not *hers*. It made him very nervous to acknowledge that…which was why he'd pushed her back.

Something inside Nic hardened. He *would* have her— but on his terms. He would force her to be honest with him and herself. There would be no drama, regrets or recriminations this time. Only satisfaction and closure.

A couple of days later Maddie was sitting in her father's study and looking at another invitation. It was addressed to her father, and it was for the Annual South American Vintners' Gala Ball in two days' time. It was in a different city each year, and this year, as luck would have it, it was to be in Buenos Aires. So near—but so far.

Maddie sighed. Something like this was just what she

needed—a chance to meet people who only remembered Vasquez as a successful estate. It was the perfect place to look for investors. But she had no hope of flying to Buenos Aires where the ball was being held. She had no money for the flight, and anyway there was a national airline strike.

Just then the phone rang, and Maddie picked it up. She flushed all over when she heard an all-too-familiar deep voice on the other end. Then she felt cold when she remembered the way he'd aborted their kiss and pushed her from him the other night. She hated Nic de Rojas for exposing her weakness and desire like that. For rejecting her.

'Yes?' Her voice was as cold as she felt.

'Did you get your invitation?'

Maddie couldn't help her stubborn streak from rising up. 'What invitation?'

'You're such a terrible liar, Vasquez. I know you're probably looking at it right now and figuring out how to get there so you can sucker some poor investor into taking on your dead-end estate.'

Maddie made a face at the phone, and then said airily, 'Oh, you mean *that* invitation? Yes, I have it…why?'

'Are you going?'

Something in his voice made Maddie's hackles rise. 'Of course I'm going. Why wouldn't I?'

'No need to sound so defensive, Maddie—I was asking because I'm taking a private jet and was going to offer you a lift.'

Maddie's jaw dropped, but she quickly recovered. After the other night she wouldn't accept anything from this man. 'No, thank you.' She injected saccharine-sweetness into her voice. 'I've got alternative arrangements made. I'll see you there.'

She barely heard him mutter something about *'stub-*

born woman' before she cut him off. Maddie's heart was thumping. She'd have to go now. She couldn't afford to show Nicolás any weakness.

By the time Maddie arrived in Buenos Aires, sticky and hot, almost two days later, she ached all over. She'd taken a ridiculously long bus journey from Mendoza, and every bump in the road seemed to be engraved on her nerves.

Maddie hauled her bag behind her and joined the masses of people all making their way to various destinations. Hers was the cheapest hotel she'd been able to find close to the Grand Palace Buenos Aires hotel, where the gala was due to take place that evening.

When she finally found her room and looked at herself in the mirror, she realised that she had a mountain of work to do to make herself look every inch the successful vintner she wanted to portray herself as being.

Nic didn't like the sense of anticipation firing up his blood. This fizzing expectancy. He was used to being in control at all times, and right now he felt off-kilter. He realised that it was because he didn't know where *she* was. He'd almost gone to her home and forced her to come with him on his plane, but a sensation of lingering rawness after the other night had stopped him.

And how the hell had she even got here? He knew it couldn't have been by air because of the strike, which was why he'd ordered the private jet.

Just then he spotted a familiar face in the crowd and he smiled warmly, welcoming the distraction.

Maddie's stomach was in knots. She took a deep breath and stepped into the thronged ballroom. She'd managed to ferret out another of her mother's dresses, and mercifully this one fitted. It was green and shimmery, it fell to the floor, and it was relatively demure, with long sleeves and a high neck. But when she walked one pale leg was exposed, thanks to a thigh-high slit. Maddie had cursed when she'd discovered it; the sooner she could afford to supplement her own wardrobe again, the better.

She'd used her practically maxed-out credit card to buy some cheap shoes and get her hair done in a salon, and now it lay in lustrous-looking waves over one shoulder. She was glad she'd spent the money when she saw how immaculate everyone else looked. She just hoped they wouldn't notice that her emerald earrings had come from a costume-jewellery shop.

And then she saw Nic across the room. Her hands tightened reflexively on the clutch bag she carried in front of her like a shield. She hated the awful feeling of excitement that danced along her veins at seeing him again. He wasn't looking at her, though; he was looking down at the woman in front of him and smiling in a way that made an awful yearning go through Maddie.

And then, to her horror, as if they were connected by some telepathic thread of awareness, he looked up and straight at her. His smile faded. The woman he'd been talking to looked over as well, and Maddie felt her belly hollow out when she recognised the same stunning blonde from the first night she'd seen him again in Mendoza.

Someone came by with a tray full of champagne and Maddie grabbed a glass inelegantly because she could see Nic taking his companion by the hand and leading her towards Maddie. It was as if she was rooted to the spot. She couldn't move, and with everything in her head and heart she cursed him—because he was going to introduce her to his mistress and make her feel like dirt.

He came closer and closer, a curiously intent look on

his face and in his eyes. Maddie was stuck like a deer in the headlights. She'd never felt so alone or exposed. She should never have come…she should have known he'd take any opportunity to humiliate her…

'Maddie, you made it…I'll resist the temptation to ask how you did it.'

Maddie's voice wouldn't work for a long moment. She could feel a curious glance from the stunning blonde, and hot, angry colour seeped into her cheeks. She'd never been in this situation before—having kissed another woman's man. And she was disappointed. Somehow she hadn't expected this kind of behaviour from him.

'…like you to meet someone.'

Like watching a car crash in slow motion, Maddie managed to look at the other woman and smile, but it felt numb. She realised then that the woman was much younger than Maddie had realised—about twenty at the most. Now she felt sick—and also, more worryingly, as if she wanted to gouge her eyes out.

'This is my cousin Estella. You would have met her at the wine-tasting evening, but she had to be in BA for a modelling assignment. She's in high demand. Not to mention that she breaks out in hives after a couple of days in the country.'

The girl looked adoringly at Nic and hit him playfully on his shoulder. 'Hardly hives, Nic. You do like to exaggerate, don't you?'

Maddie was aware that the girl was exquisite, beautiful, and had a sense of humour. And then it sank in properly. *My cousin.*

Maddie forced her throat to work, and tried to ignore the relief flooding her. 'It's nice to meet you, Estella,' she said scratchily.

'You too, Maddie.' She turned her sunny smile back to Nic and said, 'I'd better go and find my date or he'll be sending out a search party.'

'I need to meet this man who is going to pretend that he *won't* be sharing your hotel room tonight.'

Maddie looked at Nic and saw an endearingly stern look on his face. His cousin blushed, but rolled her eyes. 'Yes, Nic, but please don't give him the third degree. He's a nice guy, really.'

She jumped up and pressed a kiss to Nic's cheek, then was gone with a flash of blonde hair and sinuous tanned limbs.

Maddie was mesmerised by Nic's fond gaze after his cousin, so she wasn't prepared when he turned to look at her and his whole visage became noticeably cooler.

'I booked her a room for the night because I don't like her going back out to the suburbs too late. At least this way I know she's safe. Her father was my mother's brother. He died when she was small, so I've become a sort of…father figure for her.'

Maddie's belly clenched at hearing how protective Nic was of his cousin. A bit redundantly she said, 'She seems nice.'

Someone bumped into Maddie at that moment, and she winced. She could feel that she had a bruise on one hip.

'What is it?'

The sudden urgency in Nic's voice made her look up. 'Nothing. I'm just a bit sore after—' She stopped herself there. But it wasn't long before a dawning realistion came into Nic's eyes.

'You took the bus, didn't you?' He shook his head. 'Of all the stubborn—' He stopped and cursed. 'How long was it? Fourteen hours?'

Maddie cursed him, and then admitted painfully, 'Sixteen, actually. We got a flat tyre.'

He shook his head at her and then said, 'I suppose you're here to look for an investor?'

Maddie flushed. 'What other choice do I have? It's find an investor or lose everything to you.'

'You'd be a very wealthy woman.'

Something painful twisted in Maddie's chest at hearing him reiterate that he wanted her gone at all costs. It made her feel very nervous and she lashed out. 'Why can't you get it through that thick skull of yours that it's not about the money? I love my estate and I want to restore it to its full potential.'

Nic's jaw clenched. He opened his mouth, but just then the gong sounded for the gala dinner. Maddie took the opportunity to flee in the ensuing crush, grateful that she didn't feel a strong hand on her arm. She had every intention of talking to as many people as possible and staying away from one person in particular.

All during dinner Nic was aware of Maddie across the other side of the table. She was seated beside Alex Morales, one of the most successful vintners in the US—a man Nic had never particularly liked or trusted without ever having analysed why. It was a gut reaction, and it was becoming stronger by the second.

He couldn't concentrate on the conversations either side of him and he wanted to snarl at the pouting redhead across the table who seemed determined to give him a bird's-eye view of her surgically enhanced cleavage.

All Nic could imagine was Maddie's huge green eyes imploring Morales to invest in her poor vineyard, and he had to physically restrain himself from walking over, plucking her from the chair and carrying her far away.

Maddie looked at her attentive and charming dinner companion incredulously. 'You'd really like to discuss this further?'

The man smiled and oozed charm. 'Of course, my dear.'

He was a little cheesy for Maddie's liking, but she wasn't about to dismiss a potential investor because of a possibly erroneous gut feeling.

She couldn't believe she'd had the good fortune to be seated next to Alex Morales, and that he was interested in learning more about the Vasquez estate. This could be the solution to all her problems. If she could persuade Morales to invest in her she'd be free of Nic's influence.

Maddie had been uncomfortably aware of Nic's gaze on her all throughout the dinner but she'd done her best to ignore him. However, with this exciting development, she couldn't help glancing over in his direction. She hated that she met that blue gaze so effortlessly, as if drawn by a magnet. He was looking impossibly grim. She smiled and his eyes flashed. Maddie knew it was childish, but she was buoyed up to think that her problems could soon be over.

People were already getting up and moving out to the ballroom, which had been cleared for dancing with tables set around the dance floor. Morales took Maddie's hand to guide her from her seat. His touch lingered a little too long for Maddie's liking, but she quashed the flutter of doubt, telling herself she had to explore this opportunity.

He bowed slightly in a disarmingly old-fashioned gesture. 'If you'd excuse me? I have an important call I have to make, but I will be available in about thirty minutes if you'd like to continue our discussion?'

Maddie's eagerness was dismayingly obvious. 'I really appreciate this, Mr Morales.'

'Please…' He smiled, showing glaringly white teeth. 'Call me Alex. Why don't you meet me at my room—say in thirty-five minutes?'

He told her his room number and was turning away when sudden panic gripped Maddie. Their conversation had just taken a turn she really hadn't expected.

She reached for Morales's arm and he turned back, one eyebrow raised. 'Yes?'

Immediately Maddie felt gauche. 'I'm sorry, but… wouldn't it be easier to meet in one of the bars?'

Morales smiled, and it was faintly patronising. 'I have to make the call in my room, so it really would be easier if you came to me. All of the bars will be full and very loud. Of course, if this discussion isn't that important to you…'

His voice trailed off and Maddie picked up his meaning instantly, seeing her chance floating away.

'No, no,' she said hurriedly, telling herself that he sounded reasonable. 'Your room will be fine. Absolutely fine.'

He inclined his head and then walked away. Only to be replaced almost immediately by someone taller and far more disturbing. Maddie tried to walk around Nic but he blocked her.

She glared up at him. 'Yes?'

Nic's jaw was tense and his eyes were flashing. 'I don't trust that man.'

CHAPTER SIX

'Oh, please,' Maddie sneered. 'You just can't bear the thought that someone else might see the potential in my estate and want to invest in me.'

Nic's eyes flashed. 'I think he wants to invest, all right, but it's not necessarily in your estate. Where are you meeting him?'

Maddie went puce. She refused to answer and went to walk around Nic again, but he caught her arm in a big hand. Maddie gritted her teeth against the instant chemical reaction in her body.

He was incredulous. 'Don't tell me you're going to meet him in his room? Is that what that little conference was about?' Maddie went even more red and Nic exploded, 'For crying out loud, Maddie, you're too inexperienced to deal with someone like Morales. He'll chew you up and spit you out!'

Maddie reacted viscerally. Little did Nic know how inexperienced she really was—physically *and* in situations like these. But every ounce of pride demanded that she project an image of confidence. She looked up at Nic and tossed her hair back. She smiled up at him and hoped it had the same slightly patronising edge that Morales had just used on her.

'Do you really think I haven't met men like Morales before now? I know his type, Nic. He just needs to be played a certain way.'

Nic's face flushed and he dropped her arm suddenly, as if it was poisonous. Immediately Maddie felt bereft.

He sounded utterly disgusted. 'Forgive me for thinking for a second that you might be going into a situation you're not equipped to handle. If he's the kind of investor you want, and you're willing to do what it takes, then clearly I've underestimated you *and* your ambition.'

Nic took a step back from her and walked away, leaving Maddie feeling vulnerable and insecure. What exactly had Nic meant by not trusting Morales? She recalled his smooth smile and shuddered a little. Surely even if he came on to her she could just walk away?

Maddie didn't like the way Nic had made her feel slightly ashamed just now, or the feeling, for a brief moment, that he might be concerned for her safety. Maddie wasn't used to anyone else stepping in to fight her battles for her. Her brother had been the only one who'd ever stood up for her, and he'd died a long time ago.

Realising that she was standing and brooding in an empty dining room, Maddie knew she had to move. She glanced at her watch and cursed silently. It was already nearly time to meet Morales. Pushing down the sudden trepidation she felt, Maddie hurried to the lifts.

Nic was standing in one of the hotel bars with some acquaintances when he saw a flash of green out of the corner of his eye and looked to see Maddie disappear into a lift. His stomach clenched so hard for a second that his vision blurred slightly. He couldn't believe that she was actually going through with it. He'd underestimated her, all right. Underestimated her greed and her ambition to succeed no matter what it took.

Nic battled for a long moment with the seething emotions in his gut and then one overriding feeling rose up as he recalled Maddie's defiance just now, and her flushed face. Surely she wasn't doing this to get at *him*?

Nic put down his glass and excused himself. In hindsight, and when she wasn't standing in front of him and scrambling his brain cells with her proximity, her bravado seemed far too brittle.

He quickly got Morales's room number and strode to the lifts, punching the button. And then something stopped him—maybe he had completely misread the way she'd kissed him with such artless fervour? Maybe she changed her method for each man and gave them what she thought they wanted? Maybe she was playing Nic—kissing him the way she suspected would affect him most, reminding him of those gauche responses in the orchard that day?

The lift doors opened and Nic was torn. He couldn't move. Was he really going to go after Maddie and risk exposing himself all over again? He could already see her mocking face when she opened Morales's door. What the hell was he going to say when he *did* get up to the room?

'Nic! There you are. I've been looking for you everywhere. You have to come and meet Louis…he's waiting for you.'

Nic looked down at his cousin, who had just hooked her arm into his, and felt slightly dazed. Suddenly everything came back into perspective and he cursed this bout of uncharacteristic indecision. He felt nothing for Maddie except mistrust and antipathy—along with an annoying level of desire. Estella was someone he loved unconditionally. Who was more important to him?

He smiled down at her and said, 'Lead the way.' And as Estella dragged him in her wake Nic pushed aside all thoughts of the sable-haired witch, telling himself that Maddie was certainly able to handle herself.

He ignored the slightly ominous sound of the lift doors closing again behind him.

Maddie was stuck in a waking nightmare. She had locked herself inside the bathroom in Morales's suite and was shaking all over. She had no idea how much time had passed. But mercifully he'd stopped thumping on the bathroom door and calling her names a few minutes ago.

Carefully she stood up and went over to the sink. She looked at herself in the mirror. Her eyes widened in shock—her hair was a mess, her dress was torn at the neck and blood was oozing from a cut lip. She was still in shock. She couldn't really believe what had happened.

Her first indication that something was wrong should have been the fact that he was obviously more inebriated than he had been downstairs. But at first Morales had been charming. And interested. He'd disarmed her and made her feel as if she was overreacting. She'd tried to ignore the fact that his words were slurring slightly and that he was a little unsteady on his feet.

She'd launched into her spiel about the estate. But then he'd come over to sit beside her and put his hand high on her thigh. Immediately panicked, Maddie had jerked back, dislodging his hand. Everything had changed in an instant. He'd turned into a monster.

In the struggle that had ensued he'd ripped her dress and slapped her across the face. Maddie had somehow managed to push him off her and made for the only route of escape or safety she could see. She had locked herself in the bathroom. Morales had shouted obscenities, and she'd been terrified he'd break the door down. But now, after long minutes, everything was mercifully quiet.

Maddie crept over to the door and listened. Her heart leapt when she heard the unmistakable sound of snoring. With her pulse beating fast, she turned the lock silently and opened the door, half terrified it would smash open in her face.

She saw Morales sprawled on the couch, fast asleep with his mouth open wide. Nearly crying with relief, Maddie crept out—all the way to the main door. Her hands were shaking so badly she almost couldn't open it, and when it did open she all but fell into the corridor. She only re-alised then that her shoes had come off somewhere along the way in the struggle, but there was no way she would go back and get them now.

Forcing herself to keep moving, she set off to find the lift.

Nic rounded a corner in the corridor where he'd walked Estella back to her room, much to her amusement, and stopped dead when he saw a familiar figure walking to-wards him. Recognition was like a hot poker in his belly. He knew this was Morales's floor, and hadn't liked to admit that part of his motivation in walking Estella to her room had been for that reason. Had he really been hoping to bump into Maddie making her walk of shame? Well, his subconscious desire had manifested her right in front of him.

Anger rose like a swift tide of lava inside him. And something else much more potent and disturbing. *Jealousy.* An alien emotion because no other woman had ever aroused it in him.

In that moment Maddie looked up and saw him. She stopped dead and froze like a deer in the headlights. Nic heard something inarticulate like a sob coming from her throat, and then she turned and was walking back the way she'd come. Away from him.

All Nic was aware of was her *déshabillé* and mussed-up hair. And then he saw her bare feet. His anger became white-hot. Being barefoot made her look ridiculously vulnerable, but she'd just been— Bile rose in Nic's throat, and before he even knew what he was doing he was pursuing her, driven by dark and angry demons.

When he was close enough to reach out and touch her he stopped, and said with scorn dripping from every word, 'Well? Did you give Morales everything he wanted or just enough of a taste to keep him interested?' Disgust and something else—*disappointment*—lanced Nic in a very vulnerable place.

Maddie stopped too, her shoulders a tense line. She didn't turn around. 'Just leave me alone, Nic.'

Her voice sounded husky and raw, and it made Nic even angrier. She was still playing on his emotions. He reached for her shoulder and swung her round—but when he saw her face the bottom fell out of his stomach.

Instinctively he put his other hand on her other shoulder. 'Maddie…what the hell…? Did Morales do this?'

Maddie tried to look away, or down, but Nic gently tipped her chin up so he could inspect her face. He cursed volubly. Maddie jerked her chin out of his hold and pulled back. The blood on her split lip looked garish against the stark paleness of her face.

'What, Nic? Aren't you going to say I told you so? You did warn me, after all, not to trust him.'

Maddie was struggling to hold it together, to be strong. She couldn't bear it that Nic was witness to her awful humiliation. She'd never felt so frail or weak. Or useless. And she hated the lingering terror that made her want to cling onto his solid strength. She looked down, tears suddenly stinging her eyes.

He sounded tortured. 'When I said I didn't trust Morales, it was a gut instinct. I've never liked him, or his business methods, but I had no idea he was capable of violence.'

Maddie was bitter. 'Well, it would seem your instincts have been proved right.'

He asked then, 'When did he do this to you? After…?'

Maddie looked up at Nic in abject horror, forgetting about her tears. He thought that she'd *slept* with Morales anyway? How low was his opinion of her? Bile rose and she was afraid she'd be sick. And yet who did she have to blame but herself when she'd been so intent on proving to Nic that she was *experienced*?

Suddenly the fight left Maddie. The shock that had been numbing her wore off. The awful shaking that hadn't abated. It seemed to intensify all over her body. 'I didn't sleep with him. That was never my intention.' She shuddered reflexively. 'I couldn't…with a man like that…just to get something. You can call me naive, or whatever you want, but I went to his room believing that we would just talk about business.'

Maddie took a deep shaky breath, and avoided Nic's eye again. 'But then…he was all over me…and I couldn't move or breathe. He'd been drinking. I hadn't realised how much. He ripped my dress and then he slapped me…'

To Maddie's horror she started crying in earnest, great deep racking sobs that seemed to come out of nowhere and she couldn't control them. She felt so cold. Suddenly heat engulfed her and she felt herself being drawn into an embrace of solid muscle. Musky male scent surrounded her. And finally she felt safe. Unbelievably safe.

Maddie was incredibly slender and vulnerable in Nic's

arms, her slim body trembling violently. The protective instinct was almost overwhelming. He wanted to believe her so badly he could taste it.

To see her crushed like this was almost as hard as if she'd been defiant and triumphant. No one could fake the terror he could feel in her body. Nic's vision was red. His father had used to hit his mother whenever she angered him, and Nic had an absolute abhorrence of violence against women. The rage he felt towards Morales scared him with its intensity.

Yet he found it hard to believe that Maddie hadn't known what she was walking into by agreeing to meet him in his room. How could she have been so naive? An experienced woman like her? Had she just been playing out of her league? Not counting on Morales turning violent?

Deep inside Nic was shame and self-recrimination that he'd allowed Maddie to walk into that situation. That he'd let his own pride stop him from following his initial gut instinct to go after her. This woman had him so tied up in knots that he'd prefer to let her be in danger than deal with her. He was pathetic.

Nic held Maddie for a long time, until her sobs had stopped. His hands moved up and down her back, soothing her. *Déjà vu* hit him straight in his belly when he remembered another time and place, when he'd held this woman in his arms after seeing her in tears. He tensed against the inevitable pain that accompanied those memories, but for the first time it didn't come.

She'd stopped shaking and crying, and was as still as a mouse in his arms. He could feel her breath, warm through the flimsy material of his shirt. And just like that the protective instinct was dissolving in a rush of heat and arousal. Her body was moulding against his as if made for him alone. Every curve fitted perfectly into his harder planes.

Nic gritted his jaw, but he couldn't stop his body responding to her proximity, or the way it felt to have her soft breasts crushed against his chest.

When she tensed slightly and shifted, Nic loosened his hold.

Maddie realised that she'd just fallen into Nic's arms like some kind of wilting heroine and felt embarrassed. She pulled back from him reluctantly, swaying a little unsteadily on her feet. Her eyes widened on a point on his chest. 'There's blood on your shirt.'

He barely glanced down. 'It's fine.'

Much to her shame, his touch had stopped being comforting and had become something much more provocative long seconds ago—when the blood had rushed to intimate parts of her body in helpless reaction to being held by him. Her nipples were tight against the lace of her bra even now. Her skin was tingling all over and she felt hot.

He hadn't let her go completely. His hands were on her shoulders, his gaze searching hers. 'Where do you think you're going?'

Maddie met his eyes reluctantly, afraid he might see something of that shameful desire in her eyes. She felt very raw and exposed. 'I should go back to my hotel.' She shuddered reflexively, despite wanting to appear in control of her emotions. 'I want to have a shower. I feel dirty.'

When she moved to pull free of his hands completely Nic let her go, but to Maddie's horror her legs were so weak that they gave way. As if without his touch she couldn't stay standing.

Nic caught her up into his arms so fast her head spun, and he said grimly, 'You're not going anywhere. You're coming with me.'

Maddie tried to protest, but she was too weak. Being

in Nic's arms like this made her feel like the worst traitor for giving in, but she couldn't drum up the will to fight.

She was barely aware of Nic taking her into a lift and it ascending to the top floor, or their walk down the corridor and then a door swinging open onto a dimly lit room with a plush interior and stupendous views over night-time Buenos Aires.

Gently he put her down on a sofa and said, 'Will you be all right for a minute?'

Maddie nodded, feeling guilty. The minute Nic had enfolded her in his arms she'd felt a thousand times better. He stood up to his full height and Maddie watched as he picked up a phone. With his other hand he yanked off his bow tie and shucked off his jacket. He opened the top buttons of his shirt with long, lean fingers, and Maddie's mouth went dry.

He was speaking in low tones on the phone. 'Send up a first-aid kit, please? Thank you.'

He put down the phone and disappeared into the bathroom. Maddie could hear running water, and then Nic reappeared. He squatted down beside her. 'Do you feel okay to have a shower?'

Maddie's skin was still crawling when she thought of that man. She nodded vigorously and Nic helped her up from the couch.

He said, 'There's a robe in the bathroom. By the time you're out I'll have a first-aid kit to see to your lip.'

Maddie went into the steam-filled bathroom and shut the door. She leant back against it for a long moment, until the steam started to make her feel light-headed. Incredibly weary, she undressed and stepped into the shower, letting the hot water beat down for a long time before soaping up her hands and washing herself all over. Finally, when she felt clean again, she got out.

She dried herself and rubbed her hair, leaving it to hang damply down her back. Belting the robe tightly around her body, she cautiously opened the door again to face Nic.

He was standing with his back to her, looking out of one of the huge windows. Maddie's heart picked up its unsteady pace when he turned around to face her. He was drinking amber liquid from a tumbler glass but he put it down, coming towards her.

'Let me see your lip.'

Maddie put a finger to it and winced because it felt so swollen. Nic came and took her chin in his thumb and forefinger, lifting it to the light. Maddie held her breath. His proximity was setting every nerve tingling. She was intrigued and unsettled to see this side of him. He let her go and took some cotton wool and antiseptic from the first-aid kit.

'This might sting a bit.'

He touched the cotton wool to her lip and Maddie sucked in a breath, her eyes watering, but she said nothing.

'At least it's stopped bleeding. It'll have gone down by tomorrow.'

Maddie said, half jokingly, 'You're familiar with split lips, then?'

To her surprise Nic's jaw tightened. He just said, 'I've had a few in my time.'

Then something else caught Maddie's eye, and before she knew what she was doing she'd taken Nic's hand in hers. 'What's happened to your knuckles?' They were badly grazed.

When he tried to take his hand back Maddie held on firmly and looked at him.

Nic answered tightly, 'While you were in the shower I paid a visit to Morales.'

Maddie gasped. 'You hit him?'

Nic's face was hard, making a shiver run through Maddie.

'I stopped myself from knocking him senseless. He's lucky he got away with a bruised jaw.'

Overcome with a burgeoning and volatile emotion, Maddie bent her head and pressed a kiss to Nic's bruised knuckles. She looked up again and said huskily, 'I hate violence, but in this case…thank you.'

Nic's eyes were so blue Maddie felt as if she was falling, even though she was still standing. A taut stillness came into the air around them—until Nic said, 'Morales is claiming that you slept with him.'

For a second Maddie almost didn't understand what he was saying, and then the words sank in—and the way Nic was looking at her. She dropped his hand, suddenly aghast that she'd just kissed it. She'd been looking at him like some lovestruck groupie and he still thought…

Maddie felt sick.

'You think I'm lying.' Her voice was flat. She moved back, conscious of being in a hotel robe with nothing underneath. And of having exposed herself. How could she have forgotten for a moment, just because Nic had been slightly chivalrous and protective, that he still didn't trust her, that he thought the worst of her? He'd done nothing he wouldn't have done for any other distressed woman. She'd just read an ocean of meaning into his actions…

In the ensuing silence Maddie looked away. Even if she reiterated her innocence it would be her word against Morales's. She looked back at Nic again, and said half defiantly, 'What do you care anyway?'

Nic felt a heavy dark weight lodge in his gut. He *had* believed Maddie, out there in the corridor, when she'd been so obviously distraught. But when he'd confronted Morales just now and the man had drunkenly goaded Nic by saying, 'Jealous, de Rojas? Because she slept with me and not you?' Nic had seen red. He hadn't been so angry in years. Before he'd even known what he was doing his fist had connected with Morales's smirking face.

It burned Nic inside to know that he'd been driven to violence—not so much by what the man had done to Maddie as at the thought that she might have actually slept with him.

Just now, when she'd taken his bruised hand in hers and kissed his knuckles and then looked up at him, he'd felt as if he was drowning in those green depths. Losing himself in her. Again. The last time he'd lost himself with this woman she'd annihilated him.

He assured himself that he was not that young man any more. But it was as if she'd peeled back a protective layer of his skin, exposing his innermost self all over again.

Pushing down that heavy weight even further, Nic said coolly, 'I care about the fact that a man abused you. Beyond that it's none of my business.'

Maddie was incredibly hurt by Nic's mistrust, and couldn't believe that she'd been so seduced by a little tenderness. Once again Nic was proving just how naive she was—as if Alex Morales hadn't already drummed it into her.

'You're right.' She hoped she matched his cool tone. 'It is none of your business.'

Maddie went to go back into the bathroom to get her dress.

Nic said from behind her in a curt voice, 'Where are you going?'

She turned around. 'I have to return to my hotel. My bus back to Mendoza leaves at six tomorrow morning.'

Nic emitted a curse that made Maddie blush. And then

he said curtly, 'You're not going back to that hotel. It's too late. And you're coming home with me tomorrow. You will *not* be taking a sixteen-hour bus journey again.'

Maddie felt like stamping her foot. Why couldn't Nic just disapprove of her and let her go?

Volatile emotions were rising, making her voice wobbly. 'I might have believed you care if you hadn't just accused me of sleeping with a man to secure his favour. A man capable of violence! Quite frankly my cockroach-infested hotel room is a more enticing prospect than staying here to suffer your judgemental condemnation.'

Nic slashed a hand through the air. 'Dammit, Maddie, I'll get another room. But you're *not* leaving this hotel— and if I have to lock you in here, I will. Tell me where your stuff is.'

Maddie looked at Nic and fumed—inwardly and outwardly. She put her hands on her hips. 'Damn *you*, Nic de Rojas. You think you're so perfect? How dare you pretend to be honourable when you clearly think me nothing better than a street—'

Nic closed the distance between them in seconds. Suddenly he was too close and Maddie backed away, her pulse leaping in her throat. He was blisteringly angry— but Maddie sensed that it wasn't with *her*. That threw her.

'Your hotel and your room number, Maddie. I'm not going to take no for an answer.'

To her everlasting mortification, when Maddie thought of navigating Buenos Aires to get to her fleapit of a hotel, and that tortuous bus journey tomorrow, she wanted to cry. She was still feeling extremely fragile and vulnerable. Nic thought she had sold herself this evening for her estate, and yet he'd insisted on looking after her—as if she was an unsavoury package he had to take care of. She could see the glitter of determination in his eyes, and wouldn't put it past him to lock her into the suite.

She swallowed and gritted out finally, 'It's the Hotel Esmerelda. Room 410.'

Nic was returning to the suite after booking another room for himself and getting Maddie's things from her hotel. He'd wanted to get away from her so that his brain might start functioning again in a vaguely normal manner.

Deep down he didn't really believe that she'd slept with Morales…but when she stood in front of him and those green eyes were on his the need to put up a wall between them felt like the most important thing. He'd had no defence when he'd seen her so upset and vulnerable, and the speed and ease with which she got under his skin terrified him.

Nic steeled himself outside the suite door. He had her one small suitcase in his hands, pathetically light. Any woman he knew travelled with a veritable entourage to carry their luggage. But not Maddie.

When he opened the door and went in all was hushed. He'd half expected to see her standing defiantly where he'd left her. He explored further and came to a halt. She was curled up on the couch like a little lost soul, black hair fanned over her shoulders, her head resting on one arm.

Nic's chest constricted and he put down the bag. He walked over and bent down beside her, but she didn't stir. Overcome with a feeling too huge to push down, Nic tucked some black silky locks behind her ear. She was so pale, her eyebrows starkly black against her skin. That garish cut looked even more lurid.

Unable to help himself, Nic bent forward and pressed a kiss to the corner of her mouth where it was cut.

Maddie was asleep, but in her dreams something amazing was happening. She felt cocooned in safety and warmth and something else—something much hotter. Desire. She dreamt that Nic was touching his lips to hers gently, lingering as if he couldn't force himself to pull away.

Maddie struggled up through layers of consciousness and opened slumberous eyes. She was looking directly into Nic's vivid blue eyes, intent on hers with a seriousness that connected with something deep inside her. She wasn't even sure if she was dreaming or not.

She moved her mouth experimentally, loath to lose that connection of his warm firm mouth on hers. Gently he applied more pressure, and Maddie's lips opened slightly. Her eyes fluttered closed, because the sheer intensity of his gaze was too much. She felt the tip of his tongue exploring, and a deep mewl sounded in the back of her throat. Instinctively she sank back even further into the couch, aware of Nic's broad chest close to her breasts.

The pressure of his mouth on hers became stronger, and a fire started fizzing in her veins. Maddie angled her head and Nic's hands and fingers sank into her hair, cupping her head so that he could stroke his tongue inside her mouth and tease hers.

Maddie felt buoyant. Euphoria was infecting her blood. When Nic's mouth left hers and he trailed his lips down over her chin and neck her head fell back, her belly tightening with need. If she was dreaming she never wanted to wake up. She could feel his head descending and he pulled open her robe. Maddie felt air whistle over the exposed slope of her breast, and her hands were on Nic's shoulders, as if to hold him in place.

She raised her heavy head and looked down to see Nic's own dark blond one close to the pale swell. With his hand he was exposing her breast fully now, and cupping the plump mound with its tight pink nipple. A callused thumb circled the darker areola and then flicked the tip. Maddie sucked in a breath, her hands tightening on Nic's shoulders. Her body was arching towards him, instinctively seeking more.

When his mouth moved down to take the place of his thumb and surrounded her with a moist sucking heat she gasped out loud. Never had she felt such an intense building need within her…at least not since that cataclysmic week after which everything had changed and been tainted.

Her urgency seemed to be transmitting itself to Nic. His mouth became rougher and his hand moved down, sliding under her robe, over her belly and down. His mouth came back up to find hers, but they'd both lost sight of the fact that Maddie was injured—because pain bloomed as soon as Nic's mouth crushed to hers.

It was like a shower of cold water being thrown down on them both. Maddie yelped with pain and Nic sprang back as if shot. Maddie put her hand to her mouth and felt the warm trickle of blood again. She all but scrambled off the couch, feeling totally disorientated. *How* had she ended up kissing Nic?

Maddie wasn't even comforted by the sight of his own flushed cheeks and tortured expression. She went to the bathroom and straight to the mirror. There wasn't much blood. She sucked in a shaky breath and wet the corner of a facecloth to hold it to her mouth. Her eyes were huge and glittering, her cheeks hectic with colour. Her chest was rising and falling as if she'd just been running, and down lower, between her legs, she was slippery, hot and aching. His hand had been so close…those long fingers almost touching her right there. She pressed her legs together as if that would push down the desire.

When she felt a little more in control of herself she went

back outside to see Nic standing like a statue, watching her warily.

'I think I'd like to be alone now.'

Something savage crossed Nic's face, and in two long strides he was right in front of her. 'You wanted it too, Maddie. Don't pretend you didn't.'

Maddie flushed. Okay, so she'd woken up to find Nic's mouth on hers, but the kiss had been supremely gentle. She could remember the moment when she could have drawn back and pushed him away, but weakly she'd wanted to pretend that she didn't have to make the decision to stop and had exerted pressure back, changing it into a very mutual thing.

The hurt of his low opinion of her was still raw. Maddie had to protect herself. For him this was just sexual attraction. He didn't even care that she might have slept with another man only hours before.

Nic reached his hand out as if to touch her lip and Maddie jerked back, making his eyes flash dangerously.

'It's fine. Please, Nic, just go.'

He looked at her for a long moment, a muscle pulsing in his jaw, and then finally he stepped back. 'Eight in the morning I'll come and get you. Be ready.'

Maddie nodded.

Nic turned and walked towards the main door, and then he turned back. Ominously he said, 'We're not done with this, Maddie. Not by a long shot.'

CHAPTER SEVEN

MADDIE was grateful that Nic seemed preoccupied the next morning, and their journey to the airfield was made largely in silence. He'd looked at her assessingly this morning, and Maddie had had to submit to his inspection of her mouth, her chin in his hand as he'd tipped her face up to him.

Just the touch of those fingers to her face had had her heating up inside like an exploding thermostat. He'd let her go and declared, 'The swelling has gone down. A couple more days and you won't even see it.'

Maddie had bitten back the childish urge to tell him that she could have figured that out for herself, but a weak part of her had *liked* his concern. Even if it was only perfunctory.

The small private jet was all cream leather seats and pristinely carpeted luxury. Maddie was intimidated by this further evidence of Nic's wealth. He, however, was nonchalant, his large frame dominating a two-seater couch along one wall. Maddie chose a seat at right angles to Nic.

When they were airborne, and Maddie had turned down the offer of champagne, the silence grew taut between them. Maddie wished she had a book or something to pretend an interest in. She was far too aware of Nic brooding just feet away, and felt like asking snappishly what was wrong.

She risked a glance over and her heart flipped in her chest. Instead of a censorious blue gaze she saw his head tipped back and his eyes closed. His jaw was tense, though, so he couldn't be asleep. She could see the dark fans his lashes made on those defined cheekbones, the faint stubble already forming on his jaw even though he was freshly shaved.

His shirt was open at the neck and Maddie had a tantalising glimpse of dark blond chest hair dusting dark olive skin. She looked back up and blanched when she saw him staring back at her. She'd just been caught ogling him like some lust-crazed teenage girl.

Despite his relaxed pose, Maddie could sense that inwardly he was alert, like an animal poised to strike. Immediately she felt nervous.

'I have a proposition for you.'

Maddie felt even more nervous. She cleared her throat and crossed her legs. 'What kind of a proposition?'

His eyes flicked down briefly to follow the movement of her legs, and Maddie pressed her thighs together unconsciously. Nic took his arms off the back of the couch and moved forward, resting his arms on his thighs.

'I think you've proved how determined you are to save your estate.'

Maddie flushed to think of the awful helplessness she'd felt in Alex Morales's room, how easily he'd dominated her. How easily he could have hurt her far worse than he had.

Defensively she said, 'I wouldn't do what I did last night again. It was stupid.'

Nic shrugged minutely. 'You were just out of your depth.'

Maddie stung at Nic's rebuke, but it was true. She wanted to get them off the subject of last night. It reminded her of too much raw emotion. 'What is it you want to propose?'

For a split second Maddie had an image in her head of Nic kneeling at her feet, looking at her with a tortured expression and asking her to marry him. Hot colour seeped into her cheeks, making his gaze narrow on hers, and Maddie wished she could just disappear.

'You still insist on seeking an investor—you won't sell?'

Maddie tensed. She shook her head. 'I'll never sell.'

'So,' he prodded, 'you'll keep looking for an investor?'

Maddie nodded. 'I have to.'

Grimly Nic said, 'That's what I was afraid of.'

Wary now, Maddie said, 'What do you mean?'

Nic was shaking his head. 'You're not going to find it easy. Morales is undoubtedly making sure your name is muck. If he told *me* last night that you'd slept together, then he'll be spreading the word to others too.'

Maddie felt sick. She wanted to shout and scream her innocence to Nic, but she knew he wouldn't listen to her.

'So…what does that mean?'

Nic said, 'It means that unless you go to Europe and seek out your contacts there you don't have a hope of getting an investor.'

Maddie felt sicker. She had no money for a trip like that, and she couldn't go and ask her old boss for help. He had a flourishing business, but not enough to invest the kind of money she needed. And she'd left him after he'd put her through college. She could hardly ask him for a handout when he'd already been so generous.

Maddie looked at Nic. She felt incredibly bleak. 'So what is this? An exercise in showing me how hopeless my case is?'

Nic looked at Maddie. He had her exactly where he wanted her now. Well, not *exactly*. Where he really wanted her was on her back, underneath him, begging for release. But this was a means to that end. He felt ruthless, but he quashed the feeling. Last night had proved to him how out of control he was around Maddie as soon as he came within touching distance.

He had to have her. But he had to protect himself in the process. He needed to control this vulnerability. And what he was about to propose offered him that protection.

Nic watched her reaction closely as he said, 'I will invest in your estate.'

The colour seemed to leach from Maddie's cheeks at first, leaving her skin like porcelain and her eyes huge. And then, as she took a deep breath, colour rushed back, staining those cheeks red. His groin throbbed in response.

She shook her head. 'No way. You want something. You want to ruin me.'

Nic smiled. 'I have to admit that at first I just wanted you gone…but since you've come home life has certainly been more entertaining.'

Maddie resolutely turned away and crossed her arms over her chest. Nic's eyes were helplessly drawn to where her breasts were pushed up, clearly defined under the thin T-shirt she wore. One long lock of black hair curled down, tantalisingly close to the slope of her breast, and he clenched his jaw. He had to have this woman. He would go insane if he didn't.

Maddie seethed inwardly. So Nic thought she was *entertaining*? She heard a movement and in seconds he'd come to sit in the empty chair opposite hers. His long legs were stretched out on either side of hers, effectively caging her in.

'What do you think you're doing?' Maddie gritted out.

Nic smiled easily. 'I'm going to make you see that you have no option but to give in to my proposal. Unless you want to see your estate fall apart and your staff left with nothing after their long years of hard work.'

Maddie's mouth had opened, but now she shut it again. Hernan and Maria. They had nothing but the security she provided them with. Not even pay.

As if reading her mind, Nic said softly, 'If you let me invest in the Vasquez estate, Hernan and Maria will be secure. I will set up a pension plan. Hernan can work on the vines again. You can hire a new head winemaker.' Before she could say anything he went on, 'You need new barrels, and we both know how much they cost. The last I heard your father was still using a basket press.'

Maddie flushed hotly. Her father had favoured the old-school methods. Defensively she said, 'The basket press is coming back into vogue.'

Nic inclined his head. 'I'm not denying that. I use one myself for certain grapes. But you can't use a basket press alone. It has to be a sideline to a much more modern operation. It's a luxury—like hand-picking your crop.'

'*You* still hand-pick,' Maddie shot back.

'Yes, I do, but again that's only for certain grapes. Most of our picking is done by machines now.'

Maddie felt an ache near her heart. What Nic had on his estate was a blending of the old and the modern, which was exactly the way she would love to see things run on the Vasquez estate.

He went on relentlessly. 'Not all your vines are ruined. You have a hope of a respectable harvest next year if you take care of your vines now and cut them back. And what about the vines that have produced something? How are you going to harvest them with only yourself and Hernan?'

Maddie felt a sinking weight in her belly. She couldn't take her gaze off Nic's. It was glued there in some kind of sick fascination. He was chipping away at all the walls

surrounding her, showing her the huge gaping holes where
they all threatened to fall down on top of her.

'I'll draw up a contract, so it'll be a legal document. I
will invest in your estate, see to the provision of labour
and materials, new machinery. I will oversee the production of your first fully functioning harvest, whether that's
next year or the year after, and then I will stand back and
let you take over.'

Maddie looked at him suspiciously. 'You'll walk away?'

Nic smiled cynically. 'Not without a large share of the
profits each year, Maddie, until the investment is paid off.
You won't see much of an income for a while, but it'll give
you your estate back and protect your staff.'

Somewhere deep inside Maddie a tiny seed of hope
and excitement was blooming. What Nic was offering was
more than generous.

The tiny seed disappeared at the thought of Nic over-
seeing everything, being autocratic.

'You'd turn the Vasquez estate into a subsidiary of your
own.'

Remarkably, he shook his head. 'That's not what I'm
interested in. I quite like the idea of helping foster some
healthy competition again, and I'm interested to see how
you would develop things.'

Somehow Maddie couldn't see Nic deferring to her
judgement. Suspiciously she asked, 'Would you state that
in the contract?'

He nodded once. 'Of course. It'll all be laid out in black
and white. You can read over it with your own legal people.'

Maddie held back a moment of hysteria. She had no
money for legal people. She and Hernan would just have
to vet it as best they could. That thought gave her a jolt.
Was she already taking this as a given? She hated it that

Nic could manipulate her so easily, but at the same time she wasn't stupid enough to cut her nose off to spite her face.

Stiffly she said, 'I'd have to think about it.'

Nic smiled tersely. 'There's not much to think about, Maddie. I'm offering you a chance to sink or swim.'

After that comment, Nic settled back in his seat and stretched out his legs, trapping Maddie even more. He put back his head and within minutes was snoring softly. Finally Maddie could relax slightly. She uncrossed her arms. Her head was buzzing with all that Nic had just said and offered.

She looked suspiciously at his benignly sleeping face. He had to have an agenda. It couldn't be this simple.

She looked out of the window at the vast pampas lands underneath them. This was what she'd always wanted more than anything—a chance to work on her own estate. It had been denied her her whole life, and when her father had finally offered her the chance it had come too late. And now Nic de Rojas, the most unlikely person on the planet, was offering her a second chance. Not only that, but she had a responsibility to her staff. Hernan and Maria couldn't live on the estate indefinitely. Soon they would want to retire. They were old and weary.

Maddie sighed again, and then finally let her own weariness suck her under into sleep.

'Maddie...'

Maddie woke with a start. She'd been dreaming about Nic. Her cheek was tingling, as if someone had just touched her there. When her eyes focused, Nic was bending down so close to her that she could see the small lines fanning out from his eyes. She felt too hot, and knew instantly that it had been an erotic dream.

Scrabbling back into her seat as far as she could, she saw his jaw clench.

'We're landing in a few minutes. Buckle up.'

Maddie buckled up with trembling hands, relieved that Nic had moved back over to the couch. She could breathe a little easier when he wasn't in her direct line of sight.

They landed softly and within minutes were in Nic's Jeep, heading out of Mendoza and towards Villarosa. Maddie felt as if she'd done ten rounds in a boxing ring—mentally and physically. She snuck a look at Nic's rigid profile. He looked so stern. Had she just imagined what had happened on the plane? Had he really told her he'd invest?

When the familiar lines of the Vasquez estate came into view Maddie breathed a sigh of relief. Nic stopped at the steps leading up to the main door. He indicated the house. 'Renovation of the house would be part of the investment too.'

Maddie's heart thumped. She hadn't imagined it. She looked at him warily. 'Why are you doing this?'

Nic's face was suspiciously expressionless. He shrugged minutely. 'I have the means…and I don't like to see a good vineyard turn to dust.'

Maddie struggled to understand. She couldn't do this unless she knew *why*. She turned in her seat to face Nic. 'But our families…the feud…we've fought for so long. How do I know you're not going to just take me over completely?'

Nic's mouth tightened, and something ambiguous flashed in his eyes. 'You once told me that the feud meant nothing to you.'

Maddie felt very vulnerable thinking of that time. 'You said the same thing. But then…it all blew up again.'

Nic looked impossibly stern. 'Our parents are dead, Maddie. It's just us now. I'm willing to move on if you are.'

Maddie didn't trust him for a second. She saw something else light his eyes and immediately her insides tightened.

'There is one condition to my offer—and it won't be in the contract.'

Instantly Maddie's hackles rose. She breathed out. 'I knew it was too good to be true. So what is this condition?'

After a long moment, during which Maddie's nerves were screaming with tension, Nic finally said softly, 'One night with me, Maddie. One night in my bed to finish what was started eight years ago.'

Maddie looked at Nic disbelievingly. She knew what was between them. It crackled in the air the moment they came within feet of each other, and she'd been moments away from begging him to take her only last night... But somehow she'd been hoping that she could ignore it.

Now Nic had laid it between them. He had made the business proposition about this heat between them. She shook her head. Her throat felt tight. 'Whether you believe me or not, a man offered me a similar deal last night and I turned him down. What makes you think this is any different?'

Nic leant forward, and Maddie couldn't move back any further. The door handle was pressing painfully into her back. Nic was so close now she could feel his breath on her face. He trailed a finger down her cheek and lower, pushing aside the top of her T-shirt to rest it where the pulse was nearly beating out of her skin. His forearm touched her breast, making the nipple spring into aching hardness, pushing against the fabric of her bra.

Nic smiled, and as if he knew exactly what was happening to her body, he subtly moved his forearm back and forth against that turgid peak.

'This is different, Maddie, because you didn't want him.

You want me…so badly I can smell it. And *that's* why you'll do this.'

Panic rose up inside Maddie, almost strangling her. She reached behind her and fumbled for the door handle, almost landing on her backside outside the Jeep in her haste. Nic was out too, and coming towards her. It took a minute for Maddie to realise he was holding out her bag. She grabbed it from him inelegantly.

Nic smiled and just said, 'You know where I am, Maddie. I look forward to hearing from you. That is,' he added softly, 'if you're interested in saving your estate and being honest with yourself.'

And then he got back into his Jeep and drove off, leaving a small cloud of dust in his wake.

For almost a week Maddie battled sleepless nights full of demons and Nic's voice saying, *Be honest with yourself.* She spent the long days facing the fact that without funds she and Hernan could make nothing even of the small harvest they could bring in.

She went round and round in her head, endlessly replaying her last conversation with Nic word for word, and always with a flash of heat she came back to him saying, *'You want me…so badly I can smell it. And that's why you'll do this.'*

She did want him. She couldn't deny that. She wasn't that much of a hypocrite. It scared her the way the days dragged, and how her mind kept returning to him like iron filings to a magnet. She hadn't realised how accustomed she'd become to seeing him, or expecting him to turn up. And when he didn't…she didn't like the feeling of emptiness.

Maddie desperately tried not to think about his *condition* to the investment proposal, but invariably she would

think about it. In a way, the thought of doing it like this…
where the lines were clearly marked in the sand, with no
false emotions involved, no false seduction…should actually make it easier.

Maddie knew that when it came to Nic de Rojas she was
weak. He could have put on an elaborate act, pretended to
seduce her. And she would have fallen for it. She knew she
would have. And in the process she would have shown him
how ambiguous her feelings were for him. This way there
was no ambiguity. She was protected. She would gain closure finally, and shut the door on that part of her life. The
awful memories surrounding what had happened might
finally fade into the background and she could move on.

Maddie weakly blocked out the fact that she'd have to
deal with him every day for a long time to come if she
agreed to this. It would make the prospect of closure all but
redundant. But as the days passed Maddie was no closer
to being able to pick up the phone and change the course
of her life irrevocably.

At the end of the week, late in the evening, Maddie
was sitting in her father's study, brooding that she was
only able to see the documents in front of her because Nic
was paying for the electricity, when Hernan came in. He
looked concerned.

'I'm worried about you…and this place.' He was shaking his head. 'We're backed up against the wall, Maddie.
There's nothing you can do. You'll have to sell up.'

For a moment Maddie clung to that like a life raft. 'But
what about you and Maria?'

She could see how Hernan paled slightly in the dim
light. He shrugged, but Maddie wasn't fooled by his non-
chalance. 'Don't worry about us, *niña*. We can take care
of ourselves. You're not responsible for us.'

Maddie felt hope die and a heavy weight almost crushed

her. She knew how much this estate owed Hernan. He was such a gifted viticulturist that he alone had been responsible for the quality of their grapes, which had allowed her father and his chief winemaker to come up with the successful blends that had led to their wealth and security. She couldn't turn her back on Hernan now, or his wife. And she knew she couldn't turn her back on the very legacy she held in her hands.

'We might not have to sell...'

Immediately Hernan sat up straight. 'What do you mean?'

Maddie laid out the bare facts of Nic's investment plan without mentioning his private little caveat which affected only her.

Hernan looked at her incredulously. 'But...you will say yes, won't you? It's a chance to save the Vasquez name— the *only* chance.'

Maddie looked at Hernan. 'It's such a huge step to take. How do I know I can trust him?'

Maddie knew she wasn't talking about the investment itself now. She was talking about whether or not she could trust Nic not to sleep with her and decimate her completely. She was talking about whether or not she could trust herself not to lose herself completely if she took that cataclysmic step.

Hernan sagged in his seat and suddenly looked ten years older. Maddie immediately forgot about everything. 'Hernan, what is it?'

He looked up eventually, and his face was ashen. 'The truth is, Maddie, Maria isn't well. She needs treatment— treatment that we can't afford.'

Maddie got up and went over and put her arms around Hernan. He said to her with tears in his eyes, 'We didn't want you to worry... We thought the only option would be to sell and we would leave and go to our son in Buenos Aires.'

Maddie immediately shook her head. She knew that Hernan and Maria hated the city. Their lives were here. Their son in Buenos Aires was not well off, and had a family of his own to look after.

'There's absolutely no way you're going anywhere. If I agree to this deal with Nic de Rojas, I'll make sure you're both looked after—and especially Maria.'

Hernan took her hand in his old and worn ones. 'But we don't want to put you under pressure...we're not your responsibility.'

Maddie squatted down so that she could look at Hernan properly. She squeezed his hand and said, 'I know that, Hernan, but you are due something for all your years of service. You deserve medical care, at the very least, and security. I can provide that now.' She took a deep breath. 'I'll call Nic de Rojas tonight.'

Hernan gripped her hand tightly, the sheen of tears still in his eyes, and Maddie felt emotional. She'd done it now. No going back. She couldn't even if she wanted to. These people were more important to her than her own petty personal concerns.

The following evening Maddie was driving over to Nic's estate, an overnight bag in the back. She was so tense she felt as if she might crack apart, and she forced herself to breathe deep. It had been a tumultuous and emotional day.

The previous evening she'd rung Nic and told him she'd agree to the investment with the proviso that he met a condition of her own—that Maria be taken care of with the best medical care as soon as possible. Nic hadn't hesitated. He'd agreed immediately, and it had struck another blow to Maddie's misconceptions about him.

That morning Nic had appeared with his own doctor, who had consulted with Hernan and Maria. Maria had been taken into the best private clinic in Mendoza that very afternoon, and the relief they'd both felt had been palpable to Maddie. She'd been incredibly emotional as she'd watched them leave.

Maddie was aghast at how relieved she'd felt to see Nic arriving that morning, along with intense fizzing excitement in every cell. It had felt as if she hadn't seen him in months, not days. When she'd seen him up close, though, he'd looked a little worn and tired. Maddie had had to quash the ridiculous urge to ask him if everything was all right.

When Hernan and Maria had left Maddie had faced Nic, feeling extremely vulnerable. 'Thank you for taking care of Maria…it was important to Hernan and to me.'

'Don't mention it.'

Reluctantly she'd asked him, there on the steps of the house. 'So what happens now…?'

He'd just looked at her with an expression so intense that Maddie had gone slowly redder and redder.

'You will come to me this evening. Eight p.m.'

He'd said nothing else. He'd walked to his Jeep, got in and left.

Maddie forced herself to concentrate on the road now and tried not think about what the night would bring.

Nic was pacing in his office. He did not like to admit how close to panic he'd been by yesterday evening when Maddie had finally rung. The very walls of his house had been closing in on him, and he hadn't liked his clawing desperation to see her again. He'd hated not knowing what she was up to—had she gone looking for another investor? Had she somehow miraculously secured an investor without his knowing?

Nic had agreed as soon as she'd mentioned wanting Maria to be taken care of. He would have agreed to anything except Maddie reneging on their own personal part of the agreement. That she would be his for one night.

One night. Nic stopped pacing and looked out over his vineyard which was disappearing into the dusk, the colours melding and blurring. One night. He could do this. One night was invariably all it took for him to grow bored with a woman. So why would Maddie be different? His conscience pricked. Who was he kidding? Maddie had been different from the moment his hormones had realised she was growing up.

Nic ran a hand through his hair impatiently and turned around. A sheaf of papers sat on his desk. It was the investment contract. It epitomised everything Nic couldn't articulate about this woman who had come back into his life. This woman who he wanted more than the breath he took into his body. He hadn't realised how starved he'd been for her until he'd heard her voice on the phone the previous evening. Even though she'd been cool, he'd been burning up just to hear her.

And then when he'd seen her today…he'd wanted to back her into the wall of the house and take her there and then. His desire was like a wild beast, clawing at his insides.

This contract meant that Maddie would not turn around after tonight and claim that she'd been *bored*, or that she regretted what happened. Because she couldn't. She wanted her estate too badly. And she wanted Nic too badly too— even though he knew without the contract she might deny it. This way she couldn't. He would not be exposed again. Never again.

So why, when Nic looked at the sheaf of papers on his desk, did they seem to mock him?

Maddie looked warily at the big pink box with the red satin bow which sat on the bed as if it might jump up and bite her. She'd arrived at Nic's house and been met by Geraldo, who had greeted her warmly and shown her up to a sumptuous suite of rooms—as if they didn't both know she was there to spend the night with Nic.

He'd indicated to the lavish box on the bed and said, 'A gift from Señor de Rojas. He'll see you in the dining room at eight. If you need anything in the meantime please don't hesitate to call.'

Eventually, aware of time passing, Maddie opened it up and peeled back layers of blood-red tissue paper to reveal what seemed to be acres of dark grey satin folds. She lifted the dress out and gasped. It was stunning. No woman could be immune to the beauty of a dress like this. The material was heavy, and yet as light as a feather. Strapless, it had a ruched bodice and a high waist, and it fell in swathes of satin and chiffon layers to the ground.

More was hidden in the tissue paper in the box: silver shoes with diamanté straps and dark grey underwear, lacy and ethereal. There was also a velvet box, and Maddie opened it to reveal stunning teardrop diamond earrings and a matching bracelet. Something very fragile inside her withered slightly when she looked at the incredible bounty of luxurious goods laid out on the bed. But then Maddie chastised herself. Nic was actually doing her a favour, treating her like a mistress. All she had to do tonight was play a part—perhaps that would help her to stay intact and immune to emotion.

At eight o'clock on the dot Maddie was standing nervously at the door of the room a shy young girl had indicated. The dress felt unbelievably decadent against Maddie's bare legs. She'd put on the underwear simply because she had nothing else to wear that wouldn't ruin the line of the dress. The jewellery felt heavy and cold against her skin.

She'd put on the minimum of makeup and left her hair down—primarily because her hands were shaking too much to do anything more elaborate. Taking a deep breath and trying to remain in a detached frame of mind, Maddie knocked lightly on the door before opening it.

The scene inside was impossibly seductive, with candles flickering and a small table set for two. It was a different room from the one they'd eaten in before, more formal. It took a second for Maddie to register Nic standing by the window, his hands in his pockets. He was dressed semi-formally in a white shirt and dark trousers, hair slicked back and damp, as if he'd just had a shower.

'You wore the dress.'

Maddie gripped the handle hard and struggled to maintain her equilibrium in the face of this seductive scene. She bit back the need to remind him that she was just playing the part he wanted. 'Yes, thank you.'

Nic inclined his head and smiled faintly. 'You can let go of the door. I won't bite. I promise.'

Heat bloomed inside Maddie at the thought of Nic's teeth nipping her sensitive flesh. She let the door go abruptly just as a staff member came into the room. After conferring with Nic for a moment the man left again, and Nic walked over to the antique sideboard which held different bottles of drink.

She watched as he poured some champagne into two flutes. He came and offered her one and she took it.

He tipped his glass to hers, eyes unnervingly intense. *'Salud.'*

'*Salud,*' Maddie echoed, and took a sip of the sparkling effercescent drink, tearing her gaze away from Nic's to look around the room.

'Your mouth has healed well.'

Maddie looked back to Nic and instinctively touched the corner where it had split. It *had* healed.

'You look beautiful tonight.'

Something uncomfortable was prickling across Maddie's skin. She wasn't used to this—to compliments. To Nic being so effortlessly urbane around her. She didn't know how to behave. And all she could think of was how beautiful *he* looked.

'So do you,' she answered huskily, and then blushed and looked down. 'That is, not beautiful but handsome.'

Oh, God. Maddie took another quick sip of her drink before she could make a complete blithering idiot of herself. She wasn't sophisticated. Surely Nic could see that?

To fill the yawning gap in conversation Maddie asked if Nic had had any news from the hospital about Maria, and he told her that they were still doing tests. Maria had gone to the local doctor with chest pains and they were concerned that it could be a heart problem.

'Thank you again,' Maddie said huskily. 'Hernan didn't know where to turn, and they couldn't have afforded the kind of care they're getting now.'

Sounding serious, Nic said, 'I pay for health insurance for all my employees. Maria and Hernan will be included in that too.'

Maddie had the suspicion that Nic would have helped them anyway. It made her uncomfortable to acknowledge this, so she said, slightly acerbically, 'Just like I'm going to be an employee?'

He chided her. 'Business partners, Maddie…'

Nic drained his glass of champagne and put it down,

gesturing for Maddie to be seated at the dinner table. It was ornately set, with gleaming silverware and crockery so delicate-looking that Maddie was afraid to touch it. The champagne was fizzing in her blood, making her feel slightly light-headed.

The whole scene was intimidating to Maddie.

Especially when Nic looked so sophisticated and at ease across the table from her.

Discreet staff came in and served them with their starter—a light soup. A sense of panic and claustrophobia was rising inside Maddie, and the soup became like treacle in her throat. It was as if they were both ignoring the elephant in the room. The fact that Nic expected them to have dinner and then go upstairs and have sex. At that moment Maddie couldn't even imagine Nic's expression changing from the stern one he'd had since she'd arrived.

Maddie was aware that her own wish to remain detached was fast dissolving.

More staff arrived to take their starters away. Maddie felt agitated and hot.

Nic frowned at her. 'Are you okay? You look a little flushed.'

It was the dispassionate way he asked that galvanised Maddie. She wanted to scream, *No, I'm not okay!* She stood up abruptly, making some of the crockery knock the wine glasses. It sounded like gunshots. She put out a trembling hand, only realising then how agitated she was. The sparkle of diamonds at her wrist was like cold fire.

'I…I can't do this like this. Pretending that this is normal when it's not.'

CHAPTER EIGHT

NIC was just looking at her. Maddie's skin was prickling all over. She started to take off the jewellery, all but ripping the undoubtedly expensive earrings from her ears and the bracelet off her wrist. Immediately she started to feel lighter.

'All this. It's not *me*. I can't sit here and act like nothing is happening…'

Nic stood too. Someone came into the room with a tray and Nic sent them a glowering look, making them disappear again. He looked back to Maddie, the expression in his eyes feral. 'Something's happening, all right. You will *not* do this, Maddie. It's too late to back out. If we don't have tonight, you have *nothing*.'

Maddie backed away from the table and stumbled slightly. She bent down and took off the shoes with heels like weapons. Her heart was hammering and she craved air, and space, and something more tangible than what was in this room right now.

'If we do this we do it my way. I can't do it like this…' She flung out a hand. 'This seduction scene, it's all fake… we both know that's not what this is about.'

Maddie turned and all but stumbled out through the door, picking up the dress, half running and half walking to the main front door. She heard a curse behind her and

Nic following. She didn't even know where she was going, but she got out through the front door and looked to her left, saw the stables in the distance. Suddenly she knew.

Maddie was in the stables and leading a horse out of a stall, putting a bridle on, when she heard an ominously low, 'What the hell do you think you're doing?'

She took a deep breath, turned to look at Nic and nearly quailed. But she straightened her shoulders. 'I'm not leaving. But if this is happening, it's happening my way.'

Maddie found a box and stepped up to swing herself up on the saddleless horse. Now she was looking down at Nic and her heart tripped. His hair shone dark gold under the lights. A horse whinnied nearby.

He seemed to battle something inwardly, and then he cursed again and she saw him throw off his dinner jacket and lead his own horse out of the stall. It was a massive black stallion. She saw the play of his impressive muscles underneath the thin material of his shirt and something euphoric bubbled up inside Maddie. She kicked her heels and her horse moved out of the stables. Outside, the sun had set a short time before and the sky was a beautiful bruised lilac colour, still quite light.

Rows and rows of vines stretched as far as the eye could see, and in the distance were the huge vats and outbuildings which housed the hub of Nic's empire. Maddie turned in the other direction and kicked the horse into a trot—away from the house, towards the border between their estates.

When she had enough space she picked it up to a canter, and soon she heard powerful hooves behind her. Maddie had always felt free on a horse. She didn't look back, half afraid to see Nic bearing down on her. The cooling evening air caressed her hot bare skin. The satin folds of the dress fell and moved around her legs with the motion of the horse.

She felt the huge black presence of Nic's stallion come alongside her, and then Nic was reaching forward to effortlessly take Maddie's reins and bring her and her horse to a juddering halt. She had to press her thighs tight to its back to stop from falling off.

She spluttered, 'What do you think—?'

'Where the hell are we going?' he asked, anger vibrating from him in waves.

Maddie's mouth opened and closed, her breath coming rapidly. She refused to let herself be intimidated. 'You *know* where we're going.'

For a split second she thought she saw something bleak cross Nic's face, and then it was gone and his eyes spat blue sparks. 'I'm not going there with you.'

Maddie yanked her reins out of Nic's hands. 'If you want me—if you want this night—then we *are* going there.'

Nic looked at Maddie. His breath was searing through his lungs and it wasn't because of exertion. He was burning up. She looked magnificent. He'd been in a daze since he'd seen her arrive in the dining room, more beautiful than any woman he'd ever seen before. When he'd thought she was walking out on him he'd been so panicked it had made him feel weak.

He wasn't in a daze now, though, when he thought of what she was suggesting, and he snarled, 'What *is* this? Some pathetic attempt to be poetic? Well, it's lost on me. I'd sooner have you in my bed. Or back there in the stables would do fine.'

Maddie clamped down on the pain she felt when he spoke so crudely. She shook her head and her horse pranced away a little, sensing her agitation. 'No, it's there…or nowhere.'

Suddenly she'd whirled the horse around and was cantering off at speed again. Nic cursed volubly. There was enough light in the gathering dusk but she could still miss a rock or stone and be thrown in an instant. Giving in, he spurred his own horse on to follow.

When he reached the orchard, *déjà vu* nearly made him dizzy. He'd consciously and unconsciously avoided this place like the plague for years. Maddie's horse was riderless, tied to a small tree, and she was standing there— just waiting. Exactly as she had been all those years ago. Except now she was a mature woman. Her shoulders were bare and white in the dusk, her hair like black satin. Her breasts were full against the silk of her dress.

He swung off his horse, feeling tight inside, and secured him to another tree. He walked towards her. Her eyes were huge. Her face was pale. He felt acutely exposed, but he was reluctant to let her see how much being back here affected him.

Now that she was standing here Maddie couldn't believe she'd made this mad dramatic gesture. She'd acted from a visceral need to break out of that oh, so polite dinner as if nothing was wrong.

Her voice was husky, her senses already reeling at Nic's scent and proximity. 'This is where it started and where it ends. Tonight. For ever.'

Nic looked huge in the gloom. As if he'd grown several inches and his muscles had become even bigger. Once again she had a bittersweet rush of emotion at the knowledge that he'd once been much more vulnerable. But then he came towards her and Maddie's breath caught in her throat.

He stopped a couple of feet away and watched her, and then drawled laconically, 'Well, what are you waiting for?'

His insouciance after the intense anger she'd just witnessed made her want to lash out. For a moment she had believed that coming back here might have affected him emotionally.

She was completely unprepared for this, despite her show of bravado. He thought she'd slept with Morales the other night, so he had the erroneous idea that she was some grand seductress, when she'd never done anything like this in her life. And the reason she'd never done it was standing right in front of her. The scar of that last traumatic day after such a heady, perfect week was etched into her psyche. It had inhibited her from seeking out male company, too scared of rejection and irrationally scared of horrific revelation.

Sudden anger flared that Nic hadn't had to go through any of that…he'd blithely got on with his life. That anger galvanised Maddie to march up to him. She grabbed his shirt in her hands and pulled him down towards her.

Maddie searched blindly and inexpertly for his mouth, eyes shut tight against the reality of what she was doing, telling herself that she could divorce all emotion from this event.

For a long moment Nic seemed just to suffer under Maddie's gauche ministrations, and she nearly sobbed with frustration against his closed lips. Surely he must be realising how inexperienced she was? He couldn't be turned on by this?

But then he took control, and everything changed in an instant. Hard arms of steel wrapped around her, binding her to him like a vice. His mouth opened and grew hard, plundering hers with an expertise that awed her, his tongue tangling hotly with hers, forcing her head back onto his arms. Exposing her throat to him.

Everything within her was becoming languid and hot, while an urgent need clamoured for attention between her legs. Her breasts were swelling against the silk of her dress and her arms were crushed against Nic's chest.

When he finally pulled away she felt drunk. She couldn't open her eyes for a long moment. His hands came up and framed her face. She finally opened her eyes to see two blue oceans right in front of her. Two hot and stormy oceans.

His thumbs traced her cheekbones and then he dipped his head again to hers, his mouth touching more softly this time, teeth nipping gently at her lips, making them sting before soothing them. There was something so unexpectedly tender about this that Maddie could feel the bottom dropping out of the pit of her stomach.

It reminded her of when he'd been so gentle and seductive before…before it had all turned sour. She felt tears prick the backs of her eyes and desperately fought not to let them fall. Nic's mouth caressed and kissed her throat and shoulders, moving down. His hands dropped to her back, moulding her waist and hips, coming down to cup her buttocks through the silk of her dress, lifting her slightly so that his erection was cradled between her legs.

She gasped and tried to pull back, the intimate move suddenly shocking. But he wouldn't release her, those blue eyes blazing down into hers as he subtly moved his body back and forth against her until she was breathing rapidly and moving restlessly against him.

Hunger was rising in her, erasing thoughts of the past, gnawing and desperate. She nearly sobbed with relief when she felt him lower her down to the soft grass underneath the trees, following her. Now Nic loomed over her like a golden-haired god. Eyes devouring her, slipping down, taking in her chest rising and falling rapidly.

He lifted a hand and smoothed the back of it over the top of her bodice. Maddie sucked in a breath when his knuckles brushed the swell of her breast. He reached around underneath her back and found the zip. Maddie lifted slightly to help, sucking in a breath when she felt him pull it down as much as he could.

Slowly he peeled the dress down to expose one breast, and Maddie bit her lip, fighting the urge to cover herself. She could see Nic's cheeks become flushed, his pupils dilating, and a heady feminine energy rushed through her. He *wanted* her. Unconsciously she moved, so that her breast pushed forward, and the ghost of a small smile played around his mouth. Reverently he cupped and moulded the pale flesh, making Maddie close her eyes. A rough thumb rubbed back and forth over one tight, puckered peak.

She didn't even realise she'd said anything until she heard his throaty, 'What do you want?'

She opened her eyes. The lids felt heavy. 'I want…' *You,* she wanted to say, but she stopped. It felt so raw.

'Do you want me to taste you?'

He didn't wait for an answer. He looked feverish now, his eyes glittering fiercely, his big hand and long fingers still caressing her breast and making her want to shout out with frustration and pleasure all at once.

He came over her more fully, pressing her down into the ground, his erection feeling even bigger and harder now. He dipped his head and his mouth unerringly closed around that taut peak, and then Maddie did cry out. It was surrounded with fierce sucking heat. He was relentless, tugging it into his mouth, tongue swirling around it until it was so stiff and tight and sensitised that she cried out again, her hips moving restlessly against his.

Almost roughly Nic pulled down the bodice, fully exposing both breasts now, and paid homage to the other thrusting peak, driving Maddie mad with pleasure. Her head was thrashing back and forth, and she could feel one of Nic's hands move down and start to pull up her dress, bunching it around her thighs. She couldn't speak or think. She could only feel.

He shifted slightly and his fingers touched her where her panties felt damp between her legs. His head came up, and cool air whistled over the wet peak of her breast. Maddie was overheating.

She looked up to see Nic staring at her. His fingers started to move back and forth, pressing her panties against where she was so wet. She moaned. She felt so exposed and yet she craved it.

'You're ready for me, aren't you?'

Maddie nodded, feeling vulnerable all of a sudden. She felt as if she'd been ready for him for years. Aeons.

'Tell me how much you want me right now.'

Maddie couldn't think when he was touching her so intimately. She'd dreamt of this moment for so long and it was overwhelming now to be experiencing it. The words came out. She couldn't stop them. 'I want you, Nic…so much. I've always wanted you…'

His hand stilled for a moment. Maddie couldn't fathom the cynical look that crossed Nic's face.

'You'll say anything, won't you?'

She shook her head, nearly crying out when his hand and fingers started moving again, harder this time, as if he was angry and sensed her hunger. 'I don't—'

She gasped when she felt him slide one finger inside her panties, close to where the secret folds of her body hid the full extent of her desire and vulnerability.

'Yes…you do. But it doesn't matter any more. Nothing matters except this.'

And with a guttural growl he bent his head, his mouth finding hers in a drugging heady kiss while one finger thrust deep inside her damp heat, making her scream into his mouth. Now she was utterly exposed and undone. There was no going back, only forward.

Maddie was barely aware of her hands ripping at Nic's shirt. She only knew that she craved to see his chest, to feel it next to hers, rubbing against her breasts. And all the while his hand was between her legs, which were splayed outwards. One finger became two and Maddie nearly passed out. The pleasure was so intense.

And then he was tugging her panties down, taking his hand away for a moment, putting her legs together to undress her. Maddie felt feverish now. Hot all over.

His shirt was swinging open, his chest broad and tautly muscled. A smattering of dark golden hair covered his pectoral muscles and arrowed down to his pants in a tantalising and utterly masculine line. He sat back for a moment and she saw his hands come to his belt. With wide eyes she lay back and watched as he opened his pants, tore down his zip and yanked them down. His briefs were tented over a long and thick bulge. Maddie could feel nothing but intense excitement.

She vaguely heard foil ripping, and saw Nic's erection spring free as he ripped down his briefs. He rolled on a condom and came back over her, spreading her legs again to accommodate him as easily as if she were a pliable doll. Maddie was vaguely aware that her dress was bunched up around her waist and pulled down under her breasts. She didn't care.

Nic's hand was between her legs again and she cried out at the contact, her chest coming up into contact with Nic's. 'Please,' she sobbed. 'Please…do something.'

She didn't even know what to ask for. All she knew was that she needed *more*.

Nic shifted his weight onto his hands and Maddie's legs fell open wider. She could feel the thick blunt head of his penis as he started to push into her. Her muscles contracted at the alien invasion and her eyes grew wide. She knew she wanted this, needed it, but a sudden instinct that pain was inevitable seized her muscles.

Nic sank in some more, and pain hit like a steam train crashing into her chest. Maddie sucked in a shocked breath. The pain was white-hot.

Nic frowned and cursed softly. 'You're so tight...'

Instinctively, as if Maddie knew that the only way was to go through it, she arched up, forcing Nic to impale her a little more. She cried out at the shocking, rending pain. But her hands were on his buttocks and a fierce determination gripped her.

She looked up into Nic's eyes and saw the dawning understanding. '*Dios*, Maddie...you're not...?'

'Don't say it,' she said fiercely, feeling sweat break out on her brow. 'Don't you dare stop now.'

For a long moment tension gripped them both. The broad head of Nic's shaft was barely inside her and the pain was clearly devastating, but all he could see was her flushed cheeks and that stark determination in her eyes. So many things were hitting him at once, but the biggest one was a feeling of exhilaration. She was *his*. She would become his right now and no one else's.

He thought she'd been playing a part even when she'd told him how much she wanted him. This revelation smashed that assertion to pieces and left Nic spinning off in a direction he couldn't even begin to look at now.

Nic found some control from somewhere and gritted out painfully, 'This is going to hurt...but it won't last, I promise.'

Maddie looked up at him, tousled and flushed and beautiful. She bit her lip and said, 'Okay.'

The trust in her eyes nearly broke him in two, and with

sweat forming tiny beads on his chest Nic gritted his jaw and drove himself into her reluctant flesh. She cried out. Her hands gripped his buttocks fiercely and Nic nearly came right then at the feel of her body clamping so tightly around his.

She was crying in earnest, tears trickling out of her eyes, but still she was not pushing him away. Nic felt weak at her show of bravery. He put his forehead to hers and then pressed a kiss to her mouth. He could taste her salty tears and crooned softly, 'It's okay, *querida*, that's the worst bit…just try to relax…let me move and it'll feel better… I promise.'

Maddie felt light-headed from the pain, but there was something deep within her melting and reacting to Nic's tender words. Something that she'd shut away long ago coming to life again. She felt like a warrior. She wanted to embrace the pain with this man. She pressed a kiss to his shoulder, as if to tell him she trusted him. She couldn't speak.

Slowly she could feel her flesh adapting to his, relaxing ever so slightly from its tight grip around him. He sank in a little more—unbelievably. Eventually she could feel his pelvis snug against hers. And it didn't hurt as much. The pain was being replaced with sensations. Flutterings along nerve-ends.

Slowly Nic started to withdraw, and instinctively Maddie clutched at his tight buttocks as if to stop him. He pressed a kiss to her mouth, which felt swollen and bruised. 'No, sweetheart…trust me…let me go.'

Maddie relaxed her hold and he continued to slide out, so slowly that little exquisite shards of sensation started to flutter through her lower body. When he was almost entirely out he drove in again, and this time his passage was smoother, increasing those flutters.

Maddie's hips moved. She rolled them, forcing Nic to curse and say, 'Stop, Maddie…this is hard enough…I won't last…'

She stopped, in awe of his strength and size, and the extreme gentleness he was showing her. She tried to stay as still as possible as he taught her flesh and her body how to respond to him, but an urgency was building, the pain was being washed away by pleasure. A kind of pleasure she'd never felt before.

Digging her heels into the soft, fragrant earth beside his thighs, Maddie couldn't stop herself from moving—just as Nic's own movements became faster and more urgent. Blood was thundering through her body. Her heart hammered. She was straining, searching for something but she didn't know what.

She felt Nic put a hand between them—right there, near where he was driving in and out with relentless precision. Each thrust getting harder and faster and deeper.

Maddie wrapped her legs around his slim hips, deepening the penetration even more, just as his thumb found her sensitised clitoris and stroked it. Pleasure exploded with unstoppable force inside Maddie's whole body, radiating outwards from that thumb and his own driving flesh. It was like an endless wave, so breathtaking in its magnitude that Maddie was incoherent, bucking wildly beneath Nic as he ground himself into her and shouted out.

His whole body went taut for a long moment, every sinew and muscle locked. She could feel him pulsing and throbbing inside her, and then he was spent, and his whole weight came crashing down, crushing her to the ground.

Maddie wrapped her arms around him and knew in that moment that she loved Nic de Rojas. She'd never hated him. She couldn't. She'd fallen for him from a distance as a lovestruck teenager, and that had become a solid reality

when she'd stood before him in this place all those years
ago. Now…after giving herself to him completely…it was
cemented deep in her cells for ever. And he would break
her heart into tiny pieces even as he showed her paradise.

Maddie was barely aware of their journey home along the
trail, lit now by moonlight. She was only aware that she
was sitting within the cradle of Nic's strong hard thighs
on his horse while he held the reins of her own, leading
it home.

One arm was clamped around her waist, and she
couldn't stop her head from sinking back into his chest
as extreme lethargy washed through every bone and cell
in her body.

Having Maddie sitting so close to where Nic still ached
was a form of torture so delicious he never wanted it to
end. His brain was reeling from an overload of pleasure
more intense than anything he'd ever experienced or
could have imagined. Even the memory of thrusting into
Maddie's tight embrace had his libido raging again, and
he had to grit his teeth to counteract it.

So many thoughts were vying for dominance. But one
superceded them all. *She'd been a virgin.* She hadn't slept
with Morales. Even though deep down Nic had believed
her, there'd been a tiny part of him unwilling to give up
a kernel of doubt. As if the minute he trusted her she'd
laugh in his face.

She'd given herself to him more passionately and
unself-consciously than the most experienced woman he'd
ever bedded. He'd never forget that blazing look of trust
when she'd been in such pain but had not shied away from
it. She'd embraced it like a pagan warrior.

He'd only become aware afterwards that he'd still been
half dressed. His trousers had been around his ankles and

he'd bunched her dress around her waist. He'd been like an animal in heat.

Everything was spinning out of Nic's control. His chest felt too full. And yet he couldn't stop his arm from tightening around her even more, or the exultation that whispered through him when her soft breath sighed over his skin.

Maddie only came to again when she sensed she was being carried in Nic's arms through the quiet house. She could barely lift her head. That delicious lethargy was weighing everything down, including her mind, where dangerous thoughts hovered. Everything was still and hushed and quiet.

Maddie looked up to see the stark planes of Nic's face above her. Without thinking about what she was doing, she reached up and cupped his strong jaw. She could feel him grit it against her hand.

Then she heard a door hit a wall, and she was being carried into a dimly lit and unashamedly masculine room. Nic's bedroom. Once again sanity hovered on the edge of her consciousness, but Maddie was a coward. It was as if they were in a bubble and she couldn't bear for the bubble to burst yet.

Nic put her down gently on the side of the bed and Maddie winced when sensitive flesh came in contact with the soft surface.

Immediately Nic was crouching at face level. 'Are you sore?'

Maddie felt inexplicably shy and blushed. 'A little… but it's fine.'

Just looking at him now was making blood rush back to all her extremities. Making her *want* all over again.

Nic pressed a swift kiss to her mouth, and then said, 'Give me one minute and I'll make you feel better.'

She watched speechlessly as he stood up and strode towards the bathroom. She only noticed then that she had all but ripped his shirt off like some demented madwoman. Her heart swelled in her chest, and once again she blocked those dangerous tendrils of reality from intruding.

Nic was back and coming towards her, stripping off his ruined shirt, revealing that huge expanse of glorious, hard-muscled chest. Maddie's insides clenched down low. Lord, he was even more beautiful than she'd thought.

He reached for her and, as if she was full of magnets aligning themselves only to him, she was effortlessly swept into his arms. She curled up tight against his chest, relishing the profound sense of protection in his embrace.

Steam was building up in the bathroom and Maddie could hear the shower running. Gently Nic let her down, and she found her legs to be ridiculously wobbly. They got even worse when he pulled her zip down and tried to pull down her grass-stained dress over her breasts. Instinctively Maddie's hands came up. She looked up into wry blue eyes.

'Don't you think it's a little late for modesty?'

Maddie tried to smile but it felt brittle. Slowly Nic took her hands away and peeled the dress down. Maddie's cheeks flamed. His eyes devoured her hungrily and she watched as he lifted his hands to cup the full mounds of pale flesh. She bit her lip when she felt her nipples responding, growing tight with need again.

In an instant Nic's hands had dropped and he stepped away, saying gutturally, 'I can't stop touching you...'

Acting on instinct, Maddie stepped forward and lifted his hands to cup her flesh again. 'I like it... Don't stop.'

His eyes met hers, and they were blazing. She could feel his hands tremble slightly and a wave of tenderness washed over her.

Nic spoke abruptly, taking his hands away. 'No...if I start now...

'I won't have you on the floor of the bathroom.'

He quickly dispensed with her dress and his own clothes, and then led her into the huge shower stall and under the powerful spray. Maddie let her head drop back as the water cascaded down, and murmured luxuriously when she felt Nic's soapy hands running all over her.

By the time he was done she was leaning weakly against the wall of the shower and begging him to stop.

With stark need stamped on his face he handed her the soap and said, 'Your turn.'

Lord.

Maddie took the soap and lathered up. Nic rested his hands high, either side of her head, so that he formed a cage around her, and gave her his body. As Maddie smoothed soapy hands over his shoulders and down his chest her eyes grew wide. And when she got lower and saw the proud jutting swell of his erection they got wider. Fascinated, she wrapped one slick soapy hand around him and exulted in his sharply indrawn breath. He was all silky skin encasing pure steel.

As much to distract herself as anything else, she ordered him to turn around and he muttered, 'Spoilsport.'

Maddie faced his back and lifted her hands, but they stilled in horror when she saw the lurid white lines slashing across his powerful muscles. They extended from his neck down to his waist.

As if he'd just realised what she was looking at, he whipped around so fast her head spun.

She felt sick as she looked up into his white face. 'What are those marks?'

He just looked at her for a long moment and said nothing, but he reached for the control and switched the shower off. He stepped out and hitched a towel around his waist, handed her one. She took it wordlessly, a chill skating over her skin.

She stepped out and briskly rubbed her hair, before putting the towel around her own body and following him into his room. He was standing at his window, arms folded, looking outwards. Maddie stopped uncertainly. This was completely uncharted territory.

'Nic?'

She could see his muscles tense even more, and those scars stood out in vivid relief. She had a flashback to that moment eight years before, when his father's men had had to beat him to get him to come with them, and dread turned her blood to ice. She forced her legs to move and stood in front of him. She looked up.

'It happened that day, didn't it? Those men…they beat you?'

Nic was looking resolutely above Maddie's head and his jaw was clenched. Her heart ached.

'What do you care?' he asked coolly.

All signs of passion were gone. Rejection emanated from every tense line in his body. He'd never been more remote. Exactly as he had been that day when she'd gone back and seen him…and hadn't been able to hide her horror.

Maddie was in turmoil. 'I just…I want to know what happened…'

He looked down at her then, and his eyes were like two ice chips. She shivered.

He raised a brow. 'You *really* want to know the sordid details?'

CHAPTER NINE

MADDIE nodded even as her heart thumped. They couldn't be any more sordid than what she'd been through in the aftermath of that cataclysmic afternoon.

Nic's voice was devoid of any expression. 'My father's men brought me back to the house, where they informed him of who I'd been found with and what we'd been doing. My father was angrier than I've ever seen him. He brought me out to the yard in the middle of the stables and ordered the men to hold me down so he could whip me.'

Maddie just looked at Nic. All she could see in her mind's eye was his face when she'd seen him the following day...before he'd turned so icy and cruel. He'd been pale. He must have been in agony, yet he'd come back... to see her. Perhaps he hadn't meant those cruel words he'd uttered? Perhaps he'd just been protecting himself against her extreme reaction.

The revelation made Maddie feel weak inside even as Nic continued in that toneless voice, 'With the benefit of hindsight I can see how making love to his own ex-lover's daughter must have pushed a button or two, though I didn't know that then.'

Maddie started to tremble violently, unable to expunge from her mind the horrific image of him being whipped.

And all because of what they'd done so innocently. The ripples had been catastrophic.

Nic caught her expression. 'You don't have to put on a horrified act, Maddie. I would have thought you'd appreciate the melodrama our actions inspired. Isn't that what you were looking for to alleviate your boredom?'

Melodrama! Boredom! Maddie nearly cried out loud. He had no idea. He'd been horsewhipped. Because of *her*. Maddie couldn't stop her emotions from boiling over. She put a hand over her mouth and fled for the bathroom, just making it to the toilet in time, where she retched over the toilet bowl.

She felt his presence behind her and begged weakly, 'Just leave me alone. Please.'

His voice sounded tight. 'No. Let me help...'

Before Maddie could protest she was being lifted up and a cool wet cloth was being pressed to her face. Nic handed her some toothpaste on a brush and she brushed her teeth. When she was done he took her hand and led her back to the bedroom. Maddie pulled her hand free from his and sat on the edge of the bed.

Nic stood apart and looked down at her, his expression guarded. 'You're an enigma, Madalena Vasquez. You set out to tease me years ago, and when I tell you what happened to me it makes you physically ill.'

His jaw clenched then, as if he were remembering something, and Maddie could see him start to retreat. She knew exactly what he was remembering: her cruel words. She desperately wanted to erase them for ever.

Huskily she said, 'I never set out to tease you, Nic, or to humiliate you. I promise on my father's life I had no plan, no agenda. When you followed me that first day I was terrified—but exhilarated. I wanted you...but I would never have set out to seduce you just for fun.' Her voice grew husky. 'That week… It meant something to me.'

Nic reached out and caught her arms in his hands, pulled her up to face him. He bit out through a clenched jaw, 'Don't try and rewrite history, Maddie. You seduced me because you were bored. That week was a diversion— nothing more.'

Maddie shook her head. 'No,' she whispered. 'It wasn't. I *wanted* to see you again.'

She felt herself teetering on the edge of a precipice. At the last moment she knew she couldn't tell him everything, so she'd furnish him with half a truth. She took a shaky breath. 'When we were discovered that day and I was taken home, my mother was livid. We had a huge fight and she told me about the affair she'd had with your father… My father overheard…'

Maddie comforted herself that what she was saying wasn't a complete fabrication; she was just ommitting certain information.

She went on, 'When I saw you the next day I couldn't tell you about the affair. It was too sordid. I was ashamed, and I was afraid of what would happen if they thought I was still seeing you. I had to make you leave, so I said the most hurtful things I could think of, but they weren't true…'

Maddie felt more exposed than she'd ever felt. She'd just revealed her heart to him. She looked away, terrified he'd see the emotion, see the lie in her eyes. What she *wasn't* telling him. The darker truth.

He released her and tipped up her chin, spearing her with that laser like gaze. 'Before your father came a few weeks after that, and my mother and I found out about the affair, I'd always assumed you and your mother left so quickly because you wanted to get away from here—and *me*.'

Maddie shook her head, her heart aching at the thought of how Nic had interpreted events. She suddenly felt sick again. Maybe Nic already *knew* the awful thing she'd carried with her for so long?

Hesitantly she asked, 'What did my father say to your parents, exactly?'

Nic stepped back, raking a hand through his hair impatiently. His whole body radiated tension. 'It was my mother he wanted to speak to.' He smiled bitterly. 'After all, my father already knew. My father was away that day. I just remember finding her hysterical, ranting about your mother and my father together. I had to get the doctor and he sedated her. A couple of days later she took an overdose of pills and left a note telling my father that she knew everything. It was bad enough having found *us* together, but after my mother's suicide the old enmity was truly alive and well again. Father's rage eventually led to his own heart attack…'

Maddie's stomach churned. It didn't sound as if his mother had elaborated on *everything*. If her father *had* told Nic's mother the full ugly truth she must have taken the information to her grave. Maybe it had been too horrific to comprehend. There was no way Nic's father wouldn't have used that information for his own ends to get back at her father or his son, she suspected, if he'd known.

Maddie couldn't help herself from reaching out to touch Nic's arm. 'I'm so sorry.'

Nic smiled, but it was tight and bitter. 'My mother wasn't exactly stable at the best of times. She most likely suffered from something clinical, like bipolar disorder, but it was never diagnosed. It didn't take much to push her over the edge.'

Maddie felt as if she was treading on eggshells. 'It must have been hard growing up with that…inconsistency.'

Nic emitted a curt laugh and pulled back from Maddie's touch. Her hand dropped ineffectually.

'You could say that. If Father wasn't trying to toughen up his runt of a son, Mother was weeping silently in a corner.'

Maddie's heart clenched at hearing Nic refer to his physical weakness again. Galvanised by something she couldn't name, Maddie said with a touch of defiance, 'Yet you overcame it and proved him wrong…'

Something bleak crossed Nic's face. 'Even then he couldn't respect me. I think it angered him to know that I'd prevailed.' Nic's mouth twisted. 'It just meant that he had to get his men to hold me down to thrash me. He no longer had the satisfaction alone.'

Maddie felt tears spring into her eyes. She'd had no idea he'd been so brutalised by his father.

Nic must have seen the brightness in her eyes and he quickly closed the distance between them, hauling her body into his.

A huge lump was in Maddie's throat, an ache in her chest. Nic looked ferocious.

'I think it's time we stopped talking and remembered what this evening is about…'

Nic's mouth was on Maddie's before she could respond. Tears were running down her face, but he was ruthless, intent on sucking her back under to a place where no words were needed. Maddie eventually gave in, her arms snaking around Nic's neck and the ache in her heart intensifying even as the tears eventually dried on her cheeks and her sobs of emotion became sobs of need and want under Nic's masterful touch.

* * *

When Maddie woke the following morning it took a long time for her to register where she was and what had happened. Her body ached, but pleasurably. Between her legs she was tender and slightly sore.

Maddie groaned. It all came back. The dress; the dinner; the orchard…and back here in Nic's room. She opened her eyes wider and looked around. She wasn't in Nic's room, in his bed any more. Even though dawn had been breaking outside when she'd finally fallen asleep.

He must have brought her back here, to the room she'd been shown into yesterday evening. Immediately Maddie felt vulnerable at the thought of Nic depositing her here while she slept, as if he was done with her. As if he couldn't bear to be with her for a moment longer. And with sick realization, Maddie knew why. He had to resent her for making him open up, for telling her what he had. He'd been through so much. The thought of him returning to the orchard that last day with his back ripped apart from a whip made her want to cry all over again.

A knock sounded on the door, making her flinch. Maddie squeaked something, half terrified it might be Nic—she wasn't ready to see him. Not when she was feeling so emotional. But it was the same girl who'd shown her to the dining room the previous evening. Relief flooded Maddie when she came in with a breakfast tray.

Maddie sat up, acutely self-conscious of her nakedness under the sheet. The girl put the tray on a table and then said shyly, 'I have a message from Mr de Rojas—he says that he will see you at your home this afternoon.'

The contract.

Maddie felt a hard ball lodge in her belly. She thanked the girl and when she'd left got shakily out of the bed, wrapping a towel around her. She went to the window and looked out. The view took in the eastern slopes of Nic's vineyard, with the snow-capped Andes mountains in the distance. It was stunning.

And then she saw him, striding down a row of vines in the distance. She shrank back, even though there was no way he could see her from where he was. But in that moment he looked up in her direction. Maddie ducked, her heart beating furiously. Humiliation burnt her up inside as she huddled there pathetically.

He couldn't even be bothered to come and tell her himself. The night was over. He'd got what he wanted, which was to see her as exposed and rejected as she had made him feel all those years before. If he had felt anything for her once, it was long gone.

Nic cursed himself for looking up at Maddie's bedroom window, and for fancying for a second that he might have seen her. She'd been dead to the world when he'd left her in the bed, her pale skin marked and lightly bruised from where he'd gripped her in the throes of passion.

Even now his blood rushed south, hardening his body, and he cursed out loud. He ripped a grape off the vine and bit into it, wincing slightly. Eduardo, his head winemaker, was looking at him, and Nic suddenly needed to be alone.

He said curtly, 'Another couple of days before we pick these. I'll find you later to check the others.'

Eduardo took the hint and nodded, walking away, and Nic breathed out a sigh of relief. His head was so tangled and snarled up since last night. Maddie was the first woman he'd fallen asleep with, whose touch he'd instinctively sought, wrapping his body around hers as if loath to let her go. *That* more than anything else had galvanised him into bringing her back to her own room to put some space between them.

He hungered for her even more acutely now that he'd

tasted every bit of her. Another first. Usually his desire was dented very quickly.

Last night had veered off the tracks in a big way the moment Maddie had stood up from the dinner table and started taking off the jewellery and shoes. And then…the orchard. Even now Nic could remember the panic he'd felt when he'd realised that was her intention. And yet at the same time something had resonated deep inside him—a need to get out of the falsely polite structure he'd insisted on with the dinner.

When he'd seen her standing among those trees it had felt terrifying, but completely right. As if there could be no other place for them to seek closure, no matter how exposed it made him feel. But all of that had fallen away as soon as he'd started kissing her. And when he'd discovered her innocence…

Nic's insides turned molten even now. She'd been a virgin. She was his and no one else's.

Nic hadn't even realised his hand was full of grapes until he felt the sticky juice oozing between his fingers. He looked at his hand and saw that it was trembling slightly. He recalled the tears in Maddie's eyes when he'd told her about his parents. That effortless feeling of affinity she'd evoked. Exactly as she had once before…

Past and present were meshing dangerously.

Sleeping with Maddie last night should have been a clinical exercise, and it had been anything but. It had morphed into something completely different. It proved to him how dangerous she was—how easily she slipped under his guard and elicited information from him. Exactly as she'd done before.

Even what she'd told him about *her* version of events that week was too huge for him to digest right now. It put a spin on things that threatened everything.

For a moment Nic felt panic steal over him—a completely alien emotion. And then he remembered the contract. Relief flooded him. The contract put a boundary around last night and around *him*. And more importantly it put a boundary around Maddie, keeping her at a distance from Nic.

Maddie was operating at a level of numbness which was working very well for her. She was blocking out the previous night's events, and if some lurid images snuck through her ironclad defences she closed her eyes and meditated on something else until they disappeared.

It was lonely in the house without Hernan and Maria. She'd spoken to Hernan on the phone earlier and had been devastated to learn that Maria would need an operation. Maddie had told Hernan to stay with Maria for as long as he needed. They were hoping that the operation would take place the following week.

Feeling restless, and not looking forward to a visit from a triumphant Nic with the contract, Maddie set out to check the cellars. She needed to start making an inventory of the things she needed. No doubt Nic would expect her to be well prepared for when his funds became available now that they'd be on a purely business footing.

Maddie felt no great sense of excitement that her estate was going to receive an injection of funds. It all felt flat now, meaningless.

When she remembered how she'd felt in Nic's arms last night in the orchard—the wave of love that had come over her—she assured herself that it was just because he'd been her first lover. Heightened emotion.

Maddie resolutely forced Nic from her mind yet again, and concentrated on making notes. More time had passed than she'd realised when she noticed that she was stiff from bending over and squinting at barrel labels. She'd been hoping that she might find a hidden gem of a barrel full of untouched wine, but no such luck.

Then she heard a distinctly bad-tempered-sounding *'Maddie!'*

For a perverse moment Maddie considered hiding among the barrels, as she and her brother had used to do when they'd been small, but she squared her shoulders and called out, 'Down here.'

She heard him before she saw him, and already her skin was tingling and she was remembering—and biting her lip trying *not* to remember. And then he appeared, in a loose shirt and jeans, hair dishevelled, looking so gorgeous that her lower body instantly grew hot and tingly.

Maddie couldn't speak, but it appeared Nic had enough to say for both of them. He strode towards her, eyes flashing with displeasure. 'How the hell does anyone know where to find you? Why don't you have a mobile phone? You could have been anywhere on the estate—'

He broke off and came closer, eyes sparking down into Maddie's, and to her utter chagrin she felt ridiculously emotional and close to tears.

'Well, I'm here, as you can see.' Maddie hated that she was so raw.

Nic seemed to temper his own response. 'I couldn't find you. I looked all over the estate... If anything happened to you—if you fell and sprained an ankle or anything...' He stopped and cursed. 'I need to know where you are.'

Maddie's treacherous heart leapt at *'I need to know where you are'*, but just as quickly she ruthlessly drove down that insidious emotion.

She stepped back and said coolly, 'Let's not pretend you're actually concerned, Nic. You just don't have time to spend looking for a business associate. Did you bring the contract?'

Nic seemed to blanch before her eyes, but then colour rushed swiftly back. His response surprised her, but he seemed to control himself. 'Yes, I did. It's upstairs in your father's study.'

Nic let Maddie precede him out of the cellar, and used the opportunity to get himself back under control. All of his earlier assurances had died a quick death when he'd come to the estate and hadn't been able to find any trace of Maddie anywhere. Panic had escalated as he'd imagined her lying somewhere, helpless. With so much out-of-date machinery in this place anything was possible.

And then, when he had found her, the relief had been overwhelming.

By the time he was following her into her father's study Nic was firmly back in control. He watched as Maddie sat down and pulled the contract towards her. She scanned it briefly and looked up at him with that cool expression on her face. It made Nic's blood boil and his loins ache. He wanted to see her undone again. Right now.

'Hernan won't be back for a few days. I'll have to wait till he gets here to go over this.'

Nic saw Maddie's throat work, the slight pink colour suffusing her skin. *Good.* She wasn't as cool as she looked, after all.

Nic dragged his attention from Maddie's physical response. 'I heard about Maria earlier. She's receiving the best of care, and the physician is confident it's a routine enough operation. He doesn't envisage any complications.'

Maddie said carefully, 'That's good… But this will have to wait until Hernan is back. I can't bother him with it now.'

Nic felt something like relief flow through his system.

A reprieve. He suddenly hated that damn contract. He conveniently pushed aside the memory of the panic he'd felt that morning. All he wanted was Maddie.

Maddie did not like the look on Nic's face as he prowled closer to the heavy oak desk. He put his hands down on top of it and said throatily, 'That's absolutely fine with me. But until the agreement is signed this isn't over.'

Maddie gulped, all pretence of insouciance fleeing. 'What isn't over?'

Nic came around the table and tugged Maddie out of the chair so she was standing flush against his body.

'*This.*'

And he wrapped his arms around her and pulled her so tightly into him that her curves melded into his hard muscles like the pieces of a jigsaw. Maddie made her hands into fists and hit out ineffectually, but Nic's mouth was on her jaw and trailing hot kisses down her neck to where the pulse was thumping out of her skin.

She groaned weakly. 'Nic…*no.*'

Nic's answer was to bend and lift her into his arms, making her squeal. He looked at her. 'Where's your room?'

Maddie was torn, already breathing heavily, her whole body aching for this man's touch. She knew a thousand and one reasons why she shouldn't do this, and yet the moment seemed fragile and illusory, as if it was a dream. There was a lightness between them for the first time.

'Upstairs, second door on the right.'

Nic's face was grim, but the heat in his eyes mesmerised Maddie. She hated herself for being so weak.

When Nic brought her into the sparsely furnished room with its plain double bed everything seemed to fall away. Past, present and future. There was only now, and this crazy, unexpected reprieve. She could recognise now that she was relieved that she hadn't signed the contract yet. Until she did she was a free woman—not beholden to Nic de Rojas.

Nic was opening the buttons on her shirt, and Maddie lifted her hands to do the same to his. Nic pushed her shirt off her shoulders and down her arms. His went the same way. Nic reached around and tugged Maddie's hair free of its band, so that it fell around her shoulders. In an endearingly gentle moment he spread his fingers through the silky strands of her hair, hands cupping her head, massaging it gently. He tipped her face up to his and something inside Maddie quivered ominously.

'This isn't over…not yet…'

And then Nic was kissing her, drugging her. With deft hands he unfastened her bra, letting it follow their shirts to the floor. Then he was cupping both breasts in his hands, massaging their firmness, trapping her nipples in his fingers, making Maddie moan into his mouth.

He took his mouth from hers and lifted one voluptuous breast so that he could swirl his tongue around the hard tip. His arm had come around her back, supporting her, arching her into him. Maddie's hands were in Nic's hair, mussing it up.

When he deposited her on the bed and opened her jeans she lifted her hips to help him. Her knickers disappeared too, but Maddie didn't have time to be embarrassed. She was too hot, waiting impatiently for Nic to finish taking off his own clothes, revealing his impressively taut body.

Maddie breathed in, sighing with deep-seated pleasure when Nic came down beside her. One hand pushed her thighs apart so that he could stroke with his fingers where she ached most.

Maddie couldn't have articulated a coherent thought

even if she'd wanted to. By the time Nic had donned protection and was pushing into her hot moist core, Maddie knew she would take this for as long as it lasted. And deal with the fallout later.

When Maddie woke much later it was dark outside. She was alone in the bed, and instantly cold when she recalled what had happened. Within minutes of seeing Nic again they'd been in bed. That had *never* been a part of the plan. It was meant to be one night and then she'd sign the contract…except she remembered now that she hadn't signed it. Guilty relief curled through her. It was as if they could ignore the inevitable for as long as the contract didn't exist. But Maddie knew that as soon as it was signed everything would change.

She tensed when she heard a faint noise from downstairs. The kitchen was two floors below her room, but the sounds sometimes carried up. She got out of bed and pulled on her jeans and shirt, smoothing her hair as best she could.

Creeping downstairs, she heard tuneless whistling as she got closer to the kitchen. She stopped at the door and her jaw dropped at the sight before her. Nic was in his shirt, which was buttoned up wrong, and the low-slung jeans with the top button still open, deftly tossing pancakes. His jaw was dark with stubble.

He spotted her and stopped whistling. 'How do you like yours?' he asked. 'With cream or chocolate or strawberries?'

Maddie went in and felt as if she was in some kind of twilight zone. Faintly she said, 'Where did you get all this stuff?'

Nic answered easily. 'I went out.'

Maddie looked at him, aghast. 'What time is it? How long was I asleep?'

Nic consulted his watch. 'It's nine p.m. and you were out for about four hours.'

Maddie blanched. 'You should have woken me.' She looked away, not wanting him to read in her expression or her eyes that she was relieved to see him still here.

Lightly he said, 'You looked far too peaceful.'

What Nic was thinking was that he didn't like how much he wanted to see the delicate purplish signs of fatigue gone from under Maddie's eyes. When he'd woken it had taken all of his restraint not to wake her with a kiss, or pull her back into his hardening body.

He'd come downstairs, and when he'd seen the pitiful state of affairs in the kitchen guilt had swamped him. He'd gone shopping for the first time in years. And as he'd shopped Nic had realised that for the first time in a long time he felt unaccountably lighter.

Without the contract between them Nic had seen a barrier being removed. They could continue this affair... because surely after another couple of nights he'd get that familiar sense of ennui and be able to move on from her?

Nic's jaw clenched now as he acknowledged that if anything his hunger for Maddie was only sharper. He could smell their mingled scent in the air and it was like the headiest of perfumes. Suddenly he wanted to swipe all the ingredients and shopping off the counter and take Maddie there and then.

Maddie sat down gingerly on a stool and watched Nic prepare another pancake. He'd already prepared about six. Half jokingly she said, 'How many are coming to dinner?'

He looked up, and Maddie felt speared by the intensity of his gaze. He smiled a crooked smile. 'I used to make tons of these when I worked in the vineyards in France during a European summer. We had to take it in turns to cook…communal living,' he explained. 'I was doing my Master of Wine course.'

Maddie shook her head. 'That's such an achievement. Your father must have been proud of that…' When Maddie saw Nic tense she cursed herself inwardly. But he spoke after a moment.

'He died just after I got my results. He didn't appear to be impressed.'

Maddie felt exposed at this acknowledgement of the lack of love he'd faced from his own father. Something that was all too familiar to her.

'So, have you made your mind up yet?'

She saw him hold up a jar of chocolate spread in one hand and a carton of cream in the other. To Maddie's intense shock, because she'd never thought of herself as an erotically minded person, she immediately had a vision of Nic putting some chocolate spread on her nipple and then licking it off.

Cheeks flaming, she blurted out, 'Cream and strawberries. Please.'

Nic just looked at her with a knowing glint in his eye and put the chocolate down, saying, 'Maybe you'll try that one later.'

Completely mortified, Maddie said nothing, and waited for Nic to serve her a pancake oozing with cream and strawberries. He handed her a glass of sparkling clear wine and Maddie took a sip, letting the effervescence take her far, far away from the reality that this was very finite and all too transitory.

'Nic, what is this? What are we doing?'

Nic closed his eyes momentarily, as if that might help block out the memory of Maddie's husky voice a short while before. He'd just pulled on his jeans and shirt and turned around to see Maddie resting back on her elbows in the bed, looking deliciously tousled and flushed. The sheet had barely hidden the curves of her breasts and inevitably, even though so recently sated, his body had started to hum with energy and renewed desire.

Who was he kidding? Here in his Jeep, driving away, it was still humming.

Three days had passed now. Three days and heady nights when time had seemed to blur and lose focus as soon as Nic drove into the gates of the Vasquez estate. He had gone there each day, ostensibly to talk to Maddie about what she wanted to do with the vineyard, but as soon as he saw her they inevitably ended up in bed. The desire between them was insatiable.

Damn, damn, damn, damn. Nic hit his fist off the steering wheel.

Maddie was under his skin, in his blood. In the very place he'd wanted to keep her out, and in a place no other woman had got close to. Since that week in the orchard, when he'd come so close to allowing himself to be emotionally vulnerable for the first time in his life, he'd kept his heart closed off to everyone around him. He'd learnt his lesson and he'd learnt it well.

Despite that, Nic knew he had to revise his whole memory of what had happened eight years ago. Maddie had been innocent—not even aware of her own power. Yet her words still stung. The vehemence with which she'd uttered them was still vivid and the way she'd been physically sick when he'd touched her. But he had to concede now that perhaps it had just been overwrought teenage dramatics in the aftermath of hearing the bombshell news of her mother's affair.

Her words resounded in his head again like a taunt: *'Nic, what is this? What are we doing?'*

He'd gone back over to Maddie in the bed and taken her face in his hands, pressing a long, lingering kiss to her mouth. When his heart had begun thundering and he'd known he was fast hurtling towards the point of no return he'd pulled back and said, 'Until the contract is signed, *this* is what we're doing.'

She'd stiffened and pulled at the sheet, forcing Nic to stand up.

'And then it's over—just like that?'

Nic had looked down into those wide green eyes and seen something that had made him profoundly nervous. It was a reflection of himself as a younger man, laying himself bare for ridicule. He couldn't go back there—not for anyone.

He'd spoken past a huge constriction in his chest. 'It can't be anything else…not if you want this investment.'

Maddie had paled, but then she'd looked him dead in the eye. 'I just wanted to be sure there was no confusion.'

Suddenly Nic had felt anger rise at her coolness. He'd bent and pressed another kiss to her mouth, only satisfied when she gave a helpless little mewling sound revealing her lack of control.

He'd stood back from the bed. 'I'll be back later, to go over some business details with you.'

With defiance evident in her voice, Maddie had said, 'I'm going into the clinic to see Maria this afternoon. Her operation has been brought forward to tomorrow.'

'Well, then,' Nic had gritted out, 'I'll come and get you and we can go together—after we've discussed business.'

Nic was well aware that once Maria's operation was over and she was in recovery, Hernan would come back to

Villarosa and look over the contract. And Maddie would sign. And this edgy truce between them would be over.

Because Madalena Vasquez was linked to too many emotions and memories for it to become anything else.

CHAPTER TEN

MADDIE felt a vibrating in her jeans pocket, took out the mobile phone Nic had given her, and scowled at it before answering.

All she heard was an autocratic, 'Where are you?' and instantly her insides were melting and blood was rushing to the sensitive parts of her body.

She gritted her jaw. 'I'm at the vats.'

She ended the connection, feeling very shaky. She had been ever since that morning, when Nic had laid it out so baldly—that this affair would last only until the contract was signed and then return to a platonic business relationship. It should be making her feel happy. Surely she wasn't naive enough to think it could be anything else?

Maddie knew that for her own sanity she should be grateful. There was too much history between them. The feud might not exist any more but it had wreaked too much havoc to be healed by them alone...

She sighed now, and nearly jumped out of her skin when she heard a soft, 'Don't fall in.'

Maddie whirled around to see Nic on the catwalk. She'd been so engrossed that she hadn't even heard his Jeep, or his arrival on the steel catwalk. She turned away, scared he'd see how raw she felt. 'I did fall in once...when I was about nine.'

She heard Nic gasp audibly. 'How on earth did that happen?'

Maddie smiled wryly. 'I was playing hide-and-seek with Alvaro, my brother. Hernan was here, helping with the hand-plunging. I was fascinated and leant over too far to have a look…and fell in. Luckily Hernan fished me out again straight away.'

Maddie touched her head and looked at Nic with a wry smile. 'He managed to catch my hair…I was more upset by the pain than by the fact that I could have drowned in fermenting red wine.' She dropped her hand. 'Hernan brought me home and he and Maria cleaned me up. They never told my parents…' Maddie shuddered lightly. 'If they had, my father would have locked me in my room for a week with no food.'

Nic's voice was tight. 'Did he do that a lot?'

Maddie shrugged and picked at some flaking pieces on the huge and now empty vat. 'Sometimes…if something angered him. It was more frequent after Alvaro died. He was an angry man…angry that he had a useless daughter who he couldn't pass his legacy on to.'

Suddenly conscious that she'd been babbling, Maddie changed the subject abruptly. 'These vats are in need of serious upgrading. Father got them in because he wanted to go back to concrete tanks.'

Maddie looked at Nic when he didn't say anything straight away. Then, to her relief, he said, 'We can get rid of them if you like and go back to steel. It depends on which you think is best…'

Maddie followed Nic back down to ground level and they spent the next hour discussing the various merits of upgrading the current facilities or replacing everything with the most up-to-date modern equivalent.

By the time they were on their way to the clinic in Mendoza, Maddie was feeling far more under control.

That control became shakier, though, when she witnessed Nic's concern for Maria and his insistence that she receive the best of care. He was going out of his way for people who hadn't even been his own employees.

Maddie was largely silent on their way back to Villarosa, after leaving a worried but valiantly optimistic Hernan at his wife's bedside. She wasn't prepared when Nic asked, 'What made your father change his mind?'

Half absently she said, 'About what?'

'He threw you and your mother out, turned his back on you. So why did he suddenly leave it all to you?'

Maddie tensed in her seat and Nic looked at her. For a long moment she couldn't speak. All she could think of was that awful afternoon and the horrific things she'd learnt. Feeling bile rise, she blurted out, 'Stop the car, please…'

Nic pulled over into an empty layby that was near a local beauty spot lookout, with the Andes rising majestically in the far distance. But Maddie was oblivious. She stumbled out, feeling as if a huge weight was bearing down on her.

Nic got out too and touched her shoulder. 'Maddie, what is it?'

Maddie jerked back, her eyes wide.

Nic felt Maddie jerk back. She was so pale, and her eyes were…horrorstruck. *Déjà vu* slammed into him. She'd looked at him like that before. She'd flinched like that when he'd touched her.

She spoke thickly. 'There's something…you don't know. Something else that happened after we…after we were caught.'

She whirled around and faced out to the view. They were the only people there, and it was quiet.

Nic felt his insides constricting, growing tight. As if to ward off a blow.

Through a tight jaw he asked, 'What don't I know?'

Maddie stared unseeingly at the view. 'I don't want to tell you,' she said in a low voice.

She felt Nic put his hand on her shoulder again and pull her round to face him. He dropped his hand then, as if loath to touch her, and a sense of inevitability washed over Maddie. Perhaps she did owe him the full explanation? This would bring them full circle.

'Tell me *what*, Maddie?'

Still some part of her resisted. 'I never told you because at first I couldn't. And then…then I didn't want you to have the awful blackness of it in your head, poisoning you like it did me.'

Nic shook his head, obviously completely confused. And then he looked grim. 'Maddie, we're not leaving here until you tell me what this is about.'

Maddie looked around. She felt weak all of a sudden, and went over to sit on the low wall.

Nic's hands were in his pockets. He just looked down at her.

She started hesitantly. 'I didn't tell you everything that happened when I got back to my house…after we were caught. I did start to have a fight with my mother as I told you…she was livid.'

Nic took his hands out of his pockets and folded his arms. 'Go on.'

Maddie focused on a point in the middle distance and drew in a deep breath. 'She told me that I wasn't to see you again, and I told her that she couldn't stop me.' Maddie looked at Nic then, and said softly, 'I wanted to see you again… But then she started to tell me about the affair. I didn't know what it had to do with *us* and I tried to walk out…but then she told me something else…'

Keeping her eyes on his, Maddie relayed to Nic the full extent of what her mother had told her.

'That's why I couldn't see you again…and my father had overheard every word.'

Nic felt as if he'd been punched in the gut. He looked at Maddie stupidly. And then he felt nauseous. It burned its way up, held down only by extreme strength of will.

Maddie stood up, seeing the reaction on Nic's face. 'When we went to Buenos Aires my mother agreed to get a DNA sample from my father. He gave it to her with the proviso that she would get nothing from the divorce. I got the test done and found out that I am…*was* his daughter. But of course it was too late to tell you any of this. Too much had happened. I was still traumatised by the possibility…' Maddie stopped and swallowed painfully. 'I sent a letter to my father, but never heard from him until just before he died.'

Colour was beginning to seep back into Nic's cheeks. He uncrossed his arms and ran a hand through his hair. He couldn't look at her, and Maddie felt it like the sting of a whip.

'My God, Maddie.' Nic went and stood at the low wall and looked out over the view.

Maddie turned to face the same way. She couldn't look at Nic. She bit her lip so hard she could taste blood. 'That last day…I didn't even realise I'd headed for the orchard until I got there. That's why when I saw you I reacted the way I did. How could I have told you what my mother had put in my head? It was too horrific.'

Nic sounded grim. 'Your father must have told my mother. It has to be the reason she took such a drastic step.'

Maddie nodded. 'I suspect so, yes. And I'm sorry.'

'For God's sake, Maddie, it was hardly your fault.'

His curt tone made Maddie flinch. She'd held this knowledge in for so long, and now it was out and she'd tainted Nic's head with it too. An awful helpless shaking started in her legs and rose up, taking over her whole body.

'I'm sorry. I never wanted to tell you—I shouldn't have said anything.'

Maddie heard Nic curse, and then he was turning to her and pulling her into his arms, his hands on her back, pressing her against him, stilling the awful shaking until it was just tiny tremors racking her body. She couldn't even cry.

Nic was rubbing her back now, and her hair, soothing her as if she were a wild unbroken horse.

After a long moment he pulled away and put his hands on her shoulders. He looked her in the eye. 'I'm glad you told me.'

He kept looking at her until Maddie nodded reluctantly. Then Nic took her hand and led her back to the Jeep, putting her into the passenger seat as if she were a child, securing her seat belt. Maddie felt numb, slightly removed from everything.

A grim-faced Nic got in beside her and they drove back to Villarosa. When Maddie saw Nic take the turn for his own estate she said, 'Where are we going?'

He looked at her. 'You're coming home with me tonight.'

The inevitable heat deep within Maddie started to thaw some of the numbness. It felt as if something had shifted between them as soon as she'd uttered the heinous words. When he'd held her just now his touch had been platonic. Maybe he could never desire her again with that knowledge in his head? Even though he knew it wasn't true—it was poisonous.

They got back to Nic's house. Without a word he just took her hand and led her up to his room. Maddie felt incredibly insecure and confused. She pulled free of Nic inside his bedroom door, too many evocative memories crowding her head. 'What are we doing here?' She was ashamed of how badly she wanted him.

He came and stood right in front of her. 'We're going to exorcise those demons right now, right here,' he said.

Maddie looked at him and her heart beat fast. 'What do you mean? How?'

He cupped her face in his hands and pressed close against her, so she could feel his body hardening against hers.

'Like this.'

And then he kissed her. But this was unlike any kiss they'd shared before. It reminded Maddie of how he'd kissed her for the first time—how badly she'd wanted it after the long week of building tension. He'd been so intimidatingly sexy and yet disarmingly clumsy. Like when he'd fumbled with the buttons on her blouse before opening it, and his cheeks had flushed at seeing her breasts.

It was as if past and present interlocked. Maddie was being lowered down onto the bed and Nic loomed over her. He opened her shirt and pushed it apart, pulled down the lacy cup of her bra, forcing her breast to pout up towards him.

Maddie arched her back instinctively, silently begging him to touch her.

He looked at her steadily. 'I've never forgotten how you tasted that day…the sweetness of your skin, your breast. I could have drowned in your scent…'

Maddie ran her fingers through Nic's hair, an unstoppable tide of emotion forcing her to rise up and take his face in her hands, her mouth searching for his. Each touch and moment was imbued with echoes of the past, of the way Nic had touched her that day for the first time.

They passed the moment when they'd been stopped before, and kept going. Clothes were shed and lay in a tangled heap, on the floor or under their hot slick bodies on the bed. When Nic lay between Maddie's legs his mouth was on her breast, one big hand trailing up the outside of her body, luxuriating in her satin-smooth skin, dewed with sweat.

'Nic, please…' she begged, rolling her hips impatiently.

Shifting his big body only slightly, Nic thrust into Maddie, and her whole body stilled as she looked up at him and relished the moment when their flesh joined.

'Keep your eyes open,' Nic instructed gutturally.

Maddie couldn't take her eyes off him as he slowly started to thrust in and out, taking them higher and higher and further away from the ugliness of what had happened.

When Maddie's orgasm broke over her it felt transcendental, spiritual. As if it was washing something away. Nic's gaze was searing her alive, burning into her as his own body crescendoed and his release broke free. Maddie felt the warmth of it inside her and instinctively clasped her thighs tighter around Nic's hips.

After a long moment Nic fell into an exhausted slump beside Maddie. He hugged her close, arms wrapped right around her. All he could think of before sleep and blackness claimed him was how intense it had felt to have no barrier to his release going deep into Maddie, and how tightly her legs had clasped him to her in that moment.

Maddie woke and looked at Nic. He was so much more relaxed in sleep. He was always so tightly controlled. Her heart lurched and she suddenly longed for a time when she would see him relax and smile…and laugh. Perhaps he would…with someone else. Not her. He'd been softer once—she'd seen it in his eyes, along with hope. But she was the reason that softness and hope had been replaced by cynicism. When she thought of how vulnerable he'd been when they'd met, underneath all his arrogance...her rejection must have cut too deep for him ever to forgive.

Maddie didn't want to wait for Nic to wake and react to her presence. She knew something had changed last night. They'd crossed a line. The past had been well and truly dealt with. This affair had always been about old scores, lingering desire... The contract had provided a kind of reprieve, but it would be signed soon and then Nic would be relegating Maddie back to the periphery of his life.

Maddie had to face up to her conscience, which was riven with guilt. She'd slept with Nic using the contract as an excuse because she'd believed that it was the only way she could sleep with him. He'd never have wanted her without the contract. He wouldn't have lowered himself to seduce her just for desire's sake.

She had to get out of there before she forgot that and started wishing and hoping that perhaps...in another world...if they hadn't shared such a tangled history... eveything might have been different.

The fact was that ultimately Nic had got his hands on the one thing he wanted most, and that was the Vasquez estate. In the end he'd prevailed, and got personal revenge into the bargain.

When Nic woke the sun was high outside and he felt completely disorientated. The bed was empty beside him and he closed his eyes. The bittersweet relief that went through him to find that he was alone was palpable.

The last thing he remembered was waking during the night and finding Maddie soft and sexily pliant in his arms.

He'd been hard and aching and she'd woken, pushing her buttocks against him, urging him to take her.

He'd slid into her from behind. It had been quiet and intense.

His head reeled anew when he thought of what Maddie had told him yesterday. He'd acted from some visceral place, bringing her back here to make love in a need to negate the awful words. When he recalled what it had been like to lock eyes with her as they'd made love he felt dizzy, even though he was lying down.

Maddie's revelations put a spin on the past that Nic wasn't sure he could really assimilate. Her reaction that day…he had no defence against it any more, nothing to hide behind. He knew he would have reacted exactly the same—might possibly have been even more brutal than she'd been to him. And the fact that she'd been burdened with the knowledge…it made Nic feel sick.

She'd wanted to see him again. If her mother hadn't told her what she had, the following day at the orchard would have been very different. A cold sweat broke out on Nic's brow as he lay there and contemplated how different things might have been…and could be now. And there his mind immediately shut down. His body was locked with tension.

He'd come full circle with Maddie. They'd reached a truce. He could forgive her now and move on. He'd invest in her estate, help her get back on her feet. And that had to be enough. He simply could not contemplate an alternative, because that meant challenging the walls of defence he'd needed to exist for so long. Since his mother had smothered him with anxiety and his father had brutalised him. And since he'd spent that week with Maddie and felt his heart beating for the first time…

The concept of love had been alien to him until he'd met

Maddie. And then it had become mangled, and had withered inside him after her cruel words and brutal rejection. No matter what he knew about that day now, he couldn't undo the damage. And Maddie was inextricably bound up in all of that, so she could never be a part of his future.

Nic's bones ached when he thought of relegating Maddie to his past. He jack-knifed off the bed and took a stinging cold shower, assuring himself that finally he could move on—but he could only do it by leaving Maddie behind.

Maddie walked out of the clinic feeling tired but happy. Until she saw a familiar Jeep pull into the car park. Unconsciously she started walking faster and put her head down. She cursed when she heard, 'Maddie!'

Slowly she turned around. She didn't feel ready to face Nic yet. It had been two days since she'd left his bed, and she'd not seen him or heard from him. The message was clear: it was time to move on.

She schooled her features into a bland, polite mask. But still when she saw him she couldn't stop that impulse she had to devour him with her eyes. Her heart spasmed, her arms tight across her chest. 'Nic.'

'How is Maria?'

Maddie smiled tightly. 'She's going to be fine. The operation was a success. She'll need to recuperate here at the clinic for a few days, but she's been very lucky. They're very grateful to you.'

Nic waved a hand as if to brush aside the considerable expenses he'd met for Maria's operation and care. 'It was nothing,' he said gruffly.

Maddie's chest felt constricted. 'Was there something else you wanted?'

He looked at her for a long moment, and she felt an icy feeling of foreboding.

'The other night…we didn't use protection.'

Maddie went cold and then hot. She hadn't even thought about it afterwards. Mortified, she babbled, 'It's fine. I got my period today.'

Nic looked grim. 'That's good…'

Wanting to escape, Maddie said, 'Hernan is coming back to the estate tomorrow. He's going to check over the contract, so I should have it signed the day after, if he thinks it's okay.' Maddie felt like a fraud for delaying the inevitable: she'd looked over the contract and it was more than fair—and generous.

Nic nodded. 'I'll come and pick it up myself.'

'Goodbye, Nic.' Maddie turned quickly and headed straight to her Jeep, hating the stinging in her eyes. She knew it was silly, but somehow *now* felt like the moment when whatever link they'd shared for the past eight years was finally broken.

'Maddie—'

Maddie's steps faltered and her breath stopped. Blinking back the moisture in her eyes furiously, she turned around again. Nic hadn't moved. The planes of his face were stark, and he said, 'I'm sorry that—'

Maddie put up a hand, bile rising in her throat at the thought that he was going to give her some platitude. 'Don't, Nic. Just don't. You don't have to say anything. It's done.'

And she turned and half ran, half walked to her Jeep. She and Nic had been seeking some kind of closure and now they had it. Whatever she'd felt move between them the other night had been nothing more than an illusion, a reaction to heightened emotion.

So, she asked herself on the way home through a veil of tears, if this was closure why did it feel so *un*closed?

* * *

Maddie sat looking at the contract. It was early in the morning. She and Hernan had gone over it all last night and he'd concluded that she wouldn't have got a better deal from anyone else. With Nic's investment the entire estate and house would be completely renovated and updated—something her old-fashioned father had fought against all of his life. His resistance was one of the main reasons the estate had fallen apart.

Hernan and Maria would be well protected and looked after. Nic was going to bring in a project manager and a new head winemaker. He would also hire new cellar hands and seasonal grape-pickers, as well as the machinery needed to mass-pick grapes.

Maddie knew she had no choice but to accept this investment—not just for her sake but for the sake of the local economy. The Vasquez estate had long been an employer of locals and it could be again. Not to mention the huge debt she owed Hernan and Maria, who needed support now more than ever. She couldn't deny that she wanted the estate to flourish again. It was just a pity that she wouldn't be there to witness it.

With a heavy heart Maddie picked up a pen and signed on the dotted line. And in doing so she sealed her fate—because she couldn't remain here now. She couldn't renege on this deal, but she also couldn't go on living here, seeing Nic every day, living with his casual dismissal of their affair. She'd sold her soul and heart to him—and she'd used his investment in the estate as an excuse to hide behind.

What had happened between them amounted to nothing more than a ream of paper written in legalese.

Maddie tried to write a note to Nic, but no matter what she said it came out trite and ridiculous. In the end she gave up and simply wrote:

Nic, I am handing full control of the estate and all decisions to Hernan. He is the best person to oversee the work to be done.
Yours, Maddie.

Even that made her scowl. She folded it and put it in an envelope and left it on top of the contract, with her note to Hernan. And then she left her home.

Nic watched the dawn break, casting a pink light over the snow-capped Andes in the far distance. His jaw itched with stubble. His eyes stung. He hadn't slept all night. He hadn't slept since he'd woken in the empty bed the other morning.

The view he now looked upon, which encompassed the vastness of his estate, usually never failed to fill him with a sense of satisfaction, but for weeks now it had failed to move him. He'd become distracted and had lost interest in work—which had been his one *raison d'être* for ever.

Only yesterday Eduardo had had to repeat himself three times before Nic had registered what he was saying, and then Nic had snarled at him like a bear with a sore head. Nic had, of course, apologised profusely—he'd never lost his rag like that before—but the level of control he'd been wielding for years was deserting him spectacularly.

And Nic knew the moment it had started to desert him. When he'd seen Madalena Vasquez walk through the doorway in that hotel in Mendoza. He'd known *then*, even before he'd recognised her, that everything had changed irrevocably.

And just like that, as the pink light spread across the Andes, Nic knew what it meant—and what he had to do if he wanted to gain any sense of control or sanity back. All of this—his struggle with his parents, his health—meant absolutely nothing now. Because from the moment he'd seen Maddie Vasquez on her horse eight years ago and followed her to the orchard, she'd controlled his destiny.

She'd made him trust, and then she'd broken him apart and reformed him with her brutal rejection—which was now so understandable. But she was the only one who could heal him, make him take a chance on trusting again...

From the moment she'd come home he'd been slowly thawing, coming back to life inside and fighting it every step of the way. The pain of it was almost unbearable. But now that pain was as necessary to him as breathing.

Nic hadn't even realised he was moving until he was in his Jeep and driving out of his gate towards Maddie's estate. He barely noticed the one other vehicle on the road—a taxi. When he got to the house it felt silent, and Nic knew with a sick feeling why it felt like that.

He went into the study and saw the notes and the contract. He put the letter for Hernan aside and opened the one for him and read it. Slowly he put it down and picked up the contract. He looked at the last page. Maddie's name was scrawled on the bottom line.

With an inarticulate roar of rage Nic flung the contract against the book-lined wall and the pages went everywhere. He turned and stormed out, eyes wild.

Maddie shuffled forward in the queue at the ticket booth, counting her money. She had just enough. When she got to Buenos Aires she would try to persuade her aunt to let her stay for a couple of weeks while she tried to find a—

'Running away, Maddie?'

Maddie's brain froze mid-thought. She looked around to see Nic standing there, arms crossed across that broad chest. His calm and reasonable tone belied his wild look: his hair was messy, his eyes were bloodshot, and his jaw was stubbled with dark blond beard. And he was utterly, utterly gorgeous.

Maddie quickly turned back to face the queue again, and tried to will down the heat seeping into her cheeks. 'I don't know why you bothered to come here, Nic. And, no, I'm not running away.'

She went forward a few steps and Nic kept pace beside her.

'Could have fooled me. Did you realise you couldn't hack it? That you don't really care for your estate that much, after all?'

Maddie rounded on him, bristling. 'You *know* that's not true. I love that estate.'

'Then why are you leaving?'

Maddie flushed. She was becoming aware of people nudging each other, because inevitably they recognised one of Mendoza's foremost citizens. All they'd have to do was recognize *her* and then they'd have enough fodder to gossip about for months. *De Rojas has run Vasquez out of town!*

Reluctantly Maddie stepped out of the queue and moved away, so people couldn't hear them. She rounded on Nic. 'I don't need to be there for you to invest in the Vasquez estate.'

Nic was grim. 'It's part of the deal.'

Maddie felt like stamping her foot, and emotions weren't far from the surface. 'Nic, I'm leaving, and there's nothing you can do or say to stop me.'

Resolutely she turned to join the back of the queue and start again. Then she heard Nic say rawly from behind her, 'What if I said I don't want you to go, and it's got nothing to do with the investment?'

Maddie stopped, and her breath grew very shallow. She wasn't even aware of the interested eyes of onlookers flitting between her and Nic. She'd misheard him—or he didn't mean what she'd thought he meant.

She took an experimental step forward and heard, 'Maddie, *dammit.*'

And then Nic was in front of her, planting himself squarely in her way. She looked up. The muscle in his jaw was ticking.

'Nic…?'

'I don't want you to go because I've just realised how much I need you.'

Maddie's hands were gripping her bag. Something fluttered ominously in her chest but still she thought he had to be talking about the investment.

'But Hernan will be there. He can handle it…'

Nic nearly exploded. 'I'm not talking about the investment. I don't care about that. I only offered to invest because you seemed so determined to throw yourself in harm's way. And the contract—' Nic stopped abruptly and cursed out loud before admitting, 'The contract was a way for me to have you in my bed without admitting that I was terrified you'd reject me again.'

He reached out a hand and touched Maddie's cheek. She felt his hand trembling. *Déjà vu* washed over her.

'I messed up, Maddie, because I was too cowardly to admit how much it made me *feel* when you came back here.' He shook his head. 'Your rejection that day…it was like having my heart torn out of my chest and ground into the earth. Nothing mattered after that. I closed myself off. In the space of that week I fell for you so deeply…'

Maddie's vision was blurring. She brought her hand up over Nic's on her face and held it there, willing him to trust her. 'Oh, Nic…I'm so sorry that happened. That my mother poisoned my mind…that I couldn't tell you. I wanted you so badly. I fell for you too. And I know that's why you can't possibly forgive me.'

Resolutely Maddie took Nic's hand down and dropped it. She stood back. 'That's why I'm leaving. I'm not strong enough to live near you, loving you, knowing that you're getting on with your life…and you have to move on.'

Nic sounded slightly dazed. 'You love me? Even now?'

Maddie nodded and fresh tears blurred her vision. 'You were always in my heart and thoughts. I told myself when I came back that I hated you for being so autocratic, and for making me believe that what had happened between us eight years ago was pure lust on your part. But it was a lie. I agreed to that stupid contract because on some level I thought it was the only way you'd have me…'

Maddie looked down and wiped at her damp cheeks. She clutched her bag and took a step around Nic—only to feel him take her arm in a strong grip.

She couldn't even look at him. 'Please, Nic…let me go. You can't make me stay. Not now.'

He didn't listen. He turned her around and tipped her chin up. Maddie saw his face and her heart stopped. He looked young…and free of those awful shadows. A smile curled the corners of that beautiful mouth and her heart started again, making her feel light-headed.

Gently Nic asked, 'Have you listened to a word I've said?'

Maddie felt confused. What *had* he said?

Suddenly Nic took her bag out of her hand and dropped it to the ground. And then, before she could take in a breath, he was down on one knee in front of her, holding her hand in his.

Looking up at her with those intensely blue eyes, he said throatily, 'Maddie Vasquez, I love you. I was fascinated by you before I ever met you, and then when we did meet I fell deep into your heart. I've never stopped loving you, no matter how hurt I was, and I only realised that when you came back home. I told myself I hated you, that I wanted revenge…but I wanted *you*. And I wanted your heart. But I was too cowardly to admit it…'

Maddie was stunned into silence, sure that she had to be dreaming. The queue had long since broken up, and they were now surrounded by an avid crowd of spectators. Maddie heard someone close to her sigh theatrically.

'Maddie Vasquez…will you please marry me? I can't move on with my life unless I know you're going to be in it. I want us to have babies and grow old together, to be the ones to bury this ancient feud for ever. I love you.'

Maddie started crying in earnest, emotion rising up within her and making her shake. Nic stood up and pulled her into his arms, cradling her and soothing her. Eventually, when she could, she pulled back and looked up at him. He still looked wild, and trepidatious. She could see the old fear in his eyes—the fear that even now she'd walk away…

She reached up and put her arms around his neck.

She pressed a salty kiss to his mouth and said on an emotional sigh, 'Yes, I'll marry you, Nic de Rojas. How could I possibly do anything else when I love you so much?'

The cheers of the crowd made Maddie bury her head shyly in Nic's chest, and then she felt him lifting her into his arms and striding out into the glorious sunshine.

One year later

'No,' Nic said patiently. 'We *are* married, but my wife has an extensive estate in her own name so she decided to stay a Vasquez. She's a modern woman.'

Maddie's hand was tightly clasped in Nic's. She fought back giggles when he gripped it tighter and they watched the snooty older couple walk away, radiating disapproval at this unconventiality. The people of Mendoza were only slowly coming to terms with a de Rojas/Vasquez union, but the Vasquez estate was well on its way to flourishing again under its own label.

When the couple had gone Maddie laughed out loud, and buried her head in Nic's chest to hide it. His hand was tender on the back of her neck, fingers exerting a gentle pressure, and Maddie finally looked up when she'd collected herself, loving the feeling of languid heat which invaded her bones at his touch, which would turn to something much more urgent given half a chance—even more so now than it ever had.

'Well, Señor de Rojas.' She smiled up at her husband. 'Do you realise that this is our first anniversary?'

Nic frowned. 'But we only got married nine months ago…'

Maddie looked around the sumptuous ballroom of the hotel in Mendoza and squeezed his hand. 'Not that anniversary. I mean this time last year we met again for the first time…'

Nic looked down into his wife's clear and loving green gaze and felt his chest tighten almost unbearably. It happened a lot, this physical feeling of love. That night a year ago—he could remember seeing her shape in the doorway, could remember feeling right then that trouble was in store. And he wouldn't have changed one second of it.

He smiled and took her hand, lifting it to his mouth to kiss the inner palm. Her eyes darkened and immediately blood rushed to his groin. He almost groaned out loud. They were like two rampant teenagers.

His voice was low and husky. 'Happy anniversary, my love…'

Maddie turned her face into his palm and Nic glanced up and cursed softly, wishing that they were alone. He felt Maddie sigh against his hand and looked down, immediately concerned. He saw her wry look and felt her hand come between them, to rest on the very prominent swell of her belly. She was already two weeks overdue.

She grumbled good-naturedly, 'Do you think this baby will *ever* appear? If he takes much longer I'll need a crane to get around.'

Nic smiled wolfishly and wrapped both arms around Maddie, pulling her close. 'I can think of one way we can urge him along…'

Maddie's insides liquefied at the carnal look in Nic's eyes. This past year had been a dream. She loved this man more than she'd even allowed herself to believe possible when she'd first fallen for him.

Maddie asked, 'Can we just leave? Now?'

He pressed a kiss to her mouth and said, 'We can do whatever we want.'

'But your speech…'

Nic looked round and Maddie saw him share a look with Eduardo, his head winemaker. He looked back to Maddie. 'Eduardo will take over. This…' He put his hand possessively on her belly. 'You, *us*—there's nothing more important than that.'

The next day, at five p.m., Nic and Maddie welcomed their son, Alvaro, named after Maddie's brother, into the world.

Maddie, exhausted but happy, looked at Nic cradling his son—all ten pounds eleven ounces of him—and smiled wryly. 'If we could patent your particular method of helping labour along I think we could make a fortune.'

Nic's little finger was caught in a chubby hand, and he looked at his wife and said mock seriously, 'Next time I'll make sure to put much more effort in.'

Maddie groaned softly. 'The way I'm feeling right now, there won't *be* a next time.'

Nic chuckled, and Maddie was glad to see the colour restored to his face. He'd nearly fainted in the delivery room, his torture at being so helpless evident when Maddie was in such pain.

He came and handed Alvaro back to Maddie, who sat up and started to breastfeed. Nic leant close and whispered in her ear, 'Don't worry, Mrs Vasquez. I'll make it so pleasurable next time you won't even think about the pain.'

Maddie looked at Nic and saw how dark his eyes were at seeing her breast exposed like this, their baby suckling furiously. She felt a familiar tugging in her lower body that no pain could diminish—not even a fifteen-hour labour.

She groaned softly and said, 'What have I let myself in for?'

Nic pressed a kiss to her neck and then pulled back to look at her, one hand on his son's head. He just smiled.

* * * * *

ONE NIGHT TO
RISK IT ALL

MAISEY YATES

To my family.

Because it takes a village to support me, and you all do it with remarkable ease, very little grumbling, and a lot of love.

You can never know how much I appreciate you.

CHAPTER ONE

RACHEL HOLT'S FOCUS was pulled to the nightstand. To the ring glittering there in the bedside table light. She lifted her left hand and looked at the finger the ring had been on only a few hours ago.

Strange to see it bare after so much time wearing it.

But it hadn't seemed right to wear it now.

She picked it up off the nightstand and held it up, watching it sparkle, then turned over and looked at the man sleeping next to her. His arm thrown up over his head, his eyes closed, dark curls falling into his face. He was like an angel. A wonderful fallen angel who'd shown her some deliciously sinful things.

But he wasn't the man who'd given her the ring. He wasn't the man she was supposed to marry next month.

That was a problem.

He was so beautiful, though, it was hard to think of him as a problem. Alex, with the beautiful deep blue eyes and golden-brown skin. Alex, whom she'd met that afternoon—oh, good Lord, she'd known him less than twenty-four hours—on the docks.

She looked at the clock. She'd known him for eight hours. Eight hours had been all it took for her to shed years of staid, respectable behavior. To shed her engagement ring, and follow her... She couldn't say heart. It was hormones, clearly.

What had she been thinking? It hadn't been anything like the way she normally behaved. Not at all. She knew better than this. Knew better than to let emotion or passion overcome common sense and decorum.

There had been no decorum tonight.

From the first moment she'd seen him, she'd been completely captivated by the way he moved. The way his muscles shifted as he worked at cleaning the deck.

She closed her eyes and went straight back there. And it was easy to remember what had made her lose her mind... and her clothes.

It was the most beautiful weather they'd had since they'd arrived in Corfu. Not too hot, a breeze blowing in off the sea. Rachel and Alana had just finished lunch, and her friend was headed to the airport to fly back to New York, while Rachel was staying on to represent the Holt family at a charity event.

This vacation was her last hurrah before her wedding next month. A sowing of oats, in a respectable manner of course, as anyone would want to do before they tied themselves, body and soul, to another person for the rest of their lives.

"More shoes?" Alana asked, gesturing to the little boutique shop that was just across the pale, stone street.

"I'm going to say no," Rachel said, looking out across the water, at the ships, the yachts, that were tethered to the docks.

"Are you sick?"

She laughed and walked over to the seawall, bracing herself on it. "Maybe."

"It's the wedding, isn't it?" Alana asked.

"It shouldn't be. I've known it was coming for ages. We've had an understanding for six years and been engaged for a good portion of those years. The date for the wedding has been set for almost eleven months. So..."

"You're allowed to change your mind," Alana said.

"No. I'm not. I... Can you imagine? The wedding is the social event of the year. Jax is finally going to get Holt. My father will finally have him as a son, which we all know is what both of them want."

"What about what *you* want?"

It had been so long since she'd asked herself that question, she honestly didn't know the answer.

"I...care about Ajax."

"Do you love him?"

Her eye caught movement out on one of the yachts—a man was on the deck cleaning. He was shirtless, a pair of loose, faded shorts clinging to lean hips. Aided by the sun, the light clinging to the ridges of muscle, the shadow settling in the hollows, she could clearly see the defined, cut lines of his body.

And he took her breath away.

In one moment she had all of the passion, all of the heat, all of the deep longing she'd been growing so certain she was missing—sucked out of her by that horrendous early heartbreak—sweep through her like a wave.

"No," she said, her eyes never leaving the man on the yacht, "no, I don't love him. Not—not like you mean. I'm not in love with him. I *do* love him, it's just not...that kind."

It wasn't a revelation. But coming on the heels of that sudden rush of sensation, it was more disturbing than normal.

She'd sort of thought that maybe it was her fault. Not her and Ajax together, but just the way they were as people. Ajax wasn't a passionate man, and he never demonstrated passion with her. Quite the contrary, he barely touched her. After all their years together he never went further than a kiss. A nice, deep kiss sometimes. Sometimes a kiss that lasted a long while on the couch in his penthouse. But no clothes were ever shed. The earth was never shattered. It was never hard to stop.

And because he was a very handsome man, she'd assumed that the problem—if it could be called a problem—was with both of them. That she was missing a piece of herself, passion choked out after years of tight control. After letting her passion carry her to the edge of a cliff all those years ago, only to be pulled back just in time, so very aware of the fate she'd been saved from.

Since then, she'd kept it on a tight leash. Which made them sort of an ideal couple, in her mind.

But that wasn't true. She knew it now. In a blinding flash of clarity, she knew it.

She had passion. It was still there. And she *wanted*.

"What are you going to do?" Alana asked, sounding heavily concerned now.

Rachel's face heated. "Um…about?"

"You don't love him."

Oh. Of course Alana wasn't in her head—she didn't know that Rachel's world had just been rocked by a man more than one hundred yards away.

She waved a hand. "Yes, but that's nothing new to me."

"You're staring at that man over there."

Rachel blinked. "Am I?"

"Obviously."

"Well he's…"

"Mmm. Yes, he is. Go talk to him."

"What?" Rachel whipped around to look at Alana. "Just…go talk to him?"

"Yeah. I don't have to get on my plane for another few hours so if you need a bailout, I'm here. But I can hang back."

"Go talk to him and what?"

Flirtation, living dangerously, living for the moment—

that was all a part of a past so long gone it felt like it belonged to someone else entirely. The Rachel who had narrowly escaped humiliating herself and her family was gone. New Rachel had emerged from the wreckage. And New Rachel was a rule follower. A peacekeeper. She went with the flow and did what she could to keep everyone happy. To make sure she didn't go too far over the line and miss the safety net her father provided for her.

But for some reason, standing there in the sunshine, thinking of the safety her father provided, of the stability she had with Ajax, she felt like she was drowning in the air. Felt like there was a noose tightening around her neck, the countdown to her execution looming....

Such drama, Rachel, it's a wedding, not a hanging.

But even so, she felt like it was. Because the wedding presented her with utter, final certainty for her future. A future as Ajax's wife. As New Rachel, the one who never created a ripple on the surface, for the rest of her life.

"You have got to go and talk to him," Alana said. "You turned red when you first saw him. Like…really red. Like he lit your toes on fire."

Rachel choked. "Dramatic much?"

"So okay, I've sat back and watched your engagement with Ajax, and I haven't said much. But as you just said, you aren't madly in love with him. And anyone with eyes sees that."

"I know," she said, her throat tightening.

"Look, I know we're old and boring now. And I know that in high school we did some stupid stuff…."

"To say the least," Rachel said.

Alana continued. "But I think you've gone a little bit too far the other way."

"The alternative wasn't any good."

"Maybe not. But I think maybe this future isn't so good, either."

"What else can I do, Alana?" Rachel asked. "My dad bailed me out so many times, and I pushed him to the point where he was ready to wash his hands of me. And now? We're close. We have a relationship. I make him proud. And if Ajax is the price I have to pay for that then…I accept it."

"Does he at least make you feel like your toes have been lit on fire?"

Rachel looked at the man on the yacht again. "No," she said, the word choked out. "He doesn't."

"Then I think you owe it to yourself to spend some time with a man who does."

"Really?"

"Yes, really. I really do."

"So…I should just go talk to him? Want to bet he curses me out in Greek and then goes back to work?"

Alana laughed. "Yeah, that won't happen, Rach."

"How do you know? Maybe he doesn't like blondes."

"He'll like you because you're the kind of woman who drives men crazy."

"Not so much anymore." Flirting, toying and teasing had ended badly for her eleven years ago, and Ajax had certainly never acted as if she'd driven him crazy.

"Lies," Alana said, waving her hand. "Live dangerously for a minute, babe. Before you stop living altogether."

Rachel couldn't take her eyes off him, not even to shoot her friend the evil eye, which is what she should really be doing. "Did you read that on a fortune cookie?"

"Ever had an orgasm with an actual man? 'Cause I have. So…"

At the mention of orgasms, Rachel's cheeks burned. No, no she hadn't. She'd given them a few times, yes, but never received. "Fine. I'll go talk to him," she said. "Talk to. Not orgasm with. Lower that suggestive eyebrow of yours."

"Okay. And I'll be close. So if you…you know, need anything, text."

"Also I have mace," Rachel said. "Ajax insisted."

She winced as she mentioned her fiancé's name. But she wasn't going to do anything, not really. She was just going to go talk to Shirtless Sailor Stud. She wasn't going to do anything inappropriate.

It was all about having a moment. Just a moment. To be brave and reckless, and not so much like the Rachel she'd been this past decade. To know what it was like to chase a moment that wasn't bound up in the expectations of other people.

Just a moment. To talk to a guy because she thought he was cute. Nothing more.

She took a breath and tossed her hair over her shoulder. "Wish me...well, not luck exactly."

Alana winked. "Get lucky."

"No. I'm not cheating on Jax."

"Okay," Alana said.

"I'm *not*." The very idea was laughable. There were people who were like that. Bold people who went around *carpe*-ing *diems* all over the place. But that wasn't her. Not anymore. She wasn't sure that had ever been her. Her rebellious years had been just that. Rebellion. Not just a desire for freedom, but a desire to push against the bonds that had always held her in place. Until she'd realized just how much that behavior affected other people. Just how much it could affect her. Not just her present, but her entire future.

But just saying hi wasn't so bad. There was no harm in giving herself a moment to bask in the heat that this stranger gave off.

"Riiiight," Alana said.

"Shush." Rachel turned and walked toward the dock, her hands shaking, her body rebelling in every way against what she was about to do. Sweaty palms, heart beating so fast she was pretty sure she was going to faint, mouth watering with sickness. Yep, the signs to run and preserve herself were all there.

But she ignored them.

She looked back at Alana one more time, who was standing at the wall still, watching. Then she turned back to her target.

She would just say hi. And maybe flirt. Just a little harmless flirting. She half remembered how that went. She'd been a master of the tease back in the day. Batting her eyes and touching a guy's shoulder, all while never intending to do anything more than use his interest to boost her ego. It had been a game then. Fun.

Why not revisit it? This was her last hurrah before her marriage. A chance to hang and shop with Alana. A little time to decompress, loll by the beach, watch chick flicks in her hotel room, then enjoy a charity gala. All without her family or Ajax around.

This was just a part of that. A little time off from being Rachel Holt, beloved media figure. Rachel Holt, who was doing her best to represent her family, to do what was right.

She needed some time to just be Rachel. Not New Rachel. Not Old Rachel, either. Just Rachel.

She stopped in front of the yacht and took a deep breath that was choked off.

Then she looked up, and her gaze crashed into the most electric blue eyes she'd ever seen. Followed by a slow, wicked smile, a flash of bright white teeth on dark skin. He was even more beautiful up close. Utterly arresting. He pushed dark curls out of his eyes and the motion made his muscles flex. A show just for her. And her hormones stood and applauded. And cheered for an encore.

Stupid hormones.

"Are you lost?" he asked, his English heavily accented. The same accent as Ajax's. Greek. And yet it didn't sound the same. It wasn't as refined. It had a rough edge that abraded against something deep inside her. Struck against the hard, dry places inside of her and set off a shower of sparks that sat smoldering, building.

And all that over three words. She was doomed if she did anything other than walk away.

But she didn't. She stayed rooted to the spot.

"Um…I was…I was just there," she gestured back to the wall where she'd been standing with Alana, who was now absent. "And I saw you."

"You saw me?"

"Yes."

"Was there a problem?"

"I…" she said, stumbling over her words. "Not a problem, no. I just noticed you."

"Is that all?"

He put his foot up on the metal railing that surrounded the deck then jumped down onto the dock, the motion fluid, shocking and…darn hot.

"Yes," she said. "That's all."

"Your name?"

"Rachel Holt."

She waited. For recognition to flash through his eyes. For him to get excited at being in front of someone who had a certain level of media fame. Or for him to turn away. People did one of those two things. Rarely anything else.

But there was no recognition. Nothing.

"Well, Rachel," he said, that voice a rush of liquid that pooled low in her body, "what is it you noticed about me?"

"That, um…you were hot," she said. She'd never been so forward with a man in her life. Though, honestly, she wasn't sure if she was being forward or being an idiot. She was good with people. The consummate hostess. Everyone, even the vicious press, liked her. A reputation that had been carefully cultivated—and fiercely guarded.

But she was a lot more experienced at offering people cold beverages than she was at offering them her body.

He arched one dark brow. "That I was hot?"

"Yeah. Haven't you ever had a woman come on to you before?" Her face was burning and she couldn't blame the afternoon sun. She wasn't supposed to be hitting on him, and yet these were the words leaving her mouth.

Stupid mouth. Almost as stupid as her hormones.

"Yes, but not in quite such a charming way. Did you have an end goal in mind for this?"

"I thought…" Suddenly she did. Suddenly she wanted everything, all at once, with this stranger. Wanted to touch him, kiss him, feel his fingertips forge a trail of fire over her bare skin as he took her to levels of ecstasy she'd never believed were possible for her to want, let alone feel. "I thought we could have a drink." A drink. A cold beverage. That was back in her comfort zone and maybe a bit smarter. Especially since she didn't even know his name. "What's your name?" she asked, because since she was engaging in naked fantasies about the man, it seemed polite to ask.

"Alex," he said.

"Just Alex?" she asked.

He lifted a shoulder, the muscles in his chest shifting with the motion. "Why not?"

Why not, indeed? It wasn't as though there was any reason for him to be anything else. Who cared what his last name was? She'd never have occasion to use it. She'd never introduce him at a party, or need to refer to him in conversation. She'd never see him after today.

"Good point. So, a drink? Or…would your boss get mad?"

"My boss?"

"The owner of the yacht."

He frowned and looked behind him, then back at her. "Oh. No, he's gone up to Athens for a few days. I'm just supposed to check in on things now and again. No need to stay tied to the dock."

"I suppose not. You won't float away." She laughed, then felt immediately stupid. Like she'd regressed to being an eighteen-year-old girl rather than a twenty-eight-year-old woman. Of course, she hadn't been giggly or ridiculous over men at eighteen. She'd learned better by then.

Apparently all good sense and life lessons were out the window now.

He wrinkled his nose and squinted against the sun, an oddly boyish gesture. It made her feel even warmer. "I don't suppose. Though I have in the past."

"Have you?"

"Sure. That's how I ended up here. I spend a lot of my life floating."

She felt the layered meaning in his words. And in a strange way, felt like she'd heard more honest words from this stranger, this man she'd known all of five minutes, than she'd ever heard out of the man she was planning to marry.

"So," he said, "drink?"

"Of course."

"Let me just get a shirt." He tossed her a smile and climbed back up onto the boat. It took all of her willpower not to say "oh, no, please leave your chest bare." She figured that would be pushing it. Especially since, no matter how much she might want him, she knew she'd never do anything about it.

A drink was all it would ever be.

They'd gone to the bar next and ordered a couple of sodas. She'd texted Alana to let her know everything was fine and that she wasn't axe-murdered. But she didn't send a text when she and Alex walked around town for hours, or when they ended up having dinner on the pier, laughing and talking over seafood and pasta. She didn't text Alana about how he lifted his fork to her lips and let her taste his entrée, about the way their eyes had met in that moment and it had sent a snap of heat through her.

Or when he took her to a club later that night.

She hadn't been to a club since she'd had to sneak in with a fake ID. Clubs like this were a hotbed of scandal and sex, and all sorts of things her father and Ajax would never have approved of. The sort of place the press would crucify her for going to.

Alcohol, loud thumping music, sticky dance floors filled with bodies. There had been a time when she'd loved it. But not after she'd become aware of what she was inviting. Not since she realized the sort of trouble she could get herself into. Since she realized she'd been walking down a path that only had one ending, and it wasn't a happy one.

But just for now, she was going to put good behavior on hold. She felt secluded here, insulated by whatever magic spell Alex had cast on her the first moment she'd seen him. No one around was looking at her, expecting her to behave in a certain way. She didn't think she was in any danger of exposing herself the way she'd done in the past.

Somehow, with Alex, it felt exciting. It felt dangerous— a hit of adrenaline she used to crave. One she'd denied herself for far too long.

It all did. The whole day. It was like being on a vacation from herself, and she loved it. Or maybe it was a vacation *to* herself, but that was a step further into the philosophical than she wanted to get.

"This is so fun!" she shouted, trying to make her voice heard over the thumping bass.

"You are enjoying yourself?" he asked.

"Very."

He took her left hand and the touch of his skin against hers sent a lightning bolt shooting from her wrist to her core. "I have been meaning to ask about this," he said, tilting her knuckles so that her engagement ring caught the light.

Looking at it made her stomach crash into her toes. She didn't want to think about that. About reality. Not at all.

"I'm not married," she said.

A wicked smile curved his lips, blue eyes glittering in the dim light. "I wouldn't have cared if you were. I would have maybe just asked how big your husband was. And if he was connected to organized crime in any way."

The thought of Ajax being connected to anything as sordid or exciting as organized crime was hysterically funny. He was far too staid for anything that outrageous. He was the calming, steadying influence in her life. Or at least that's how her father saw him. And she couldn't really imagine him mustering up any rage for Alex being here at the club with her.

Ajax wasn't really a club kind of guy. If she'd asked him, he would have probably waved his hands and said to have fun while he went back to sorting numbers into columns or whatever it was he did all night in his office that gave him such satisfaction.

"Um…you don't need to be concerned. Besides, we haven't done anything we should be ashamed of," she said. "I haven't…violated any vows."

"Yet," he said, his grin turning wicked. "It's still early."

"So it is," she said, her heart thundering hard.

"Do you want to dance?"

She looked at his outstretched hand and she felt an ache, a need, tighten in her belly. Ajax had never once danced with her. Had never even asked. And until that moment, she hadn't realized that she'd been missing it.

In that same moment, she realized that this wasn't just a request for a simple dance.

She knew that this was it. The deciding moment. That

if she said yes to this, she wouldn't say no again for the rest of the night.

But maybe that had been true hours ago. Maybe from the moment she'd locked eyes with him, saying no had been an impossibility.

"Yes," she said, the word torn from her, scraping her throat raw and leaving in its place a sweet, light relief. She had decided. Tonight she was going to embrace life, whatever that meant. "Yes, Alex, I want to dance."

CHAPTER TWO

HE KISSED HER for the first time out on the dance floor. There were people all around them, the crush of bodies intense. And she let them push her into him, let them drive her against him so that she could feel the hard heat of his muscles against her chest.

When she was pressed against him, she looked up, angled her head toward his. She knew she was begging for it and she didn't care. Because she needed this. More than air. It didn't matter what happened tomorrow, or in the month leading up to her wedding, not if she didn't survive this night.

And it felt like she might not if he didn't touch her. If she couldn't taste him.

But he didn't make her beg for long.

He dipped his head and claimed her mouth, his tongue forcing her lips apart. She opened to him, took him in deep, kissed him until she was dizzy. There had never been a kiss like this. Not for her, maybe not for anyone. One that stole her every thought, her every worry. One that reduced her to nothing more than need, nothing more than a deep, physical ache that demanded satisfaction.

She wrapped her arms around his neck and clung to him, her body moving against his, no longer in rhythm with the music, but in rhythm with her own desire. She forked her fingers through his thick, curly hair, held him against her, poured all of herself, all of the desire that had been building in her for so many years, into a kiss that she shouldn't be having. A kiss that was forbidden to her.

And that just made her angry. More determined to get what she needed tonight. What she would never have after tonight. This was her last chance.

A secret thrill. A secret bit of adventure. No one ever had to know.

"Come back to my hotel with me," she said, against his mouth, unable to part from him for even a second.

He didn't answer—he only kissed her again, and she realized there was no way he'd heard her, not over the music.

She pulled his head down and put her lips against his ear. "I have a hotel room. Come back with me."

That was all the encouragement he needed. Faster than she could change gears, Alex was dragging her off the dance floor and out into the warm summer night. He paused outside the club door, pushed her against the wall and kissed her, the motion and the kiss savage, explosive. Perfect. She arched into him, rubbing her breasts against the hard wall of his chest, trying to find some satisfaction for the need that was tearing through her like a beast.

"Now," she said, her eyes closed tight. "We have to go back now. I need… I can't…"

"I agree."

"It's close. I think it's close. I'm dizzy, actually. The city is sideways. It's hard to tell where the hell we are."

Alex laughed and pressed his forehead against hers. "I know exactly where the hell I am."

"And where is that?"

"With you. I don't need to know anything more."

She exhaled sharply, tried to ignore the stab of emotion in her chest. This wasn't supposed to make her feel. "Wow. You do say the best things. You really do."

He took her hand. "Lead the way."

She did. And somehow, right then, she felt more like herself than she ever had. Like the two halves of her life, the woman she was in public and the woman she was in private had merged together for the first time.

She felt brave. She felt certain.

She felt happy.

A whisper of who she'd been before she'd learned to shut herself down. Before the Colin debacle. And blackmail. Before she'd had to face her father and tell him what she'd done. And what the fallout from it might be.

I can't protect you anymore, Rachel. These choices you're making are dangerous. People, men, will always try to take advantage of you because of your connections, the press will always hunt you because of who you are, and you're courting it. No more. If you keep on like this, I will not cover for you again. I love you too much to enable you this way.

And less kind words from her mother. *A woman in your position can't afford these mistakes. It's not only immoral, it's dangerous. Think of what the press will say. About you. Us. I haven't spent all these years helping propel us to this position in society to watch you tear it down with stupid behavior!*

Angry words spoken in private. A side of her mother only Rachel ever saw.

But she'd taken those words, balled them up and stored them in her chest, kept them close, ever since.

Except…except this moment.

But it was different. It was out of time, out of the real world entirely. And Alex didn't even know who she was. He didn't want to use her. Didn't want to get her into a compromising position so he could sell photographs, or a dirty video.

Even Ajax, one of the kindest people she knew, wanted her for her name more than anything else.

But that wasn't Alex. Alex just wanted her.

That simple thought pushed everything dark away from her mind. Everything in the past, everything in the future. There was just now. And now was perfect.

They started walking down the sidewalk, then they were running, laughing. She bent and kicked her shoes off, carrying them in her free hand as she ran barefoot down the stone walk.

They stopped in front of the hotel, the lights from the lobby casting a glow on Alex, on the fountains in front of the building. "Oh, yes," she said, breathing heavily. "I'm in a nice hotel."

"So you are." He laughed, the sound reverberating through her body.

"Don't feel awkward or anything."

"I don't," he said.

Of course he wouldn't. It was hard to imagine him feeling awkward anywhere. "Good. I need to know at least three more things about you before we go in, okay?"

"Depends. Are you going to do a credit check?"

"I swear not," she said, "I won't even fingerprint you. But…you're a stranger, and I can't have that."

"Really? And what is it that will make me not a stranger?"

She squeezed her eyes shut for a moment, and when she opened them, Alex filled her visions. "Favorite color?"

"Don't have one."

"Come on. What color is your bedspread?"

He laughed. "Black."

"Okay. How old are you?"

"Twenty-six," he said.

"Oh." For some reason the answer sent a little thrill through her. "Well, I'm twenty-eight, I hope that doesn't deter you."

"Not in the least," he said. "I might, in fact, be more turned on now. If such a thing is possible."

Her pulse kicked into a higher gear. "One more thing," she said. "Would you rather…sleep under the stars, or in a beautiful suite?"

"Either. As long as you were with me. Preferably in a state of undress."

The air rushed out of her lungs. "Well, that was the perfect answer."

"Can we go in?"

"Yes," she said, of course, since there was no way she was saying no now. "You aren't a stranger now, so it's all good."

"I'm glad," he said.

They went into the hotel and passed quickly through the lobby. She pushed the button and stood in front of the elevator, waiting, her nerves building as each second ticked by.

As soon as they were inside, as soon as the doors closed behind them, he pushed her back against the wall, his mouth hungry on hers, his hands roaming over her curves.

She could feel the hard press of his erection against her hip, could feel his arousal, not just there, but in every line of his body. The tense hold of his shoulders, the thundering of his heart, the urgency in his kiss.

She'd never in her wildest fantasies imagined herself here. Like this. With a man kissing her like he was starving for her. She never imagined she would be kissing a man as though she was starving for him, in truth.

Her past experiences included fizzy, alcohol-flavored kisses and heavy coercion. This wasn't alcohol going to her head. Nor was it coerced. It wasn't about rebelling against her neat and orderly life. It wasn't about a sense of duty. It was about her.

They were at her floor not nearly fast enough and all too quickly. Any slower, she might have died—or he might have just taken her straight to heaven with her clothes on. She was close, so close, and she knew it.

She might not have ever considered herself overly passionate but she had a sex drive. And since Ajax was patiently waiting to take things to the next level, that meant she was an expert at satisfying that sex drive on her own.

Orgasm she knew. But having it entirely out of her control? That was a whole different matter. She'd given Colin pleasure, but he'd never really touched her. And anyway, that was eleven years ago, and the extent of her experience with men and any sort of nudity.

Now she was here, and Alex was definitely touching. And her pleasure was all in his control. It was both exhilarating and terrifying.

She walked out of the elevator into the hall, her legs shaking. She dug through her purse, trying to find the little key card she'd thrown in there earlier. Why had she been so careless? She hadn't had this in mind, that's for sure. She hadn't known there would be urgency. She had all the urgency and no flipping key....

She scraped the bottom of her purse with her hand and came up with the card. "Oh, thank God," she breathed. "That was sacrilege, wasn't it?" she asked, looking back at Alex.

"Why?"

"Thanking God because I found the key so we could... well, this is fornication, isn't it?"

"It will be in five minutes," he said. "Right now it's just lust."

"Pretty powerful stuff." She turned to the door and slid the key in the slot. The light turned green. "So, I guess we go in now."

He stopped and touched her cheek with the tip of his finger, the gesture so tender it shocked her. "You're very pretty when you're nervous."

Her face heated. "Well, that's nice of you to say."

His blue eyes locked with hers, so sincere, so focused. As if he could only see her, as if she was the only thing that mattered. No one had ever looked at her like that, not ever. "I mean it."

She coughed, her throat suddenly tight with emotion. "Well…thank you. But I'm less nervous when you kiss me. Maybe we should go with that?"

He didn't have to be asked twice.

He pulled her into the room and onto the bed. She was flat on her back, the mattress soft beneath her, Alex hard over her. She didn't have time to be nervous. She was too turned on, too in the moment.

There was nothing boyish about him now. The humorous light in his eyes was gone, replaced with something dark, feral. Dangerous.

And she liked it.

"I will be slow the next time," he said. "I promise. I like foreplay." He rose up onto his knees and stripped off his shirt. "And there will be some. Next time. Next time, I promise." Then he reached into his shorts pocket and took out his wallet, pulling out a condom and throwing the wallet down onto the floor, followed quickly by the rest of his clothes.

She didn't have time to be nervous—she was too busy looking at him. He was incredible, so much more than she'd imagined a man might be.

And she wanted… She just *wanted*.

He tugged the top of her dress down, bared her to him, lowered his head and sucked one nipple deep in his mouth as he pushed her skirt up over her hips.

He hooked his fingers into the sides of her panties and tugged them down her legs, then drew back for a moment, opening the condom and rolling it on quickly before he positioned himself between her thighs.

He put his hand beneath her bottom and tilted her up to him as he thrust deep inside her. She winced against the pain, fighting the urge to make a sound. Because she didn't want to ruin the moment. Even with the pain it was the most beautiful moment ever. The most exciting and wild thing that had ever happened to her.

It was perfect.

If he noticed, he had no reaction. And she was glad. Instead, he thrust deep inside of her, pushing them both higher and higher until she was gasping. Until she was fisting his hair, the sheets, whatever she could get hold of so she didn't fly off the bed and shatter into a million pieces.

The pain faded quickly, every thrust pushing her closer to the point of release. But it wasn't an easy push. It wasn't a gentle journey to the peak. It was fire and thunder—her release almost ripped from her as it hit, suddenly and before she could take a chance to breathe.

She shuddered out her release, clinging to his shoulders, legs wrapped around his calves. She was sure her nails were biting into his skin, but she didn't care. She couldn't.

He went still above her, a hoarse sound on his lips as he found his own pleasure. And then he was up, moving away from her and into the bathroom.

She lay there on her back, her dress pulled down over her breasts and up past her hips, trying to catch her breath, hands over her eyes. "Oh, dear Lord, what have I done?"

He came back in, the condom managed, the look on his face grim. "Now, you should have told me *that*," he said.

"Told you what?" she asked, sitting up and trying to put her dress in place. Though he didn't seem concerned with his nudity at all.

"That you were a virgin."

"Oh. That. Well. I *could* have told you. It's just that…"

"Just that what?"

"I didn't want to. How stupid is that?"

He walked over to the bed and took her left hand in his, holding it up so she was eye level with her engagement ring. "Whoever gave you this? He's an idiot."

Rachel came back to the present, her eyes on the ring, just like they'd been in that moment after her first time with Alex.

They'd been together at least four times in the hours since then. And he'd been telling the truth. He did like foreplay. Not only that, he was good at it. Darn good.

She put the ring back down, a smile curving her lips.

She sat up slowly, the muscles in her body complaining. Alex had given her a little bit more exercise than she was used to. That made her smile widen. Which was stupid, maybe, but she felt…different. Giddy. Alive.

Half in love.

She closed her eyes. No. She didn't want that. That was such a stupid cliché. She didn't actually know the man. She'd been naked with him, that was all.

Except it was easy to remember how it was to dance with him. How it felt to hold his hand as she walked barefoot down a city sidewalk. How she'd been different with him. More alive.

Happy.

So maybe it wasn't so stupid that she felt half in love. It was scary, though. She'd been…not in love, but infatuated with a guy before, with hideous results. But that had been different. It felt like another lifetime. Like it had happened to another girl.

She'd changed over the past eleven years. In ways that were necessary, but in ways that had left her feeling like she was trapped in skin that had become far too small.

And sometime last night, she'd changed again.

She got out of bed and stumbled to the bathroom, taking care of early morning necessities and looking at herself in the mirror. She looked… Her hair was a wreck. She was pretty sure the dark mark on her neck was a hickey.

She smiled. She should not be enjoying this. But she was.

Real life could be dealt with later.

She pushed her hair back and walked out into the hotel room again, and stopped when she saw Alex's wallet on the floor. It was open, from when he'd taken out the condom and thrown it onto the ground. After that incident, he'd procured protection from the concierge. Much to her chagrin.

Well, and delight, if she was completely honest. She'd absolutely benefitted from the acquisition of a box of condoms.

She bent down and picked his wallet up without thinking. It was an expensive wallet. Black leather with fine stitching. Like something her father, or Ajax, would own. Strange because his clothes were so worn. Because he worked on a boat.

Her eyes skimmed over to his ID. He had an American driver's license. Which seemed odd. Because he was Greek, no question. Though, perhaps his employer was American.

Okay, snoopy. Not really your business.

And it wasn't. They weren't trading life stories so it wasn't really fair for her to be looking at his personal property.

Before she could snap the wallet shut and put it on the table, she read his name. Not on purpose. But she saw it, and then all she could do was stare.

She knew his name.

And for a full thirty seconds, she didn't know from where.

Alexios Christofides.

She heard the name in Ajax's voice. A growl, a curse. He'd been nettling Ajax for months. Buying shares in his business, reporting him to the IRS for suspected tax wrongdoing, reporting him to environmental agencies. All false accusations, but things that had cost time and money.

He wasn't a cabin boy, that was for sure.

And he wasn't a stranger.

She'd been seduced by her fiancé's enemy.

She thought the floor might shift beneath her feet and fall out from beneath her like sand, dropping her back into the past, in a moment so close to this one it made her want to scream.

Colin, so angry over her refusal to sleep with him, revealing who he really was. What he really wanted from her.

If you don't want to put out, that's fine. But I have all those nice pictures of you. A very compelling video. Of what you did for me. I don't need sex. A little money from the media will be even nicer.

She'd thought she was smarter. More protected. Different.

She was the same foolish girl she'd always been. Worse, even, because this time the villain had succeeded in his seduction. He'd more than succeeded.

What she'd done with him…what she'd let him do to her…

"Alexios?"

The man in her bed stirred and Rachel tried not to pass out. Tried not to vomit. Or run screaming from the room.

She had to know what had happened. She had to know if he knew who she was.

Of course he does. Like he's here by accident? You can only be a naive fool to a certain point, moron.

"Alexios," she said his name again and he sat up, a wicked smile curving his face. When he actually looked at her, the smile faded.

As if he knew, even half asleep, that he wasn't waking to the postcoital scene he was hoping to be a part of. As if he knew that his response to the name had been wrong.

He'd probably already forgotten which woman he'd been in bed with. Which hotel.

That made her want to be violently ill. Or just violent.

But for the moment, she had to stay calm. She had to get answers.

"Rachel," he said, his voice as strong as whiskey and good sex, going straight to her head and making her toes curl. "You should come back to bed."

"I don't… No." She put her hand on her forehead. "Not right now. I…"

His eyes met with her hands. Where her fingers held his wallet. He looked back up at her, one black brow arched. Something in his manner changed. In an instant, he changed.

He pushed his dark curls off of his forehead and for a second she thought she was looking at a stranger. A naked stranger.

Then she realized that was what he was. She didn't know this man. Not at all. She'd fooled herself into thinking they'd shared something. That their souls had met, or some such idiocy. But they hadn't.

It only underlined her stupidity. Her weakness.

Last night, she'd felt like herself. Freed from all the layers of protection and expectation. Somehow slipped free of those well-meaning, soul-binding words spoken by her parents all those years ago. She'd felt real. Well, real Rachel was, it turned out, incredibly stupid. There was a reason she'd been kept in hiding.

"You know who I am, don't you?" she asked.

He stood, the covers falling from around his waist, his body, his beautiful hard body, on display for her. And even now it made her heart leap into her throat. Like it was trying to climb out so it could get a look at the view.

"Why were you looking at my wallet?"

"It was on the floor. I picked it up. I thought, 'nice wallet for a cabin boy.' Clearly far too nice. So now you might as well tell me the truth."

"I know who you are," he said. "Imagine my surprise when you found me before I could find you. Imagine my further surprise when I realized I didn't need a week or a special event to seduce you. You were a lot easier than I expected."

"To what end?" she asked, her heart thundering, her hands shaking. "Why would you… Why…?"

"Because I want what he has. Everything. And I've had something very special to him now. Now we both know I've had you first."

"You bastard," she said, scouring the room for her clothes. "You…! This is *my* hotel room." She stopped collecting her clothes and started getting his instead. "Get your clothes and get out." She threw his shorts at him, then his shirt. "Out!"

He started dressing. "I don't know who you think your fiancé is, but I know who he is."

"And I know who you are! A… A… I can't even think of a bad enough word for what you are. And you're no kind of man."

"You and I both know I am."

"The ability to trick a woman into letting you put your hard penis inside of her does not make you a man!"

"Did I trick you? Or did I, like you, not tell you everything. I hardly forced you into bed."

No, he hadn't. And that meant it was her fault. Her stupid, stupid fault.

"But you…seduced me knowing that you would ruin my engagement. With the express intent of doing it!"

"And you thought my seducing you would leave it intact? Is that it? Or are you just pissed because I planned it?"

"Yes! I am pissed that you planned it. I thought we had

something… I thought…" Her throat closed off, emotion, anger choking our her words.

"Such a virgin, Rachel," he said, his tone dry.

"No, I'm not, and I think we both know it. Because of you!" And even before that she'd lacked innocence. Which meant she should have known, she *did* know. But he'd made her forget.

"Because of you, *agape,*" he said, tugging his slacks up and doing the button. "You made your choice. Don't be angry with me because I outed you as being faithless."

Before she could measure her response, his wallet was sailing out of her hands, skimming his ear, hitting the wall behind him. "Out!" she screamed.

She had just destroyed her engagement. The future of her family's company. All for sex. Sex with a man who'd been using her. Tricking her. Trying to hurt Ajax…

Ajax, who hadn't deserved this treatment at all. Who cared for her. And her father… After all he'd done for her…

She pressed her palms into her eyes, trying to keep the tears at bay. "Out. Out. Out," she said.

"Rachel…"

"You ruined my life!" she screamed, flinging her arms wide. "I thought you were different. I thought you made me…feel something and you were just lying. I blew up my life for you and it was a lie!"

"I never promised you anything. You made a mistake. Unhappily for you."

"Don't call him," she said, her stomach sinking. "Just don't call him."

"I don't have to," he said. "You won't marry him."

"One night with you and I'm going to leave the man I've been engaged to for years? I hardly think so," she said. Only a few moments ago, she would have. Just a few short moments ago.

She would have exposed herself to scandal, exposed her

family to it. She would have destroyed everything she'd spent years rebuilding for him. What had she been thinking?

And now...what had she done? What was wrong with her? She hadn't thought, not for a moment. She'd been feeling. Lost in some inane fantasy that had no hope of ever coming true.

Now she was sitting here, all of it burned down, ash at her feet, the hero of the story revealed as a villain.

"Just go. And please don't contact me. Please don't call him, don't... Don't."

"Now, why," he said, his lip curling, "would I agree to that? I got exactly what I wanted. I am a man who makes careful plans, *agape,* and I don't plan on changing them just because you shed a tear."

He strode across the room, to the hotel door, and walked out. He didn't even look at her again. Didn't spare her one more glance as he closed the door behind him.

Rachel sank onto the floor, her knees giving out entirely. And it was then she realized that she was still completely naked. But it didn't matter. Putting on clothes wouldn't make her feel less exposed. Wouldn't make her feel less... dirty.

That's what it was. She felt dirty.

She'd betrayed Ajax.

That was the truth no matter who Alex really was. But his betrayal was like salt in her wounds, as they would be salt in Ajax's.

Ajax...

She would have been prepared to end the relationship if there had even been a chance that...

That Alex wasn't a lying, horrible, hideous bastard. But there wasn't. He was. And that meant she had to go back home. The wedding had to go forward. Her life had to go forward. As if this hadn't happened.

This was why she'd avoided passion. This was why she'd avoided doing things that were risky, and crazy. Because when she took chances, she got hurt. Because when she trusted, it came back to haunt her. On her knees, her chest burning so bad she could hardly breathe, she remembered exactly why she'd taken to hiding herself.

Never again. She would go back to Ajax, to safety. And if Alex told him about tonight, she would beg for his forgiveness. She stared ahead, eyes dry and burning like her insides.

She would forget the heat and fire she'd discovered tonight. She would forget Alexios Christofides.

CHAPTER THREE

HE'D TOLD HIMSELF he wasn't going to the wedding. He'd told himself so as he'd boarded a plane in New York that was headed for Greece. He'd told himself so as he'd reclined in first class, accepting more glasses of wine than he normally would during travel.

He'd told himself so as he drove from the airport to the Holt Estate, where he knew the wedding was being held.

Everyone knew where the wedding was being held. It was international news. The wedding of enigmatic businessman and heartthrob Ajax Kouros to the beloved Holt Heiress. Photos of the event would cost a premium, the world waiting with bated breath for information, for a glimpse.

It had been shoved in his face on every news publication since he'd left Corfu. Since he'd been thrown out of Rachel Holt's bed.

Rachel.

He couldn't think of her without aching. That soft skin, that smile. The way she'd made love with him, all enthusiasm and clumsy motions. She had been inexperienced—well, non-experienced—but she had *wanted* him.

Never in his life had he been wanted like that. Not just in a sexual sense.

At some point over the course of that night he had forgotten. That he wasn't just Alex. That she wasn't just Rachel.

He had been a man, who wanted a woman. Not a man twisted and bent on revenge.

But her sweet voice piercing his sleep with *Alexios* had brought him straight back. And then it had all gone to hell. He hadn't enjoyed that moment. Hadn't enjoyed her realization that he was Ajax's enemy.

That fact had surprised him. And then when she'd asked, with tears in her eyes, that he not tell Ajax, he damn well hadn't done it.

And what was the point of going to all that trouble to have Ajax's woman if he didn't let him know it? He'd clearly passed the point of seducing her up the aisle so he could rob Ajax of his acquisition of Holt, a fact he'd learned was contingent on the marriage, so at the very least he could stop their marriage and deprive him of the company that way.

And yet he hadn't made the call.

It was a mystery to him. As was the fact that he was now at the Holt Estate with an expertly forged invitation. A forged invitation that allowed him to be one of the few guests admitted early to enjoy canapés and a tour of the grounds.

He'd had his personal assistant start working on the invitation a couple of weeks ago. Merely a precaution. And it had turned out to be a good thing, since he was here.

He hadn't been planning on coming, but it was always nice to cover your bases. If there was one thing Alex knew for sure, it was that life had no place for the lazy or the honest.

It was best to be hardworking and morally flexible.

He handed the invite over to the woman standing at a podium. She was dressed all in black, her blond hair pulled back into a neat bun. Everything about the décor, from the ribbons to the flowers, was restrained. Elegant. Nothing unnecessarily frilly or romantic.

The picture of the woman Rachel seemed to be in the

media, but not the woman he'd met that sun-drenched day in Greece.

He was filing that away. It could be useful information.

The woman scanned a code on the back of the invitation—that had been the tricky part, but his PA was friends with an acquaintance of Ajax's PA, which made getting in to reproduce the sequence on the codes possible—then smiled at him brightly when it made a nice sound that gave him the impression it had been approved, and gestured behind her.

"Follow the path to the garden. You'll find that refreshments are already being served, Mr. Kyriakis."

Nice alias. Seeing as he'd lived his entire adult life with one, he knew a good one when he heard it.

"Thank you."

He followed her instructions, and the neatly groomed path, to the back of the house. It was expansive, with rows of chairs set up facing an altar and the sea. Everything was white. Crisp and pure.

Again, very like the Rachel the media was so fond of. Nothing like the woman he'd experienced.

The woman he'd experienced hadn't seemed so pure when she'd been with him. Legs wrapped around his hips, her breath hot on his ear as she'd moaned her pleasure.

Heat washed over his skin. Prickles of sensation that bloomed from his neck and down his arms. He flexed his fingers, tried to shake off the sensation. It wasn't as though Rachel was the first woman he'd had.

There were any number of options available to a young man who found himself out on the streets and unsupervised from the age of fourteen. If nothing else, hooking up had often given him a bed to crash in, and he'd had no complaints about that.

So why on God's depraved earth was he so fascinated by a night of sex with a virgin? He couldn't fathom it.

Perhaps it was extra satisfying because he had taken her from Ajax. Because he'd robbed him of what he had been surely saving as a wedding night prize. Why else would he have left her untouched?

Just thinking about the man, being this close to him, made his stomach burn. If he hadn't decided years ago that assassination was a bad plan, he would have been considering it now.

Well, he was imagining it, but he wouldn't really do it.

He was a bastard—life had made him that way. But he wasn't entirely cold-blooded. Unlike Ajax.

Unlike their father.

No matter his position now, Ajax had been there, just as Alex had been. A young teenager who had taken advantage of the excess on offer.

The women, like Alex's mother, who would have done anything for their next fix. Who were slaves in every way. Victims. Living in poverty while surrounded by opulence. Kept on a leash of addiction, and in his mother's case, a strange attachment to the master of the manor.

A twisted thing she'd called love. The kind of love that, when severed, had left her to bleed out onto the floor. A crimson stain in Alex's memory that he could never wipe away.

Years and success wouldn't change that. Wouldn't bring her back. And yet Ajax stood at the top now, unaffected. With a family. A woman who had always appeared, to Alex, at least, to love him.

He looked unscathed, unspoiled. Ajax could pretend at respectability all he wanted but Alex knew the truth.

Because the truth was in him, too. But at least he never played as if he was anything other than a bastard. Ajax played as though he'd walked through it all and come out clean.

Alex *knew* he would never be clean.

He curled his fingers into fists and looked up at the house. There was a small group of people headed inside, led by a woman wearing black, which was clearly the uniform of the event staff.

He started in their direction, melting into the back of the group. Everyone was rapt, paying close attention to what the woman was saying about a fresco on the exterior wall that had been moved from an old church. Blah blah. He didn't care.

Greece was old. Like that was news.

He'd spent nights in more crumbling ruins than he could count. He was a fan of mod cons. As long as they didn't come at the price of living under the roof of a violent, sexually deviant psychopath.

Yeah, he'd preferred the ruins to that. He preferred the street to that. Starvation and cold and everything else that came with it.

He had run from that life. From all that it represented. He would not become a part of it.

He followed them into the house and as soon as they rounded the first corner, he separated from them and headed up the stairs. No one stopped him. Because he looked like he belonged. A right he'd earned, if only recently.

This was his world now. He was no longer someone who could be stepped on by the rich and powerful.

He *was* the rich and powerful. He went where he liked, he did what he liked.

"I have something to give the bride," he said to a passing servant. "Where might I find her?"

"Miss Rachel is in her suite. Down the hall and just to your left," the woman answered without blinking.

Because he looked the part. He spoke with confidence. And as a result, no one questioned whether or not he belonged.

He nodded once and continued on down where the woman had indicated.

He hadn't been going to come. But he was glad he had.

She'd never prayed so hard for her period to come in all her life. She'd never prayed for it to come. She'd taken it for granted. The cramps, the teariness. It had started when she was fifteen and it had gone on, regularly, for all the time since. Just a little signifier that it was the middle of the month. Nothing more.

Well, not right now.

Now the absence of it was about to send her into a panic attack. She'd been walking around her bedroom in her bra and panties for the past twenty minutes, a tampon on the nightstand, right next to an unopened pregnancy test.

Neither had been used at this point. One month since her night with Alex. One month of alternating between cursing his name and lying in a dark room just staring at the ceiling, unable to cry because tears were a release she wouldn't allow herself. A rush of emotion, too uncontrolled for the likes of her.

And then her period hadn't come. Even after it had passed fashionably late, she'd still been praying the floodgates might open and forth would come the crimson tide, and that the pregnancy test could remain unopened. But no such luck.

Tampon or test. She was going to be opening one of them in the next few minutes.

And it was rapidly becoming clear which.

She was already six days late. This little song and dance between her and those two items had been going on since the first morning.

She finally reached down and grabbed the pregnancy test.

And suddenly the world just sort of tipped to the side

and she saw herself clearly, standing there, almost ready to marry another man while she was potentially pregnant with Alex's baby.

And she knew there was no way she could get married today.

Her hands started shaking, her throat going dry. *Oh... Jax, please forgive me.*

So now she was just going to have to...tell him. Right before the wedding. But there was something she had to do first.

"Okay," she said to the little white-and-pink box. "Let's do this."

Her bedroom door swung open and she whirled around, clutching the box to her breasts in an instinctive attempt at modesty. Until she realized she was advertising that she was holding a pregnancy test and whipped it behind her back, her thigh crossing over the front of her other thigh in an attempt to hide that she was in very brief panties.

Then she froze, because she realized who her intruder was. For almost a full second, she was frozen, caught by those arresting blue eyes. Again.

It was almost like all that thinking about him had just... conjured him here. But at the worst possible moment.

His hair was shorter. His body wrapped in a custommade suit and not in those thin, faded work clothes she'd first seen him in.

How strange to think it was the other Alex that had been a disguise, while this was the real him. It hardly seemed possible.

Then suddenly, she was hit by the bright, clear smack of reality. She hated Alex. *Hated* him. It was her wedding day. He was here. And she was afraid she was pregnant with his baby.

"What the ever-loving hell are you doing here?" she asked.

He seemed frozen. As she'd been only a moment before.

"At least close the door," she said, realizing that anyone who walked by was going to see her standing there in her undies.

He obeyed, stepping into the room.

"I am *naked*," she hissed.

"You're not."

"Close enough."

"Not anywhere near close enough." He was looking at her. Intently. As though he was trying to gauge the opaqueness of her underwear.

"Stop that! And what are you doing here?"

"I am here for your wedding, *agape*."

"Weird. I don't think Ajax penciled his mortal enemy onto our guest list," she said, her fingers curling tightly around the pregnancy test still hidden behind her back.

She was trapped. Standing there in lacy bridal undies, unable to do anything for fear he'd see the test.

"He might have. Did you look to see if I was listed under Enemy or Mortal?"

"I was looking in the *A*'s for As—"

"I won't let you marry him," he said, his voice turning into a feral growl.

"What?"

"You don't know what he is."

She lifted one shoulder, the casual gesture at odds with her internal panic. With the fact that when he'd burst through that door he'd blown through her carefully cultivated, calm façade, yet again. "I've known the man for more than fifteen years. I think I know who he is."

"You've never even slept with him."

"I'm gonna," she said, edging away from him toward the bathroom, "tonight."

He strode toward her, blue eyes like chips of ice. He

put his arm around her waist and hauled her up against his chest. "You will not."

"Yes, I will," she said, words pouring out of her now, with no thought of control or decorum or any of the other stuff she was usually so attached to. She was lying, because before Alex had come in, she'd decided she couldn't do it. But she wanted to…hurt him if it was possible. To cause him some kind of discomfort because he sure had caused enough for her. "I'm going to have sex with him—" a shiver of displeasure coursed through her at the thought "—tonight. I'm going to let him inside of me. I'm going to do all the dirty naked things with him that I did with you!"

And then he leaned down and kissed her. As if he had every right to do it. As if she didn't have a wedding scheduled to happen in just four hours. As if she hadn't told him that she hated him and never wanted to see him again.

As if there was no reality. No Ajax. No vengeance gone wrong. No angry words. As if there was nothing more than passion. Fire and heat. She wrapped an arm around his neck, the other still behind her back, and parted her lips, let him slide his tongue against hers.

She kissed him back because for some reason, when Alex touched her, she couldn't think.

Because suddenly a month since the time they'd been apart didn't matter. And neither did anything else. Nothing but the kiss. The heat that flooded her body, her mind, her soul.

She wrapped her other arm around his neck and hit him in the ear with the edge of the box. He jerked his head back and looked to the side, and she followed his line of vision and froze.

Oh. Bloody perfect.

"What is this?" he asked, pulling back, his hand encircling her wrist.

"Nothing."

He arched a brow. "Try again."

"It is a…gift. For a friend."

"A gift for a friend?"

"Yessss," she said, drawing the word out to give herself time to think of more to add to her very stupid lie. "Because she asked for something that could tell the future and I thought…Magic 8 Ball or pregnancy test? And I went with pregnancy test because it gives specific yes or no answers to very specific questions."

"Do you think you're pregnant?"

"Right now? I think I'm absent a period. Which under normal circumstances would be like, 'Hey, great timing, because I'm supposed to be getting married.'"

"But?"

"Under the circumstances of 'I slept with my fiancé's enemy a month ago' I find it a bit worrisome, and yes, I think I might be pregnant."

"Go and find out," he said, moving away from her. "Now."

"So now I'm supposed to pee on your command? What if I don't have to go?"

"You were about to go—don't play that way."

His jaw was set, his skin pale. He wasn't taking this much better than she was. "Honestly, Alex, what do you care if I am?"

"I care because I will be a part of that child's life."

"You will not be," she said, the words coming out before she had a chance to think them through.

"You think I'm going to let that man near any child of mine?" he asked, rage rolling off him like a force field, pushing her back. "I know what happens to children who get near the Kouklakis family. I doubt you do."

"Ajax is…he's not a Kouklakis. He's…"

"Got an alias. How foolish are you? He's changed his name."

"I don't…"

"Go and take the test."

She didn't even have it in her to argue with him now. She nodded slowly, holding the box in numb fingers as she backed into the bathroom. Alex watched Rachel's retreating form, his heart pounding so hard he thought it might hammer through his chest and flop onto the bed, leaving a crimson stain on that pristine white duvet of hers.

A child.

His child.

This wasn't about revenge anymore. It hadn't been, not from the moment he'd claimed Rachel as his own. He wanted her, and he would have her. That was why he was here.

And because he refused to allow Ajax Kouros anywhere near a son or daughter of his.

No, Ajax didn't deal in human or drug trafficking, and Alex knew that. He knew, from the extensive research he'd done on the subject, that Ajax's business was entirely legitimate.

But bad blood was bad blood. Alex knew it. He felt it. He'd been born with the same blood as Alex, and he would never truly escape it. Alex hadn't, why should Ajax?

He shook it off. That thought. That burning sensation he felt whenever he imagined poison running through his own veins.

Things had changed for him.

Alex had made his fortune playing the stock market, first with other people's money, and now with his own. He was a gambler by nature, and doing it in the realm of the financial had been lucrative. Because like any good gambler, he had a skill for it. It wasn't pure luck, it was research. Memory. A natural feel for it.

It had earned him millions. On his twenty-sixth birthday, only six months ago, he'd netted his first billion.

He wasn't powerless anymore. He never would be again.

The bathroom door opened and Rachel appeared, white-faced, blue eyes watery.

"What?" he asked.

"There were two lines."

"Well, what does that mean?" he asked, tension making his heart race, pumping too much restless energy in his muscles.

"It means that I'm pregnant. And before you ask—it *is* your baby, I won't lie to you about that."

"You will not marry him."

"You know there are like…a thousand wedding guests coming? A hundred reporters?"

"You have two options, Rachel," he said, the adrenaline that was spiking through him making his mind run quickly. "You leave with me, now, don't speak to anyone. Or you go forward with the wedding. But mark my words, if you do that, I will stop the ceremony and I will tell everyone that you are pregnant with my child. That I seduced you in Corfu and that you gave it up to me in record time. Even without a paternity test, your precious Ajax will know. Because I'm the only man that's had you. And a due date with that big of a gap from your wedding night won't lie."

"The press…"

"The press is here, and they'll hear and report every word I say. But the decision is yours."

"It's not mine," she said, crossing her arms beneath her breasts. She was still wearing nothing more than her underwear. "I'm in an impossible situation here. I can't go back. I can't fix this. I can't…" she paused. "I could get a…" She looked away from him. "I could make it go away."

His stomach clenched. "No."

She shook her head, her blue eyes filling with tears. "You're right. I can't. I just… I can't."

"Come with me."

"And what?"

"Marry me."

CHAPTER FOUR

"You're insane," Rachel said, aiming the air-conditioning vent at her face as Alex's red sports car peeled out of the driveway of the family estate.

Holy crap. She'd done it. She was running away from her wedding. She had…almost nothing. A few clothes, her favorite shoes. Her computer, her phone, her books.

But when he'd told her about the options, it was like seeing ahead, straight and clear. She could go out there, dressed all in white, the virginal bride, and promise herself to Ajax, knowing she was carrying another man's baby. Knowing the press would slaughter all involved if Alex strode down the aisle after her and told everyone in attendance what she'd done.

That was something she'd known she couldn't do even before she'd confirmed the pregnancy.

She knew the position she was in. She'd been made so fully aware of it that day in her father's office when he'd told her he would no longer shield her from the scandal she was exposing herself to.

She'd managed to stay perfect in the eyes of the public and because of that the media had placed her on a pedestal. That meant that any whiff of scandal would send a mob of reporters out to knock her straight off it.

Nobody liked a paragon, not really. They only kept her around for the chance to see her fall. She'd been spared that fate. Her father had protected her from the consequences of her actions, and after seeing the extent to which she could have ruined things for herself she'd decided that she would be playing the part of dutiful daughter, and wife, for the rest of her life.

And all she'd done was delay the inevitable—she saw that now.

It would be vicious when they found out about this, and no matter how she played this, she would come out the villain. She knew it for certain. But she didn't have the strength to have it happen in front of an audience. To let Alex say his piece like that, in front of all those guests and reporters, without any control for what was said or how.

The thought of it… It felt like her whole life, the life she'd taken such great pains to build from the time she was seventeen, was slipping through her fingers. She had become The Holt Heiress. Rachel Holt, style icon and media sweetheart. Eternal hostess, role model and…and what else she didn't know.

That night with Alex had brought something out in her she hadn't known had existed, and she was paying for it dearly now.

Stepping off that straight and narrow path had proven to have some pretty permanent consequences. And right now, she was taking a temporary leave of absence from those consequences. Because this way, she didn't have to look at Ajax's face when he found out. Or her father's.

Or Leah's.

She took her phone out. "I have to text Leah at least." She thought of her sister, who was all set to be maid of honor in the wedding. Her lovely, sweet sister who'd always gotten such crap from the press, but who was one of the best people Rachel had ever known.

It made her sick to think how Leah would worry.

How her father would worry.

And Ajax…

She had ruined everything. She was going to panic. She was officially on the verge of a panic attack.

"Don't text them until our plane is about to leave. And why am I insane?"

"Because *everything* is insane!" She exploded. "And you want me to marry you. I am not marrying you. I don't know you. I don't like you, either."

"How can you dislike me if you don't know me?"

"Fine. I don't know you very well, and what I do know about you, I don't like."

"You like my body."

"And if you were only a body, maybe that would matter. But there is, unfortunately, a personality beneath those hard muscles and it freaking blows."

"Does it?"

"You're a liar. You're hell-bent on ruining my fiancé's life, and I don't even know why, and you used me to get revenge on him."

"And then didn't do anything about it."

"You came today."

"Yeah, so I might have done something. But I wasn't going to come to the wedding so I wasn't planning on doing anything anymore. It's just…it's just that then I ended up coming. And it was a good thing I did."

"It was not."

"You would have married him then?"

"No."

"I thought not."

"Why do you hate him, incidentally? It seems like this might be really important to my future." She looked down at her hands and noticed they were shaking.

"As I told you, Ajax Kouros is a created name. A created identity. Hell, mine is, too, for the most part. Christofides is anyway. I was never called by a last name at all."

"How is that possible?"

"I was the son of a woman who couldn't remember her real name. Or if she did, she chose never to use it. 'Meli' was all she ever called herself. Honey. I think it was a double entendre of some kind. We lived in Ajax's father's compound. The infamous Nikola Kouklakis."

"What?"

"I suppose you've heard of him."

"The depth of that trafficking ring was...horrendous. When it was broken up a few years ago..."

"Yes, it was shocking. So many people. So many lives ruined. My mother wasn't one who was kidnapped. She was seduced. By the drugs. By the money. By love of some kind. We lived in the compound. As did Ajax. I remember seeing him and thinking he was quite something with his suits. The cars. But I learned very quickly to be afraid of him, because he was the big boss's son. Because what if he saw me causing trouble?"

"Alex...I don't... This can't be."

"What? You think I goad him for fun? I goad him because I don't think he deserves any of what he has, not while so many of us live with the lasting wounds of where his fortune came from."

"But he didn't earn any of it from...anywhere bad. He came to my family when he was a boy. He got work with my father. He built up from nothing."

"You don't know him like I do. You think you do, Rachel, but you don't know him."

"I do."

"Why had you never slept with him?"

"He's not...very passionate. And I figured I wasn't, either, so fine."

He chuckled, a dark, humorless sound. "I witnessed some of his behavior back at the compound. He was with the women there. He's certainly not passionless, and knowing his background I find it worrisome more than anything that he hasn't touched you. Perhaps he was just going to savor your virginity."

Her face heated, anger and anxiety shooting through her. "He didn't know I was a virgin. I had a...a relationship before him, and I didn't... I obviously didn't sleep with him, but it wasn't chaste. Okay? And Ajax and I never discussed it, so he really didn't know."

"Trust me, *agape,* he knew."

"*You* didn't."

"I only knew you for an afternoon."

"It had some lasting consequences," she said, leaning against the window of the car and watching the scenery fly by. "Why am I going with you again?"

"You don't want me destroying your reputation in the press? Or destroying Ajax at the altar, though I can't imagine why."

Her head was swimming. She couldn't even imagine the Ajax she knew, the man who seemed to spend twenty-four hours a day in a crisply pressed suit, prowling the halls of a drug house and mingling with prostitutes. It didn't make sense.

"I only know what I know about him."

And that of all the things that she felt right now—which were blessedly cushioned by shock or she would be rocking in a corner— heartbreak wasn't one of them. So the other thing she could add to the list of Very Obvious Things She Knew was that she did not love Ajax, for certain.

That part of her was relieved to be fleeing the wedding, even if it was with Alexios Christofides.

Even if she was having his baby.

Her stomach pitched. No, she wasn't relieved about that. She couldn't even really think about all that.

"You aren't going to hold me prisoner, are you?" she asked when the car pulled up to the airport.

"If I wanted to do that, I would have done it back in Corfu."

"I suppose."

"There's no *suppose* about it. I had you wrapped around my finger, *agape mou.*"

She gritted her teeth and opened the door to the car. He followed, and an employee came out for their bags. Not the normal treatment, even when *she* flew, and she was accustomed to first class.

She whirled around to face him. "Actually, Alex, no matter what you say, no matter what your plan was, I'm fairly confident I had you wrapped around mine."

"You had me by something, but it wasn't my finger."

She curled her lip. "You're despicable. Now which terminal are we going to?"

"We are taking a private plane. All the better for us to discuss our issues."

"Why do I feel like I'm in the presence of the big bad wolf?"

"Because of my big…teeth?"

She made a face. "Maybe it's your ego, did you ever think of that?"

"It could be that," he said, obviously completely unbothered by her insults.

"I don't like you," she said. For some reason, with him, the honesty flowed.

"I know, but you still want me, and that really bothers you."

Her hackles rose, because, dammit, it was true. "Not half as much as having your baby bothers me."

"Then why are you coming with me?"

She shook her head and stopped walking. "Because… because as angry as I am at you, this isn't all your fault. Not really. I blew up my future. I put a bomb in the middle of it and now it's so wrecked there's no putting it back together. If I stay, I expose my family to more scandal than if I go quietly."

"And how it affects your family is what really matters to you?"

"It matters. My mother was the most lovely, gracious woman around. No one ever found fault with her. My father is so…decent and my sister gets hell from the press for no reason other than they wanted a punching bag and they picked her. I can't make things worse for them."

"What about you?"

"Fine. Me, too. I don't want cameras in my face, and lots of questions asked. And…Alex, you're the father of this baby, whether I like you or not. And I feel like you deserve a chance. Not marriage, mind you, but a chance."

"So what is it you want?" he asked.

"To know you, would be a good start."

"I take it you don't mean in the biblical sense."

"I already do, and it got me nowhere but pregnant and out of a wedding, so let's just hope that the other kind of getting to know you goes better."

"If you expect me to sit around and talk about my feelings, you're out of luck. If, however you would like to get to know me more closely in the biblical sense…"

"I'm thinking of two words here, Alex, and they are brought to you by the letters *F* and *U*."

"I had the impression you were a docile little thing, based on media reports. And also that you weren't very smart."

Heat streaked across her cheekbones. "I suppose you did, but then that's the way the media likes to show me, I guess." Partly by her design. "Simple and accommodating."

"And you aren't."

"Not on the inside," she muttered.

But she'd learned to be. After all the parties had started catching up with her. After Colin and his sleazy seduction that had concluded with her agreeing to some drunken, pornographic photos and a brief video.

One she'd had to confess the existence of to her father. If there was anything more horrifying on the face of the planet she couldn't think of it. Hard evidence of just how stupid she was being. And as her father had pointed out, she was lucky that the worst of it was the photos. Going off alone, drunk with a man who was essentially a stranger could have ended much worse.

Then there had been the partying, the drugs she'd been experimenting with. The fact that she'd been driving herself home under the influence...

She'd deserved the dressing down her father had given her. The threats of being cut off. And as she'd looked at the pictures of herself with Colin...it had been a full-color exhibit of her bad choices.

The wake-up call she'd badly needed. And after the photos and video had been managed, after Colin had been paid off, her mother had gotten sick. Rachel had thrown herself into caring for her mother, driving her to appointments, keeping her company, helping her plan her parties. Helping host them.

And then on the other side of that, after her mother's death, had been Ajax.

Her father had expected her to marry him. Of course, her father also hoped she would love Ajax. Either way, she'd known what she was supposed to do.

Ajax treated her like she was fine china he was afraid to break. Unlike Alex, who seemed to think she could withstand all manner of rough treatment. Brute.

She sniffed. Loudly.

"What?" he asked.

"You aren't very nice to me," she said, walking ahead of him, following the cart that held their luggage. "Interesting you claim Ajax is such a villain but he treated me like a—"

"Nun."

"—a princess."

"You aren't a damn princess. You're just a regular woman."

"Ajax thinks I'm a princess."

"In about four hours Ajax will think of you as that traitor who left him at the altar."

She clenched her teeth together tightly. She couldn't argue with that. And she couldn't blame all of this on him, not when she absolutely had a stake in the guilt. But she really, really wanted to.

The conversation stopped when they approached a sleek jet parked on the runway. The door opened—a carpeted staircase waited to ease their entrance.

"Swank," she said, going up the stairs and into the plane, where her tart descriptor was proven to be an understatement.

Everything was beautiful beyond belief, polished and plush, from the cream-colored floor to the soft leather couches.

"There's champagne chilling," Alex said, coming in behind her. "Of course, you can't have any. Bad for the baby."

"Are you always this insufferable?"

"Are you?"

"No, I never am. I'm actually extremely pleasant, all the time. It's just that you make me… There really isn't a word strong enough to express the anger-slash-anxiety I feel when you're around."

"Attraction?"

She narrowed her eyes. "That's not the word."

"You're sure?"

"I am *so* sure."

"Then why did you kiss me earlier?"

She sat down on the couch, suddenly feeling taxed. "You also make me crazy. I do stupid things when you're around."

"I'll take that as a compliment."

She crossed her arms. "I wouldn't. Can you at least get me an orange juice?"

"That, I could manage." He pushed a button on his arm rest and gave the order.

She leaned back and crossed her arms. "Where are we going, anyway?"

"Back to my house. Away from the media firestorm that will no doubt ensue when they realize the bride has failed to show up for the wedding of the century. You'll have to face the fallout eventually, but why not put it off for a while?"

It really did sound good. To avoid reality for just a bit.

"You can text your sister now."

Oh, yes, that was a bit of reality she really couldn't avoid. Otherwise her family would be sending the police after them. For a couple of seconds she entertained the idea of letting them arrest Alex for kidnapping. But that was a news story she didn't really want her child going back and reading, so she decided against it.

Rachel pulled out her phone, her fingers hovering above the letters on the screen. What did you say when you did something like this?

"Why aren't you texting Ajax, by the way?"

"Because I'd rather roll around in honey and get thrown into a badger den."

Short and sweet, Rach. Don't tell all yet. She looked across at Alex, who was now sprawled in the armchair like a lazy big cat. Twitching his tail, waiting for his prey to make a false move.

Yes, the less she said about the situation, the better. She knew next to nothing about it except that she couldn't marry Ajax. And that she had to figure out what she was going to do about Alex.

I'm not coming. I need to be with Alex. I'm sorry. Please
tell Jax that I'm sorry.

She took a deep breath, then hit Send on the exhale.

"Done. I told them."

"What exactly?"

"That I'm not coming. Nothing more. Well, I mentioned
you. Your first name."

"We'll see how long it takes Ajax to send a hit man."

"Actually," she said, as the plane engine started and they
began to taxi around the runway, "I'm curious."

"About?"

"Why didn't you stop the wedding? Why didn't you
call Ajax and gloat? Why weren't you hanging your sheet
stained with my virgin's blood out your window like some
kind of marauding knight or whatever?"

He cleared his throat. "You kicked me out—I didn't have
time to take the sheet."

"And that foiled your evil plan?" He said nothing in response. "I'm serious," she said.

"Did it occur to you that maybe things changed because
you were the one who found me?" he asked.

The stewardess came in with a tray of drinks. What
looked like a scotch for Alex, the jerk, and an orange juice
for her. She thanked the woman and wrapped her fingers
around the glass, letting the coldness seep into her skin.

"I... No," she said. "I hadn't really thought of it. But...
it is true. I am the one who found you."

"Strange, don't you think?"

"Maybe." More than strange. But there was no denying it. There was no way to accuse him of putting himself
in her path, either. She'd seen him first. She'd approached
him. And unless his ego was even bigger than she imagined, he'd had no way of knowing she would have to go
and talk to him when she saw him. That she would be hit

with a bolt of attraction so intense it left her stunned and utterly senseless.

"I was there for you," he said slowly, swirling the contents of his glass before taking a sip. "I won't lie about that. I was there to find you and seduce you. But I had a plan, you see. You had a fundraiser later in the week."

"I ended up not going." She looked down into her juice.

"I know," he said.

"How?"

"Because I went."

"Oh." She cleared her throat. "Why?"

"I don't know," he bit out. "But I was going to meet you there, at that fundraiser. And seduce you with my wealth and fortune. Seduce you away from my rival, slowly. Publicly. I was going to bring you over to my side of things and make him watch powerlessly as I did so."

"And then what was supposed to happen to me?"

He shrugged. "That was of no concern to me. But instead, you found me on a dock after I'd just come in to Corfu. What are the odds of that?"

"Heck if I know," she said.

"I wouldn't know, either."

"So what… So that's why you didn't tell Ajax? That's why you didn't call weeks ago and have the wedding called off?"

"I was as seduced as you were," he said. "Though I hate to admit it. If I'd had any respect for my own plan I would have followed it. Instead…"

"Instead we met and spent the day together and then we…"

"Spent the night together."

"And then it all went to hell," she said.

"When I came to your house today… What I came for… It had nothing to do with revenge. I was there for you."

Their eyes locked, electricity crackling between them, her heart pounding so hard she thought she might pass out.

Her phone buzzed and she looked down. She had a message from Leah.

Alex who? Anyone I know?

Well, what was the point in lying? It was going to come out. The press would see her with Alex. She would have to explain eventually that she was pregnant. And who the father was.

She might as well let the bomb drop in stages. She typed in a reply.

You don't know him. Alex Christofides. Unexpected. And I'm sorry.

It was sort of a lie. Leah wouldn't know him. But Ajax would. And the way she'd phrased it made it sound like she didn't know who he was. Also a lie.

She was big into self-protection at the moment.

Well, who wasn't? Except for Alex. That was a strange thought, but when she looked back at their night together...

When she'd confronted him, he'd been honest. About why he'd seduced her. About who he was. It didn't make a lot of sense, really.

"Why didn't you defend yourself?" she asked. "Why didn't you lie?"

"Because I couldn't think," he said.

It pained Alex to admit it, but it was the truth. He hadn't been able to think up a lie with her looking at him as though he'd personally stabbed her in the chest. Because somehow, during the course of their day together, his seduction had been genuine.

He had wanted her. It had been easy to forget just who

she was. Who she belonged to. He didn't look at her and see Ajax Kouros's fiancée.

He'd looked and seen Rachel. So soft and elegant, with wildness that ran strong beneath.

He'd seen her. And he had wanted her with every piece of himself.

So he'd taken her, and when she'd confronted him, he'd been able to do nothing but speak the truth because he'd deviated so far from his plan he had no idea how to get back to it. He should have lied. Appealed to her. Kept to the original plan.

But he hadn't, and it was too late to go back now.

He would have let her go if it was what she'd wanted. But things were different now. She was pregnant and that meant he had to keep her.

He ignored the slug to the gut that rebelled at the idea of allowing her to marry Ajax, pregnant or not. Of course, had she wanted to do so, he wouldn't have stopped it. He could have let her go.

The inability to do so would imply that she was special. That he had feelings for her.

Alex didn't have time for feelings.

He'd made time in his life for two things: making money and getting revenge. Everything else was an incidental. A distraction he couldn't afford.

Of course, now that there would be a child he'd have to make room for a third thing.

Because he would be damned if any child of his left to be raised by a stranger. If any child of his wasn't in his sight at all times.

Alex knew about all the evil in the world, and if there was any way for him to shield his own child from it, he would do so.

As though his own life depended on it.

CHAPTER FIVE

HIS ISLAND WAS BEAUTIFUL. He would never get tired of it. Of the fact that it was his. Of the fact that he now owned a place he possessed total control over.

Back in the compound, everything had been shared. Perhaps *share* was too generous a word. It had been fought over. There had been a serf class in the compound. The women, the security guards. And the security guards had had guns, which put the women square on the bottom rung.

And beneath that...

The children of those women.

Many of them had been given away by their mothers. Sold, Alex now realized, for drugs. He had spent many years feeling astonished, grateful, that his mother hadn't done so. That she'd put some sort of value on him. That he'd stayed safe.

A miracle, it had seemed.

But then he'd found out the truth. And the truth hadn't been rainbows and a mother's love. No. The truth had been poison.

He was the monster he'd always despised. A tool that kept his mother near her favorite addiction. Not heroin, but Nikola Kouklakis himself.

The older man had, of course, kept her there since she was the mother of his son. Since *Alex* was his son. But Alex had discovered the truth and when his mother was no longer useful it had all come crashing down.

And Alex had run. Run away and never looked back.

And when he'd finally stopped, when he'd won enough card games that he had some money—money and this island—met enough people that he'd forged business connections and learned about the stock market, when he'd finally reached the pinnacle of success, that was when he'd looked back for the first time.

He'd looked back at all of the pain, all of the injustice, and then he'd looked at the one man who had risen above it. Clean, pristine and well-respected. Rich as god with a beautiful woman hanging on his arm.

And he'd known that next on his agenda was making sure that Ajax Kouros knew helplessness. That he knew fear. That he knew what it was to lose the things he loved.

And while he hadn't destroyed the other man's business yet, not for lack of trying, he did have Ajax's fiancée.

And though he wasn't actively using Rachel as revenge at the moment, that thought almost made him cheerful.

"Where are we?" Rachel asked as the plane touched down, white sand and turquoise sea rushing into view.

"An island near Turkey. I call it…" And he realized that earlier he'd told her his mother's name. It made him feel exposed, to tell her what he called the island when she would know why. He cursed his moment of sentimentality. Cursed the fact that he still cared so much for a woman who'd never loved him back. Who had ended her life rather than spend her days with him. "I call it Meli's Hideaway," he said. "And before you ask, no, my mother never saw it. She…died just before I left the Kouklakis compound. But if she hadn't…this is where I would have taken her. So she could have a rest, finally. Though she's resting now, I suppose." If she had given him a chance. If she had trusted in him at all. If the idea of being with him hadn't been a torture she couldn't bear.

"I'm sorry," she said, her voice muted. "My mother passed away, too. It's hard. Really hard."

"Life is hard,' he said, lifting one shoulder in a casual gesture.

"What? That's it?"

"I'm sorry," he said. "Life is hard and then you die. Is that better?"

She shook her head. "Not really. You're not exactly enjoying the journey, are you?"

He stood up as the plane came to a stop. "Enjoying the journey is for another sort of person, from another sort of life. Someone like you, *agape*."

"Well, I won't deny that I have a great family. That I've been blessed to have a lot of nice things. Yes, I do enjoy the journey." She was lying, though. He could sense it. Strange because when he'd met her in Corfu, she had exuded light. Joy. But he didn't see those things in press photos of her.

It was like she was hiding that light most of the time.

"Were you going to enjoy spending the rest of your journey with Ajax?"

She nodded, her posture stiff. "Of course I would have. I care about him deeply."

"But you don't love him."

"Oh, bah. Why are you people so fixated on love?" Alana had tried to talk her out of the wedding at the eleventh hour. Citing love as the primary reason. "I like him. I love him in a way. Sure it's not an all-consuming kind of love, but—"

"But you aren't crying your eyes out just at this moment, either," he said.

"I have a lot on my plate here," she said. "I just found out I'm pregnant." She paused and swore. "Pregnant. Oh...I can't *even.* I can't even take all of this in. And I just ran out on my wedding. And I'm in Turkey. With you."

"We're not in Turkey. We're on my island."

"Yeah, big effing difference to me just at the moment."

"If it's any consolation, I feel similarly…run over. Is that how you feel?"

"Run over by a train, yes."

"This doesn't have to be difficult," he said. He was about to propose marriage again. Yes, she'd brushed his mention of marriage off the first time, but she'd been shocked. She would come around, he was certain of it.

One thing he knew for sure, and that was that he refused to be a shadowy figure in the background of his child's life. He would not be that man. He would be as different from his own father as humanly possible. As different from everyone in his family as humanly possible.

If you can be.

No. He wasn't the same. He would love his child. He wouldn't want to own his child, wouldn't keep that child around simply to keep a link between himself and the person he was…obsessed with.

He would never be either of his parents.

"How is it going to be easy?" she asked as the door to the plane opened and a rush of thick, warm air filled the cabin.

"Perhaps it will fall somewhere between easy and difficult?"

"Perhaps," she said, walking toward the exit.

"You don't sound convinced."

"I'm not." She descended the stairs and he followed, his eyes on her curves, the way her white capris cupped her expertly. He was still a man, after all, regardless of how intense the day had been.

And she was still a temptation. It had nothing to do with how provocative her clothing was. It wasn't, in truth. She exuded class. A kind of untouchable, crisp elegance that a man like him had rarely been exposed to.

Rachel Holt had come by her style and poise due to a lifetime of being immersed in wealth and culture, of being aware of cameras watching her every move.

Nothing like the way he'd grown up.

It was part of what he found so enticing. That prim little exoskeleton of hers. Perfect hair and makeup, even just after finding out she was pregnant and running out on her wedding. But he'd cracked all that open. Had seen her skin flushed pinker than that top she was wearing. Had seen her hair in disarray, her skin glistening with sweat...

He'd had those expertly polished nails dug deep into his shoulders, and that was something he couldn't forget.

He shifted and tried to ease the pressure caused by his growing arousal. Nothing helped. Not when he had the back of Rachel Holt as his view. The rest of the island just didn't seem to matter. And neither did anything else.

"And why is that?" he asked.

"Because I...don't think I like you." She looked up and around at the cypress trees that spread around them to create a canopy of green, and at the white sand beaches beyond them.

"There are some incredible ruins on this island. Colonial and Ottoman."

"I was just in Greece. Ruins, we have them."

"I am aware," he said. "I was trying to make conversation."

"Do you live in a ruin? Or do you have an actual house?"

"I have a house, but some people would argue I live in ruin."

She snorted. "At this point, some people would argue that I do, too."

"You are giving off a bit of a fallen-woman vibe," he said dryly.

"Am I?" She sniffed her wrist. "I don't feel any different."

He turned and looked at her. "Not at all?"

Her cheeks flushed a deep rose. "No."

"Interesting. Would you like to walk to the house or drive?"

"You're in a tux," she said. "You're hardly dressed to walk."

He looked down. "Indeed not. I'm a little disoriented. Could be because in New York it's early morning. Which means I've technically been up all night."

"You came from New York?"

"Yes."

"Why?"

He looked at her, at those cheeks, still flushed from the sun and from…from whatever memories had come into her mind when he'd looked at her. "I came for you."

"That simple?"

"Yes."

"Why did you come for me?"

"I don't know," he said, and it was the honest truth. "Because I don't want him to have you. Because I want you for myself. Because I think you're beautiful and as of now you're the only woman I can imagine having in my bed, and considering I would like to have sex sometime soon that's very inconvenient, and even more so if you were to marry another man."

She blinked. "That's almost flattering."

"Almost. A walk, I should think." He took his jacket off and cast it onto the sand, then rolled his shirt sleeves up. "It might do something to shake off the time change."

"Lead the way then."

He started down a path that took them down near the beach and could have sworn at the absurdity of getting sand in his custom-made shoes. Shoes he'd bought with his own money and not the money earned by other people's suffering. There, a reminder that he had transcended his blood in some way.

"So what do you do in New York?" she asked.

"I gamble with other people's money."

"What?"

"I deal in investments," he said. "And I'm very good at it."

"Isn't that a bit unstable?"

"Sure. Can be. But I've made enough of a profit that I'm sitting on stable assets of my own, and I've made some wise purchases and investments myself."

"Including an island."

"I won this," he said.

"You won it?"

"In a card game. It was one of the more interesting gambling experiences of my life. Yes, I was a literal gambler there for a while. At first with other people's money."

"How?"

"Card counting is a particularly useful skill. I happen to have the gift. I was a kid living on the streets doing card tricks for tourists and a rich guy picked me up, offered to kit me out to play in the casinos with his money, for a cut. I said 'of course,' naturally."

"Naturally," she said.

"I won a lot of money. And I got to keep part of it. Rented myself an apartment, started offering up an underground service. Until I had enough money to go gamble for myself at least once a week."

"And?"

"I ended up in a high rollers' game. There were things in that pot by the end that you wouldn't believe, including a night with a man's wife, which I turned down, by the way. But the island… I took the island."

She looked hard at him, blue eyes glittering. "You're really twenty-six, Alex?"

"Yes. And I was eighteen when I was doing that. From there, I figured I better decide what to do with the money I'd earned. So I walked away from the casino and started looking into investing. And I proved to have a knack for that so I thought…why not do it for other people? An extension of where I came from."

"A self-made man," she said.

He laughed. "None of us are really self-made, Rachel. We're made with the aid or misfortune of other people. In my case, people had to lose money so I could gain it. Now, the people I make money for are aided by me, as I am by them. You are made by your father, by the media, and you were to be finished by Ajax, am I right?"

"Finished?"

"It's how you were going to spend the rest of your life in comfort. You found a man who would close the loop neatly on everything you've built."

"I don't think of it that way."

"No?"

"No." She wobbled in the sand and he reached over and caught her arm, holding her steady. She froze for a moment, her eyes falling to his lips. She swallowed hard. "I don't think of it…of him…that way. It's not how it is."

"Then how is it?"

"I don't know. He's a friend. And…maybe like a brother, almost, which I can see right at this moment is so ridiculous it's… I don't know why I thought I could marry him. I don't know why at all. I thought caring could be enough. I thought it was enough."

"Only because you'd never had passion." He'd been the one to show that to her.

"Don't be so smug—it's nasty. Truly, I wouldn't crow about it if I were you. Is there an easier conquest than a woman who's still a virgin at my age? 'Hard up' doesn't even begin to describe it."

"That's not what it was though. I myself was not particularly hard up, as you call it, and I still felt the electricity between us."

She stopped short, arched one eyebrow. "Oh, really?"

"Yes," he said. "Don't deny that you felt it."

"No, I mean, 'oh, really, you weren't hard up?' What does that mean? When was the last time you were with someone else?"

"Jealousy, Rachel? I didn't think you liked me."

"I'm not jealous. I'm curious."

"And if I tell you, you won't be angry?"

"I've been angry at you for a solid month, Alexios. I'm not making you any guarantees on that score. You could breathe funny and make me angry at this point."

"Don't be dramatic. It had been a couple weeks by the time I met you."

She sniffed loudly as she'd done at the airport, a sign of her pique, he was realizing. "It had been twenty-eight years when I met you, but whatever."

"Are you saying I'm special, Rachel?"

"Heck. No. I am not saying that. I am not saying that even a little bit. I'm just saying—some of us don't run around with our pants around our ankles all the time."

"And you're sure that Ajax was celibate the whole time you were together?"

"I…I just… I… Yes."

"Probably you're delusional," he said. "As you were about marrying him in the first place."

"Okay, Alex, answer this question. Has there been a woman since you were with me?"

"No." She looked far too triumphant when he admitted that. This honesty thing where she was concerned really had to stop.

She seemed to bring it out in him. He'd held back next to nothing since he'd met her. He'd told her. About why he'd seduced her, about his mother, about why he hated Ajax.

Well, he'd told her most of it. There were things he couldn't bring himself to speak out loud into an empty room. Much less share with with anyone else.

His house came into view. He'd had it custom built when the island passed into his control. It was completely modern. Square, with hard, clean edges, windows that faced the sea. There was no gilded excess, no old-world opulence.

That would have reminded him too much of the Kouklakis compound. And he had no interest in that. It was too much in his mind as it was.

Stale, filthy opulence. And a carpet stained with blood.

"It's certainly different," she said.

"Is it?"

"Very…minimalist."

"I'd had enough Persian rugs and intricate carvings to last a lifetime. I wasn't interested in living in it for the rest of my life."

"Oh."

"What about you?" he asked. "What sort of architecture do you prefer?"

Rachel paused on the path, his question hitting a nerve for some reason she couldn't really identify. "I don't know."

"You don't know what sort of house you would have liked to live in one day?"

"Ajax's house," she said, bristling. "And his penthouse in the city. All nice places. And nothing not to like about them."

"And before that?"

"I had an apartment. In New York." She'd liked her apartment a lot, but she'd given it up before the wedding, naturally. But it hadn't been a place for entertaining. It had been a place just for her. Giving it up had been a lot harder than she'd anticipated, in truth, but it wasn't worth crying over. "And when I come to Greece I stay in the family vacation house."

"If you were going to have a home built, what would it be like?"

"I don't know, okay? I've never thought about it, but what does it matter? I was going to have a beautiful home with Ajax. Now I may very well end up being homeless because I just walked away from a deal that was essential to both my father and to Ajax. Because… Because…"

Suddenly her fists tightened. "You knew," she said, her tone getting cold. "You knew and you're over here pretending to be all honest and 'marry me' and crap, but you knew."

He didn't blink, his blue eyes focused on her.

"Whoever marries first gets my father's company. That's what you want. It's not me, or hurting Ajax by taking my virginity or whatever else. It's that you were going to try and get me to marry you so that you could screw him out of Holt. You're trying to take my family business!"

"Rachel…"

"You—"

"If I had wanted that, if that was the route I'd decided to take, I would have sweet-talked you back in Corfu when you saw my ID. As it is, I let you go."

"And then you came back. Were you going to make some sort of declaration of love and try to woo me away from the wedding and to…Vegas or something?"

The thing that was so unsettling about that prospect was the fact that it might have worked. That if she hadn't found out she was pregnant, if he'd walked in and kissed her, and told her that he hadn't stopped thinking about her for the past month, that he loved her, she would have probably dropped everything and run away with him.

Because she had feelings for him. Feelings that she

couldn't quite understand or deal with, but they were definitely feelings. Stupid, *stupid* feelings.

Feelings that should be utterly choked out by this most recent revelation.

"I don't understand. Even if the past that you share— that you say you share… Even if it's true I don't know why you would want to destroy him so badly."

"Of course you don't," he said, walking in front of her, toward the house, "because you live in a dream world, little girl. You don't know anything about the way the world works. And you should be thankful for that."

CHAPTER SIX

RACHEL LAY DOWN on the white down-filled blanket and stared at the ceiling. She would ask for him to take her home if she wasn't such a coward. If she wasn't so afraid she didn't have a home to go back to.

Even if she did, it would be crawling with reporters, ready to get the juicy dirt on why she'd left Ajax at the altar. And the lame thing was there was tons of juicy dirt. If the bride being pregnant with another man's baby wasn't a great scandalous headline, she really didn't know what was.

Society wedding of the century became farce just that quickly and the press would absolutely adore it.

There was a knock on the door. Not Alex, (A) because he wouldn't have knocked, and (B) because it was soft, a woman's hand, she was almost certain.

"Yes?"

The door opened a small woman with dark hair came in. "Mr. Alex has requested that you join him for dinner out on the terrace."

"Oh, has he now?"

"Yes," the woman said, either not picking up on Rachel's annoyance, or choosing not to acknowledge it.

"When does he expect me?"

"Ten minutes, miss."

"Tell him it will be twenty—I need to dress for it. And tell him not to let that go to his head."

The woman nodded and backed out of the room. Rachel felt like a shrew. A sweaty, mean one. She was hot from the walk, still, and in a foul mood.

A quick shower did wonders for the sweaty part, but the meanness still seemed to be simmering beneath the surface, even while she slipped into a simple black shift dress and a pair of black heels. She fastened a string of pearls around her neck and looked at her side profile. Her hair was neat, in place as it should be. Her makeup looked good.

She looked normal. Like the Rachel she was accustomed to seeing in the mirror every day.

Which was so strange because she didn't feel like normal Rachel. She hadn't. Not since that day she'd locked eyes with stupid Alexios Christofides.

She let out a harsh breath and exited her room to find the maid standing there waiting for her.

"I will take you to Mr. Alex."

"Thank you," Rachel said, even while she thought that he was only sending her an escort to make sure she didn't bribe his pilot to get her off the island.

That was when she realized how stuck she was. With each step across the white marble floor and out toward the terrace, she felt a rope tightening around her neck, her pearls suddenly feeling heavy, like they were choking her.

She reached up and unfastened them as they walked, wadding them up in her shaking hand, holding them down at her side.

"Miss Rachel," the maid said, announcing her as though she were a duchess of some kind.

Alex stood and her heart squeezed. No matter how angry she was, he never failed to leave her utterly speechless. He was wearing a simple white button-up shirt, unfastened at the collar, the sleeves rolled up past his forearms.

His skin looked a deeper bronze in that color, a glimpse

of chest hair visible through the open neck. He looked so effortless. So ridiculously sexy.

It wasn't fair.

It wasn't fair that her body was drawn to a man like this. A man who had tricked her, used her and basically had her held captive on an island. What the ever-loving heck was wrong with her? Was she punishing herself for past sins? Or was there something that drew her to men who wanted to…use her?

She sat down, and he took his seat.

"I trust you had a nice rest?" he asked.

"I don't think you really trust that. I'm sure you know I spent the past hour quietly freaking out in the privacy of my bedroom."

"I suppose that's only fair."

"I've just found out I'm having a baby, on top of everything else, so yes, it is only fair."

"That is why I proposed marriage," he said. "Not to get Holt away from Ajax, but for the sake of the baby."

"Great. Fine. But please know that I will not marry you. Not for the baby, not for anything. At the very least not until my sister is married and I am certain, one hundred percent certain, that you won't get Holt because of my indiscretion. I will not allow you to hurt Ajax or my family in that way." A startling thought occurred to her. "And if you go after my sister I will be forced to remove your male member from your body with a very dull pocketknife, and don't think I won't do it. I might have been spoiled from birth, but I'm also from New York, and we don't mess around over there."

"I have no desire to go and seduce your sister," he said, leaning back in his chair, looking out at the ocean. As though they were discussing the weather, and not her desire to castrate him. "My plans, my priorities, have changed. My loyalty is to the child, not to my vengeance."

"Well, it's very early in the pregnancy, and things can go wrong, so, yet again, marriage is off the table."

"Fine. For you, maybe it is, but not for me. I'll continue to enter it into the discussion at times I feel are appropriate."

"You are a massive pain in the rear, do you know that?"

"I absolutely do," he said, lifting a glass of wine to his lips. Yeah, and he was drinking wine in front of her. He knew he was a pain. And he seemed to revel in it.

"Well, stop it." She took a sip of water from her glass.

"Probably not. That's twenty-six years of bad habits you're asking me to break immediately, and I doubt it's going to happen."

"Another good reason to avoid marrying you."

"Why is it you agreed to come with me?"

"I'm a massive coward," she said. "Among other things."

"What other things?"

"An idiot. That's the other thing I am. I can't believe I fell for your charm and that boyish curly thing your hair does when it's wet and your...sparkling blue eyes."

"Are you preparing to compose a sonnet about me?"

"Shall I compare you to a horse's ass?"

"Is that your attempt at poetry?"

"Yes. I thought it was good."

"Brilliant." He took another sip of wine.

"I have to ask, Alex, because it doesn't make a lot of sense to me—what does a guy like you want with a baby?"

"I don't want *a* baby," he said. "I want *my* baby and that's an entirely different thing."

"Just a bit-of-sperm different at this point. It's not like you know the child, not like you could even...feel him or get an idea he was inside of me for...months and months. I would think walking away from it would be really easy for you."

"Why is that?"

She lifted a shoulder. "Because a lot of men do. It's not

an insult, it's just that…well, a lot of men do. And since you just picked me up with the idea of getting revenge on Ajax and that's all done, I would have thought it wouldn't serve your purpose to be involved with the child. Especially since I won't marry you and let you take Holt from Ajax."

"This is a matter of honor."

"You have honor? Where was your honor when you were stealing my virtue in Corfu?"

"This virtue I stole," he said, leaning forward, "where was it when we were in Corfu? Virginity I remember. But I sort of remember you flinging it at me. I don't really remember me stealing it."

She sniffed. "What. Ever. The thing is that I'm not really sure what's in this for you and that makes me nervous. I've removed a couple of carrots and yet here you are still, like there's another treat for you to catch—and I'm concerned about exactly what treats you think you're going to be…getting from me. Because none. The answer is none."

"I want my child," he said, setting his wine glass down, his palms flat on the table. "Because I know how the world is. Because I know what it's like to grow up without a father. I know what it is to look at trees making shadows on your wall, and to not simply wonder what sort of evil things a bogeyman might do to you, but to know, with utter certainty, every horrible thing that could become of you. What it is to know that if the bogeyman ever did come there would be no one to protect you. My child will never know these fears. I will protect him. I will give him shelter with me, security. When I'm there, he will never worry. Not about one thing."

She looked down at the table and a plate of fish and rice was placed in front of her. It didn't look appetizing in the least. Her stomach was too full of knots and anxiety for her to take a bite of anything.

And Alex's speech had only added to the knots. She didn't

want to see the good in him. It was far too dangerous. She wanted to be angry. To look at him and see a mustache-twirling villain bent on tying her to the tracks in an attempt to defeat Ajax, who she was still trying to place in the position of hero.

Not that she could believe that Ajax was a villain, not in the least, but…but it wasn't like she was longing for him to ride in on his white horse, either.

"That's really good of you, Alex."

"It's basic human decency," he said. "Every parent should want to be there for their child. What about you, Rachel? Were your parents there for you?"

"Yes," she said. "Always. My father has always been involved in my and my sister's lives, and when Ajax came… He loves Ajax like a son. And so did my mother."

"You said your mother died?"

"A few years ago. She was ill. That's one reason I never went on to higher education or anything. I had to help. Leah was young and…and she needed to live her life. My mother wasn't the easiest person for me to get along with, but she was sick and she needed someone. So I can't possibly resent that I spent that time with her." She fiddled with her fork. "But then…well, then Ajax expressed the desire that we might…"

"Why did you put him off for so long?"

"I can see now, clear as day, that my saying I wanted to 'live a little' first was mainly because I just didn't feel anything for him. I dated some other men, but didn't have serious relationships with them because even though I knew Ajax wasn't putting an exclusive claim on me it felt like I would have been cheating." And she'd felt far too burned out to go there, but she wasn't going to bring that up. "And then we made it official and we've been engaged for years and…it was comfortable. To wear his ring and go on with life like it hadn't changed." She looked into her water glass. "And now *everything's* changed."

"Well, not everything. You aren't married."

"And I'm not going to be."

"Because you don't trust me?"

"There's that, but there's the fact that this isn't even close to being about trust. My father has promised ownership of Holt to the daughter who marries first and to the man she marries. He won't go back on a promise."

"Refreshing," Alex said, a dark light in his blue eyes.

"Yes, well, you don't get to benefit from it. Sorry."

"Too bad."

"I'm exhausted," she said, standing. "I think dinner wasn't the best idea. I'm going to my room."

"Fine. Shall I have your plate cleared?"

"Yes," she said. "And have cookies sent to my room. And decaf coffee. I don't want to eat healthy."

He arched a brow. "You are a rebel, Rachel Holt. How did the media ever paint you as anything else?"

"Shut up, Alex." She turned and walked back into the house, stalking to her room. She flung open the door and then slammed it with equal fervor.

She needed something. She needed…cookies. And to open a window so that she could breathe. She walked over to the other side of the room and flung the curtains open, then shoved the windows wide.

The breeze coming in off the ocean didn't help relieve the pressure in her chest. It didn't help anything.

She felt like she was going to burst. The pressure behind her eyes was so intense she could barely stand it.

But there was no release. She had worked so long to keep her emotions, her desires, anything too wild or demonstrative in check, that she couldn't let it out even now.

She couldn't even be herself when she was alone.

The scary thing was, she was pretty sure the only time

she'd been herself for more than a decade was during the night she'd spent in Alex's arms. Naked in every single way.

He hadn't deserved that. It had been a lie for him.

She took a deep breath, gulping the air down like water. She squeezed her eyes shut, hoping for tears, desperate for a crack in the foundations she'd built.

Nothing came.

Damn that Alex. She was so angry at him, so hurt by everything he'd done. And still she craved those moments of release, those moments of feeling like she was home in herself, that only he'd ever given her.

Well, that was too bad. She wasn't ever going to be back in his arms, ever again.

So she would just have to deal with that.

He married me, BTW.

Rachel stared down at the text from her sister, her body numb. She'd married Ajax? *Leah* had married *Ajax?*

When she'd started texting with Leah that morning she hadn't expected this. Leah had been checking on her, and she could get why, because running off like this was out of character for her, and because, yeah, she had a feeling they knew full well who Alex was.

But to find out Leah and Ajax had married? She didn't even know how to process that.

She got up from her position on the floor and went to her computer, typing in Ajax Kouros as quickly as she could.

And sure enough.

Ajax Kouros Weds Replacement Bride

"Well…wow."

She picked up the phone and typed in Holy crap. Just Googled.

You're happy? You didn't love Ajax did you?

Her sister's response came quickly. Leave it to Leah to worry about her, even still. Rachel couldn't imagine her sweet younger sister with Ajax. Hell, *she* was the one who was worried.

As for the love part…

Not like that. Not the kind you need to marry a guy. You know?

She hit Send. It was a lie of omission in a lot of ways. Because she would have married him. If things hadn't changed. If not for the baby.

The baby. All of this kept hitting her in little pieces. She had a feeling if it hit her all at once she would be completely buried by it.

Do you love Alex?

Her sister's message hit her right in the chest. Because it brought her back to that night. To those feelings. Feelings that were so different from anything she'd ever experienced before.

I need to be with Alex.

She typed it, but didn't hit Send right away. It was the truth. She had to figure out how they were going to make this work, what they were going to do.

She'd stayed up half the night reading, browsing the internet and eating cookies and basically trying to figure out what had gone wrong in her world and how she was going to fix it.

She knew one thing for sure: That she had to give Alex

a chance to be in his child's life. Beyond that? She had no clue.

She finished out her conversation with Leah and tossed her phone down onto the bed.

Oh, great. And there went her line of defense. Her "No, Alex, you villain! I cannot marry you!" was going to be so much weaker now.

Although, it was nice to know that Holt was secure. That it would still go to Ajax, because even though she hadn't wanted to marry him, she hadn't wanted him to lose anything, either.

But Leah… Oh, she hoped Leah would be happy. That she knew what she was doing. Leah had always been fond of Ajax. They'd always gotten along, but she hadn't gotten the idea that her sister wanted to marry him.

Maybe she was wrong. Maybe they were both better at hiding who they were than people realized. Rachel was sure her sister would never believe that she was a bad girl living inside of a good girl, and that both entities had a penchant for cookies. That she'd had a one-night stand on vacation with her fiancé's enemy. Nope. She was sure no one would guess that.

There was a knock on the bedroom door, and this one, she guessed, was Alex. Though she was a little shocked the man knew how to observe things like knocking. It was a social nicety she wouldn't have credited him with.

"Come in," she said, straightening and hoping she didn't look like she'd had an all-night cookie and internet bender, even though she had.

Alex strode into the room, as usual, his charisma filling up the small space in a way that was shocking.

"They got married," he said.

"So I saw," she returned, and she was sure they were talking about the same people.

"Are you okay?" he asked. It was shockingly sensitive,

all things considered. A lot more sensitive than a man who was just out to use her should ever be.

"I'm…fine. Worried about Leah. I didn't want her to… to marry someone she didn't love for me."

"Maybe it wasn't for you."

"Of course it was," she said.

"The whole world doesn't revolve around you, you know."

"No, I'm well aware of that. I get used a lot. But what I want doesn't ever seem to be that important."

"Are you sorry you aren't married to him?"

"Am I sorry that I'm not trapped in a loveless marriage with him?"

"You could be trapped in one with me," he said. "It might take your mind off her."

"Nice try, but I actually think that I might relish my newfound freedom."

"What do you mean?"

"I have screwed everything up. When the press find out…well, when the press find out, I'm not going to be their princess anymore. They love me, sure, but they love Ajax and the wayward woman will always be the villain. My father will be so disappointed that I…that I didn't learn. Leah's had to marry someone she doesn't love because of me. I've messed up everything. I have…no reason at all, in all the world, to keep doing what's expected of me. Or rather to start again. I'm ruined," she said, laughing. "Utterly ruined. And there's no point even trying to backpedal. To try and legitimize myself by marrying my baby's father when it won't change the circumstances. My father can't pay anyone off and make this go away."

"So you're ready to go and face the press then?"

"I am absolutely not," she said. "I…I want you to know that no matter what…whether I was pregnant or not, press or not, whether you had come or not…I wasn't going to marry him."

"Is that the case?" he asked, his voice rough.

"Yes. I can't. I…I can't. But that doesn't make me brave. I would still be hiding, without the baby. I'm a coward, and I feel totally fragile and I want to hide out for a while and figure out…what all *this* means. See what…what happens with the pregnancy."

"Do you have any reason to believe you'll miscarry?" he asked. He looked disturbed by the idea, which was strangely touching. It was easy to imagine he was digging in and doing the right thing because of his past experience, but he almost seemed to want the baby. Almost seemed like he would be sorry now if it didn't happen.

And she felt a little bit shocked by the revelation that she would be sad if something happened. That she wanted the baby, no matter the circumstances.

"No. Not any reason beyond statistics. I mean…they happen, don't they?"

"I suppose. But it hardly seems right to plan for one."

"I'm not. I'm just being cautious."

"I have to go back to New York for the work week. I have several clients I need to meet with and it has to be done in person."

"Why can't you Skype them or something?"

He leaned against the door frame, arms crossed over his broad chest. "I'm new in town still. Comparatively. That means I have to play by other people's rules sometimes."

"You must hate that."

He smiled that wicked, enticing smile. "I hate rules. But you have to play the game. And the game has been good to me so far. It's how I've earned my money. It's how a kid from a brothel ended up being a billionaire."

"Well, have fun in New York," she said. She didn't want

to probe deeper. Didn't want to find out more about him. Didn't want him to seem so human.

"You aren't going to come?"

"Was I invited?"

"Of course. You want to stay here then?"

She did, weirdly. She should go home and face the music. Her father. Everything. But she wasn't ready for that yet. She wasn't ready to share her and Alex's...*relationship?* Whatever it was, with her family. When she told her family she was pregnant, she would have to confess that she'd had that little indiscretion and she wasn't ready to tell them yet.

Wasn't ready to expose that part of herself, a part she'd only just discovered. A part Alex had uncovered.

She hadn't even known she was capable of being swept away on a tide of desire, and she wasn't really ready to let anyone else in on her revelation.

"Yes."

"By yourself?" he asked.

"Sounds ideal, actually."

He pushed off from the door frame. "Well then, please yourself."

"Shall."

"I will see you next week."

She nodded slowly. "Okay. Next week, then."

"Then...then we'll decide what we're going to do."

She nodded, holding back a groan. She wasn't ready to decide anything.

"No guarantees."

"People do not tell me no, Rachel. I warn you of that right now."

"Funny, I've told you no quite a few times."

"Yes. But before you said no, you said yes. Pretty emphatically. I'm sure I can get you to say it again."

CHAPTER SEVEN

HE WAS SO TIRED he wanted to lie down and not get up for three days. But he didn't want to lie down alone. He wanted to lie down next to Rachel. To pull her curvy body against his and just hold her while he slept.

That was probably the jet lag talking, but oh, well.

It was morning on the island, late night in New York. What he had to do was drink an espresso and suck it up. He was young—there were plenty of people his age who partied every night and went to work the next morning.

For some reason, though, half the time he felt old.

Maybe it was the strain of being a respectable business-man when he knew that it just wasn't programmed into him genetically. He would have been better off selling his body for cash or selling other people to turn a profit.

He shut down that line of thinking and walked into the house.

He could hear singing. Coming from the kitchen. It was off-key, and it was horrible. Warbling about wanting to make someone feel wanted.

He followed the noise like a bread crumb trail, and at the end of it was a blonde with her hair piled high on her head in a messy bun, dancing around the room in short pajama shorts with an empty mug in her hand.

"Good morning," he said. "Is the coffee made?"

She stopped then flailed, her arms flung wide. "Ack!"

"Sorry to interrupt."

"You scared me. I didn't know when you'd be back."

"I texted you." That was how he'd kept in touch with her over the past week. The occasional text just to make sure she was okay. Sometimes she'd even responded without an insult.

"I hadn't checked my phone yet."

"I'm so disappointed you weren't waiting for contact from me with bated breath."

"Sorry." She went over to the coffeemaker and set about filling the empty mug.

"Thank you," he said.

"It's for me."

He shot her his deadliest look and went to the cabinet and picked out his own mug, then poured himself a cup. "I don't think you appreciate how much I need the caffeine."

"I'm supposed to limit it, but I can't seem to shake the need for an early morning cup. But the doctor said that was okay."

"Doctor?"

"Yes. I managed to secure myself a covert doctor visit while you were gone."

He leaned against the counter. "And?"

"Knocked up, as we thought."

"And?"

"It's early. No point doing an ultrasound or anything like that."

"But everything is fine. And you can drink a coffee."

She curled her fingers like talons around her mug, her eyes glittering evilly. "I can drink a coffee."

"Okay. Don't cut me or anything."

"Hiss."

"You just said hiss."

"Hissing at you would be overdramatic. It was like a pre-hiss. A warning."

He looked at her, in her pajamas, her feet bare, toenails bright pink, her hair piled high on her head, and laughed. She was the most absurd little thing he'd ever encountered.

"What?" she asked.

"You're so weird."

"I am?"

"Yes."

"Why are you shocked by it?"

He shrugged. "The press makes you look like some… staid and stable ribbon-cutter."

"Ribbon-cutter?"

"Like you go to openings and stand there and cut the ribbon."

"Hmph. That's your bad for believing the media's representation of me! They only see a small bit of who I am, and they report on a piece of that. They don't know me or what I do at home."

"Is that their fault or yours?"

"What does that mean?"

"You're very guarded, Rachel, and while I have to say you don't seem to be around me, in general, I think you are. Does anyone know you?"

Rachel paused with her coffee mug halfway to her lips. She was unhappy because seeing Alex walk into the kitchen had sent her heart way up into her throat, even worse than it had done when he'd sent her text messages during the time he'd been away.

"Alana probably a little."

"Alana?"

"My friend. The one I was in Corfu with. The one who encouraged me to go and talk to you. She was my maid of honor along with Leah, actually. Well, she would have been had I gone through with the wedding."

"And she knows you?"

She winced. "Mostly." Alana had been there for the wild

past. They'd passed a liquor bottle back and forth between them in her Mercedes. They'd cleaned up their act together. But Alana didn't know that Rachel felt like she was suffocating beneath her skin.

She shopped with Alana, she talked shallow crap with Alana. She and Leah had warm chats where Rachel felt obligated to seem stable and to give advice. She and her father had a similar relationship. She always felt like she needed to seem happy, so that he wouldn't worry that something was wrong again. That she might be sliding back into her old ways.

Then there was Ajax…and with him she had to be… well, calm and fine and…and…things. With Ajax she was the woman she pretended to be for the media. Poised and steady. She could never do anything that might point in the direction of her very covered up, fairly sordid teenage years. She could never flail or cuss.

She did both of those things around Alex. With alarming frequency. And she wasn't sure why. Maybe because he'd seen her naked. Or maybe because she'd been naked since she met him. Metaphorically.

"I've just never… Everyone has their expectations. And what they need from me. You, on the other hand, well, I don't need to be a certain way around you because I don't even like you, and also we're stuck together, so what you think about me or want from me doesn't really matter."

His eyes went blank. "I don't really know what it's like to have someone have expectations of you."

"Oh. Well, it's not bad. I don't really mind it or anything. It's just that…it means that I make sure I behave a certain way in certain company is all. And yeah, I don't go around saying weird things in public or around people who wouldn't get it. So I'm…restrained in certain settings and…"

"Fake," he said.

"What?"

"You're fake. And that's okay, I am, too. I mean, I know how to be. Witness how we met. And how do you think I survive a week of meetings like this? I don't go in telling them where I'm from. I make sure to temper my language. I've learned how to dress in a way that reflects who I am now, and what I do now, not in a way that reflects who I was. Or where I'm from."

"I'm not fake."

"Don't look so upset."

She realized she was frowning with great ferocity. She didn't bother to stop. "How can I not be upset when you're telling me that I'm fake?"

"Because it's a life skill. Chameleons do it. It's how they survive. It's how *we* survive. You don't want to walk around showing the wrong colors, so to speak. You have to learn how to blend in."

"Deep, man."

"It's the truth is all. And you do it, so you obviously, instinctively, know the benefits of it, whether you like it or not."

"It's…being appropriate in your surroundings. It's not fake."

"Is it authentic?"

"Does it… What does that mean?"

"I'm not judging you, Rachel, I'm observing."

Her phone started buzzing against the hard marble tile and she grabbed it, looking at the screen with no small amount of dread. Because she hadn't talked to Ajax at all since his wedding with Leah and she hadn't talked to Leah on the phone. Or her father. And she didn't know if she could handle any of them.

Fortunately the caller ID showed that it was Alana. Alana, who she was prepared to deal with at least. They'd talked a little bit during the week, and while she hadn't broken the pregnancy news, her friend had guessed that Alex was the reason for the wedding no-show and had been nothing but supportive.

"I have to take this. In an authentic manner." She hit the green button on the screen. "Hi. What?"

Alana was talking so fast that Rachel could hardly decode what she was saying. "A huge order. Like…huge, and I can't fulfill it if I can't buy the materials—I'm only getting half paid up front. And you're not even going to believe this! A pipe burst in the shop upstairs and flooded me completely. I have ruined inventory, things that I can't just replace and my insurance thinks her insurance is responsible and vice versa and it's just absolute madness!"

"What can I do?"

"There's the obvious but I hesitate to ask."

"Well, since I'm part owner in the business, it makes sense that I help, especially since— What is this huge order?"

"It's costume stuff, which I don't love to do, but I'd get a film credit. It's for a really big French film and—"

"Say no more. I'm coming over. We'll get it all worked out."

"You don't have to come if you're still deep in issues with your mystery man."

Rachel looked up at Alex. "Let me worry about that." She hung up. "I have to go to Cannes."

"What?"

"My friend Alana has a boutique there. Technically, *I* have a boutique there. I own most of it. But I'm a silent business partner, as it were."

"How is it I didn't know that?"

"No one knows that," she said. "Not even Ajax. And yes, I felt a little guilty about it, but I believe in her skills as a designer and I wanted to support her. So I set her up with a boutique. And we've been turning a decent profit the past few years. She's having a crisis now, though—burst pipe upstairs—and we have damaged clothes. So I need to go and see what all happened, and try to help her get everything put back together."

"That's easy," he said. "Throw money at it."

"What? Like just pay someone to go and fix it all?"

"Why not?"

"I have a budget. What? I do. I have a trust, yes, but I have to live off of it. And I just stopped living in the apartment my father paid for. And I've just burned some bridges, so all things considered, I should throw a mop at it, not money. It needs to get done quickly because she has a chance to pick up a major client, but not if she's underwater. So to speak."

"I could pay for it. You know, if you were my wife I would feel obligated to pay for it."

"Oh, no! I'm not your wife, though. I'm not even your fiancée. You know what? It feels really good not to be someone's fiancée. It really does."

"I'm happy for you."

"You don't sound it. So anyway, as I'm assuming I'm not a prisoner, I need to get a plane off this island and get myself to Cannes."

"Are you coming back?"

She bit her lip. "I don't know. I might stay with Alana for a while. This, you and me, is probably going to end in shared custody."

He frowned. "That's not how I want it to end."

"How do you see this ending?"

"With our family together. You with your child, me with both of you. You in my bed."

She choked on her coffee, coughing and sputtering, bracing herself on the counter until she could suck in a breath that wasn't blocked by liquid. "What?" she finally managed to rasp.

"What did you think I meant when I proposed marriage?"

"Something not so…intimate."

"And why not? We're good together, *agape*."

"Whatever. You only slept with me because you were being revenge-y. And you were wanting to steal Ajax's woman and his business and whatever. It had nothing to do with me."

A muscle in his jaw ticked. "I suppose. But things have changed. You're the mother of my child and all things considered…"

"I will never be a convenience. Not for any man. Not ever again. You talked about being fake. Fine, maybe I've been fake. I didn't even know it, though. That's the thing. I didn't know…how far from love what I felt for Ajax was, and I'll never put myself in that position just to make other people comfortable. I'm done making other people comfortable. I'm going to make me and my baby comfortable. Beginning and end of story."

"Well, then, I suppose I should drink more coffee and pack."

"Why?"

"Because, apparently, we're going to Cannes."

"We?"

"I'm not done with you, Rachel. Not by a long shot. And hey, this time, I'll pay for the hotel room. Since you paid for the last one."

Her ears burned. "Did you not just hear what I said?" She really needed him to not be suggesting they pick up where they left off in Corfu, because she was genuinely afraid that she would be too weak to tell him no. That she would say "yes, yes, take me!" and lie down on the nearest flat surface so he could have his wicked way with her, and that would accomplish nothing.

It would be fun, though…

Maybe. But she wasn't going to have any more of that kind of fun with him. She had, in some strange way, been set free by all these crazy turns of events, and she was going to make the most of that freedom. Not head toward another loveless engagement.

"I heard you. I'll get us a penthouse suite with separate bedrooms. It will be very luxurious and private and it will not interfere with your budget."

"Well…thanks. But why?"

"Because I am not going to give up on you, *agape mou*. On us."

"Because you love me so much?" she asked, her heart hammering, her palms sweaty. She'd asked it to put him off. To mock him. Instead, she found herself standing there shaking, a part of her praying his answer would be yes.

"Not at all. Love isn't in the cards for a man like me, Rachel. I wouldn't even know where to begin. But a family… I thought I would like to try."

She swallowed hard. "But I need more than that, Alex. I need more than just you trying. I'm not going to be your happy family experiment, it's not fair."

"You don't have a happy family, experimental or otherwise at the moment, so why not?"

She tried to ignore the punch to the gut his words delivered. But it was impossible. Because she'd lived the past eleven years holding her family together. Being what they needed. And now it was gone.

It was gone and she didn't know what to do without it.

It was like realizing that pieces of her armor had been stripped away. Threatening to expose her. Vulnerable. So soft and easily hurt.

She crossed her arms beneath her breasts, as if that might hold what was left of her armor close to her skin. As if it might protect her.

Suddenly she was very aware of the baby inside of her,

and that, in spite of the fact she had a human in her, she'd never felt so alone or frightened in all of her life. As if everything, inside and out, had turned completely alien.

She would take pictures of herself being intimate with her former almost-lover hitting the news any day over the feeling that had grabbed her by the throat just now.

"I…I need to go," she said. "Send the plane. I'll pack."

"No. Lucy will pack for you. You rest here and I will see to all the arrangements." For Alex, he seemed almost contrite.

"You don't have to come."

"You don't want me to?" he asked.

"No."

"You can't always get what you want, *agape*."

CHAPTER EIGHT

"Show-off," she said, looking around the penthouse and walking toward the window, looking out at the ocean below.

The flight to Cannes had been quick and uneventful. The uneventful part he credited to the fact that Rachel had ignored him the entire time.

"What? The hotel room you put me up in was very nice. And the room service was excellent."

Something flashed in her eyes that he didn't like. Pain. Shame. "You aren't authorized to joke about that night," she said. "I don't like the reminder that you used me."

"No more than you used me. You were engaged to another man, after all. You were hardly blameless."

"You knew, though. I didn't trick you."

"Can we not have this fight again? The one where you tell me all the things I did to wound you? I felt…guilty, after it happened, Rachel. That's why I didn't call. That's why I didn't storm your wedding. It's why I came to see you and not him."

She frowned. "You felt guilty."

"It turns out that when you seek revenge on someone you hate…because of the way they treated women—the way they treated people in general—and you use someone in order to do it, you come out feeling a lot like the thing you despise."

It was the truth. He'd never allowed himself to fully

form the thought. To examine exactly why the whole incident with her left him feeling dirty. Empty. It was because it was another piece of evidence for the trial being conducted over his soul.

Innocent or guilty. Victim or predator. Which was he?

He didn't even know the answer. And it burned.

"A conscience, huh?" she asked.

"I'm maybe not as bad as you think. I'm maybe not as good as I think, but…also perhaps I'm not completely amoral, either. Which is good to know."

"Do you want to be…good?"

He frowned. "I don't know. I know what I don't want to be."

"So you really… You really think you grew up in a brothel with Ajax."

"I did," he said, his chest tightening. "He wouldn't remember me. I was a boy when he left. Maybe eight. But I remember him. And his father."

A leaden weight settled in his chest. As it did whenever he thought too much about…everything. When he had moments of wanting to call Ajax's father "my father."

He swallowed past the bile that was rising in his throat. *Bad blood, right? That's the way it works.*

It must. Except it didn't seem to work that way for Ajax. Ajax, who'd acquired a family when he'd left the compound. Ajax, who'd had no trouble finding love.

He·couldn't think about it. It gave him a headache. It was too complicated. Too hard.

"He never told me about his life before he came to work for my family," she said. "I mean…nothing. He never said a thing about it and now…now I think it's a bit strange. But honestly, Alex, if you knew him…he's so serious. He never does one thing out of line. I can't even imagine the man you're describing."

"He was little better than a boy," Alex said, his voice

rough. "I suppose I imagined he hadn't changed much as a man. That when I met you you would have stories of him in excess, and that he would be the same."

"He doesn't even drink. He's the most outrageously decent man I've ever known, and no, he doesn't inspire great passion in me. But he's a friend. He's not a bad person."

"But he was," Alex said, feeling the need to justify himself. "He was."

"Or maybe he just had his moments? Like you said, what happened with me...it wasn't your best."

"No," he said.

"It wasn't mine, either. But I don't think it was my worst. Well, it depends on how you look at it. It wasn't the worst thing that's ever happened to me. It was definitely the worst thing I've done. Because I didn't keep my promises, and that was... That wasn't right of me."

"What was the worst thing?" he asked, his throat getting so tight he could scarcely breathe.

"I don't want to talk about it. Actually, what I should do is run and check on Alana."

"I'll go with you."

"You don't need to."

"I want to. I want to be a part of your life. And I'm frustrated because I'm not really sure how to accomplish that beyond lying to you."

A crease dented her forehead. "What would you say?"

"What?"

"If you were going to lie to try and keep me in your life, what would you say?"

He looked at her, at her flawless face and the deep blue eyes that carried a wealth of depth and hurt behind them. Hurt he didn't want to add to, even though he knew he already had.

"I would tell you that I loved you. That my life would

be nothing without you. That I needed you. More than my next breath."

Her blue eyes shimmered, tears pooling in them and he wished for a second that what he said could be true. But he didn't know how to feel those things.

And even if he could...

He would never risk them.

For some reason that resolution pushed forward an image of a baby. A squalling, delicate newborn whose cries screamed need. Need for him.

It made his chest feel strange. Tight and heavy. A strange sort of helplessness crept around the edges. The kind he hadn't felt since he was a boy, surrounded by evil he knew he could never combat.

And the people who should have been protecting them— protecting him—they were the monsters.

There was no hopelessness deeper than that. And he'd felt it every day, a feeling that had only intensified the day he'd learned the truth. The day he'd run.

And now you're going to be a father.

The thought was enough to buckle his knees. To send him straight to the ground.

"Well," she said, bursting through the haze of his thoughts, "that would certainly be dramatic." She swallowed visibly. "And of course I wouldn't believe you."

"Wise. That's what you call learning from your mistakes."

She flinched. "I suppose so. Now, I'm going to go and deal with Alana's crisis. Alone, actually. Yes, I'm going alone, so find something to amuse yourself."

"Did you just tell me to amuse myself?"

"Yeah. I can give you some spending money if you like."

He frowned. "You need it more than I do. But your attempts at flippancy over the past week have been amusing. If flawed."

"As have been your attempts at being a decent human being. All right. I'm going."

"Where is her shop?"

"I'll text you."

"And I'll find it. When should I expect you back?" he asked, crossing his arms over his chest.

"When I'm back."

"So I won't know if you've been backed into an alley by the paparazzi or if you're just running late? That doesn't work for me. Estimate a time or at least give me your location."

"Are you…worried about me?"

"The baby," he bit out, the word making his stomach ache.

"Well, of course. That's what I meant."

"Yes," he said.

"Thanks. I'm… Thank you. I'm going to go. I'll be back here by seven. If I'm not, I'll text you."

He nodded and watched her walk back out of the room, his stomach flipping over itself. Maybe he should be thankful for her refusal to marry him. What did he know about being a father? What did he know about being a husband?

All he knew was that he felt a need to be close to her. To protect her. And he knew, with a total certainty, that he would feel that way about the baby.

He meant to offer them protection. But he had no idea who would protect them from him. No, he would never harm them with his hands. But…

He had always pictured Ajax's veins being filled with black poison. When he'd been a boy and he or Nikola would walk past him, it was a strong vision he'd had. That they were something different than men. That if you cut them, evil would pour out. They exuded it. How could it not be a physical thing beneath their skin?

And then he'd found out the truth.

If their blood was black, then his was, too.

Because it was the same blood.

Worse, he'd seen Ajax lose that legacy. Had seen him walk away and create a new life. He'd seen his mother, desperate to cling to the man she'd loved.

The men he'd always considered evil seemed to have no trouble binding people to them.

The same legacy had been coursing through his veins since birth, and yet no one had ever chosen to stay with him.

It made him fear that the only thing he'd inherited was the darkness.

The skin on Rachel's arms prickled as a breeze blew across the water and over her. She and Alana had just closed up shop after assessing the damage, and Alana had gone with her boyfriend back to their apartment.

Rachel had just been standing out in front of the store, looking across the harbor at the yachts, at where blue sky met blue water, rich colors fading together.

She breathed in deep and the breeze set the hair on the back of her neck on end and brushed a tingling sensation over her, down to her fingertips. It wasn't fear. But it was something she couldn't ignore. Something urgent, little bursts of it popping through her until she turned her head.

And then it all made sense.

Alex was walking toward her, hands in his pockets. He was dressed casually, nothing like he'd been that day on the yacht, but still much more relaxed than Alex the Businessman. A pale blue shirt open at the collar and a pair of dark jeans.

"I'm glad to see you've not been buried beneath photographers."

"Oh, well, thank heaven for the off-season. None of the locals would dare break their cool by raising an eyebrow at my presence, much less interrupt their day by setting the paparazzi on me."

"Thank God for people far too blasé to care for a bit of scandal."

She laughed. "I suppose."

The moment was strange. Like that time a month ago in Greece playing over again. Different setting, different time. But the pull was there. Whether she wanted it to be or not, it was there. Engagement ring or not, it had been there. Conniving plot to seduce her to get revenge on Ajax or not, it had been there.

Even now, with the baby and all the baggage, it was there.

She knew he felt it, too. She could see it in those wicked blue eyes. He was thinking of sex and sin and all the wonderful things they'd done together. She didn't know how she knew it, only that she did. Only that for some reason she had a connection with him that she couldn't explain. One she didn't want at all.

Why couldn't he just be that jerk who'd seduced her? Or, if she couldn't summon up the rage to think of him as a jerk, why couldn't he just be the cause of her pregnancy? A distant figure until they had to work out a shared custody agreement? It's not like he could do anything for her now anyway.

But there was more. She hated that there was more, but there was. This deep, sexual connection that somehow felt like…more. Why did it keep going with him? Why, no matter the depth of feeling she was willing to admit she had with him, did a small voice inside of her keep whispering *it's more?*

Stupid small voice inside of her.

"Dinner?" he asked, another echo from the past.

"Yes." She felt the yes slip off her lips and a deep ache

slide down deep inside of her. Her body responding to the consent.

For dinner, you little hussy. Dinner. Down, girl.

He held his hand out, and she didn't take it. Because if she did, she knew she was really, really sunk. She had no business touching him. No business even flirting with the idea of engaging in intimacy with him again.

The fact that he was a lying liar aside, they had too much going on to confuse it all with more sex.

As if things could get more confused, but whatever.

"Where are we having dinner?" she asked. Because it seemed to her they were just going back toward the hotel.

"I hate to see a perfectly good terrace wasted, so I thought we would dine at the suite."

"You make it sound so fancy."

"It is," he said. "It's very fancy. And dinner should be waiting for us already. And I will be having juice, along with you."

"That's…well, that's awfully sensitive of you."

"You sound surprised."

"I am," she said, walking next to him, acutely aware of the way they both held their arms at their sides as they walked. Acutely aware of how they weren't touching when their fingertips were so close.

That wasn't how it was supposed to work. She was supposed to not touch him and have all the attraction magically resolve. Her shell was supposed to protect her. All those years of self-denial. Of never letting her passion out. Learning to be risk-averse, learning to keep every emotion, every desire, every need shoved down deep and covered by a layer of smooth, impenetrable steel. All of that should have helped her now. Should have preserved her.

But it wasn't and she couldn't understand it. How eleven years of hard-won control had just suddenly melted as if it had never been there in the first place.

They walked into the hotel in total silence, then took the elevator to their floor. The double doors to the terrace were open, a wash of pink evening light painting the living area.

She walked through the suite and outside. The table was set for two, a bottle of sparkling grape juice in an ice bucket, wrapped in a linen towel as if it were fine champagne. And their plates were covered with a silver dome, everything set and ready.

As though Alex had wanted to make sure they weren't disturbed.

"This is romantic," she said, her tone about as dry as sand.

"Is it?" he looked around as though the notion surprised him. "I just asked for dinner for two and that we not be disturbed. For privacy's sake, as we are discussing personal matters and you are a bit of a public figure. Romance never came into it."

"Naturally not. Come to think of it, you aren't much of a romantic, are you?"

He shook his head. "I've never had much practice with it. But I would like to think I romanced you that night we were together."

"You seduced me. Completely different. I wasn't looking for romance."

"So you were looking for sex?"

"No," she said. "But I think that's why it worked."

She sat down and grabbed the bottle out of the bucket, eyeing the cork warily. "It has a cork."

"Yes."

"These things freak me out. You do it." She handed him the bottle and he took it, working the metal cage off the cork so that it popped up. She winced at the sound. "Gah. I always expect it to fly out and poke someone in the eye."

He laughed. "Not likely. But then, caution isn't a bad thing."

"That's certainly been my motto in life."

He arched a brow as he poured her a glass of the sparkling juice.

"It has been. For…a while. Because…because bad things happen to you when you put yourself out there, you know?"

He nodded slowly. "No," he said, the words at odds with the gesture. "I don't. Because I never put myself out there."

"So you never have girlfriends, do you?"

"No. One-night-stand stuff. Sometimes women who hang around for a couple of weekends. Nothing more than that."

Strangely, it didn't really bother her to hear him say that. She would have been more disturbed in some ways if there had been a woman in his life that he loved.

And she really didn't want to know why that was.

Silly since she'd been in love before. Even if it had turned out badly. Sillier still because she didn't love Alex and she didn't want him to love her, either. But nothing about her feelings for him were logic-centered. None at all.

"That seems smart," she said. "I mean, in some ways. It wouldn't really work for me, I bet, because the guys would go to the press." She hadn't meant to tread that close to the truth of her past.

"It must be inconvenient. For my part, as rich as I am, only financial magazines seem to care."

"It surprises me because your face would sell magazines."

"I'm content out of the spotlight."

Her heart bumped into her breastbone. "If you're seen with me…I mean, when people find out…you'll be in the spotlight. You know that, right? Your anonymity is sort of over."

"I can deal with that," he said, pulling the covers off of their dinner to reveal some sort of fish dish. It had crispy skin. And a head. Oh, Lord, it had a head. She didn't mind fish, usually, but after spending so much time in Greece and then on his island, she was concerned she was going to grow gills.

"I love the sea," she said. "I'm underwhelmed by seafood, to be honest." She poked at it with her fork. "Daaaaang. It has a head."

He laughed at her, then bent across the table and took her plate, and his, and put them back by a nearby tray. "Hold that thought."

He went back into the hotel room and she couldn't help but watch his butt as he went. She looked away and back down into her drink and she didn't realize he'd returned until he spoke. "I ordered a pizza. What's the point of all this pretension?"

She laughed. "A pizza?"

"I was promised it would be here in ten minutes."

"Tell me there are no anchovies on it, because if there are, we haven't solved any of my problems."

"No anchovies. Promise."

"Good. What did you get?"

"Pineapple."

"I love!"

"Me, too."

A strange sort of calm settled between them, and it felt more disturbing than the tension from earlier. This wasn't like it had been a month ago. Not entirely. There was an edge of comfort, of domesticity to this that hit a nerve in her.

They tried to make clumsy small talk until they heard the knock at the door and he went off for the pizza, setting the box on their table.

She laughed. "So much for romance."

He shrugged. "This is better. It's real, anyway."

"True." She flipped up the lid on the box and took out a piece of pizza, chewing through the burn of the first bite.

Worth the pain to get the cheese at the optimum point. "So," she said, after she swallowed. "Do you get pizza often?"

He looked down, then back up, and she was hit, once again, with the full impact of his beauty. "Do you want to know a secret?" he asked.

"Yes."

He leaned in, the look in his eyes intent. "After I left my...the compound, I didn't have any money. So I slept where I could and ate what I could, and I still felt better about it because I wasn't a part of that horrible place."

"I can understand that."

"But once I started making money, and I got my own apartment...I didn't want to buy filet mignon or lobster. I'd had all that. Living in that house... It was the darkest pieces of glamor and excess. Junkies throwing up in the halls, people having sex in public. But then we'd sit down to some formal dinner like this insane family or something. Anyway, I never wanted to revisit that. I'd never just had a pizza. I ordered it almost every night for a...a long time."

He looked down and took a bite of pizza, the gestures and expressions boyish now. It was strange; sometimes he seemed so young. Sometimes he seemed about a thousand years old. And she could relate, because sometimes that was exactly how she felt, too. Too young, too old and never just right.

"What did you have on the first one?"

"The pizza?"

"Yeah," she said, her stomach tight. "I'm sure you remember."

The left corner of his mouth quirked upward. "Yeah. Pepperoni. Black olives. It was New York style. Of course, at the time I'd only dreamed of New York. I live there now. The pizza's much better than this."

She laughed. "Yeah, I know. I spent at least half my childhood there. Most of my adult life. I've been fortunate to travel a lot from an early age."

"I barely left the Kouklakis compound until I was fourteen."

"What?"

"There was…nowhere else to go. And they didn't really want anyone talking to us. Questioning us. There weren't very many children. The ones that were there had to be careful. Careful to try and go unnoticed by anyone who might want to use us, people who came for parties and things. Careful about what we said. The wrong words could set the police down on Nikola and that would have been unforgivable. Death for certain."

"He would have killed…children?"

"He would never have gotten his own hands that dirty. But he would have used someone else's. I always knew that my life was in a tenuous place as long as I was there. I always knew." He took another bite of pizza. "But I got free. I got pizza. It has a happy ending, yes?"

"Does it?"

"What do you mean?"

"Well, it's not over yet. Right now we're just sitting here eating pizza. It's not going to fade to black or anything."

"True."

"There are a lot of potential outcomes for all of this. And I'm not sure if any of them are wildly happy."

He grunted, a short, frustrated sound seated in the back of his throat. "Because you're looking for something I can't give you. You could be happy if you just—"

"If I what?"

"—compromised. You were willing to do it for Ajax and you didn't even want him. You weren't having his baby. Well, you are having my baby, and you do want me, so I don't see any reason that you shouldn't want to marry me instead of him. What changed?"

She looked down. "I think I did. Or maybe I didn't change, maybe I just became more afraid of what might happen if I kept living my life as someone else, someone safe, and less afraid of what might happen if I made an effort to find some happiness."

"I think I made you pretty happy for extended periods of time in bed," he said.

She coughed. "Well, there's that."

"I want you, Rachel."

"What…now?" She looked around them, at the blue-tinged air slowly falling darker as the sun sank below the horizon line.

"Every moment since the first time I saw you. And that's not me lying to keep you here, that's me telling you the truth. That's me confessing. Frankly, I know this isn't going to get me anywhere with you so you have to believe that it's honest. Because I know that it doesn't mean anything to you that the moment I saw you, I forgot Ajax's name, and every thought I ever had about revenge. Because all I could think about was getting you naked then and there. Not romantic, maybe. But all I know is that it didn't matter then who you were. I mean…not in the sense of who you were to Ajax, or the media, or what your marriage had to do with him acquiring Holt. It only mattered…who you were. Which I know sounds stupid, but in my head it made sense."

Rachel's heart was pounding hard, echoing in her head. She leaned forward, grabbed his collar and tugged him to her, kissing him on the mouth. She didn't know what she was doing or why. Only that she couldn't stop.

And along with her heartbeat, his words reverberated through her. *It only mattered who you were.*

He cupped the back of her head and pulled her in harder, taking the kiss deeper, his tongue sliding against hers, sending a wave of lust down through her body. Nothing was settled. And she shouldn't be kissing him. Shouldn't be making things confusing by throwing a match on their simmering physical chemistry.

But he'd said he wanted her. And everything in her responded to that. It fought to break free, to push past the boundaries she'd placed around herself, a neat little fence that kept her safe and hidden.

Because he wanted that part of her. He didn't want her to hide it. Didn't want her to keep it behind a locked door. Didn't want her to keep her passion from him. And she wanted to give him that. Wanted to give it to herself, this moment of freedom. Another chance to grab it. To try and feel something.

She'd spent so long not feeling. This was like coming to the surface of the water and breathing in air, filling her aching lungs when she hadn't even realized what she'd been missing.

She hadn't realized how much pain had been caused by holding herself under. Because it had been a slow-growing pain, easier to deal with than the idea of having herself exposed to the media, of being used by a man she'd thought she loved.

Still, it hurt. And she was only now seeing just how much.

"I have garlic breath," she said when they parted, breathing hard and hoping it wasn't too offensive.

"I probably do, too."

"Well, I didn't notice so I guess we're good."

"Stop talking, Rachel."

She nodded. "It would be for the best."

She moved away from him and away from the table so it wasn't between them anymore. He rounded it, pulled her to him and kissed her like he was starving. She wrapped her arms around his neck, clung to him.

He tightened his hold on her, propelling her backward until she was pressed up against the rough stone wall of the hotel. "I need you," he said, kissing her cheek, her neck, her collarbone. "Rachel. *Theos,* how have I survived this long without touching you?"

She wanted to cry, and she wanted to come, and she couldn't figure out, in the end, which need would win out. It all felt too big for her, too much. Too much for a girl who was used to hiding in her shell, to feel stripped and exposed like this.

But she couldn't stop. She couldn't.

She pulled his shirt open, not caring that it scattered buttons everywhere, not caring that she could hear the sounds of traffic below, that they had nothing to cover them. She pushed his shirt off his shoulders and ran her hands over his chest, the hard muscles, the rough hair.

"You're so hot," she said.

"We've had this conversation before."

"I know, but I have to say it again because it's all I can think about when I see you. When I touch you. You make me… Alex, I don't understand this. I didn't think this was how I was. Not anymore. I thought it was gone."

He dipped low and kissed her, forcing her head against the wall, the hard surface behind her the only thing keeping her from melting into a puddle on the ground. One of his hands slid low, down to her thigh. His fingers dug into her skin, his grip tightening as he lifted her leg and held it up over his lower back, bracing her with his hand and the wall behind them.

He moved against her, the hard ridge of his arousal hitting her in just the right spot. She tightened her grip on him and moved with him, amping it up, pushing herself closer and closer to the edge.

He pressed a kiss to the center of her breasts, his tongue tracing a line down to the edge of the fabric of her dress. Then he continued down, still holding her leg as he lowered himself, draping her thigh over his shoulder as he settled onto his knees.

He pushed the skirt of her dress up, exposing her to him. "Remember, I told you I liked foreplay, but that first time…I took you too fast. I need to make up for it now."

"I… Oh." He slid his finger beneath her panties and stroked her where she was slick and so very ready for him.

She could feel his breath against her skin, hot and tantalizing. He ran his finger over her flesh, leaving a trail of fire in its wake. "Good, baby?" he asked.

"You told me not to talk," she said. "And now I can't. So don't ask questions. It's not fair."

"What's not fair is the fact that I'm shaking," he said, tugging her panties to the side, leaning in closer. "You do that to me, you know?"

She'd suddenly forgotten how to do anything but lean against that wall. "I didn't… I—"

Then his lips made contact with her bare skin and she couldn't think, couldn't breathe, and she definitely couldn't speak.

His tongue slid over her slick flesh, teasing her clitoris, sliding down deep inside of her. She flattened her hands against the wall, trying to find something to hold on to. Her fingers scraped against the stone, the rough surface biting her knuckles.

He moved his hand, his large palm cupping her butt, pulling her harder against his mouth as he intensified his attention on her body, his lips and tongue working dark magic on her, driving her closer and closer to the edge.

She put her hands on his shoulders, clinging to him, in an attempt to keep herself anchored to the earth.

He slid a finger deep inside of her and she tilted her head back, the stars in the darkening sky blurring, then he added a second and everything seemed to combust, the bright lights overhead bursting into a million fireworks.

He released her then stood, his body pressed against hers as he kissed her deeply, the evidence of her own desire on his lips. "Inside," he growled.

She turned away from him and fumbled for the door into the room. He slid it open and he walked in behind her, sweeping her hair over her shoulder, his lips on the back of her neck as they walked inside.

Then he gripped her shoulders and turned her to face him, kissing her lips. "Can't wait," he said, tugging at her dress until he slipped it from her body, then pulling her panties down her legs, while she worked on the closure to his jeans. He stripped them off, along with his underwear, leaving him blessedly naked.

He gripped her thighs and tugged her up so that her legs were wrapped around his waist before lowering them both to the carpet. The door was still open, the traffic noise and ocean breeze coming into the suite, but she didn't care.

There was nothing but this. Nothing but Alex.

"Please, Alex," she said. "I need you."

He positioned himself and slid inside of her, filling her, stretching her. She felt right for the first time in weeks. Or maybe more truthfully, she felt right for the first time in eleven years. More herself.

And then it was all wiped away as she gave up emotion for pleasure. There was nothing but their fractured breathing, Alex saying rough, coarse things in her ear. In English, in Greek. Words she'd never heard before. Words that sent a shiver of illicit longing through her, that heightened her desire, amped up her arousal.

After the orgasm he gave her outside, she was shocked that she had another one building already. But with each stroke, each rough, whispered word, he pushed her higher, faster.

He put his hand beneath her lower back, lifted her hips off of the ground and thrust harder into her, the sound of skin on skin overtaking the traffic noise from the street below.

He thrust into her one last time, a hoarse sound rising in his throat as he came. The sound, his loss of control, the look of tortured pleasure on his face, was so intense that she felt it as it echoed through her, grabbed hold of her own pleasure and expanded it, pushed her over the edge, their orgasms blending into one until she couldn't tell where hers began and ended, until she felt like they'd genuinely become one.

When it was over, the traffic noise came back into her consciousness. He rolled away from her, lying on his back on the carpet. A breeze blew through the door, chilling her bare, sweat-slicked skin.

"Well," she said.

"Yes." She looked over at him. He was on his back, his arms up, hands beneath his head.

"I suppose that was inevitable," she said, sitting up, drawing her knees to her chest.

"Clearly it was," he said.

"Obviously. Because it happened."

He turned and rose up, cupping her cheek. "Yes, it did."

"It didn't fix anything," she said, a cold feeling stealing into her chest.

"No, but I don't suppose sex ever stood a chance of fixing anything."

"I thought we might…" She stopped talking, because she didn't know what she'd thought. That it would steal the mystery? Break the bond? That it would bond them? Answer the questions and reservations she'd had?

No, she hadn't thought any of that. She'd thought of nothing but need. Her need to have him, the way he'd looked at her. The way he'd wanted her.

Not the façade, but her.

But now, with the haze of orgasm fading slowly into the

background, she was acutely aware of the fact that she was, yet again, naked with a man she didn't know. Yet again, she was exposed with him.

This time she'd gone and shown just how needy she was. For some kind of acceptance. It made her cringe. She knew better than to show this much of herself. Than to be anything more than self-contained.

Her mother had been that way. So perfect. So gracious. And she'd tried. Rachel had always tried, and never quite lived up to it all. She'd failed eleven years ago, on purpose and with blazing, spectacular glory because at the time it had seemed better than trying so hard and still not measuring up.

And she'd failed again with Alex.

"I think I need…"

"A cigarette?" he asked.

She laughed. "No. Oh, man…I haven't had a cigarette in…more than a decade."

"But you've had one? I'm shocked."

She took a deep breath. "I think you're too easily shocked. Everyone has a past, you know."

"Oh, believe me," he said. "I know about pasts."

"Yeah, I'm sure."

"You seem far too…good, to have a past," he said, frowning.

"I seem good? After that? I need to work on my moves."

"I just mean…you were a virgin. You've never had your name in the paper for anything even remotely scandalous."

"By design. All of it. Anyway, since when does virginity equal goodness? Mine's certainly not a reflection of that. It was…fear, mostly."

"You didn't seem afraid that night with me. Though you did tremble a bit."

"I hate you."

He stood up, naked still and entirely unconcerned.

"I'll bet the people in the building across the way are getting a show."

He turned and waved. "Probably."

"Good grief, Alex, have you no shame?"

"No. A product of my upbringing, I'm afraid. Hard to have shame raised in the environment I was."

"But the people across from us might have shame."

He grinned and bent, grabbing his black underwear and tugging them back on. "There, how's that?"

"Better for some," she said.

"Not you?"

She felt her face get hot. "Not really."

"How is it you kept all this passion hidden for so long?"

"I hid it so well, I even hid it from me," she said, hoping to redirect the subject. Away from things like this. Away from drunken parties and stupid decisions. "Plus... Look, I've made some crappy decisions, okay? And I almost got burned seriously and permanently because of it. Who am I kidding? I did get burned just...privately. I learned my lesson, though. I learned that you can't just do things without consequences catching up with you."

"Do you have lung problems from all your smoking?" he asked, his tone dry.

"If only that were the case."

They looked at each other for a second. She was still naked. And he was mostly naked. And she realized they knew so little about each other.

She knew about his past, but the only thing that felt real, the only thing that had seemed as if it was connected to a real emotion and not just a cold, hard fact about the way he'd grown up, was his honesty about the pizza.

They didn't know each other. He didn't know her. But then, as he'd already pointed out, no one really did.

And here she was, having just shared herself with him in the most intimate way, pregnant with his baby, no less, holding tight to shame that was so deeply embedded in her, trapped beneath that layer of steel.

"Do you know what I used to love?" she asked, because she was naked anyway, so there was no reason not to say it.

"What?" he asked.

"Driving really fast. I was…such a jerk behind the wheel. Really dangerous. Alana and I used to cruise around a lot when we were in Greece. We didn't really get the chance to drive in the city so when we were here…? All bets were off. I had this great car. It was red and sleek, and it went… well, it went fast, let's just say that. And we'd cruise with the top down and flirt with guys at stoplights. It made me feel like I wasn't Rachel Holt, this big disappointment to her mother. I hated all the things she wanted me to do. I just wanted to do something *I* wanted. And for a while, I just wanted to…forget that I cared and…drive fast."

"That's normal…isn't it? I don't really know since I didn't have what you'd call traditional teenage years, but even so, I think I've seen things like that in movies."

"Sure, I suppose it's normal. But that doesn't make it smart or safe. Especially not when you've been drinking. Which…we did. It was stupid. I was stupid and I…I don't know what I was doing. Rebelling against a life that was too…sedate, I suppose. A life I didn't feel like I was excelling at. I just wanted to feel something. Something exciting and dangerous. The wind in my hair, bubbles fizzing through my blood… I liked to flirt, too."

"You were an innocent, so it's not like—"

"There is a lot of ground between innocence and not having had intercourse, Alex. I would think a man like you would realize that," she said tightly.

"Oh." He looked…unhappy with that.

"Does that bother you? That you aren't the first man I've been intimate with? Though I'm not really sure you can call a quick blow job in the back of a car intimate. But

I make very poor decisions under the influence of drugs and alcohol, let's put it that way."

"This has never been in the papers. Everyone talks about you—"

"Like I'm the sainted Holt Heiress who spends her days sitting on a cloud playing a harp? I know. And it's not by accident. My father… He covered for me. He paid off every cop that pulled me over, he bought any incriminating club photos. He kept me from being exposed. And then…" Her throat tightened, a sick sense of shame pouring through her, choking her. "I did something…really stupid. That seems to be the only descriptor I have for that year of my life. One year, Alex. Out of…twenty-eight. I acted out and I almost lost everything. I almost changed the way people saw me forever. I…I know I did change the way my mother and father saw me."

"What happened?" he asked, his posture suddenly stiff, something in his stance deceptively, unnaturally still. As though energy were building in him, coiling tightly beneath the surface of his skin, ready to pounce at any moment on an imagined enemy.

Too bad the only enemy was her. The things, the desires, in her.

"Everything kind of came to a head—bad choice of words, you'll see why in a second—when I met this guy at a club. Colin. I really liked him. We met up and danced a couple of weekends in a row and he asked if I wanted to 'get out of here,' which, you know, means that a guy wants something from you. I was drunk and feeling like giving it because he was hot and I liked him. A lot. He was handsome, and he had a nice smile. He thought I was pretty." She rolled her eyes then looked down at her hands. She didn't want to look at Alex right now.

This reminded her of standing in her father's office, sweating and shaking, about to embarrass herself fatally, because she didn't know what else to do. Because if she didn't expose herself to her father, she would be exposing herself to the whole world.

"Anyway, I ended up in the backseat of the car with him. Which... You know what that means. We parked at the beach. At least it wasn't a back parking lot somewhere—that makes it less sordid. Kind of. He got out his video camera. Pre the days of cell phone recordings, and thank God because the whole thing was much more concrete back then, not this nebulous digital web that could have had it in a thousand places immediately."

"What did he do?"

"He filmed me. He asked and I thought, why not? I thought it was hot that he wanted to commemorate the event. I was drunk. I was seventeen. And right when he asked me to do it I thought maybe I even loved him, because being drunk and seventeen is basically all it takes to feel like you love someone. He wanted me, and I... Well, what I really loved was being wanted. For me, you know. Because, clearly, my blow job skills were the essence of me as a woman."

"He videotaped you..."

"Going down on him. Yes. And the next morning I woke up with a raging headache and very little memory of it. Until he came around the villa the following evening looking for things to go further. I said no because...I didn't feel ready for sex yet. Which maybe doesn't make a lot of sense but...I just knew I wasn't. He got mad and he threatened me. Because he had the video and he was going to send it out. To the media, to the internet. And I was...so afraid that he would. That...*that* would be out there. Me...doing that. Thinking about it makes me panic even now. I just...can't imagine anything more exposing or humiliating. Though telling my father about it and begging him to bail me out was a close second."

"And what happened?"

"He made it all go away. He protected me, because that's what he's always done. But he…he was so disappointed, I could tell. And that was when he told me he wasn't protecting me anymore. He told me that anything could have happened to me. Driving drunk, going off with strange men… He said I was going to get myself killed and he wouldn't watch while I did it. He wouldn't enable it. No more help. No more money. No more family. He said I had to behave myself, or lose everything. And…I have. Until now. Probably I'm cut off, I suppose, but…but…"

"That's why you aren't calling home."

She nodded silently. "I don't want to know." Her eyes stung, but still, there were no tears. "I don't want to see him look at me that way ever again. Like I'm a…lost cause. I don't know why I did all that stuff, not really. But I know why I stopped. Because I wanted more out of my life than what I was going to get partying until my brain fell out of my ear."

"And that more was marrying a man you didn't love or even want to sleep with?"

His words hit her, cold and hard in the chest.

"Apparently, what I was really waiting for was to meet a stranger and have a one-night stand with him and get pregnant with his baby. My goals were much loftier than a mere loveless marriage."

He cleared his throat and looked out the window. "Did your father tell you what a worthless asshole that man was?"

"What?"

"Did he tell you what a horrible person that man was? Because it seems to me that all of this was about the situation you put yourself in, and while I get that there were poor decisions on your part—and I'm the proud owner of many poor decisions so I'm not throwing stones—he was the one determined to take a private encounter public. He was the one who was threatening to expose you."

"I… He wasn't there to be lectured, I was."

"And you were the one who had to change."

"I really did though, Alex. I was trying to take a long walk off a short pier."

"I agree with that in terms of the substance abuse. Drugs mess things up, Rachel, in ways I'm sure you never saw in a club. But you're clean now, I assume."

She nodded. "Yes. I was never a heavy user. Mainly I drank too much alcohol. But I have a one-glass limit on wine now. And a no-glass limit at the moment."

"What were you trying to fix?"

"What?" she asked.

"Everyone I've ever known that's been on drugs or who partied till they couldn't think—and I've known a lot of them, considering my background—has been running from something. Medicating for some reason. What was yours?"

"I don't… I…" She blinked rapidly and looked away from him. "I didn't worry so much about being good enough when I was doing all that. I felt…happy. I felt good."

"And since you stopped?"

She lifted one shoulder. "Until recently, I knew I was good. Feelings didn't really matter."

"So you exchanged one form of denying your feelings for another? New solution—don't change your feelings, just don't have them?"

"I'm sorry, Alex, but this is something you couldn't possibly know anything about."

"Is that right?"

"Yes. I don't mean to be cruel, but who has any expectation of you? When I found out who you were I knew I'd been used because your name is synonymous with epic bastardry. You'd already tried to ruin Ajax with those tax fraud allegations."

He quirked his lips into a half smile. "And the odds that they were true seemed high. They would have been with many corporations."

"Sadly for you, Ajax does things so by the book it's almost unreal."

"A surprise, considering."

She suddenly felt even more naked than she had a moment ago. She wrapped her arms around herself and shivered. She should get her clothes, but she had a feeling that they wouldn't make her any warmer. Any less exposed. He knew now. He knew the worst of her.

And she knew...what he thought was the worst of Ajax. And she knew about the pizza. But she didn't know him.

"Tell me something about you," she said. "What are you ashamed of?"

He looked away from her. "I'm not ashamed of anything. I don't have shame."

He looked back at her, their eyes meeting, his expression fierce. "I've seen too many things...done too many things. And I don't regret them. Because they've made me who I am."

"That's such a line. We all regret things. I regret getting into the car with Colin. I regret drinking that much. I regret letting him videotape me."

"And it changes nothing, so why bother with it?"

"Because it did change something. It changed me."

"Ah, yes, and you're so happy and well-adjusted now?"

"No. I've proven, yet again, that when you follow your... emotions and hormones and...things that aren't logical, stupid things happen."

"Is that how you see the baby? As something stupid?"

"I didn't say that."

"You said stupid things happen."

"Are we going to stand here and pretend I made a stellar

decision in sleeping with you when I was engaged to some-one else? I don't have it in me to lie like that."

"Just to omit the truth when it suits you."

"Shut up, Alex."

"You just asked me to share about myself."

"Then do that. But don't throw stones at me. I can't take it right now. I just…spilled my guts to you and I can't take your criticism on top of it."

Silence fell between them. A thick blanket that offered no warmth or comfort. Just a heavy awkwardness that made her skin break out into goose bumps.

He shook his head. "Sorry, I'm not overly shocked by your revelations since I used to catch live performances of what you did in that video in the halls of…of the Koukla-kis compound. When I was a child," he finished, the word hard and bitter. "I was protected, but only to a degree. You want me to tell you about things I'm ashamed of? I don't even know what shame looks like."

He turned away from her, his posture rigid, the defined muscles in his back standing out, tension radiating from him. "I've seen my own mother on her knees in front of a man. I've seen her beg and cry and offer favors for a chance to stay." He turned back to her. "To take care of me, I thought. Because of love, I thought. But that wasn't it. At least it wasn't because she loved me. It was because she loved heroin and the man who owned it all. It was never for me. Fine, do you want to know what shame re-ally feels like? Finding out your own mother loves drugs and sex more than she loves you. That's shame. That burns, Rachel, in a way you can't possibly imagine. You want to know what I know about family? There you are."

"Alex…"

"Don't," he bit out, crossing to her. "I don't need your pity. I am not that boy. I am not a victim. I got out by the skin of my teeth—I scraped my knuckles raw climbing out of that prison. I didn't escape clean, but I escaped."

"Is that why you hate Ajax so much? Because he got out and he's done well for himself? Because he's unaffected?"

"Of course that's part of why I hate him."

Because Ajax was so normal. And Alex was so broken. He didn't say the words but she felt them between them. And she believed him.

"What happened when you left?"

He reached out, cupping the back of her head and pulling her forward. "I do not want to talk anymore."

"Alex—"

He kissed her, his lips hard, crushing against hers.

"Don't be afraid with me, Rachel," he said, his hands skimming over her curves. "Don't hide from me."

"Alex," she said again, his name a plea this time. For what, she wasn't sure. For freedom? For a moment unleashed from the cage she'd locked herself in.

"There's no shame with me," he said against her lips. "None at all."

His words pulled at something inside of her, at a need she'd been denying for so long. Rooted out the guilt that had been tangled around her soul like a creeping vine.

"You want me," he said, kissing her neck, her collarbone. "Tell me that you want me."

"I can't…"

"Tell me what you want," he said, his voice firm as he lowered his head and sucked her nipple deep into his mouth.

"We just did this, like, a half an hour ago," she said, gasping, her head falling back.

"Yes. I know. And you want me again already. Because you're passionate, Rachel, no matter what you think. Because you have desire. So much. And it's beautiful."

Her throat closed, something shifting in her chest. She took a sharp breath, trying to hold back the sudden, unexpected rush of emotion. She didn't have time for it. Not now. Not when Alex was kissing her like this. Not when he was taking that old memory she'd just shared and twisting it, changing the way she felt about it. Changing the way she felt about herself.

"Tell me what you want," he growled.

"You," she said.

"Tell me how I make you feel," he said, raising his head, his teeth scraping against her neck before he sucked the gentle curve hard, drawing away the sting.

"I…I want you, Alex."

"Like no one else?"

"No one else."

He put his hand between her thighs, his thumb sliding over her clitoris while he pushed a finger deep inside of her. "Tell me," he said again, a ragged edge to his voice that told her there would be no arguing with him. That told her she had to obey.

"I—" The words stuck in her throat, embarrassment, and self-protection slamming down and keeping her from saying anything.

"Tell me," he said, "or you don't get to come."

"Alex," she said, trying to be exasperated while his hands were working magic on her body. While he was holding her apart from paradise.

"I don't have time for you to hide, *agape.* You want me, or you don't. But you have to tell me." He added a second finger, amped up the movements, pushing her closer but still not taking her there. And he knew it.

"I…I want you inside of me."

He smiled, wicked, naughty. Thrilling. "I am inside of you."

She shook her head. "That's not what I mean."

"Say what you mean."

"I don't…"

"You want my cock?" She nodded, biting her lip hard. "Then tell me."

Heat flooded her face—embarrassment and arousal. So silly when she was being so intimate with him. When they'd done even more only a half hour ago, why couldn't she say what she wanted? Why was it so hard to be honest? With him? With herself?

"I want your cock inside of me," she said, the words coming out in a rush.

He cupped her chin, held her face steady while he kissed her deep. He withdrew his fingers from her and lifted her up into his arms, carrying her into the bedroom and depositing her on the center of the bed, pushing his underwear down his legs and coming to join her.

He parted her thighs and gripped his thick erection, pressing himself to the entrance of her body, guiding himself in slowly.

She arched, a harsh cry escaping her lips as he filled her. Stretched her. She felt so close, so needy—incredibly, considering what had happened earlier. But she couldn't get enough of him.

She'd been waiting for this, for him, all of her life.

As soon as she had the thought, she pushed it away. She pushed everything away. The barrier she kept between herself and the world.

She forgot to feel shame. She forgot to curb her emotions. She forgot to be quiet and dignified. Instead she clung to his shoulders, dug her nails into his skin and wrapped her legs around his hips.

Instead she bit his neck and cried out her pleasure, riding the wave of pleasure to ecstasy. He pounded hard into her body until he stiffened, a hoarse cry on his lips as he found his own pleasure, as he poured himself into her.

Afterward she lay there, shaking. Feeling vulnerable and

exposed. Like a creature that had been dragged out of its den and forced into the sunlight, uncovered, unprotected.

And she started retreating as quickly as possible. Did her best to try and rebuild her defense system.

But his arms were around her and he was kissing her neck, her shoulder, the curve of her breast. It made it impossible to retreat fully. Because he was holding her captive.

"You can't possibly want to do that again," she said. "I'm completely spent."

"That's one of the perks of younger men," he said, pinching her nipple lightly. "We can go all night."

"I can't. I'm exhausted." Physically, she could have him again. She already wanted him. How could she ever get tired of a man like him?

But emotionally? She didn't have the strength. Because he'd done something to her. It was more than unleashing a wild part of herself she hadn't known existed. It was more than just sex. She was stripped naked, down to her soul, and there was no way she could go through any more just yet.

It was all starting to catch up with her. The reality of her actions, from the moment she'd met him until she'd told him so bluntly what she'd wanted from him.

She looked at him, their eyes clashing. He was so beautiful. A man built to tempt even the most righteous of women. And she'd never been all that righteous. She'd only been pretending.

This man was the father of her baby.

Her stomach lurched, the thought butting up hard against her compromised defenses. Oh, good Lord, the baby...

She shivered, a dry sob in her throat. But still there were no tears.

"What's wrong?" he asked.

"I don't know...I...I was thinking about the baby."

He froze behind her, then his hand drifted from her breast down to her stomach. "How are you feeling about it?"

Scared. "Okay. I mean…it's a lot to deal with."

"Naturally. And what are your plans?" he asked. "If you don't marry me, what do you think we'll do?"

"I don't want to talk about this right now." She felt scrubbed raw, and she didn't think she could even handle thinking about the pregnancy in terms of it producing an actual baby at the end, much less how Alex and her relationship with him would squeeze in around that.

"Then when, Rachel? You're pregnant with my child. You continue to end up in my bed. Marriage is—"

"Is that what this is about?"

"What?"

"You…putting the moves on me. Is it just so I'll agree to this…marriage thing?"

"This marriage thing," he said, moving away from her and getting off of the bed, "is the best chance our child has at a normal life."

"Oh! So we're normal? What in all the world makes you think that?"

"I didn't say we were, but a normal family structure is the best chance this child has."

"And you want to prove something to Ajax?"

"This has nothing to do with Ajax! When I went to that wedding, I went for you. You could have been marrying my very best friend and I would have come to take you. Because you're mine. It's that simple."

"I'm yours? Why?"

"Because," he said, his words tight. "Because you're having my baby."

"You didn't know I was."

"And because I want you."

"To be who you want. To do what you want."

His lips curled. "I asked what you wanted. And you told me. Oh, baby, did you tell me."

"Shut up, Alex," she said, turning away from him, those words starting to become familiar.

"Because you still want to pretend that you're a cyborg?"

"Because I can't deal with all of this right now!" she said, exploding. "With the baby. And with you…and…and my family… I can't." She got out of bed and started hunting for her clothes.

"We have to deal with it sometime."

She had that feeling again. As if the pressure was too much. As if she was too full of…everything and as if there was no release on the horizon. As if she was drowning inside of herself.

"Not right now," she said. She looked around and realized her clothes were in the living room. "Crap."

She pulled the blankets off the bed and gathered them around her body, covering up her curves. "I'm going to bed," she said.

"Fine."

"And I'm not marrying you."

"Yet," he said, his blue eyes boring into hers. Oh, those eyes…

"Why does it matter to you? You don't know anything about normal. You said yourself your experience with family is…is horrible, so why would you care?"

"Because I will give better than that for my child. I can't fix anything that happened to me. I can't…make it go away. But I can make sure no son or daughter of mine is exposed to what I was. That they'll always know who their mother and father are. That we'll both be there for them. If that's not what you want…perhaps you should give custody of the child to me."

Her entire body recoiled at the thought. "No. I would never give up my baby."

"You said yourself you aren't sure how you feel about it."

"Because I'm afraid. Because I know what a huge responsibility it is! Because I don't want to…raise a child who grows up like me and I don't know how not to do that. How to protect a child without smothering them. How to guide them without making them feel like their choices are all bad….how to protect them when they genuinely are being an idiot. I don't even know who I am, Alex. How am I supposed to deal with the life of another human being?"

"With me," he said, his voice rough.

"No offense, but I'm not sure adding screwed up to screwed up is going to equal anything more than a mess."

She turned and walked out of the room, her chest swollen, her body aching.

She didn't know how to fix this. She didn't know what she wanted. Right now she could hardly remember how to breathe.

CHAPTER NINE

It had been two weeks since Cannes. And two weeks since they'd last had sex. And Alex was pretty sure his head was going to explode, if parts farther south didn't first.

He had no idea how to reach her. He'd never wanted to reach a woman before, not in any way beyond the physical. But Rachel… He wanted something more from her. Without having to give more than was comfortable. Surely that wasn't completely unreasonable.

She didn't want all he had to give anyway.

Not if she had any concept of what it might mean.

Hell, he wasn't sure he had a complete concept of what it might mean and he didn't aim to acquire one.

Still, she was staying with him, even if she was wandering around sniffing indignantly at him half of the time. She was hiding, and he knew it. But he found he didn't care, so long as she was close. Barring the small blip of a headline about them cavorting in paradise, which had something to do with them being snapped together having dinner in Cannes, no one had picked up on what was actually happening, and considering the tenuous situation, that was fine with him.

She seemed pale, though. More so than when they'd first met, and he hated the idea that he might be the cause of it. Shouldn't be surprised, though. That came back to him.

To what was in him. A boy that no one could love, a man who was fundamentally flawed down to his very genetics.

That black blood filtering through his veins. The image he could never quite shake.

He saw her sitting out on the terrace and walked through the room, out the door, to join her. "Good morning," he said.

"Hi."

"Ready for the doctor to come?"

"Yes. It seems pretty extravagant to have her do a house call."

"Until you're ready for the story to break, we need to keep it as low key and close to home as possible. I assume you aren't ready?"

"No. I haven't told my father yet."

"Have you spoken to him?"

She nodded. "Very briefly. He's worried. I told him… I told him that I was just enjoying a little bit of fun. He said…" She blinked rapidly. "He said that was fine. That it was about time I did. Why is he so supportive of me? Even when I make such stupid mistakes?"

"Why shouldn't he be?"

"I don't know. I guess it would make more sense if he'd just get mad."

"Why? You're a grown woman. You can make your own decisions."

"I'm not sure if I make good ones."

A maid appeared in the doorway. "Dr. Sands is here."

"Great. Send her in," Alex said.

Dr. Sands, Rachel's doctor, whom he hadn't met yet, came out onto the terrace smiling. It felt so strange to have a doctor standing there. To know that this was about the baby.

Sometimes—well, all the time—it was so much easier not to think about the baby.

But then, if there was no baby, Rachel would have no reason to be there.

That made his throat tighten with a strange kind of terror.

"Hi, Rachel. Shall we go upstairs and get started?"

Rachel looked at him, her eyes wide.

"Are you afraid I'll come?" he asked. "Or afraid I won't?"

She lifted a shoulder. "I'm not sure."

"I'm going to come."

"Okay."

A loose summer dress and a sheet were Rachel's accessories for the appointment. She knew it was technically too early to need another appointment. She was close to eight weeks, but there was little point in checking things out. Except she was nervous.

About everything. Afraid everything was fine. Afraid it wasn't.

And on the verge of losing her mind completely. The pressure in her chest had built to a maddening degree. So that just breathing every day was a chore.

It had been two weeks since she'd been with Alex. Two weeks. And she'd denied herself the only release that had given her any relief. Because he was too much. Because he wanted too much.

"Go ahead and lie down on the bed, Rachel, it will be pretty quick. I understand that you were wanting to see if we could see the heartbeat. I can't make any guarantees. If we don't see anything, it could all still be fine, but we'll give it a look."

She nodded. "Thank you. I know it's early but...we have...things to deal with."

Dr. Sands gave her a sympathetic smile. "I know. It's okay, we'll figure it all out."

"Alex, could you stand up...well, not down there?" Rachel asked as she moved into position for her exam.

Alex came to stand by her head as the doctor prepared the ultrasound.

Rachel winced both at the cold and the intrusion and waited for everything to come up on the small screen of the portable machine.

"There we go," Dr. Sands said. "See the flutter of movement there? That's the heartbeat."

Rachel looked at the black space on the screen, at the little lines of white and flickering brightness that signified life.

"It all looks good. Of course, there are no guarantees at any stage," she said, looking her in the eyes, "so you don't want to make any decisions that are too life-changing. But you're healthy, and there's no reason to believe anything will go wrong, okay?"

Rachel nodded. "Okay. That's great. Good."

"I'll let you get cleaned up. Alex? Perhaps you'd like to come with me. And if you have any questions it would be a good time—"

Their voices faded when the door closed and Rachel stood up, her hands shaking as she went into the bathroom and dealt with the gel mess left behind by the ultrasound.

Then she knelt down in front of the toilet and threw up.

Morning sickness in the afternoon maybe. Or just shock.

She sat down in the middle of the floor, her knees drawn up to her chest. What had she gotten herself into? She was pregnant and there was really no denying it. There was a heartbeat. Inside of her. She'd never been so afraid in her entire life.

She didn't know how to do this. She didn't know… She couldn't do it.

All she could picture now was the doctor putting the baby in her arms and her handing it right back.

She pushed herself up, standing on shaking legs. She felt like a newborn fawn. A newborn fawn that was in no way equipped to care for a baby because she was…well, she didn't feel like she was a grown-up yet. Didn't feel like she could be a mom.

Miserable, she crossed to the sink and started brushing her teeth. At least her breath would be better, even if everything in her was still in disarray.

She took a deep breath, gasped for it, and went back into the bedroom. She was okay. She would be okay. She didn't need to cry.

She never cried. She hadn't cried in years. She wasn't about to start now. She hadn't cried since her mother had died. Her mother…

That's not where it goes, Rachel.

No, Rachel, you're doing it wrong.

You're too loud. Too rowdy. You shouldn't go out at night. You shouldn't wear that dress.

Rachel, how could you do something like that? Didn't I teach you to wait for your husband?

Rachel blinked rapidly, trying to shut out the memories. The critical voice in her head. The voice of the woman who was perfect and graceful to everyone. Everyone but her.

Because Rachel couldn't do anything right. Rachel wasn't ever going to be able to do things the way they were supposed to be done. Rachel would never get it right. Ever.

She'd tried to kick against it, to rebel, and in the end she was the only one who'd been hurt. And she'd come out the other side trying so hard to be better. Trying to keep herself from being too big…too loud…too *her*.

She was trying so hard not to be herself.

The dam that was holding everything in, that had been holding it all in for years in spite of the mounting pressure, finally burst.

A tear slid down her cheek.

The first tear in years. And now she didn't think they would ever stop.

She walked over to the bed, clutching her chest, her shoulders shaking as the dam burst on the past ten years of emotion, held so tightly in her, in a tight, heavy ball that she'd resigned herself to carrying around inside forever, broke open and poured out all over the place.

She wondered if you could drown in your own tears. She was seriously afraid she might. Or at least that she might die from not being able to catch her breath. Every attempt at breathing became another sob, until she was gasping, shaking and having a complete and utter breakdown.

Maybe this was what happened when you kept it all in. Maybe the breaking point was inevitable.

She was certainly broken. No question.

She was dimly aware of the bedroom door opening.

"Rachel?" Alex's voice, her name followed by a sharp curse. "What's wrong? Is everything okay? Are you okay?"

"I can't do this, Alex!" Her words came from somewhere deep inside of her, came out without her having a chance to even think them first. She only felt them.

"Yes, you can."

"No, I can't. I can't…ever do things the way they're supposed to be done. I mess them up. When I feel too much I make mistakes and when I…when I don't feel at all I feel like I might as well be doing nothing at all. I don't know what I'm supposed to do. I don't know how to love a child, and follow my heart, use my emotions, without making bad decisions. And if I…if I keep on like I have been and just don't care…then what's the point? I can't. It's too hard. I'll mess it all up, I know I will."

His arms were around her, holding her close, his lips on her temple, fingers laced through her hair. Their last confrontation, the angry words, didn't evaporate, but for the moment they were on hold. "Rachel, you can do this. You can."

"It's a lie, Alex. It's always been a lie. I'm not perfect. I hide all these pieces of myself, and I don't show anyone. I don't know how to give everything because I'm so damn afraid of it. Because if I do…it still won't be good enough. It won't ever be good enough."

"Why do you think that?"

"Because it never was! Not ever. Not for her. I tried, Alex, I put everything on hold because she was sick. I helped plan her parties, I chose Ajax because he was safe and easy and he wouldn't disgrace me or our family. I tried to appear polished and to always smile, just like she did. But all I could ever be was a pale imitation. All I could ever manage was lukewarm cocktail shrimp and a party that was barely mediocre. She was this… She made everyone so happy at parties. She made everyone's life easier and I just…made things harder because I was distracted and couldn't finish, or just because I don't have that thing that she had. I fake it, but I don't have it. Not really. The press sees it, they think I'm so like her but I… She was never happy."

"That isn't your fault, Rachel, you aren't her clone. It doesn't mean you're a failure, not in any way."

She nodded. "I'm just all…messed up inside, Alex."

He stroked her hair, his body a solid wall of reassurance for her to lean against. "Aren't we all?"

"Well, *we* are."

"As you said. Screwed up and screwed up."

"A mess," she said.

"But it's the mess we have."

"I know," she said, sniffing loudly. "I haven't even cried for… This is the first time in eight years."

"I haven't cried since I was a boy," he said.

"How long?" she wanted to know. She wanted to know how heavy the burden inside of him was. Hers had been nearly unbearable.

"Probably about twelve years. A boy of fourteen—I might have cried then."

"Why?"

"You want my secrets now, *agape?*"

"I'm leaving snot trails all over your shirt," she said, leaning back. "I think we have no reason to keep secrets. And I wanted them once already. But you didn't give them."

She thought back to their night in Cannes. He'd deflected then. Both times. And he'd done it with sex.

"Then you can have them now," he said. "Leaving the Kouklakis compound was the single hardest thing I ever did. The worst day of my life. My mother was dead. I felt very alone. Afraid of what was ahead. I wanted to escape and yet I feared the freedom. I knew I couldn't stay because…because of what I would become if I did. I cried that day. It was the only home I knew, and I loved it as much as I hated it."

"Your problems are so much bigger than mine," she said. "I must seem like a nutcase to you."

"No. I don't see it that way."

"How?"

"Because it hurts you. If there's one thing I've learned from being in the position I've been in, being around the types of people I've been exposed to, it's that people have common pains. They come from different places, but they are the same sorts of hurts."

"Forgive me, Alex, but you're one of the most amoral men I've ever met. You used me to get back at Ajax, you were going to crash my wedding—"

"Maybe. I was undecided. Though…it is likely I would have stopped you from going through with it. Because… as I said, you are mine."

"You…don't make any sense to me," she said. "You act like you were raised by wolves…and then you go and say things like this. You go and say things that are so insightful, and that make me feel like I just might not be alone, or that I might not be the big ball of crazy I tend to think I am."

"You probably are still a...ball of crazy," he said, the words sounding so funny and off rhythm in that accent. "But a very charming one."

"Thanks. I appreciate that."

"Well, I can't have you questioning what you think of me too deeply. It might make you rethink too many things, right?"

"Maybe I should." She rose up onto her knees and moved to where he stood at the edge of the bed. Her heart was pounding fast, the emotion flowing through her making her dizzy.

She knew she shouldn't touch him. She knew she shouldn't want him. Nothing was settled. There was still too much baggage between them. But when she was in Alex's arms...she was so much closer to the woman she really was, rather than the woman who was just pretending.

Right now, she didn't have the strength to pretend. She leaned in, eye level with his chest, and kissed the bare skin revealed by his undone top button.

"Rachel." Her gaze met his. He looked like he was in pain, his eyes closed, a deep groove between his brows.

"I'm not going to hit you," she said, stretching up higher and kissing his neck, "I just want to kiss you."

He reached out and grabbed her wrist, held her back from him, his eyes. "Only if you're absolutely certain you want me to push you back onto that bed and take you hard and fast. Make you mine. Make you scream."

"I think I do," she said, her voice trembling, her whole body trembling.

He captured her face with his other hand, his expression intense. "That isn't good enough. You'd better be completely certain."

She swallowed hard. "I want you, Alex."

"Why?" he asked, his voice sharp.

"I don't know why," she said, a tear sliding down her face. Another tear, nothing significant about this one, since it was the hundred-somethingth tear in an hour instead of the first one in eight years. But still, it felt significant. Everything about this moment did.

"Try to tell me."

"Because you're the only man that's ever made me feel this way. Because you're the only man I've ever wanted, *really* wanted. You make me feel like myself. And I don't think I've ever felt like just…me, before. Everything I've done, from rebellion to behaving, has been for other people. You were the first thing I ever did for me."

"I see." He traced her jawline with his fingertip. "Am I still a mistake to you, Rachel?"

"I don't know yet."

"What? You need to…make me one more time before you're sure?"

"I might need to get to the end of…everything before I know for sure."

"And in the meantime you want to make love with me?"

She nodded slowly, his hands still holding her. "Yes. Does that make me… Is there something wrong with me?"

"There's something wrong with both of us. Because whether I should or not, I'm going to have you tonight."

"When you say things like that… Alex, it's enough to drive a woman totally insane. And in a good way."

"Is it?"

"No one else has ever wanted me. Not really. Not me."

"I do," he said. "Feel how much?" He put her hand on his chest, over his heart, then guided it downward, over his denim-covered erection. "Do you feel that?"

"Yes," she said, squeezing him. "Impossible not to."

"Then you can't be in any doubt of how much I want

you. Want this. If you're sure of one thing, be sure of me. Of how much I want you."

"You really do say nice things."

"I'm honest. When I want to be."

"That instills a lot of confidence," she said, moving her hand over him, cupping him through his jeans. "I think you should take these off."

"In a moment. I want to watch you take your dress off. We're always in a hurry. I don't want to rush this."

"I might not give you a choice," she said, moving away from him to the center of the bed and sliding a strap from her shoulder. "I might jump on you."

"I welcome the challenge," he said. "You wouldn't be half so much fun if you weren't always pushing me."

"You actually enjoy my back talk?" she asked, pushing down the second strap.

"I more than enjoy it. It turns me on. I've seen enough passive, hollow-eyed women, bent on doing what they're told just to get a fix. Of a drug. Of a person. I don't want that from you. I don't want empty compliance or…that thing that you've been doing where you try to make everyone's life easy at the expense of what you want. I want fire."

She smiled and tugged at the zipper on the back of her dress, letting it fall down, revealing her breasts. "I think I can give you that."

She was trying to keep it light, keep it sassy, but it was hard to do when she felt as if she might cave in on herself. As if all the emotion that was inside of her was going to expand too far, and when everything came to a crashing halt, she would just fold right in.

She pushed the dress over her hips. The sunlight was bright, filtering in through the window, and she was naked now. But she didn't feel awkward. She felt incredible. Because he did want her. Because he didn't want her as the woman she was when she put on her mask and tried to become the perfect hostess. The one who never sent a ripple over the surface of anyone's life.

He was okay with her not falling in line. With her not being perfect.

"I'll never be perfect," she said, the words spilling out of her mouth. She was physically naked, so she might as well be emotionally naked, too.

"I don't know what you're talking about. You look completely perfect to me."

"You're just saying that because I'm naked," she said. "But that's not what I mean. I mean…I'm never going to be everything that my mother was. I try. But I can't sing on key. And I don't like big fancy parties that much. I like to stay home in my pajamas instead of going to galas. I hate those stupid art shows that she used to sponsor. Generalizing, but I kinda think that modern art is pretentious and I never want to have to go host anything like that ever again."

"Then why do you?"

"Because I don't know how else to be…valuable."

"Right now, touching you seems like it's more important than air. I feel like if I don't touch you, if I don't have you, I might die. How's that?"

"That feels good. Not an overarching life goal, but good enough for now."

He put one knee on the edge of the bed and tugged her toward him, kissing her deeply, his arm tight around her waist, hand resting on the curve of her butt as he explored her slowly with his lips and tongue.

"You are," he said, pausing to kiss her again, "the most incredible woman. The most beautiful. The most frustrating. You are, I hate to say, a terrible singer. But how could you ever doubt your value?"

He kissed her neck and she shivered, whatever words she was going to say drying up on her tongue, stolen completely by his touch, by her desire for him.

Alex advanced on her, strong arms guiding her fall to the soft mattress as he came to rest over her, one of his hands pinning both of hers above her head.

"You've said that I made you do things that weren't in your character," he said, "but you have turned me into a man I barely know. I dream of you. Of the softness of your skin. The sounds you make when you come. I think about you the way you told me what you wanted from me." Her face heated at the memory. "You are a distraction," he said. "One I never expected to deal with. I can't even think of revenge, and *agape,* I was able to think of revenge when I was starving on the streets, when I made my first million, my first billion. I have always been able to think of it. And for the first time my head is so full of other things, other desires, that I can't. That is what you do to me. That is powerful. You have done more than make me act out of character—you've changed me."

She wiggled, wanting to touch his face.

'No," he said, tracing her nipple with his free hand. "I'm not letting you free just yet."

"Why?" she asked, panting, out of breath, needing him so badly she thought she might go crazy.

"Because I want to take my time." He lowered his head, sucking her nipple deep into his mouth. "I want to savor you."

He lifted his hand to cup her cheek and she nipped at his finger. He paused, a smile curving his lips, his finger hovering just above her mouth. She sucked it in deep, the expression on his face taking on that slightly pained look, then as she released him, she bit him gently.

"You are dangerous," he said. He bent and kissed her, bit her bottom lip as they separated. "But so am I."

"I never doubted you were dangerous," she said, trying to catch her breath. "But I'm not."

"You don't think?"

"No."

"Liar. You are completely deadly. To my sanity. To my senses. I don't even think I can breathe right when I look at you."

His free hand roamed over her curves while he held her still. She arched and squirmed, trying to find satisfaction. Trying to find release. But he held her, held the power to bring her to orgasm or not. And he was definitely enjoying teasing her at the moment.

"Please, Alex."

"Please what?" he asked, kissing her neck, the curve of her breast. He settled between her thighs, the denim rough on her skin. And she moved against him, desperate for satisfaction.

"Please let me…"

"Please let you…? Remember, you have to ask. Don't hide from me, Rachel. Tell me what you want."

"Please let me come," she said, her cheeks getting hot with arousal, not embarrassment.

"Good things come to those who wait," he said.

"I've been waiting. I've been waiting for two weeks."

"So have I," he said. "And I want to enjoy the experience."

He moved away from her on the bed and tugged his shirt over his head. She watched the play of his muscles rippling beneath golden skin as he worked on his belt and shrugged his pants and underwear down his legs.

"I want you," she said.

"I know."

"I mean…get off the bed."

"I don't take orders."

"You should take these. Now get off the bed."

He obeyed, standing close, and she moved over to the edge, on her knees. "I want this." She lowered her head, her heart hammering hard. And she realized she really did want this. She wanted to taste him. Not because it would pleasure him, but because she wanted it. Wanted him in her mouth. Her tongue flicking out to taste the head of his shaft.

Strong fingers gripped her hair, gently pulling her back. "You don't have to do that."

"I know." She met his eyes. "I want to, Alex."

His hold on her loosened and she bent down again, taking him into her mouth. The sharp hiss of his breath, the tenseness in his whole body, sent a sharp pang of pleasure straight to her stomach.

She was so very aware that this was Alex. The past wasn't with them. There was nothing shameful tied to what she was doing for him, because she wanted it. Because it wasn't selfish taking and coercion on his end.

"Stop, Rachel."

"Why?"

"We're savoring, remember?"

"I know I am," she said.

He growled and she found herself flat on her back. He had one arm wrapped around her, the other cupping her chin. "You push me to the edge of my control."

His kiss was hard, demanding, his tongue sliding over hers, the slick friction sending a wave of lust through her body.

"I'd hate to see you out of control then," she said, panting as they parted. "I'm not sure I could take it."

He chuckled, the sound void of warmth. "Perhaps not." He tightened his hold on her and repositioned them so that they were on their sides with him behind her. "Then again...I might be able to do good things with my loss of control."

He cupped her breast with one hand, turned her face toward him with the other and kissed her lips. She could feel his erection, hard and hot against her back.

He took his hand from her breast and positioned himself at the entrance to her body, testing her before sliding in deep. She let her head fall back against him, tasting him as deeply as she could in her current position.

His hand drifted between her thighs, stroking her clit as he thrust inside of her. He held her to him, his arm tight over her chest, his breath hot on her neck as he whispered dark, sensual words in her ear.

Alex liked to talk dirty. And he did it so well. Telling her how good she felt and all the things he wanted to do with her, in explicit detail.

She was hot all over, pleasure coiling low and tight inside of her, breathing a near impossibility.

"Come for me," he said. "You wanted to. Now you have my permission."

It shouldn't have been sexy. But the words, low and husky and so commanding, pushed her over the edge. A hoarse cry escaped her lips as he thrust into her one last time, pleasure pounding through her like a wave, enhanced by the pulse of his shaft as he found his own release.

She lay back against him, breathing hard, her body tingling with pleasure, her lungs burning. Her heart was pounding hard, and it hurt. Because it felt heavy, swollen. She couldn't begin to put a name to what it was, only that it made her feel happy and desperately sad at the same time.

She wanted him. In every way. Wanted to have this, to keep him with her. And she knew that it wasn't going to happen. She'd refused him. And he was young. He would meet someone new. He would make a family with her. He would do this with her.

And she could only think of one thing to say.

"I'll marry you, Alex."

CHAPTER TEN

ALEX WAS SURE that he hadn't heard her correctly. He was having a hard time hearing at all, since his blood was still roaring through his ears and his heartbeat was louder in his head than any sound in the room.

And yet he had heard it.

She had agreed to marry him.

And for some reason, instead of feeling like all the pieces were falling into place, he felt a bit like he was falling apart.

"I am glad to hear that, Rachel," he said.

"It seems like a weird conversation to have right now."

"No, I think a man should be flattered if a woman decides, after sex, that she will in fact marry him. Better than last time. After which you told me you didn't want to talk about it and stormed off."

She cleared her throat. "Um…it's just…all very confusing."

He shifted, holding her soft, curvy body against his. He put his hand on her stomach, as he'd done that night two weeks ago. It was still flat. No sign yet of the baby she carried. If it weren't for the scan earlier, he would hardly believe she was pregnant.

"And now it isn't? What changed your mind?"

"If I say the orgasm will you run away?"

He could have laughed at her candor—if his chest didn't feel like it had a pile of bricks on it. "No."

"Well, it wasn't that. Not really. But it is partly this. I can't imagine trying to raise a child with you. Seeing you. And having it not be like this and I thought… I just thought, and I'll be perfectly honest with you, how if I didn't marry you there would be other women. That you might have a child with someone else. I don't want that, Alex. Which brings me to the next part—if you marry me, I'm the only woman you get."

Her demand warmed him in a strange way. That she could be jealous. That she would want to ensure only she had him. "That's just fine with me."

"Really?"

"Yes. I have no desire to ever make you feel used. And it's not just because of your past, but because of mine. Of my mother's."

"You loved her, didn't you?" she asked.

Her words hit like an arrow. "Yes," he said. "She was my mother."

"But a lot of people would be angry with their mothers for putting them in that position."

"She was a victim, Rachel. Nothing more. Sad and utterly pathetic, and I do not have it in me to be angry with her. No one on all the earth loved her but me, and I am happy to be the one who did. The one who does." The words stuck in his throat, a note of sadness in them that he despised. Still the boy who longed for her love. The boy who'd never really had it.

"My mother… When she found out about the video—" she let out a shaking breath "—my dad had to tell her because it cost so much to pay off Colin. Mind you, they had a lot of money and she never would have noticed, but he felt like it was right. She was so ashamed of me. She'd taught me better, not to let men talk me into things. Never drink, never smoke, never tarnish our reputation. She'd told me to save my virtue. And I didn't, in her eyes. I embarrassed the whole family, ruined myself forever, and it would have all been avoided if I had just been…"

"More like her." He felt a lead weight settle in his stomach. So very strange, but he felt for her. Felt her pain. Just as he felt her pleasure when they made love.

"Yes. But you…you remember your mother's flaws and you love her."

"I do," he said, his throat tightening.

"I love mine, but sometimes I think remembering her as anything but perfect, the way everyone else seems to remember her, is an insult to her memory. I'm the only one who had that relationship with her. It's almost like I knew someone different."

"They're your memories, Rachel. They aren't wrong. And you have a right to feel upset about them."

"You're better than a therapist, Alex. Of course, while dealing with all of these old issues you're giving me a set of new ones. Also, you've given me a lot of issues in general."

"Have I?" he asked. Her joke, which he was sure was only partly a joke, made him feel unspeakably tired. Made him feel like he was ruining something wonderful.

"Nothing serious," she said.

"No, just a baby and a husband. I'm not giving you anything too serious."

"Hey, one day at a time, right?"

"So your solution is not to think about it?"

"No, I think about it. Okay, I don't really. But I am right now. I did earlier."

"That was the source of your breakdown."

"I'm afraid. Because I know how badly even a good person can hurt their child. I'm afraid that I'm really not good enough. I'm afraid that I can't do it."

"You have to get some confidence," he said. "Because I was raised in a brothel and drug house and I'm pretty sure you're our child's best chance at normal."

"I don't know about that."

"You're as normal as they're going to get, anyway."

"Love fixes a lot of things," she said. "Look at how you feel about your mother."

"Love one way isn't enough," he said, his voice rough, the words he hated to voice more than anything out there in the open now.

"Of course she loved you, Alex," she said. "She probably just had a hard time showing it. Like my mother."

But his mother's words rang in his ears. The last words she'd ever spoken to him.

You ruined all of this for me! I kept you all this time for him! And now you've taken him from me. He's the only thing I love. He's the only reason I kept you all this time! Because I knew then he would let us stay! And now he wants me to go. I have nothing left!

Me, mama. You have me.

I don't want you, stupid boy! I never did. I would rather die than be without him.

"I'm sure that's all it was," he said, the words hollow, the vision of his mother making good on her threat fresh in his mind. "Everything will be fine."

And he knew he didn't believe any of what he'd just said.

She had to call home. It had been nearly two months since her aborted wedding, and still no one knew about her engagement to Alex, about the baby.

Ajax and Leah had gone through a lot of drama, which had resulted in Ajax calling her. That had been awkward.

But he'd only wanted to talk about Leah.

He loved her, which made Rachel feel good. About everything. Because Ajax and Leah were meant to be together, and now, now that Ajax had been able to confess his love, they were together.

And they were going to have a much better marriage than he and Rachel would have ever had.

So great for them, but now she had to cross the hurdle of her and Alex. Hiding out in his house. Taking occasional trips to Cannes together to check in on the expanding boutique.

The good thing was, it was successful, and Alana was considering opening up a second location. And Alex was advising Rachel on investing so she was looking into other businesses, as well. She was becoming a regular venture capitalist.

It was something she had a knack for, and she had the trust fund to start up. Plus it kept her mind off all the reality she had crushing down on her. And oh man, there was a lot of reality.

For starters, she was growing some real, serious feelings for Alex, and that was hard to deal with. It was scary, especially when so much about their future felt scary. Then there was the fact that no one knew what was going on. The fact that she would have to share.

Then there was the wedding business.

Another big wedding. Just a couple months after she'd ditched the original one. The whole thing made her feel a little weird.

Or a lot weird.

Still, she had a phone call to make.

She pulled up Leah's number in her contacts and pressed Call, taking a deep breath and sitting down on the couch.

"Hi, Leah," she said when her sister picked up.

"Rachel! I haven't talked to you in…too long."

"I know. I'm sorry, but I'm sort of working my stuff out, and I didn't really want to interrupt you working your stuff out."

Leah sighed. "Yes, there was stuff. It's good now, though. I love him, Rachel," there was a slight pause, "and that's partly why we haven't been as close as we should have been these past few years. Because I always loved him. That's my fault, not yours. It's hard to be close to someone when they have the man that you love."

"You loved him?"

"Always," she heard a catch in her sister's voice. "I've always loved him."

A tear slid down Rachel's cheek. It was so easy to cry these days. "I'm so glad you married him, Leah, because I didn't love him. I never did. And if I'd had any idea that you did...I would never have put us all through this."

"It worked out. More than worked out. I'm so happy with him."

"I'm just... I'm glad. I'm so glad."

"Okay, now you have to tell me about Alex, because I've been worried about you. We've been worried about you. Ajax, too."

Rachel smiled. "Yes, he would be. Of course."

"And Alex...he's Alexios Christofides."

Rachel hesitated. "He is."

"Did you know?"

She swallowed. "Not at first. But I did when I ran out of the wedding. I mean, that's the thing that I sort of need to tell you all." There was no easy or painless way to say it. So she just soldiered on. "I'm pregnant. Alex and I are having a baby."

"Oh... Oh, my gosh. I don't know what to say. I'll make you a candy bouquet for your shower."

Rachel laughed. "Oh, wow. Candy bouquet. Thank you. I don't...I don't think I want a shower, actually. I think I'm going crazy."

"Why?"

"Because it's not... He doesn't... He wants to marry me because of the baby. I said yes. I finally said yes because he's the father of my child and there's no other man I want to marry. So yes seemed like the thing to say. But now I've said it and it just feels... I'm scared. About all of it. Having a husband who doesn't love me. Having a baby when I can't remember the last time I held one."

"I can...see where that would be terrifying."

"Right?"

"And I know what it's like to marry a man knowing he doesn't love you. To have him look at you and know...and know it's not you he wants."

"Oh, Leah..."

Her sister paused for a moment. "If you don't want to marry him just come home."

"I think I do. Want to, I mean. I think I need to."

"Because of the baby? You don't, Rachel. We would all support you. You know that."

"I know," she looked down at her hands. Except she didn't know that. One more step out of line and she was finished. She was very likely finished already. "I do know that. I need to for me. Because as much as sometimes I feel like I don't know what I'm doing with him, I know I wouldn't be happy without him."

"That's the worst. I totally know how you feel."

"Ajax?"

"It's all good now," Leah said, sighing, "but at first... yeah. I had to make a choice. Did I want to be with him, even knowing that it wasn't going to be ideal, or did I want to be without him."

"And obviously you chose to be with him."

"Yes, and it worked out. But it doesn't always."

"I know that."

It was weird taking advice from her younger sister, but she badly needed it in a lot of ways. Because Leah was the authority on it, after all.

"I know you know, but someone has to say it. Just in case it got knocked out of your head by Alex's sweet, sweet loving, which, I'm assuming, is what drew you to him in the first place."

Rachel couldn't hold in the borderline hysterical giggle that bubbled up into her throat. "There is that. But you know…there was something else. From that first moment, there was something else."

She wasn't sure exactly what the something else was. And she was very sure she didn't want to know. Though she had a suspicion.

And like almost everything else involving Alex, it was the most exhilarating, terrifying thing she'd ever experienced.

"You love him," Leah said, in the knowing tone of someone who had been afflicted by the same thing.

Her heart sank, and a burst of joy popped inside of her at the same time. It was terrifying. And wonderful. And horrible. Suddenly it was like the walls had come down, and there was no New Rachel or Old Rachel or Rachel With the Walls of Steel Behind her Heart. There was just Rachel.

Rachel Holt, who loved Alexios Christofides more than anything. No matter what.

"Yes. I do. I love him."

"Hello, darling."

Alex walked into his bedroom, well, the bedroom he usually shared with Rachel, and stopped. She was standing there in nothing but a short lace nightgown, her expression nothing short of seductive.

"To what do I owe the pleasure?" he asked, undoing the top button on his shirt. He'd been conducting most of his business via Skype for the past couple of months, when possible, so even though he didn't leave the house, the video chats made it so he still had to dress up.

But he wasn't wearing a tie in his own home.

"Of what?"

"The seduction. Because that's clearly what's going on here."

"I told them. My sister, my father. About the baby."

He paused, squeezing tight on the button he'd been about to push through its hole, the blunt plastic edge biting into his finger. "And?" If they'd hurt her…if they'd said anything to her to make her feel like she'd dishonored them in some way…he feared his actions would be less than noble. Possibly less than legal.

Because Rachel was *his*. And no one was ever to hurt her.

"They were…surprisingly calm. But I think relieved because I explained why I did what I did. I mean, it's awkward having to say to your dad 'I met a man and I was overcome by attraction to him' but I managed. To be honest, I think he preferred it to 'Dad, I put the car in a ditch while I was drunk' or 'Dad, I gave some guy a BJ and he videoed it.'"

"I'm certain he did," Alex said, his throat tightening. He wished he could get his hands on the scumbag who'd done that to her, that was for sure.

But then he really *would* do something illegal.

"Yes, well…I feel like I can't worry anymore. About letting everyone down."

"Is that right?"

"Yes. I need to worry about me. And us. And the baby."

"Not so scared of the baby now?"

"Oh, no, terrified. Utterly terrified. But I feel a little bit more like I can breathe again. Actually, I feel like I can breathe for the first time in a long time. Because… Because if I really am okay—as I am, I mean—if I really don't just have to be a clone of my mother? Well then maybe I can focus on being a good mom because I won't be working so hard to keep my façade in place. Does that make sense?"

"As much sense as any of our issues make."

She laughed, so sweet and beautiful in a lace nightgown, blond hair spilling over her shoulder, a seductress. Giggling. There was something so perfect about it. Something so free.

He wanted to capture it, hold it forever.

But then…then she wouldn't be so free. Then she would be in a cage fashioned by him, rather than one built by Ajax or her father.

The thought unsettled him. And yet it didn't diminish the need to hold her to him. To claim her.

"I guess that's true. I mean, none of it makes sense to anyone but ourselves, right? In here, though—" she put her hand on her chest "—it's been the realest thing in my life. Trying to deal with that critical voice, trying to best it, to be better. While secretly dying of boredom. I haven't even been able to be myself inside. I haven't even had emotions that belonged to me because…I was told so often I was wrong."

"I let go of emotions because it was the safest thing." Except he hadn't let go of them, not truly. Anger, rage and that impotent longing of a young boy for some kind of affection…it was all still there. And he hated it.

Silence fell between them, the light in her eyes changed. She looked fierce. Angry. "You should never have been subjected to the things you saw. It makes me want… I want to go back and protect you and I can't. It hurts to know that I can't."

He felt like she'd reached straight into his chest, taken his heart in hand and squeezed tight. "I do not need protection."

"Maybe not now, but you did. I wish someone had done that. I think it's wonderful that you love your mother, in part because no one else did. But I wish, so much, that someone had stepped in and protected you."

"You…care about me, Rachel?" he asked. They were hard words to speak, and yet it was harder not to say them at all.

"More than that, Alex. I actually… I wanted to say—and I was going to wait until I had you all sex-sleepy, but—I love you."

Alex froze. "Say it again," he said.

They were the words he'd wanted from someone all of his life. Words that had never, not once, been directed at him. Not by his mother, not by his father, not by a lover. Now that he'd heard them he wasn't sure what they made him feel. It was something deep. Something hot and cold. Something that made him want to pick up a car and throw it into the ocean, or just pull her into his arms and kiss the hell out of her.

Instead he waited, frozen inside. Even his heart had stopped. He was certain of it. Because he couldn't breathe, not at all. The world might even have stopped turning, just waiting, on pause, for the next words that might come out of her mouth.

"I love you."

She said it again, and it all started again. His heart pounding hard, causing a shift inside of him that made him feel like he was crumbling, each beat compromising the stone walls built up around him for protection.

He couldn't think of what to say. Or what to do. And that rarely happened to him. When it did, though, Rachel Holt seemed to be the cause of it.

"Why?" he asked.

He hadn't meant to ask the question, but the minute he did, he realized it was the word pounding through his head. Because it made no sense. Because no one ever had. And he wasn't sure why this beautiful, incredible, ridiculous woman who seemed to light the world on fire when she smiled, would feel that way about him.

Not when he'd used her. Seduced her for revenge.

"Because I cried in front of you. I want to seduce you, and be seduced by you, and say dirty words for you. I can sing off-key in front of you. And you don't judge me, or look down on me. You accept me that way, and I feel like I can accept myself that way, too."

"Is that all?"

"Achieving self-acceptance isn't big enough for you? Fine, that's not all. The sex is good, too."

He didn't feel torn about what to do anymore. He crossed the room and pulled her into his arms, kissed her until neither of them could breathe. Until his lungs were filled with her. Her scent. Everything.

Until his blood was so hot with lust he thought it would scald him inside.

He felt wild. Out of control. Unequipped to accept what she'd given him and unable to return it.

But one thing he knew for certain was that she was his. Love would make her stay. He'd truly done it. He had made her love him, and now that she did, she wouldn't go.

He'd seen that growing up. He'd seen it with his parents. She would stay. His Rachel would stay.

He felt the need, the intense, unendurable need, to brand her and solidify that bond. Vows. Legal documents. He needed that marriage now. Needed to strengthen his hold.

Because she couldn't leave him. He couldn't lose her.

"Show me how much you love me," he said, his voice a growl he didn't recognize. The feelings in him utterly foreign, something that was also beyond his recognition.

"How?" she asked.

"Show me," he repeated, feeling desperate.

She pushed his shirt from his shoulders and kissed his neck, his chest, her fingers working at his belt, and the closure of his pants. Soon she had him naked, soft hands skimming over his body.

He just wanted to drown in it all. In her touch. In the moment. To never have this moment pass so that he could live in it forever.

But it was already passing, changing. And he couldn't regret it because of where it put her hands. The way that she cupped him. Squeezed him. Teased him. Her hands sure on his body, her lips soft, her tongue hot and slick.

She moved away from him and a kick of fire burst through him. Her not touching him was going to drive him insane, but he had to let her stop, because he had to see what she would do next.

He was powerless to do anything but watch her.

She took the lacy nightie off, exposed her body to him slowly. And in her eyes he saw her emotions. She wasn't pausing to make jokes. Wasn't interrupting the moment, the tension, with a comment.

It was the first time she'd simply met his eyes and taken her clothes off.

He was glad she wasn't talking because he was sure he couldn't have spoken if he'd wanted to.

She returned to him, full breasts pressed against his chest. He pushed his thigh between her legs, felt her wetness on his skin. Her desire for him.

He put his hand on her lower back and rocked against her. Her head fell back, lush lips parted, a sweet sound of pleasure escaping her mouth.

He cupped her chin, held her steady, bending to kiss her as he continued to move, continued to pleasure her.

He would give her this. Not love. But this. And she loved him, so it would be enough. Because she'd said he made her feel good. And that the sex mattered.

He would show her just how good he could make her feel. Just how much sex mattered. He would give her everything that he had to give. Everything.

He slipped his thigh from between her legs and walked her backward to the bed, pushing her down so that her butt was resting on the mattress and her legs were over the side.

"I need you," he said, the words painful to force out. "You don't know how much."

He hooked her legs over his hips and thrust into her. Her back bowed off of the bed, her round breasts thrust into prominence. He took one nipple in his mouth and sucked it in deep, until she moaned. Until he felt her internal muscles tighten around his cock.

She grabbed his shoulders, her fingernails digging into his back as he thrust into her, hard and uncontrolled. He didn't have it in him to be measured. Wasn't able to take his time.

He needed her too badly. He needed to keep going, to run from the roar of blood in his ears, to push toward a release that would make the ache in his chest go away. That would make everything clear and calm. An orgasm to purge him of all the longing and pain that were weighing him down.

He gripped her hips, tugged her to meet his body with each movement. He couldn't get enough. He didn't think he ever would. He'd never felt like this before. Like he was unraveling at the seams.

She cried out her release and it pushed him over the edge, his climax engulfing him as he leaned forward, hands braced on the mattress on either side of her as he shuddered out his release. His muscles were shaking, his body trembling. It had been the most intense sexual experience of his life.

But it hadn't taken away the weight. The pain. The confusion.

But it had left one thing deeply rooted in him. She was his.

He moved away from her, lay down on the bed beside her, his legs off the edge like hers, as he tried to catch his breath.

"I will plan the wedding for as soon as it can possibly be coordinated," he said.

"What?"

He looked over at her, watched her breathe hard. It was rewarding when she was topless. And yes, even with all of his inner turmoil he appreciated the gentle motion of her breasts. Or perhaps, because of the inner turmoil, he appreciated it particularly.

"The wedding. There is no point in putting it off. Your pregnancy is going to become evident soon." He put his hands on her stomach, it was a bit fuller than the last time he'd done that. A strange surge of pride shot through him, one he didn't want to examine too closely.

"Maybe I like the maternity bride look."

"Do you really?"

"No."

"Okay then, since you've made the decision. And since you love me...I see no reason to put it off."

"You're high-handed."

"Yes."

"You're the younger man. You're supposed to be my boy toy, but you're all alpha and stuff."

He rolled over and put his hands on either side of her, his chest touching her breasts. "You like it."

"I do."

"So don't complain. We will be married within the next couple of weeks. I'll hire a coordinator and you can submit all of your ideas to her."

"Well, that sounds...easy."

His heart seized up. "You have a complaint about it?"

"No, not at all. Not really. I already kind of just planned a wedding. For the entire last year of my life. And I ended up not going to it, so this is kind of... I don't really care what this one is like."

That hit him wrong. "You don't care what your wedding to me is like after you spent a year planning your wedding to Ajax?"

"Don't be that way. That's not what I meant. I'm just… The wedding itself doesn't seem that important, all things considered. It's what it means. It's what our lives will be after."

"And what will our lives be?" he asked.

"We'll be together."

Yes, she was his. She truly was. His muscles relaxed, his entire body getting the post-sex languor he'd been anticipating.

There was nothing to worry about. He'd been in control of all of this, from beginning to end. Sure, things had gone off the rails a couple of times, but in the end, he was getting what he wanted.

In the end, he was getting her.

CHAPTER ELEVEN

IT WAS HER WEDDING DAY. Again. How strange to have a second wedding day in just over three months' time.

But here it was, that time again.

She smoothed down the front of her wedding gown and looked in the mirror. It was a simple chiffon dress that flowed over her stomach. Her stomach which was not up to being squeezed into anything fitted. It was tender and she was already having to ponder maternity pants.

The difference this time was that she loved Alex, and she knew that being with him was what she wanted. No, he didn't exactly love her back. Or at least he hadn't said that he did, but she wanted to be with him.

And as Leah had said, sometimes you had to make choices.

They were marrying on Alex's island, rather than her father's estate. It made her feel sort of wistful and sad. Actually, the fact that her family didn't feel as much a part of it as her first wedding made her feel wistful and sad.

And Alana hadn't been able to make it, either, because she was attending a movie premiere in the States, as the guest of a celebrity she'd dressed. Great for her, but sucky for Rachel. Not that she would have ever asked her friend to give the opportunity up.

It was for their business, after all. It was Alana's career, but it was Rachel's investment. It was a nice distraction, really. Knowing that was going on halfway around the world.

Weddings, whether she loved the groom or not, made her nervous, it turned out.

But at least she knew she wasn't going to have any past lovers crashing this one.

She took a deep breath and picked up her bouquet. No, nothing was going to mess this day up. And then she and Alex would be married and the rest would...just work itself out.

She ignored the leaded weight in her stomach that said otherwise.

Alex looked out his office window, down to the grounds below. Chairs had been set up by the water, and people were already filling them. An arch was in place at the altar. There were flowers all over it. It looked a little bit fussy for Rachel. Not any more indicative of who she was than the first wedding had been. But then, she'd said she didn't want to be part of the planning, so the coordinator had taken the helm.

She'd have to be happy with what she got, because she was the one who'd made the decision not to make decisions. And he shouldn't care if it "looked like Rachel" or not.

It didn't matter. All that mattered was that the wedding happened, and quickly.

It was all about to begin. It was, in fact, time for him to head down there. He opened the door and started down the hall.

This was it. The final piece to keep her with him.

Because she made him feel new. She made him feel like he was something other than his blood. She made him feel like a man who was loved.

And he needed that. He needed her.

He went down the stairs and threw open the front doors

of the mansion, striding down the walk and toward the beach. He made his way down the aisle, ignoring the head turns of the guests. People he didn't know. All of them were Rachel's guests.

Because no one was here for him. He brought nothing in terms of connections or friendships to the marriage. He had no friends. He had clients. He had enemies.

He had Rachel.

And that was all.

She had friends. She had a family who loved her. A lightness to her, that even with her pain and vulnerability seemed to shine through.

She was good. And that wasn't something that could ever be said about him. There was a reason no one had ever loved him.

A large rock settled in the pit of his stomach, growing heavier with each step. Making each step a challenge.

And as he stood there at the head of the aisle he scanned the crowd, and his eyes met with those of Ajax Kouros. Sitting in the front row, by himself, his wife likely gone to wait with Rachel.

Ajax looked very like their father. It was a blessing in Alex's mind that he himself did not.

He wondered if they looked very much like brothers to a disinterested party. He thought he might see some similarities. The same jaw. The same chin. Ajax's eyes were dark, while Alex had his mother's eyes.

But as he stood there, a sick, horrifying feeling washed over him.

Ajax had their father's eyes. Their father's love. A love that Alex shouldn't have wanted, but that he did want. Because he'd wanted someone's love. Anyone's. And Ajax had the love of so many. His wife, his father-in-law. He had a family. He had friends.

Alex was alone.

Alex, who was conniving to trap this woman, this loving beautiful woman, into a marriage that would offer her so very little.

The way his father had kept his mother in the compound. On a leash made of drug addiction and a terrifying, unhealthy love.

Alex was no better. He had used a woman's body in a bid for revenge. And now he was tying her to him when he knew he could give her nothing but his anger, nothing but the black, wicked blood in his veins.

As he saw Ajax sitting there, Alex saw nothing more than a man. Not a monster, not a demon.

No, the demon had never been in Ajax. The demon had always been within Alex. It was the thing he feared, the thing he hated. And it was him.

That was why no one loved him. Why his mother had taken death over a life with him.

It had always been him.

He took a step back down the aisle. And another. And another, until he was walking away from the beach, back toward the house.

He stumbled inside and closed both doors behind him. And he looked up and saw Rachel coming down the stairs, with her sister, Leah, trailing behind, helping with the train of her gown.

She looked like an angel. All in white, the gentle rounding of her stomach highlighted by the soft, flowing fabric. Her blond hair was in loose curls, a halo of gold that made him ache. Made him hate the man who had taken her innocence and used it in his games.

Hate himself. More than he had ever hated Ajax. More than he had ever hated his father.

More even than he'd hated his mother as he'd watched the blood drain from her body, as he'd watched her steal herself from him.

Why would anyone ever love the creature he was? His mother must have known, even then, what he was. She had been able to love Kouklakis, but she'd never been able to love Alex. Had killed herself rather than face life away from the compound. Rather than face a life with just herself and Alex.

If there was anything more telling he didn't know what it was.

I would have saved you. He'd wept that day. So hard. Without hope. *I would have given you everything.*

It had never mattered. Because he wasn't enough. He would never be enough.

"I need to talk to you," he said.

She blinked. "What about? Is everything okay?"

"We need to talk, Rachel."

"Okay. Leah, can you give us a moment?"

Her sister nodded and headed back up the stairs, giving him a hard look that let him know she wasn't overly impressed with him. Well, she would be even less impressed after this. But it didn't matter. None of it mattered. He had just had a look in the mirror for the first time, so to speak, and he'd confirmed what the deep, clawing ache in him had always hinted at. No one hated him more than he did.

Except for maybe Rachel. But she would hate him even more if he subjected her to a lifetime of him.

"I am not marrying you," he said.

"What?"

"You heard me," he said. "I am not marrying you today."

"Why the hell not? I have a dress. We have a marriage license. What in the world is wrong with you?"

"I have something I haven't told you. Something that will change the way you feel about me. It could do nothing else."

"What you just said has already started to change the way I feel about you."

"Understandably. And you need to hear this, too."

She threw her bouquet down on the step, spreading her arms wide then slapping her hands down on her hips before crossing her arms beneath her breasts. "All right. Great. Let's hear it. Come at me, bro."

"Ajax Kouros is my brother."

That shocked her silent for a moment. "Say what now?"

"Ajax is my brother. Nikola Kouklakis is our father. We have different mothers. I have never known who Ajax's mother was, and doubtless he didn't, either."

"Why didn't he ever say anything?"

"He doesn't know. I didn't find out until years after he'd left. He left when I was eight or so, he would have been… sixteen. He never knew." He swallowed hard. "When I was fourteen I was told who my father was, by Nikola himself. I was terrified, because I'd always been afraid of him. I'd always hated him. But, he said, with Ajax gone I would have to be his heir. And then… And then he told my mother it was time for her to go because she'd outlived her usefulness there. She'd provided me with…a mother's presence, I suppose, and now he no longer needed her."

Alex paused, his heart pounding, his body shaking. He'd never told anyone about this. Had never spoken these words out loud. He hated this memory. Hated this moment in his life. Hated this truth.

"He told me how he had cared for me. How he had forbidden any of the men in the house from touching me, both when I was a boy and when I was older. How he made sure I got fed. I always thought it was her. But it wasn't. It was never her." He took a deep breath, afraid he might throw up. "I ran out of his office. I wanted nothing to do with him. With all of it. She was so angry with me. She told me…I'd ruined everything. She never wanted me. It was all for him. Everything she'd done for me had always been for him. I told her I would take care of her. I told her it would be all right." Everything turned cold inside of him.

"What happened?"

"She killed herself. In front of me. Because that future, the end of everything, was preferable to a life spent with me."

Rachel's eyes widened with horror, her view of life already darker because of him. Because of his truth. He was ruining her already. "Alex...I don't... She had problems, Alex, it wasn't you."

"It wasn't me? She loved Nikola Kouklakis, and she couldn't love me. Everyone loves Ajax. He came out of it...fine, just fine. I'm broken. Everything in me is...I am his son. All of the bad things are in me. I cause...destruction just by breathing."

"Based on what? The actions of a woman who was too broken to know real love when she saw it?"

"It's more than that. It was what my father did—he broke people. And I do it without even trying."

"That's not true. I don't care who your father is. I don't care who your brother is. What your last name is, where you came from. If your mother was a prostitute or if *you* were a prostitute. I don't care. I know who you are now. I love who you are now."

Her words burned in him, a sharp, almost refreshing sting. Antiseptic on an infection. He couldn't accept it.

"You can't."

"I do. Alex, I love you. Your mother had a lot of things going wrong inside of her, and they weren't your fault. She couldn't love you, but that was because of her own heart, not yours. There's nothing broken in you. You're a good man, and I love you more than anything."

He couldn't take it. He couldn't. All he could see was his mother's face, so haunted and broken at the thought of life away from the compound. Life with him. And then lifeless and blank as she lay there dying.

He thought of Ajax, who'd transcended it all. Who'd

found love and a life away from all of that while it all seemed to cling to Alex like creeping slime.

It would never come clean. Ever. He would only poison her, too.

"Don't be so naive," he said. "It was always going to happen this way. I didn't want Holt. I never did. I wanted nothing less than your and Ajax's utter humiliation. His leaving is part of what triggered my mother's suicide. He escaped with no consequences, and it was my job to give them to him. Now he has married your sister, the second-choice bride, because he couldn't have you. And then, I'll make you available to him now that it's too late. Now that you're having my child and he's married to someone else. Don't you see how well you were played? Don't bore me with any more of your declarations of love. They mean nothing, because you don't know who I am. You can't love me," he said, the words choked. Because he knew they were true. She couldn't love him. "You can't love someone you've never truly met."

She raised a shaking hand, a tear sliding down her cheek. "Then it's nice to meet you, Alexios Christofides."

He extended his hand and closed his fingers around hers. She was so soft and perfect he wanted to weep. This was the last time he would ever touch her. She would leave him now, and it would be for the best. For her. For their child.

Their child should never know him. Everyone was better off without him in their lives.

"I'm sure you don't mean that," he said.

"No," she said, "actually it really sucks."

"Shall you tell them all it's off, or shall I?"

"I will," she said. "I can handle this myself. You've done enough. I'll send for my things later. We won't speak again. I assume you don't want anything to do with the baby?"

His heart screamed. And he ignored it. "No."

"Great. Great, that's just...great. If you come near my family again, I will castrate you, do you understand? Because you've liberated me, and I will not go quietly. I won't let you get away with *any*thing. If you show up in our circles, I swear I will have your head on a pike. You thought your revenge on Ajax was bad? Just wait." She walked past him and pushed the doors open, the sun illuminating her. She was no innocent angel now, she was an avenging angel. Caught on fire with the light of the sun. He had to look away. He closed his eyes and he could still see the impression of her behind his lids, burned there. He had a feeling when he closed his eyes it would always be her that he saw.

The doors closed. And he heard footsteps behind him.

And then something cold hit him in the back of the head. He turned and saw Rachel's bouquet on the floor behind him, damaged now beyond recognition from hitting him. And then there was Leah, standing there looking like she was ready to castrate him in the real world.

"It's not over for you," she said. "Not by a long shot. When Ajax finds out what you did..."

"Let him come. Tell him to bring all the firepower he has. I don't have anything to lose." Not now. There was nothing left for him to lose that had any value or meaning. He'd just cut ties with the woman he... The woman who meant more to him than he could ever say. And his child. A child he would never see. Never touch. Never hold.

It's for the best. It's for them.

He walked past Leah and went up the stairs, back toward his office. He walked into the room and slammed the door behind him, locking it.

He looked out the window and saw Rachel standing beneath the awful, ugly arch all alone, explaining to all those people that there would be no wedding.

Then the world tilted beneath his feet and he found himself on the floor, on his knees. He couldn't breathe. He didn't think he would ever be able to get back up because he was crushed under the weight of it all.

He had lost her. And it was only just now that he knew he loved her.

But it didn't matter. Loving her wasn't a kindness if it meant binding her to a man who was poison down to his core. Everything he'd done to her since they'd met… He was so bitter and twisted and she deserved more than that.

She deserved everything. She deserved someone who wasn't broken.

He'd been broken from day one. Somehow…fundamentally in a way that made it so no one could ever love him. A tool for his father, a pawn for his mother.

She deserved better. Rachel deserved everything.

Hot, wet tears were on his cheeks. He didn't care. He had caused Rachel's first tears in years, and now she had caused his.

A fitting end.

Theos, but he hated that it was the end.

CHAPTER TWELVE

"MORE CANDY, RACH?"

"Yes," Rachel moaned, holding her hand out to her sister and letting her fill it with little chocolate shoes.

She was lying on the couch in Leah and Ajax's penthouse in New York, where she'd been staying for almost two weeks trying to heal from a completely shattered heart.

She'd had a rage high for the first week. A total, deep and loathing hatred for Alex that made it impossible to cry over losing him. Made it impossible to think about their last conversation in any detail that went beyond the horrible, awful things he'd said.

She'd let it fuel her, carry her, keep her from collapsing.

In front of the wedding guests, she'd done nothing to take the high road. She'd done nothing to keep them from finding out what a hideous worm he was. She had been angry.

A mother bear, feeling rage for her cub. He'd said he didn't want to see their baby. His rejection of her was bad enough, but that rejection had opened up a well of maternal emotion she'd never felt before. It had given her a momentary, honest-to-God, deep desire to hurt him. Physically. To hit him with something hard. Repeatedly.

But now the rage had subsided. And parts of their final conversation were replaying, sections she'd tried to forget. His revelations about himself. How he felt about himself.

That his mother had killed herself rather than be with him. That the underlying tone of it all was that he was a man who felt unworthy. Of everything. He had hated Ajax, because Ajax had the one thing Alex didn't think he would ever truly be able to have.

Love.

And for some reason, her love hadn't been enough. Or, maybe, he was just afraid that her loving him would hurt her somehow.

And that made it harder to rage at him.

Something had happened at the wedding. She was getting surer and surer about it. But until she figured out what to do, until she had the energy to tell Ajax that Alex was his half brother, she was going to lie around and eat more of her sister's candy.

"You okay?" Leah asked.

"No. I don't know if I'll ever be okay. I think I love him still."

"Yeah, I know how that goes. It's the worst."

Ajax walked into the room then, looking handsome, as he always did, in dark slacks and a white shirt. She could see it now that she looked at him—his vague resemblance to Alex. But he didn't have those eyes. Or that wicked sparkle.

Well, he did a little bit when he looked at Leah. And that made her happy. Because this was, by far, the happiest and most carefree she'd ever seen Ajax.

"What's the worst?"

"*You* were," Leah said. "You know, when we almost got divorced."

"Yes," he agreed, his tone overly serious. Typical Ajax. "I was the worst."

"Hey, Jax," Rachel said.

"Yes?"

"Did you say anything to Alex at the wedding?"

"No," he said, frowning. "But you have to know, I never trusted him. I'm sadly not surprised by the outcome."

"But I am. I spent months with him. I was… He was my lover. We're having a baby. I felt like I knew him better than that and none of this really makes sense to me. So maybe he was that good of an actor. Or maybe there's a little more to all of this than it seems. So I thought I would ask."

"He didn't say anything. He…looked at me, but unless he has some sort of unrequited longing for *me,* I don't see how that's valid."

"Yeah, that's not his problem. Trust me."

She laid her head back down on the couch.

"Another movie?" Leah asked, her tone pitying. Good. Rachel deserved pity. She was alone. And with child.

"Yes. And cake. Is there cake?"

Ajax gave her a look that mirrored his wife's. "I'll get you some."

She took a deep breath and stared at the TV, not really absorbing what was happening. She was miserable. She was in love with a man who didn't deserve her love. A man who needed love like a flower in the desert needed water.

Alex was drying up inside. Dying. And he wouldn't get help. He was determined to embrace all that anger and push everyone who cared about him away.

And yeah, he'd really messed her life up and it felt horrible. But he'd done some good things for her, too. And maybe rather than melting she should try and remember it.

She put her thumbnail in her mouth and started gnawing on it. "You know, Leah, I don't really want to watch a movie."

"Do you still want cake?"

"Yes, oh yes, I want cake."

"Good. Cake you shall have. What do you want to do?"

"Talk maybe?" Rachel asked. "I think…I think we spent too many years not talking."

"My fault, Rach, really," Leah said, frowning. "I was lusting after your man. That made things hard."

Rachel shook her head. "Sure, there's that. But…if we were closer, wouldn't I have noticed?"

"I don't know. But I'm not in the mood to blame you for it. Anyway, Ajax and I worked out. So it's fine."

"I was supposed to make sure I wasn't a bad influence on you, you know."

Leah laughed. "You? A bad influence on me? You're so sweet and…sweet. And I'm not. Never have been."

"Well, I wasn't for a while." She thought of drunk nights in clubs. Driving too fast. "I was a pretty big partier for a while. But you were a kid. You wouldn't remember. Dad was always on hand to cover up for me. Mom was always on hand to disapprove."

"You had a secret life!" Leah said. "I'm truly impressed."

"Don't be. I was an idiot. See, this is why they wouldn't let me tell you! You're easily influenced."

Leah laughed again and Rachel couldn't help laughing in return, until she was almost breathless with it, the need for something other than sadness and anger taking over and hijacking her emotions until she was almost in hysterics.

Leah followed suit until they'd both slid to the floor, laughing. Over nothing and everything. Rachel wiped her eyes and looked at her sister, another giggle surging through her.

"I guess if I can laugh for a little bit… Hey, it's a start, right?"

Leah cleared her throat. "Yeah, Rach, it's a start."

Rachel smiled, a feeble attempt. Yes, it was a start. But she had a feeling the road to getting over Alex was longer than she could possibly imagine. She had a feeling the wounds would get cut open, raw and fresh again every time she looked at their child.

Especially if that child ended up with those beautiful, wicked blue eyes...

She hoped they wouldn't. And she hoped they would.

For now she would take a couple hours of distraction. Her broken heart was going to take a long time to heal, but at least she had her sister. She could spend some time with Leah, doing her best to forget her pain.

Alex hated having to get dressed. Lying around his apartment, drunk and in his underwear, was about his speed lately. But here he was, shaven and showered and wearing a suit. Because he had business to see to.

Business that involved a man who would very likely kill him on sight. But at least then there would be an end to the hell he'd been living in. Death seemed like a pretty serene option, all things considered.

"Mr. Christofides." A man who was sitting behind a large desk in the ante chamber of Ajax's office addressed him. "Mr. Kouros will see you now."

"Oh, good. I don't suppose you know whether or not he's in a killing mood."

"At work, Mr. Kouros usually is."

"Well," Alex said. "Damn." He forced a smile and walked toward Ajax's office.

"Alexios," Ajax said when he walked in. "I was surprised when you said you wanted to see me, and you made it necessary for me to dodge my wife's questions because I didn't want to upset her.... Anyway, you've put me in a bad frame of mind already so if I were you, I would speak quickly. If you've come to make some sort of arch villain monologue, you're wasting your breath. I don't care."

"Hardly. I thought you might want an explanation. For everything. For why I was after your company. After you."

"You were at the compound, weren't you?" Ajax asked, sounding weary, a tired look in his eyes. Yes, Ajax felt very much like Alex did about the whole business. "In which case I understand why you might have reason to dislike me. However, you should know, and I say this not to try and absolve me of sins past but so you have some closure, I was the key part in having my father's crime ring brought down."

"I am happy to know that. To know that you were a part of stopping it. I wish I had been."

"You're young," Ajax said. "It took me time and age to do the right thing."

"I was at the compound," Alex said. "But that's not really the important part of the story. The important part is what I found out after you left."

"And what is that?"

"Your father had another son."

"That doesn't surprise me," Ajax said, though some of the color had leeched from his face.

"Well, it did me. Knocked me on my ass, in fact."

"And why," Ajax asked, his voice rough, "is that?"

"Because it's me."

Ajax paused. "You're sure?"

"*He* was. Enough to offer me his twisted kingdom when he passed, so I would say he was fairly certain."

"And that's why you've been after me? And my business?"

"I guess so. I was just blindly angry for the most part. How could you have escaped? And you had this perfect life. A family who loved you. A woman who loved you. And I had nothing. So I wanted to take it from you. Bring you down to the level I felt you should be on. The level I was on. But now I've hurt Rachel. And I'm not happy about that. I've also had a look at my own bloody self and let me tell you, it's not pretty. Rachel aside, I needed to speak with you about this. To let you know I'm not going to be pulling any more stupid stunts in the name of revenge. I'm tired. Tired of this. Tired of all the ugliness inside of me. I just want to let it go. And I'll never be the man she needs, I understand that. But I want to feel something other than... all of this anger."

Ajax grabbed a cup on his desk and straightened it, his knuckles white, because he was squeezing it too hard. "You understand, though, that because of Rachel, our relationship can't be..."

"I do. I don't think I'm the sort of man who has close family ties. At least, I don't know how."

Ajax looked down, his expression blank. "I am glad you told me."

"No more secrets. That old bastard doesn't get to have any of us anymore. No more power."

Ajax nodded slowly. "Yes. No more."

"Thank you for seeing me. This is hardly the kind of news you leave on a voice mail."

"Indeed not."

"I'll see myself out." He turned his back on Ajax and headed toward the door. Then paused, before turning back around. "Ajax, can I ask you a question?"

"Anything."

"How did you do it?"

"What?"

"How did you let it all go? How did you... How did you find it in you to ask a woman to tie herself to you for the rest of your life knowing where you came from? Knowing what's inside of us...how do you ever truly believe you'll rise above it? How can you ever believe you...deserve it when... No one has ever loved me. And I figure there's a reason for that. How do I tell her I want it when I'm afraid it will destroy her?"

Ajax was silent for a long moment, his dark brows drawn together, his focus out the window. Finally he spoke.

"Whatever our father said, whatever words he might have used, in my mind there was one thing he never did. One thing that he was missing that, had it ever taken root, would have changed the way he lived his life."

"And what is that?"

"He didn't have love, Alex. I think that's the thing that changes us. It's the only thing, at least in my experience, that can banish the monster."

"Love is what made my mother kill herself," he said, his tone flat.

"What do drugs do to you, Alex?" Ajax asked.

"They're addicting."

"They make you feel things," Ajax said, meeting his eyes now. "They make you need them. But you don't love them. They ruin you, make you think you can't live without them. Addiction isn't love. Which do you think your mother really felt for our father?"

Alex almost choked. "I…I'm not certain."

"Love is the thing that changed me," he said. "From Joseph Holt, to Leah, love was what truly healed me. It wasn't money or power. It wasn't vengeance. I didn't deserve it, either, but when I accepted it…that was when I changed. Think about it. Think about what love really is."

"I will."

"I hope you do. I really mean that."

Alex walked out of the office and down the hall, numb as he stepped into the elevator. Love. He was in love. A lot of good it did anyone.

He let out a roar of frustration and hit his fist on the button panel of the elevator, swearing roundly when it lit up several more buttons that signaled he would be taking a few more stops than he wanted on his way down to the lobby.

He leaned back against the wall, his heart pounding so hard he thought he might be having a medical crisis.

Was it so simple? Just loving and trusting that love

would make it all right? That it would bring forgiveness for everything that had happened? That it would stay? Could he truly have it, finally? The thing he'd craved his whole life?

Was it so simple to just say, "I love you, and I'm a mess and you deserve better? But please love me anyway"?

Would love light the way and keep him from going back into darkness? Would it make him a man deserving of that perfect, beautiful woman?

He pictured Rachel's face. Her beautiful smile.

Yes. Dammit. Yes. It would be enough.

He would never be worthy of her. Ever. She deserved a man who was whole. A man who would never dream of seducing a woman to get revenge on an enemy.

He wasn't that man. But he would let her cry, let her feel, and he would listen to her sing off key. He would hold her close at night and he would change their baby's diapers, because he wanted to be with her, and to share everything in this new, amazing life that he'd never once imagined he might have.

The elevator stopped. Fifth floor, of all the stupid things.

Then it stopped again.

And again.

Finally he was at the lobby, and by the time he was out on the street, he was sprinting. He was going to get Rachel. And he would beg if he had to.

But he had to take a chance.

Otherwise, all of his houses, his island, every cent of his money, wouldn't matter. Gaining all the world didn't matter if he lost the one thing he truly needed.

"Where is your dang ice cream, Leah Kouros?" Rachel muttered, rummaging through the freezer. "Why does your stupid candy company not make ice cream?" Unfortunately, her sister was down at Leah's Lollies today and was not in the apartment to hear Rachel cursing her name over her lack of frozen treats.

The front door opened and Rachel straightened. Maybe her angry mutterings had summoned Leah.

"I'm in here! How is it you have all this sugar and no ice cream? Answer me that."

"I don't know."

She turned around and dropped the spoon she was holding. It clattered on the tile floor, the sound ringing through the silence.

"Alex," she breathed. She felt like she was going to fall over. Felt like she'd been sucker punched. She hadn't seen him in nearly a month.

She put her hand on her stomach. Five months in and she was definitely looking her condition these days. "What are you doing here?"

His eyes dropped to where her hand was resting, a strange expression on his face. "Your body has changed."

"I'm pregnant," she said, "that happens. Especially since things are going well."

"They are?"

"Yes."

He let out a long breath. "I am relieved to hear it. Beyond relieved."

"I didn't think you cared."

"I'm a liar," he said, his words rough. "I care…Rachel, I mourn the changes in your body that I've missed. That it happened without me here. I should have been with you all this time. I should have been here. I should have…I should have been your husband."

"It was your choice not to be," she said, bending to pick up the spoon. "You were the one who walked back down the aisle and left me to explain why there wasn't going to be a wedding." She slammed the spoon onto the counter. "You made that decision. And then you told me it was your plan from the beginning. To use me. Because I was just a pawn to you. A pawn like I've been to everyone else. Except this was worse because with you I was honest. I told you how I felt, Alex. I showed you who I was and you took that and you abused it."

"I lied to you," he said.

"You what?"

"I lied to you because… Rachel, I got up there and I looked out in the crowd and I saw Ajax sitting there. And I knew…I hated him so much because of who I thought he was, but for some reason being up there and seeing him, my brother, made me see myself clearly for the first time. I hated what I saw. A man who used you. A man who contrived to trap you with him, even when he knew he had no hope of ever being all the things you deserved. A man who would hold you to him using any means, even your love against you. I saw myself in that moment. I saw that I was a man whose own mother couldn't love him and that she was right not to. I—" He took a deep, shaking breath. "I couldn't allow you to go through with it. Because everything that happened between us was so manipulated by me. Including your feelings. You say you love me…but that's because you're having my baby. Because you spent a few idyllic months on a private island with me."

She was sure that the room was spinning.

"Alex," she said, her voice trembling. "Are you telling me that you were acting the whole time we were on your island?"

"No," he said, "but it was so engineered, all of it. You felt trapped. I made you decide to come with me so quickly I…"

"Do you trust that I'm a smart woman, Alex?"

"Yes."

"Great. No hesitation even. So do you trust me to know my own heart?"

"Why? I sure as hell didn't know mine."

She frowned. "Poor man. Well, I know mine. I loved you. So much. And when you pushed me away...when you told me you never even wanted to see our child? I wanted to hit you with something heavy and blunt."

"That seems fair."

"I gave you my love, you...you jerk. I gave you everything. I would have—"

He pulled her into his arms and kissed her, deep, desperate. And she didn't push him away. Didn't fight him. Because she was too hungry for him. Angry, yes, she was angry. But she'd never stopped wanting him. She'd never stopped loving him.

He pushed her back up against the fridge, his hands on her waist as he kissed her. She wrapped her arms around his neck, tears streaming down her cheeks as she poured all of her hurt, all of her weeks of anguish into the kiss.

"Okay," she said, gasping for air, "we have to talk and not just have sex. The sex is fine between us. *We,* on the other hand, have problems."

"True," he said, breathing heavy.

"So why are you here?"

"Because I have spent the past month drunk and miserable. Because every time I think about never seeing our baby I want to die. And every time I think about never seeing you again...Rachel, I start praying for death to come quickly."

"Why?" she asked, her throat tight.

"Because I love you. With every broken, miserable piece of myself. And I realized this weeks ago but I kept thinking it wasn't fair to ask you to spend the rest of your life with a man like me. But...but I have to be selfish now and ask that you do. That you spend your life with me because if you don't then I'm not sure what my life means at all."

"Alex, why do you think you aren't worthy of me?" she asked. "I am... I'm not perfect. And I've fought to get to the place where I could say that and just be okay with it.

I'm not perfect. I've made mistakes. And I'll make more mistakes. I don't want a perfect man because I could never live up to those standards."

"I would give you a better man," he said.

"With all due respect," she said, "you're a jackass."

"Why?"

"Because I know what I need. I know who I am. I don't need better. There isn't better for me. For me, there's you. That's it. Alex, the moment I saw you I fell in love with you. Is that crazy? I would have thought it was crazy until five months ago when I saw you standing there, on a yacht. And you made me want things I never knew I needed."

He pulled her to him, crushed her against him, taking a sharp breath. "Me, too. Rachel, that was the moment for me, too. When you were standing there looking at me, so awkward and obviously attracted."

"Hey."

"It's true. You were. But it's okay, because that was the moment. When I knew that I needed you. I didn't know then that I needed you forever. I thought an hour. A night. I didn't know how much it would change me. But it did. And then you kept changing me these last few months. Even when you weren't there. Even when all that was left of you was how much I missed you."

"Why did it take you so long?" she asked. "Why did it take this long for you to know you loved me?"

"It was the one thing I'd never had before. I loved my mother, Rachel, but I didn't know what it was like to have her love me back. Not really. I didn't understand love as a living thing. As something that could give. She took. I gave. And in the end I was left devastated because…she ended herself rather than be with me, Rachel."

"Alex…it wasn't you. She had so many problems, honey, but they weren't you."

"I know," he said. "I do now."

"I'm glad. I'm so glad."

"Ajax helped me with that. He…he made me see. I hated him for what he had, without trying to find out why he'd been able to get it. Love. And when he told me that…it all made sense. Love is different than I thought. The love I feel for you has demanded that I change, that I give, that I sacrifice. And it makes me burn. Makes me want. Makes me hurt. Makes me so happy I… It's happiness like I never thought I could have. I had no idea what to call it, no idea what to do with it. It's love. And it's the most terrifying, wonderful thing I've ever felt before. And if you feel the same for me, if you want to do this—for the rest of our lives, knowing who I am, where I've been—then I can only be grateful. I can only try and become the man I think you deserve."

"Just be the man you are, Alex. That's the beginning and end of all I want from you. Because it's the freedom you gave to me. And it might seem like a small thing but… Alex, don't you see that you set me free? I feel like I was trapped in someone else's body, desperately trying to live up to an ideal I didn't even want to be and afraid I was failing miserably at it. You are… You are amazing. What you've given me is amazing. There is no better man to me than the man who simply wants me. As I am."

"I am that man," he said, kissing her cheek. "That I promise you. I want all that you are. All that you will be. We'll both keep changing, but we'll change together. Whatever life has in store for us, I think we can meet the challenge head on, as long as we're together."

"I think so, too."

"So, when are we getting married?"

"Not for at least six months," she said.

"What?"

"I need time to plan it. I love you and this is for life. And you love me. This is a real wedding. Also, I *don't* dig the pregnant bride look, I've decided."

"You're going to make me wait, Rachel?"

She smiled, her heart swelling. "For some things, Alex. Not for others."

A long time later they lay in her bed, limbs tangled, breathing hard. She was tracing his biceps with her fingertips, a smile on his lips. Yes, she loved this man, more than anything. Their start had been rocky at best, but they had forever ahead of them.

"You know, if we can make it through all of this, I think we can make it through anything," she said.

"I agree."

"Just as long as we're honest, from now on."

"In the interest of honesty then," he said, "may I say, I think your breasts have gotten larger. I like it."

"Wow. Romantic."

"Maybe not. But honest."

"Appreciated."

Suddenly, she flashed back to that evening they'd eaten pizza in a fancy hotel in Cannes. When he'd talked about happy endings. "You got your happy ending," she whispered.

He kissed her on the cheek and she could have sworn he left a teardrop behind. "It's not over yet."

"No," she said, snuggling closer. "It's not. And thank God for that."

"Yes. I get a whole lifetime with you. With ups and downs, with every emotion. But it will be with you."

She kissed his forearm and held his arms more tightly to her. "That's much better than any old happy ending."

He sighed, and she could hear the smile in his voice. "I agree, *agape*. I agree."

EPILOGUE

"I̲ᴛ ᴡᴀs ᴀ ʙᴇᴀᴜᴛɪꜰᴜʟ ᴡᴇᴅᴅɪɴɢ," Leah said.

"And it *happened*," Ajax added.

"You're sensitive as a blunt instrument," Leah said, beaming at her husband.

Ajax shrugged and turned to face Alex, who was standing there in a tux, his tie undone, his two-month-old son wrapped in a blanket and nestled in his arms. "Am I insensitive, little brother?"

Alex shrugged and looked down at his son. Liam didn't care that his parents had just gotten married. He was at peace, as he always was, everything in his world right. Alex's heart swelled with love, with pride. That his son had so much family to love him. That his life would be so much more beautiful than his or Ajax's had ever been.

That he would never know the harsh criticism of a mother the way that Rachel had. Never feel like he had to rebel or close up completely, rather than being who he wanted. That he would never wonder if he was loved at all. They told him every day.

"Yes, but it's part of your charm."

"Don't encourage him, Alex," Leah said.

Rachel returned then, on her father's arm. They had just finished their dance and Rachel was beaming. Her figure was still fuller than it had been before giving birth, her cheeks round. He loved it.

"How nice," Joseph Holt said, "to have all my children, and my grandson together in one place."

Alex's heart tightened as he looked around at his family. "Yes, it is," he said.

"Do you mind if I steal my grandson for a moment?" Joseph asked. "I'll trade you your bride for him."

"A deal."

He handed Liam to the older man, then took Rachel's hand, leading her out to the lit dance floor. "This wedding was much more you, wasn't it?" he asked, looking around at the simple décor. At the bright colors. It exuded joy. Just like his wife.

"Yes," she said. "But then, with you, I am much more me."

He kissed her nose. "I'm glad. I'm certainly a better me. It's amazing what can happen inside you when you start to understand love. When you replace anger with it."

"I'm glad you did, Alex, because you have so much love to give."

"I've never been as happy as I am today," he said, his wife in his arms, his son nearby.

"Then we have a new goal," she said.

"What is that?"

"To find even greater happiness, every day. As long as we live."

"With you, Rachel, that won't be hard at all."

* * * * *

ONE NIGHT
SCANDAL

JOANNE ROCK

To Mandy Lawler for all of your help and guidance. Thank you!

One

Hannah Ryder scavenged her last scrap of patience as the film director she despised zoomed in on her for a close-up shot. The bright lights were making her sweat right through the thick layers of makeup. Itchy, dry hay poked her bare skin. She lay smothered in the stuff on the floor of an old barn temporarily transformed into a movie set. The scene called for her character to fall through the loft in the middle of hooking up with a cowboy; thankfully, the stunt had been pulled off by someone else paid to do that sort of thing.

Now, Hannah had to perform the sequence following the fall after her cowboy lover had abandoned her. Her face was covered in cosmetics to look like blood and bruises. All of which was fine, if she hadn't been in her third hour of shooting reaction shots while drowning in hay that made her eyes water and her skin burn. Her makeup had to be retouched every twenty minutes to keep it from sliding off, and the flesh-toned bodysuit she wore under the hay didn't protect her in the least. Horses flanked her on either side, their impatient hooves providing a frame for the scene, according to the sadist in charge. What if one of the animals decided he was tired of a sneezing woman writhing on the floor of his barn?

Twice she was sure a spider or some other creepy-crawly had skittered up her bare leg, and a cramp knotted her calf.

She would have walked off the production days ago if she hadn't wrangled a part in this film for a very specific reason. She needed evidence of the director's sexual harassment of women on the set to help avenge what he'd done to Hannah's younger sister a year ago.

The incident had transformed nineteen-year-old Hope from a bright-eyed aspiring writer, with a coveted job as script reader and assistant to director Antonio Ventura, into a quiet shell of her former self. Hope now worked in retail, content to unlock dressing rooms for customers since it was a job that surrounded her with women. Hope didn't write anymore, and she showed no desire to leave the house for any reason but work. She startled at noises and cried when she thought Hannah couldn't hear.

The change broke Hannah's heart, and months of therapy hadn't seemed to help her sister. Hope refused to file charges, insisting she'd destroyed evidence after the fact because of conflicted feelings, and she didn't want to bring a case she couldn't prove. When months of gentle encouragement and outright coercing had proven ineffective, Hannah had taken a new approach. She'd spend time on one of the bastard's sets to see for herself if he was victimizing other females.

So far all she'd learned was that every single person who worked on his film *Winning the West* thought he was a tyrant and a megalomaniac. But she had no evidence that he was locking vulnerable women in closets to forcibly grope them the way he'd done to Hope.

Just the thought of it steeled Hannah to withstand the cramp throbbing in her calf for another minute while the camera closed in on her tears. She'd been Hope's guardian ever since her sister had moved to Los Angeles to be with Hannah. Their parents had never been much help since their high-powered attorney father had walked out on their mother long ago—taking his family fortune with him. As for their mom, she'd done her best to raise Hope and Hannah, but she'd made no secret of the fact that she was "done" once Hope had turned eighteen.

Hannah would never be "done." And she would fight for her sister even if Hope refused to fight for herself.

A horse snorted and tossed his head, a hoof momentarily pinning Hannah's hair to the floor before shifting away again. She couldn't smother her gasp, ruining the take.

But before the director could explode in rage, a tall, broad-shouldered cowboy stepped into view, casting a long shadow onto the floor where Hannah lay.

"Ventura, I need to take my horses," the man demanded, his tone uncompromising as he confronted the despot in charge of the shoot. "Now."

A murmur of collective surprise—quickly stifled—stirred the production team ringing the small barn.

Hannah stretched quietly in the sea of hay, wanting a better look at the cowboy whose arrival had diverted the director's ire away from her. The newcomer blocked the lights, providing a welcome moment of coolness for her itchy skin.

She craned her neck to see around a horse's knee.

And got an eyeful of feminine fantasy material in denim and worn boots. The hard-muscled cowboy stood a head taller than the director, his biceps straining the fabric of a gray cotton T-shirt as he reached to stroke a hand over a horse's nose.

The man's features remained in shadow, thanks to the set of his dark Stetson, but the sharp edge of his jaw and the hint of dark hair curling along the collar of his shirt were enough to make any woman long to see more. For now, Hannah settled on taking in the rest of him, from where his shirt tapered along his back, from his formidable shoulders down to his lean hips.

"You are ruining my shot," Antonio Ventura snapped at the cowboy, his dark eyes narrowing. "Now, thanks to you, I'll need the animals even longer."

The fury brewing under the quiet words made the sweat on Hannah's back turn cold and clammy, worry chilling her.

"Whether you need them or not isn't my concern." The cowboy took the reins of the one closest to him. "They're not professional actors, and they're done for today."

Hannah would have admired anyone unafraid to stand up to a bully like Ventura. But she took a special brand of pleasure in seeing this big, strong guy put the smarmy brute in his place.

"As you can see—" Ventura enunciated each word as if the cowboy was a simpleton "—they are hardly being asked to act. They're standing in the middle of a barn, just the same as they will be when you take them with you. I suggest you consult your boss before you make a choice that will cost you your job."

The dirtbag. How unfair to threaten the man's livelihood. Hannah was already mentally composing a letter to the ranch owner in the cowboy's defense.

"My choice is made." The sexy stranger gathered the other horse's reins in the opposite hand. "And since we're making suggestions, I'm going to advise you to take better care of your actors." The man's gaze fell to where Hannah sprawled in the hay. "Do you need a hand, miss?"

His eyes were blue. Clear sky blue.

Wide-open spaces, Wyoming blue.

Hannah wanted to fall right into them.

Except, she realized, she couldn't afford to thumb her nose at Antonio Ventura before she'd gathered evidence of his criminal behavior. With more than a little regret, she shook her head, a stray piece of hay poking the back of her neck as she moved.

"No. Thank you." She risked a small smile at the horseman, hoping the director was too busy seething to notice.

When she gave her boss a quick glance, he seemed to be pounding out digits on his cell phone as he paced away from the camera equipment.

"You're going to regret this show of stupidity," Ventura threatened between clenched teeth.

Around him, the production team buzzed with new life, sensing they were done shooting for the day as the cowboy guided the animals out of the wide barn door. The night air rushed in.

Hannah watched his retreat, her breath stuck in her chest as she followed his long-legged stride, an easy swagger that made her wish she would have accepted his hand when he'd offered it. What might it have been like to touch him? To keep that blue gaze trained on her a little longer?

Behind her, the wardrobe stylist cleared her throat. "Um… Hannah?"

Swiveling away from the enticing view, Hannah glanced up to find the young woman holding a robe in her hands.

"Sorry. I must have gotten distracted." She grinned conspiratorially as a production assistant shut off the hottest of the set lights nearby. Hannah didn't want anyone to see how stressed this shoot was making her. Her muscles were cramped from the strain and tension of working with her sister's molester as much as from holding the twisted pose for hours.

"Didn't we all?" the stylist, Callie, agreed. Her high, dark ponytail swung in front of her narrow shoulders as she leaned down to wrap the cover-up around Hannah, shielding her in the flesh-tone bodysuit. "I think I forgot to breathe just now."

The woman's vanilla fragrance settled around Hannah as surely as the silk dressing robe. Hannah's itchiness eased immediately from the fresh air, the cooler temperature without the set lights and being free of the hay.

She was stepping into the leather slides that Callie had brought out for her when, from the other side of a rolling cart stuffed full of electronics, a series of shouted curse words blistered her ears. Callie flinched and Hannah's eye started to twitch while they listened to the director yell at whoever was on the other end of the call.

Hannah needed to get away from here. Three hours

of dealing with that man was more than she could take. She had a private cabin on-site at the Creek Spill Ranch, close to where filming took place each day. No need to stay here and listen to Ventura's tirade when her accommodations were within walking distance.

"Callie, I think I'm going to call it a night and head back to my room," she said softly, tying the belt on her robe. It was blousy and pretty enough to pass for a caftan. "I can take off my own makeup."

"I don't blame you," the stylist muttered under her breath, her gaze moving furtively toward their boss. He looked ready to pop the vein in his temple, his face contorting as he shouted about ineptitude in his staff and incompetence in the production company. "Take some makeup wipes," Callie said, passing a small plastic packet before gesturing to Hannah's face. "You don't want anyone to think you've just been in a horrible accident."

Hannah was already peeling out a damp cloth from the pack. "You're a lifesaver." Retrieving her purse from behind one of the barn columns, she headed for the door, leather shoes slapping the bottoms of her sockless feet. "Thanks, Callie. I'll see you in the morning."

Part of her wondered if she should stick around a little longer while Ventura was all worked up and angry in case the bad mood brought his criminal tendencies out. But she was physically exhausted, her spirit weary after the trying day. She needed to de-stress tonight. Conserve some energy for tomorrow.

She'd take a soak in the tub. Maybe try some yoga. The porch of her tiny, secluded cabin had a beautiful view during the day. And at night, she could see stars for miles. But as she hurried across the ranch to indulge herself in some much needed downtime, an image of her sister's tearful face returned to chastise her.

Back home, Hope wouldn't be de-stressing tonight. And she sure as hell wasn't taking any feminine joy from admiring the way a brash cowboy looked in jeans.

Priorities quickly realigning, Hannah double-timed her steps toward the cabin. She'd shower, change and sneak back over to the barn to see what else Antonio the Ass got up to tonight. Because nothing would give her more pleasure than putting him behind bars.

Not even a diversion with the sexy horseman who'd rescued her from the shoot today.

Brock McNeill couldn't get the actress out of his mind.

Two hours after he'd removed his quarter horses from the set of the idiot director who was making life at the Creek Spill Ranch a living hell, Brock was more than a little preoccupied by thoughts of the curvy blonde covered in hay. There was something about her that appealed to him—something far more intriguing than her looks, although she was easy enough on the eyes even with the heavy blue and purple makeup meant to look like bruising.

Now, riding back through a rocky ravine to his place after a late consultation with the vet, he found his thoughts on the woman instead of on his sick filly. As the head of the quarter horse breeding and development program at the Creek Spill Ranch, Brock realized his focus needed to be on his portion of the family business now more than ever. The film shoot required it. But the timing couldn't be worse.

Because the McNeills were bracing for a scandal. A

blackmailer had promised to reveal his stepmother's secrets to the world two days from now. The whole Wyoming branch of the family was on high alert, waiting for the other shoe to drop because they'd decided not to meet the blackmailer's demands.

To make matters worse, Brock's stepmother was still recovering from a suspicious hiking accident that had put her in a coma right around the time the blackmailer had first surfaced. It was a mess.

Brock needed to protect his family. As the youngest of his brothers, born after the twins Carson and Cody, Brock had always been the odd-man out. It had been easy to fly under the radar in a big family, but the time had come to step up and prove himself now that his brothers needed to focus on their own relationships. Plus, his half sisters were particularly vulnerable because the blackmailer was hinting that their mother's marriage to Donovan McNeill was invalid. Brock needed to be there for his father, his stepmother and his half sisters.

So it was flat-out wrong for him to spend his mental energy thinking about the hay-strewn beauty on the floor of his barn. Dating an actress would only draw more attention to his family when they needed to lay low. It was bad enough his sister Scarlett had been in the tabloids recently for dating one of the film's lead actors. Besides, thinking about the woman so much was crazy, considering he'd watched her work for only half an hour or so. He'd shown up at the shoot because the ranch hands tasked with bringing the horses back hadn't returned. Brock didn't appreciate having his generosity with his animals taken advantage of, so he'd gone to set Antonio Ventura straight for himself. And gotten distracted by the woman crying tears that looked all too real.

She'd only been performing, of course. He understood that. But the tears had gone right through him, the pain in her eyes so damn convincing it had been tough to look away. What made a woman choose a job so emotionally demanding? Because—performing or not—tears like that didn't manufacture themselves. They came from somewhere deep. Seeing her like that had felt oddly intimate.

Maybe that's all it was. He'd caught a stranger in a moment that felt intensely private. Except then she'd smiled at him. The smallest twitch of her lips when their eyes met, and there'd been…

Heat.

He would swear from the look in her eyes that he hadn't been the only one feeling a connection.

Brock decided to circle back to the remote barn Ventura had been shooting in earlier, wanting to see for himself that the guy had released the actress from work. Because while Brock had succeeded in freeing his horses from the director's overheated set, he hadn't gotten the satisfaction of witnessing the blonde walk away from the grueling job. He'd rather lift bales of hay all day than spend an hour sitting in the stuff half-naked the way she had. Especially the old, super-dry variety the director had spread all over the floor. Brock guessed a bed of nails would be more comfortable.

Reining in his horse as he reached the old, small barn that had outlived its usefulness on the ranch, Brock could see filming must have stopped since the lights were dim. A damn good thing, since he would be well within his rights as a partial owner of the McNeill lands to shut down filming if the company violated safety protocols, a clause his brother Carson had the sense to put into the contract with the production company. And working in a wood barn with hot lights and overheated straw that could catch fire veered into dangerous terrain.

The doors were open, though, inviting bears and other foragers inside. Someone must have forgotten to close up for the night. Swinging down from the mare, he patted her neck before dropping the reins and stepping through the open wood doors.

A dark shadow emerged from behind a support post.

A curvy shadow.

Brock recognized the shape of her instantly. No mean feat considering she'd been mostly covered in straw the last time he'd seen her. Apparently, his imagination had done a highly accurate job of filling in the blanks where her body was concerned.

She was dressed in dark leggings and a dark T-shirt. Her platinum hair was tucked under a ball cap with the logo of a West Coast football team. With her face scrubbed clean of makeup, he could see her features better now. The long lashes over her eyes. A few freckles on her nose. Then the stubborn tilt to her chin as she spotted him just inside the barn entrance.

"I sure hope you're off the clock at this hour." Brock summoned a smile, not wanting to startle her when she was alone. "I came back to make sure your director knew enough to call it a day."

She shuffled from one tennis shoe to the other. Was she uneasy?

He took a side step to lean against the barn door, giving her plenty of space to walk out if she chose.

She folded her arms across her chest and stood her ground instead.

"So did I," she claimed, although something vaguely

defensive about the way she said it made him wonder if that was true. "I walked off the set right after you did, but the director was in such a snit, I returned because I wanted to make sure he wasn't—" She took a deep breath and let it back out as if she was forcing herself to relax. "Taking advantage of people with no seniority."

Her careful phrasing seemed…off. She was hiding something, and it didn't take a genius to see she was uncomfortable. Maybe he'd been mistaken about the attraction before. Maybe it had been all one-sided.

"That would make him even more of an ass than I already took him for," Brock said, preparing to leave, in case he was responsible for her feeling uneasy. Straightening from the doorframe, he was about to wish her a good-night when her laugh caught him off guard.

A genuine laugh. Surprise music to his ears.

Some of his tension eased as hers seemed to.

"He is. Most definitely." She took a step closer to him, a smile lighting up her whole face, transforming her from pretty to breathtaking. "I'm Hannah Ryder, by the way."

She extended her hand. Anticipation flared at the thought of touching her.

"Brock. It's a pleasure to meet you." He closed his fingers around hers and squeezed.

His hand lingered for a moment longer than necessary. Just enough to see her notice. Her pupils widened a fraction. She sucked in a quick breath.

Gratified that he hadn't been wrong about their first meeting—that there was something hot lurking just beneath the surface between them—he released her hand. He hadn't mentioned his last name, preferring to avoid the inevitable interest in his well-known, wealthy family.

Brock had been down that road before, not realizing a woman he'd cared about had been after him only for the connections. The McNeill lifestyle. Or, more accurately, other McNeills' lifestyle. Brock preferred hard work to jet-setting, no matter that his hotel magnate grandfather owned five-star resorts all over the world.

Hannah Ryder toyed with the long sleeve of her dark T-shirt, pulling it over one hand, but not before he spotted a silver ring in the shape of an eternity knot. "I didn't get the chance to thank you earlier, but your entrance was very well timed."

There was a slight husky quality to her voice that made the sound as warm and inviting as a whiskey shot. She was about a head shorter than him, maybe a little more. Dressed all in black with her hair tucked under the cap, she looked like she was trying to avoid recognition. Maybe movie people dressed that way all the time when they were off duty. She seemed about as far from his idea of a diva as possible.

"I regret that I didn't intervene sooner, before my horse's hoof landed on your hair." He couldn't act fast enough after that, knowing the animals were too restless to be trusted standing so close to her head. "You barely even winced."

She shrugged, shaking her head. "But it was enough to ruin another shot. Whenever I let my guard down even a little bit, then it's my fault the whole crew gets stuck on the set for an extra hour."

"Is it always like this?" He realized her eyes were gray under the shadow of her cap's brim.

She smelled good, too. Like soap and wildflowers. He caught the hint of fragrance as she played with the shirtsleeve, the fabric rubbing against her skin.

"Not at all. My job is usually pretty fun, but this film is making me see how much the director has to do with setting a production's tone."

Brock wanted to ask her more, but he guessed she must be tired after her long day.

"Well, for what it's worth, I thought you were fantastic today." He wasn't overstating it, or flattering her. She was good. "In fact, it was because I was so caught up in watching your performance that I didn't interrupt filming sooner."

She laughed again, the sound another surprise shot of pure adrenaline.

"So I have no one to blame but myself for my hair getting stepped on? Are you saying that if I'd been a worse actress, you would have come to the rescue sooner?" Her gray eyes twinkled with mischief.

Teasing. Flirtation.

It wasn't a game Brock had played often. Or well. But he damned well recognized it.

He let the new flames crackle through him, stunned that a total stranger could stir that level of heat. What was it about her? Hell, what was it about *him* that he was letting it draw him in?

"I'm saying, Hannah Ryder, that you're not an easy woman to look away from."

He heard the tone of his voice; it was all wrong for the moment. It brought the teasing and flirtation to a halt. The air around them changed. Got warmer.

He saw the confusion in her gaze. The surprise. A whole host of emotions flickered through her expression that he couldn't identify.

But there was one that he knew. Because he felt it, too.

Desire.

It pulsed in the charged air like a heartbeat. For a moment, he thought she might take a step toward him. Until, outside the barn, his horse whinnied softly. Breaking the moment and the connection.

"I'd better go." She tucked her chin into her chest and stalked past him. Out of the barn and into the night.

Brock watched her leave, knowing he shouldn't follow. She'd made her decision. He respected that. He needed to check in with his family anyhow, see if their investigator had any updates on the blackmailer.

Taking a deep, cooling breath to ward off the lingering hunger for Hannah, he took his time stepping outside. Only to glimpse her outline in the moonlight.

With her back to him, he could see clearly the image that she'd pulled up on her phone.

A map of the ranch.

Walking directions back to her cabin.

Brock closed his eyes for a long moment, knowing he couldn't let her make the long trek in the dark by herself. He would give his own sisters a hard time about navigating those woods on foot alone at night, and they'd been raised here, fully aware of what to look out for. How much did a West Coast visitor understand about the potential dangers of the Wyoming land?

Steeling himself against the inevitable draw of the woman, Brock stepped closer to make an offer that was going to be hell on his restraint.

"How about I give you a ride home?"

Two

The cowboy's voice smoked through her, heating her insides and sending a shiver of awareness over Hannah's skin.

Did she want a ride?

Her subconscious was going to have way too much fun tormenting her with that image in her dreams tonight. For now, she needed to stop fantasizing about sexy Brock, the rancher who turned her inside out with just a handful of words and a smoldering gaze.

Her legs were still unsteady after whatever it was that had passed between them inside the barn. She'd had meaningful relationships in her past. Men she'd loved. And yet no one had ever given her the sizzling shock to the system that she felt from being around this stranger. Swallowing hard, she braced herself as she turned around to refuse his offer.

"That's okay. I don't mind walking." Her voice was soft and breathless when she needed it to be firm and sure. "I, um, could use the fresh air."

She could also use a new libido. One that wasn't quite so susceptible to tall, muscular cowboys. It must be because of all the stress she was under with her sister. She'd latched on to a pleasurable distraction and now she couldn't quite let go.

Brock folded his arms across his impressive chest. God, his arms were amazing, too. She wanted to skim her hands up the triceps and over his shoulders. Instead, she jammed her restless fingers in the back pockets of her jeans along with her phone.

"You'd probably be fine," he acknowledged. "You must have walked over here in the dark in the first place, although the moon was higher at that hour, making the path a lot easier to follow than it will be now."

She had been thinking the same thing since she didn't remember exactly where she'd broken through the brush to find the barn. Nightfall in this part of Wyoming was nothing like it was in Southern California. Here, there was no ambient light of any kind. Just deep blackness and stars.

"I've got my phone," she argued, although she was beginning to wonder what else might be out there in the wilderness surrounding the ranch lands. She'd heard wolves—or some kind of wild dogs—baying in the distance on the walk over here. "The cabin I'm staying in is just through there."

She pointed vaguely, trying to see any kind of trail.

"I'm not sure calling someone will do you any good if you meet up with a bear. Or an elk. Or some other wild animal that wasn't expecting company at this hour."

She didn't want to be foolish. So, in spite of the out-of-control attraction, she figured the best thing to do would be to accept the ride and get home as fast as possible.

And put this encounter out of her mind.

"Is your truck nearby?" she asked, peering around the barn. During the shoot, there'd been a couple of golf carts and two trucks parked there.

A smile curved that hard mouth of his. Nodding, he relaxed his arms and walked past her, close enough for her to feel the warmth of his body, close enough for his sleeve to brush hers.

"My horse is right this way."

"Horse?" Her belly flipped.

Not because she minded riding a horse. Only because it implied a proximity that…

A shiver stole over her skin. Her nerve endings danced in anticipation of touching him. Something her brain knew was a very, very bad idea.

"I—" Her voice wasn't even there. She licked her lips. Tried again. "I'm not sure—"

"You'll be fine," he assured her, holding a hand out for her while he stood next to a dark horse with a glossy coat. "I'll help you up." He flipped the ring for her foot so it was easier for her to see. "Step into the stirrup and you'll be home in no time."

Her heart pounded a chaotic, fast beat. But stalling wasn't going to get her home any faster. She understood that much. Willing herself to remain calm, she stabbed the toe of her tennis shoe through the foothold.

Brock's hands were quick and efficient as he boosted her up onto the saddle. He didn't linger. But he might as well have been massaging her naked body for how her skin reacted under her clothes. Her thigh tingled. Her waist...

She wanted his hands there again. Before she could gather herself or prepare for more, Brock swung up onto the animal behind her. His chest was against her back. Her hips tucked into the cradle of his lap, his strong thighs bracketing hers.

There was no space. No distance. And it felt so good she couldn't have spoken if she'd tried. The only thing she didn't like about it was that she shouldn't like it so damn much.

But there was no chance to protest now as his arm curled around her waist, his hand bracing her protectively against him while he nudged the animal into motion. Hannah sucked in a gasp at the feel of their bodies moving together. In sync. Rubbing together.

It was the most erotic experience of her life, and she hardly knew the man. Keenly aware of his body, Hannah closed her eyes to try to shut out the feel of him...everywhere. But even that proved dangerous, as her mind vividly supplied even more suggestive details. The scent of him—leather and musky aftershave—drifted around her, the warmth of his body a welcome heat on a summer night that had cooled surprisingly fast after sundown. Searching for a fraction of space, she shifted in the saddle as they galloped through trees. Her movement elicited a sharp intake of breath behind her.

It was the first indication Brock might be feeling some of the wayward attraction, too. She wanted to turn around to face him, to see the expression on his face, but his palm was a firm weight against her belly, his fingers a light graze of warmth along the inside of her hip. The barrier of her leggings didn't begin to dull the intimacy of the sensation.

She didn't know how she'd walk away from him at the end of this ride. For that matter, she didn't know how she'd look him in the eye again after this. It was all so very…

Sensual.

Her heart pounded faster than the horse's hooves. She told herself it was because of the incredible stress she'd been under. The frustrated tension of seeing her sister suffer and not being able to help. The unbearable strain of working with a man she despised in order to find evidence of his misdeeds.

All that anxiety had shoved her to a breaking point, leaving her with zero reserves now, when tempted with the heady pleasure of a generous, honorable man's touch. Brock had strode into her world, putting the bully Ventura in his place, and Hannah had been intrigued. Curious. Attracted.

Now, adding to that attraction, the horseback ride tantalized her with needs she normally shoved to the backburner. These were desires she'd ignored easily enough in the past, only indulging them within committed relationships.

Brock's touch teased her with all the ways she'd gone unfulfilled. Because no man had ever ignited the sort of awareness she felt tonight. As if the slightest increase in pressure from his hands would unleash a tide of passion and desire that would completely sweep her away.

Then, suddenly, her cabin was in sight, the tiny pinprick of light from an upstairs window growing as they neared the small structure. She focused on it like a beacon in a dark sea, telling herself this churn of sensual thought would recede once she arrived there.

When Brock leaned back slightly in the saddle, drawing the horse to a halt, Hannah waited for a break in the seductive spell. But even as Brock swung a leg over the saddle and jumped down to the ground, her nerve endings still danced with awareness. Anticipation.

Glancing at him, she met his gaze for a moment, and that only worsened the heat. He reached up to help her dismount, his hands ready to assist her. And she simply fell into his arms. No thought. No planning. She slid down, her body against his in a way that set her on fire. Then she was reaching for him, wrapping her arms around his neck.

Kissing him.

His lips sealed to hers, his arms banding around her back and waist. She dangled in midair for a moment against him, her breasts pressed to the hard wall of his chest. Flames licked over her skin as their mouths fused, tongues tangling. A mindless need roared through her, a hunger to have more of this. More of him.

When he set her on her feet, he edged back to look at her, his breath coming fast.

She knew it was wise of him to separate them. To break the mesmerizing contact. To give them a moment to think about this. But there in the endless dark, with only the horse and the wind as her witnesses, she couldn't scavenge any reason to deny herself this heat. This connection. This kind of intense pleasure she'd never experienced before. Perhaps it was the inky blackness of the night that made it feel surreal, like a dream she didn't want to wake up from.

All Hannah knew was that her body went to his like a magnet drawn to a more powerful one.

A raw sound rose up in his throat as she found his lips and kissed him again. Brock wrapped his hands around her, this time with more intent and purpose. She could feel the difference in how he flexed his fingers against her, the added pressure tantalizing her all the more.

"Hannah." He breathed her name against her mouth. "Are you sure?"

"Positive." She gripped his biceps, wanting him inside where she could take his clothes off.

Straightening, she withdrew the keycard for the door from the small hip pocket sewn into her leggings. Her fingers were unsteady as she slid it through the reader.

"I don't have protection with me, but my house is just through the woods."

"I have something." An old habit inspired by a college friend's pregnancy. A good thing, because she wasn't willing to wait for him to make a trip to his place.

As she pushed open the door, she knew stepping over the threshold was a point of no return. But she had no reservations about this. It was a moment of pleasure in a year of hell. The only things she felt now were hunger and need, the desire for him so stark she couldn't begin to account for it. Her gaze met his in the dim light cast by two cast-iron sconces that flanked the stone fireplace mantel.

Extending her hand to him, she threaded her fingers through his. "Please. Come in."

Something had happened on that shared horseback ride.

A switch had been thrown. A blaze had started, and there was no putting it out now.

Brock told himself he'd given her every out. Every

option of changing her mind. And she'd refused. He couldn't fight himself and her, too. Not when he'd wanted her from the first moment he'd seen her. Not when the stress of being a McNeill was at an all-time high. He felt like the whole damn world around him was poised to collapse when the blackmailer went public.

How could he refuse a night to forget about that, just for a little while, and lose himself in the promise of what Hannah was offering?

So, stepping into her two-bedroom cabin, he closed and locked the door behind him. Gave himself a moment to try to muster some scrap of restraint, if only to ensure they made it to a bed instead of tearing off their clothes in the middle of the living area.

But Hannah was having none of it. With the same certainty she'd shown when she slid off his horse and into his arms, she came to him now. She wrapped her arms around his neck, pressed herself into him. This time, he didn't hold back, allowing the full impact of those sweetly feminine curves to work their seductive magic.

Purely potent. Totally intoxicating.

The chemistry was intense, the heat so strong he thought they might combust right there. He cupped her cheek, angling her chin higher to taste her more thoroughly. She tipped off his Stetson, winging it to an empty ladder-back chair near the door. Her ball cap had already fallen away, her silky blond waves tickling his arm, teasing along his skin.

He walked her backward, toward the dark hallway where the bedrooms were. He'd helped build this place with his brothers long ago—now it was a guest residence for visitors. Hannah let herself be led, moving with him, pausing near the kitchen bar long enough to pluck a leather handbag from the counter. She brought it with them into the darkened bedroom.

He flicked the switch by the door that lit a small gas fireplace on one wall opposite the bed, the low flames the only light in the room as he toed the door closed behind them. Hannah had already peeled off her shirt, and the sight of her creamy skin, breasts cradled in blue lace, nearly undid him.

Pulse thrumming hard, he reached for her, needing his hands on her. Her skin was incredibly soft as he drew her to him, the scent of her—something sweet and heady like orange blossoms—making him desperate to taste her. He kissed his way down her neck, searching for the source of the scent, taking his time on the journey to lick along her collarbone, nip her shoulder and ear.

She gripped the hem of his T-shirt and hauled it up his back and over his head. The pace was too fast but the hunger too keen to slow down as they undressed each other, tasting and touching as they unveiled themselves. Her creamy skin was rosy in the firelight, her hair turning from platinum to strawberry blond as it fell along her shoulder. He slid a finger beneath one bra strap, tugging it off, tracing the scalloped edge of lace before the fabric fell away.

She arched into him, the taut, pebbled peaks of her breasts almost close enough to taste. Bending to take her in his mouth, he circled the tip of one and then the other, unfastening the hook to free her and cupping the soft weights in his hands. Her moan was a sexy siren's song in his ear.

"Please, please, please," she chanted, one hand on his belt, a fingertip tracing the top edge of the leather.

Grazing his abs. Making him impossibly harder.

Torching all restraint.

She took a condom packet from her purse and put it on the bed. He eyed it before helping her with the belt. Quickly his pants were gone, his boots were gone, boxers gone.

His undressing was faster than hers, since she tangled her feet in the leggings while she watched him disrobe, her attention so damn flattering.

Brock lifted her in his arms, skimming off the scrap of blue lace around her hips before he pulled her down to the white duvet with him. She made soft, sexy sounds of approval in his ear as she speared her fingers into his hair and drew him down to kiss her. Shadows flickered across the bed beside them in the firelight, the need for her—for this—ratcheting higher.

He'd never bedded a woman so fast. Never imagined a night like this where desire smoked away reason and sensual hunger roared with predatory demand. But Hannah was right there with him, her hands shifting lower to smooth down his chest, back up his arms. All the while she urged him faster, whispering soft commands to touch her. Taste her.

He couldn't get enough of her.

When she placed the condom packet in his hands, he tore it open like a man who'd been deprived for years. He wanted to take his time. See the way she looked when pleasure overtook her.

But this thing—whatever it was between them—was beyond that. It was a fever in the blood, driving hotter and faster with every breath.

Rolling the condom into place, he met her gaze. Her gray eyes watched him, her lips parted as her breath came in fast pants. He captured her mouth, kissing her as he positioned himself between her thighs. Edged his way inside.

He caught her cry of pleasure before she arched her neck and back. Her nails dug into his shoulders, and her body went still at last. When he started to move, he took his time, building the pleasure while she adjusted to him. Her foot pinned his calf for a moment, then slid higher, an ankle hooking around his waist. He gripped her thigh and angled her body. Nearly died of how damn good she felt.

Brock waited, trying like hell to slow down. To temper the need. But then, Hannah breathed in his ear, nipping the lobe and licking his neck just beneath it. Somehow that pushed things higher, and started the banked tension building again. He reached between them to touch her, teasing out the pleasure for her, too.

He could feel that same tension in her. Her head tossed from side to side, the rest of her going still. He kissed her again, taking her lips just as the sweet squeeze of her release gripped him tight.

The spasms went on and on, nudging him over the edge and into oblivion. His shout mingled with her soft cries, a chorus of the most perfect pleasure he'd ever felt.

With a woman he barely knew.

The realization slammed home just as he caught his breath. Just as some form of reason returned. Still, the fact that they didn't know each other well didn't take anything away from whatever they'd just experienced. It had been powerful. Passionate.

Incredibly fulfilling even as it made him want her all over again.

In other words, it was pure insanity.

Brock sank into the mattress beside her, rolling her

to his side so they lay together before he drew half of the duvet over their bare bodies.

"That was the craziest thing I've ever done." Her words were softened by the wonder in her voice. The amazement. A hint of a smile curved her lips. "I don't even know your last name."

A stir of warning prickled along his shoulders. He'd withheld it on purpose, of course. But it didn't matter now. She certainly hadn't been trying to get close to him because he was a McNeill. That much had been established.

Besides, as an actress, she had her own path to fame and fortune.

"McNeill." He glanced over at her, smoothing a long blond wave away from her cheek. "Brock McNeill."

Something shifted in her eyes. A recognition, yes. But not the speculative, almost greedy kind that he'd sometimes seen over the years.

No. He could have sworn Hannah Ryder all but recoiled. There was the slightest flinch. A fractional crinkle of her smooth brow. A stillness.

As if the name meant something to her, and not in a good way.

He wanted to ask her about it. Or at least, to talk to her and make some sense of what just happened. But she was already sliding away from him.

"I'm so sorry." She shook her head. "And embarrassed. But I just remembered I have an early call on set tomorrow." She slipped out from under the duvet, turning to plant her feet on the floor. "I don't know what I was thinking. But I guess that's the whole point. I wasn't really thinking."

Perhaps her reaction didn't have anything to do

with his name. Maybe she was just feeling the bite of morning-after regret—far too soon. That much, he could understand. The attraction had caught them like a tornado, touching down with fevered intensity.

He put a hand on her shoulder. "I'll go in a minute," he assured her. "Is everything okay? Are you all right?"

"I'm fine." She nodded, not making eye contact. "I'm just… This is completely awkward, right?" Hopping to her feet, she found her shirt and slid it over her head, the dark T-shirt covering her to the tops of her thighs. "Would you mind if we talked tomorrow, when I've got my head on straight again?"

Something was off here. Wrong.

He was missing it, but he wasn't sure what he could accomplish by staying any longer when she was clearly agitated. He understood that. And she wasn't the only one feeling rattled by what just happened. He just wished he could be sure that the only thing upsetting her was how fast things had escalated between them, and not something connected to his family name. The McNeills already had enough trouble brewing.

"Of course." Nodding, he scooped his clothes off the floor and started to dress. "I'll come by the set tomorrow and we'll talk then."

She opened her mouth, then snapped it shut again. Nodding, she pulled an afghan off the end of the bed and wrapped it around herself.

"Sure." She hugged the blanket tighter while he finished dressing. "And, um, thank you for the ride home."

He couldn't help a wry chuckle as he stepped into his boots. "I sure as hell hope the ride isn't what you remember most about this night." Leaning close to her, he brushed a kiss over her cheek, wanting nothing more than to remind her that what just happened hadn't been a fluke. But he understood about early wake-up calls. "We'll definitely be talking more tomorrow. Good night, Hannah."

Striding out of the bedroom, he retrieved his hat off the chair and dropped it on his head before stepping into the night. If Hannah was hiding something from him—if she had something against the McNeills—he had every intention of finding out.

Three

Hannah knew she couldn't hide from Brock McNeill, but she was tempted to try the next day when he hadn't made an appearance on the set by midmorning. How could the hottest night of her life have gone so terribly wrong?

The sexy rancher who'd turned her inside out was a *McNeill*.

Seated in a makeup chair under a canvas tent erected near the barn where she'd been shooting earlier, Hannah tried unsuccessfully to read through a script to take her mind off of Brock. She tried to get comfortable. There was a full-length mirror in front of her, and a cup of coffee stuffed in the mesh drink holder of her chair. Dressed in her period costume—a calico dress complete with petticoats and chemise—Hannah scrolled through the script for a space Western on her phone. It didn't take a genius to know she was starting to get typecast as a ditz—a role she'd done well once and should have distanced herself from afterward. She played something similar in *Winning the West*, but she would have taken a role as an extra if it meant getting to work on an Antonio Ventura set. Shoving aside her phone, she wished she could feel outrage about her career. Instead, all she felt was anger at herself for making a selfish decision last night.

How could she have indulged herself that way, putting her own needs before her mission? It had never occurred to her that the casually dressed rancher who personally oversaw his horses could be a member of one of the nation's wealthiest families. Hannah knew all about the connection between Cheyenne's ranching McNeills and the Manhattan branch of the family and their lucrative resort chain. She'd also read up on the ties between the Silicon Valley start-up, Transparent, principally owned by Damon McNeill and his brothers.

Hannah had researched all of them carefully before she accepted the film role on McNeill land because of the secret connection between the Ventura family and the McNeills. A connection they'd all hidden so thoroughly, she wasn't sure how many people even knew about it besides her. Not that Hannah cared about the secrets and scandals of the rich. She'd simply done her homework to find out if the McNeills were potential allies or enemies in her quest for justice for her sister.

And despite all the research she'd completed—even briefly working for the Ventura family's cleaning service—she still couldn't be certain. It could go either way. Certainly, Brock McNeill had shown no liking for Antonio. They'd behaved as though they were strangers when they spoke on the set yesterday—one more reason why Hannah would have never taken Brock for one of the McNeill family.

Restless and uneasy, Hannah shot from the chair to pace the temporary makeup and dressing area. She hadn't gone three steps when Callie raced into the tent, her work apron covered with pins and her usually sleek ponytail twisted into a haphazard knot.

"There you are!" The wardrobe assistant skidded to a stop, one sandal catching on the tassels of a floor mat. Her cheeks were pink with hectic color. "Hannah, you have a visitor on set." She lifted her dark eyebrows and lowered her voice. "The hot cowboy from yesterday."

Tension squeezed Hannah's shoulders even as warmth stirred in her belly. How could she pretend the same ease with him that she had yesterday, knowing his identity? Knowing the McNeills hid a connection to Antonio Ventura, the man she hated beyond reason? Not even Meryl Streep could pull off that kind of acting job.

"He's here?" Hannah asked finally. Stalling.

She peered into the full-length mirror, wondering if her expression revealed her distress.

Callie stepped closer, looking at Hannah's face in the mirror. "He said you were expecting him. What's wrong?"

"Nothing. Just a little nervous, I guess." She forced a smile, needing to get it together before she saw Brock. If only she understood his family's link to the Venturas.

Was there a chance her relationship with Brock could help her learn something useful about Antonio? Something that would aid her efforts to unmask him for the monster he was?

Steeling herself for the performance she needed to give for the sake of her sister, Hannah hoped she could extricate herself from an intimate relationship without alienating Brock altogether. Because while she was willing to leverage a friendship to learn anything she could about Antonio, she drew the line at allowing Brock back into her bed ever again now that she knew he was a McNeill.

The rest of the world might not know the truth about the Ventura and McNeill connection, but Hannah had unearthed the secret from a coworker at the Venturas' cleaning service.

Paige McNeill, Brock's stepmother, had married Brock's father under an assumed name. She was actually the missing Hollywood heiress Eden Harris. Daughter of the actress Barbara Harris and director Emilio Ventura. Stepsister to Antonio Ventura himself.

So until Hannah knew where the McNeills stood on the issue of the family they had never publicly acknowledged, maybe it was best to treat all of them—Brock included—like they were her potential enemies.

Brock knew he should stay away from Hannah Ryder.

Publicly, it made sense to keep the relationship quiet since he didn't need to draw more attention to his family in the days—hours, perhaps—before a scandal broke. And privately, Brock had yet to figure out the expression on Hannah's face when she'd learned of his identity last night, so it wasn't a good idea to get too involved with a woman so clearly rattled by the McNeill name.

Yet here he was on the set of her film before noon the day after they'd met. After they'd parted awkwardly and she'd dominated his thoughts all night.

He paced behind the camera while the set crew

worked to change some components in front of the lens. Lights were rolled out of the open barn doors and new lights were rolled in on handcarts and dollies. Props were switched. Hay was raked and "fluffed" using methods that rendered it unusable for horses—glue, silicon spray and filler were mixed in to make the piles look bigger against the walls. The whole place bustled with activity while the actors and director were on break.

Brock had missed seeing Hannah's scene earlier in the day, but he'd been busy with his family. His brother Carson's new girlfriend—Emma Layton, a stunt woman for *Winning the West*—had shared what might be an important clue about a connection between the McNeills and the Venturas, one the blackmailer could be exploiting. Emma's mother, Jane, had been hinting at the connection in recent phone conversations. Jane Layton had worked as a maid for the Ventura families for years and had been privy to many of the family's private affairs, but Emma also confided that her mother was emotionally unstable.

So could they trust any information gleaned from Jane Layton?

The McNeill family's private investigator couldn't follow up all the blackmail leads fast enough now that the time had almost expired on the threat to expose Paige McNeill's past. Brock's father was scared his wife was going to have a nervous breakdown, since she hadn't yet fully recovered from her time spent in a coma. And Scarlett, Paige's youngest daughter, refused to speak to any of them while she nursed her anger that they'd somehow forsaken Paige by not trying to work something out with the blackmailer.

Now this.

The woman who'd so thoroughly captivated Brock last night was hiding something, and he was determined to find out what. The family suspected the blackmailer might be working on the film or have a close connection to someone who did. Could Hannah Ryder be capable of blackmail? Anger flared at the thought she might have used sex to get closer to him. He was certain the attraction was real, but the possibility of deception rankled.

He was so caught up in those dark thoughts he didn't hear anyone approach him as he held the side door open for a woman pushing a catering cart of fruit, breakfast pastries and coffee.

"Brock."

The sound of Hannah's voice behind him sent a spike of unwanted heat up his spine. He really needed to get his attraction to her under control until he figured out where she stood in this mess with his family.

Pivoting on his boot heel, he faced her.

She was even lovelier than he remembered. Her hair was pinned up on either side, the back falling in curls that struck him as a vaguely historical style—maybe because the curls were so carefully molded. She wore a frontier-woman kind of gown, too. It was cream-colored and dotted with tiny flowers. The bodice shaped her torso in an exaggerated manner that looked sort of painful—cinching her waist and lifting her breasts in a way guaranteed to draw the eye. The full skirt of her dress would have reached the floor if she didn't have the fabric tucked into the waist, probably to keep it clean when she wasn't filming.

Even her black lace-up boots with tiny heels were from another era.

He battled the urge to touch her. To greet her with a kiss, or a whispered word about how beautiful she looked. Instead, he needed to come straight to the point. He was running out of time to help his family. He needed to know why his name had upset this West Coast actress who shouldn't care about his identity one way or the other.

"Hello, Hannah." His nod was as terse as his tone, but it couldn't be helped. "We said we'd talk more today. Can we go somewhere to speak privately?"

"My next scene is supposed to start filming soon." She seemed different. More guarded.

Which was to be expected, he supposed, even if she didn't have anything to do with the blackmail scheme. He ground his teeth against the frustration of the past few weeks. He was a horse breeder and trainer, damn it. Not a sleuth.

"I need to ask you about last night," he pressed, unwilling to let it go. He simply lowered his voice more and drew her into a dark corner of the barn, between the side door and the open front doors. "About the way you reacted when I told you my name."

There it was.

A tiny flinch. A slight flare of her nostrils.

He'd been with a woman who kept secrets before. He recognized the signs, and it was an experience he refused to repeat.

"I don't know what you mean," she lied smoothly enough, but the words didn't erase that moment of honest response he'd seen on her face.

"Yes, you do." He wasn't going to drop it. And he wasn't going to let her off the hook. "My family is going through hell right now, Hannah, and if you know something about that—about the threats leveled against the McNeills—"

"I have no idea what you're talking about." She shook her head, the curls brushing her shoulders, catching on the lace detail of her sleeve. Her face paled. "What threats?"

Behind him, another dolly rumbled past with electronic equipment, but with the shouting and noise made by the crew, he wasn't worried about being overheard.

He plowed ahead. "Someone has been threatening my family. Time is running out for me to figure out who's behind those threats." He stepped closer to her, sensing movement behind him as the set workers adjusted lights overhead. "We're being blackmailed—"

His speech wavered, then halted, as something heavy cracked the back of his skull. He had a flash of awareness that he was falling. A moment to see panic on Hannah's lovely face before...

The world went black.

"Brock!" Hannah watched in horror as the big, strong man beside her crumpled to the ground.

It took her a moment to process what had happened. One of the overhead lights had broken free of the grid, hitting the back of Brock's head. The light lay smashed on the floor behind him, the heavy black housing bent on one side. Already, people were shouting, grips and gaffers scrambling to secure the grid and clear the set.

"Brock?" Hannah sank to her knees beside the fallen rancher, her fingers tentative as she touched his shoulder, fear icing her insides. "Are you all right?"

He was breathing, but he remained stone-still.

Two production assistants were suddenly beside her, leaning over him, informing her not to move him.

Because she was flustered and scared, it took her a moment to process why. He had a head injury. He could have a concussion or much worse. A spinal injury would be…

Oh, God. She laid her hand over his, taking his fingers—careful not to move his arm—and squeezing them gently.

"Call 911!" she shouted, even as one of the wardrobe assistants flashed a thumbs-up sign as she spoke into her phone.

Someone was already taking care of that.

The minutes stretched out endlessly as they waited for an ambulance. In the background, Hannah heard the second director yelling at the production staff while someone swept up broken glass. Hannah debated how to reach Brock's family to let someone know what had happened, but she couldn't seem to let go of his hand.

He'd told her someone was threatening his relatives. Blackmailing them. He'd been upset about it—to the point there was even suspicion of her in his eyes—before that light had hit him. Did he suspect her of blackmail?

The thought chilled her even more.

Had he told his family about them? About his night with her or the way she'd reacted when he mentioned the McNeill name? What if they blamed her for the accident?

None of it should matter now when Brock was hurt. But she couldn't afford to get caught up in a scandal that had nothing to do with her. Brock might suspect her of something, but she knew she wasn't a blackmailer. She only wanted evidence against Antonio Ventura, but she couldn't possibly share her secret agenda with his family. Not even to clear her name, if it came down to that.

In the distance, she heard the wail of a siren. The ambulance was getting closer.

Relieved that help was on the way, she let one of the director's assistants know that she was going to follow the ambulance to the hospital. Because no matter how awkward things had gotten between her and Brock, this was still the man who had kissed her senseless the night before. The man who'd publicly told off Antonio.

She needed to be there for him until someone from his family arrived.

"You're going to be fine," she assured him even though he couldn't hear her. She stroked her free hand over the subtle bristle of his jaw. "The ambulance is almost here."

The siren grew louder. Nearby, the production team cleared a path between the doors and Brock, moving aside equipment.

Hannah told herself she should step back out of the way, too. But before she could, she felt Brock stirring.

Relief rushed through her.

"He's waking up!" she shouted to no one in particular, her eyes remaining on him. "He's coming out of it."

She squeezed his hand tighter, watched as he lifted his head ever so slightly. Then, as if he found it too heavy, he rested his head back on the ground, but blinked his eyes open and stared up at her.

"Are you okay?" she asked him, tilting her head to meet his gaze. "It's probably better if you don't move just yet."

She searched his face, looking for clues to any sign of discomfort or injury. Needing him to be okay.

Brock frowned, a scowl wrinkling his forehead as he studied her. When he spoke, his voice was gravelly and deep, his tone oddly distant.

"Who are you?" he asked, his blue eyes never wavering from her face. "Do I know you?"

Four

Was he serious?

Vaguely, she became aware of movement around her, the EMS crew laying a stretcher next to him before gently shuffling her aside to assess Brock's condition.

Did Brock really not remember her?

She squeezed her temples, trying to figure out what that meant. Because while she'd started this day wishing she could have a chance at a do-over with Brock, she had never wanted him to be hurt.

Tension balled tight in her stomach as the EMS workers took his vitals and asked him questions, gathering information about the blow to his head. Hannah paced circles nearby, willing herself to think. To figure out what it meant that Brock didn't recognize her.

He'd stared at her as if she was a total stranger. As if they hadn't been naked together less than twenty-four hours ago.

Her gaze skittered toward him, her heart rate jumping at the sight of him. She couldn't imagine forgetting their time together. Forgetting him. She watched as he tried to wave off the woman taking his blood pressure. Brock reached for his phone, insisting he would call his own physician.

A good sign, right? Except his movements seemed a bit stilted. And when the other EMS worker asked him what day it was, Brock seemed confused.

Worry twisted inside Hannah. For a moment, she considered walking away, before his memory returned. No one would be the wiser that she'd bailed on him.

Except she wasn't that kind of woman. Besides, she should stay close to Brock in case he knew more about Antonio Ventura. Hannah's mission to help her sister came first.

If Brock had forgotten about his night with Hannah, maybe she didn't need to remind him of how far things had gone between them. She could have her chance at a do-over, only this time, she'd be his friend and not his lover.

There would be no expectation of more. No suspicions about why she'd backed away from a relationship so fast. And if a little voice inside her head warned her that it wasn't going to be easy to pretend she wasn't attracted to him?

She'd simply have to ignore it, along with the man's red-hot appeal.

Brock just lay in a hospital bed, skull throbbing, hypoallergenic pillowcase crinkling as he shifted. Some of the pain he attributed to the knot on the back of his head. But the bigger ache came from not knowing how he landed in Cheyenne Regional Medical Center.

There'd been other times in the past he'd woken up to an EMS worker hovering over him. During his rodeo years, he'd broken enough bones and taken enough blows to the head that ER trips had been regular occurrences.

But in the past, he always remembered the fall.

Today? He didn't have a clue what had happened to him. And it didn't take a medical genius to know something was really wrong, considering all the docs who'd come through his exam room to ask him questions and frown over his chart. Where was his family? Not that he expected his older brothers to come running when he fell off a bull. Or his father either, for that matter. But his half sisters normally showed up for him. Maisie, Madeline and Scarlett had always been good to him.

This time, Maisie and Madeline had both texted him their regrets that they couldn't be there because they needed to be by their mother's side before "the scandal broke." Whatever that meant. Scarlett's response was even more puzzling, since she said Cheyenne was too far to drive, but she hoped he felt better soon.

Where in the hell was his youngest sister if not in Cheyenne? He wanted to look back over his texting history—to see if he could make sense of his world again, but he was having the damnedest time operating the cell phone, which was a different model than he remembered.

He stabbed at the touch screen, wondering where the home button had disappeared to.

The door to his room opened and one of his attending physicians entered—a tall, genial guy with a thick Eastern European accent. Brock slid his phone onto the bedside table, anxious to be released so he could get home and wait for his head to clear. The whole world felt off-kilter, but if there was some kind of scandal brewing that could hurt his family, Brock needed to be with his brothers and sisters, not sitting in a hospital bed.

Brock straightened, sliding his feet to the floor.

"Whoa, Mr. McNeill." Dr. Kreshnik hurried closer, his clipboard clattering to the tile as he reached for Brock's arm to steady him. "You've had head trauma. We don't want you moving too quickly on your own."

"I'm fine," Brock protested, knowing he would feel better at home. "I don't know who decided I needed the ER visit, but I'm definitely ready to be discharged."

"I'm afraid that's not possible, Mr. McNeill." The physician frowned as he retrieved the chart from the floor. "We want to evaluate you further."

"I've been here for five hours." Time might be fuzzy for him, but he'd messaged his sisters from the ambulance so he knew he'd been at the hospital that long. The room spun a bit, but then stopped. He was still wearing his street clothes and they'd already done a CT scan. He could have the results sent to his specialist.

"You're exhibiting signs of amnesia…" The doctor continued speaking, rattling off words like "short-term episode" and "more tests."

But Brock's brain stuck on that word. *Amnesia.*

Was that why he couldn't recall what was going on in his family? Why he didn't remember the accident that brought him in here? But he knew his own name. Could remember his friends. His family.

His head throbbed harder.

While the medical expert spouted something about care plans, a soft knock sounded on the exam room door. One of his sisters, maybe?

"Come in," Brock called, needing an ally to bust him out of the facility.

But the woman who stepped into the room juggling two steaming foam cups wasn't a sister. And he thanked his lucky stars for that.

Her generous curves and platinum waves were the stuff fantasies were made of, although her outfit made her look like she'd just stepped off the prairie. Her long, flower-dotted skirt was something from another era and modest in the extreme. But the shirt she wore with it was another matter altogether, the stiff fabric as tight as a corset, nipping her waist and drawing the eye upward to her breasts.

No amount of head trauma would have kept him from noticing her. From feeling the spark of attraction.

"I can come back," she offered, hesitating just inside the door when she spotted the man in scrubs and a lab coat next to Brock's bed. "Is this a bad time?"

"Come in," Brock insisted, waving her forward even though he had no idea who she was. He had a vague memory of her sitting beside him when he first regained consciousness, an unreadable expression in her beautiful gray eyes. But before that—nothing.

Who was she?

"Ms. Ryder." Dr. Kreshnik nodded at the mystery woman. "Any luck getting in touch with his family?"

"I'm afraid not." She shook her head, the curls bouncing lightly as she moved toward Brock and passed him one of the foam cups. He noticed there was no wedding ring on her finger. "I left a message with the foreman at the Creek Spill Ranch, however, and he promised to contact Brock's brothers personally."

That was the last thing Brock needed. He'd spent a

lifetime flying under the radar of his big family, and with good reason. He had no desire to be in the Mc-Neill spotlight, especially when it sounded like his family was in crisis.

"That won't be necessary," Brock interjected. "I'll sign whatever you need to release me." The sooner he got back home, the sooner his head would stop pounding. The sooner he could figure out what was going on with his family. The fact that none of them was here with him spoke volumes.

Dr. Kreshnik frowned while Brock sipped the coffee—too sweet for his taste, but still good.

"You've had a head injury—" The doctor looked like he was winding up for a long diatribe, his pen stabbing into the top paper on the clipboard he carried.

"And I need to rest, not have more tests." Concussions could affect short-term memory. And he knew concussion protocol by heart. No doubt his head would clear in a few days. "So if you want to write up any medical recommendations you have for me, I'll be on my way. My family needs me at home." Brock turned to the woman while the doctor pivoted on his heel and called for one of the nurses. "Is your vehicle here?"

Her coffee cup froze midway to her lips; she appeared surprised to be a part of the conversation. He noticed a name—Hannah—had been written in gold marker on the front of her take-out beverage.

"Sure. Um. Yes." She lowered her drink, standing straighter. "I borrowed one of the set vehicles to follow the ambulance."

Set vehicles?

He didn't have a clue what that meant, but he remembered she had been beside him when he regained consciousness. Everything else—including what he'd been doing with her—was hazy.

"Great. If you don't mind dropping me off at the Creek Spill, I can meet you downstairs in ten minutes." He knew the hospital couldn't keep him here against his will.

Her gray eyes darted from him to the doctor and back again, but she nodded. She reached inside her handbag for a set of keys and slipped out the door.

There was something peculiar about her that went beyond her odd outfit. Something in those uneasy gray eyes of hers, but maybe it was simply worry for him.

Right now, she was his fastest ticket home so he could figure out what was going on with his family. Besides, she'd be able to provide some answers about the accident that had landed him here.

Assuming, of course, he could trust her.

Short-term retrograde amnesia.

Hannah mulled over the term as she steered the compact car onto the county route on their way back to the Creek Spill Ranch half an hour later. The orderly who had accompanied Brock outside had handed her the discharge papers with instructions for follow-up care, giving Hannah a moment to see the diagnosis while Brock buckled his seat belt for the ride. Now, chewing her lip between answering the questions Brock fired her way, she wondered what exactly the amnesia would mean for him.

Did "short-term" imply the problem was temporary? Or had he lost only his short-term memories? She couldn't even ask Brock since he was clearly still reeling from the injury. He'd asked *her* how the accident happened, why she was dressed like a frontier woman, why a movie scene was being filmed on his land and how long they'd known one another.

She was honest about how they met, and even admitted he'd given her a ride home the night before. She just skated over the part about throwing herself into his arms afterward, seizing the chance to conceal their intimate connection.

But she found it surprising that he'd forgotten her yet knew that his family needed him now. He'd said as much to Dr. Kreshnik, but it hardly seemed possible he would recall the McNeills were being blackmailed if he had amnesia. Then again, maybe he'd put things together from reading texts on his phone. She knew he'd been receiving messages from his siblings. No wonder he'd been able to verify today's date when one of the doctors had asked him about it, even though that very same question had confused him in the ambulance. Brock must have been able to orient himself with the evidence on his screen.

"Honestly, Brock, are you really sure you want me to take you home? I couldn't help but notice those discharge papers." She removed one hand from the steering wheel to point at the paperwork now resting on the console between them. "If the doctor is correct that you have amnesia—"

"I've hit my head before. Bull riding." He stretched his legs in the cramped quarters, one denim-clad knee bumping the dashboard. "I know concussion symptoms and I have a good neurologist in Denver. I'll give his office a call when I get home."

She bit her lip, unsure how much to argue. A concussion could make someone irritable. Act out of character. She'd read that much online when she'd been in the waiting room today, hoping all the while someone from his family would come take her place. No one had. But at least she'd learned a little more about head injuries, and she knew that stress could aggravate his symptoms.

"That's a good idea." She tried being agreeable as she turned off the county route onto the private road that led to Creek Spill. "But I'm not sure a concussion alone can account for how much time you've lost if you don't remember that there's a movie being filmed on your land."

Winning the West had been on-site for almost two weeks, and before that, the location scout had been staying with Brock's older brother, Cody, while she worked out the logistics for the filming.

"I'll look into it once I check on my family." He rapped his knuckles lightly on the inside of the window. Anxious? Impatient? Or maybe just agitated. "And keep going past the main house. My family will be at my father's place. I could tell from my sisters' messages today that something is really wrong at home."

The obvious worry in his voice struck a chord with her. Hannah understood all too well the way fierce family loyalty could drive a person to great lengths and behave in a way they wouldn't normally. Like checking themselves out of a hospital when they needed medical care. Or taking a job working for a man who'd molested a family member.

They had more in common than she'd realized.

"I might know something about that," she admitted, wanting to help him if only to make up for the way she'd omitted details about their relationship. "You mentioned something to me about your family before that light hit you."

She drove past the main house at Creek Spill Ranch, as he'd asked. She hoped he remembered the directions to his father's home since she didn't know where she was headed any longer.

"Tell me," he said simply, turning the focus of those blue eyes on her. "What exactly did I say?"

She shivered with awareness, feeling the impact of his gaze even as she kept her attention on the road ahead. Memories of being with him tantalized her. Taunted her with all she'd never experience again.

"I—" Her voice hitched on a breathless note. She cleared her throat and tried not to think about the way he'd touched her. "That is, you mentioned your family had been going through hell lately. That someone was threatening the McNeills."

"I knew something was wrong when no one came to the hospital." His fingers tightened into a fist, his shoulders tensing. "Threatening how?"

She hated to upset him when he was in this condition. But he had the right to know. "Blackmail."

He bit off a curse and reached to withdraw his phone from his back pocket. "There's got to be some clue about what's going on in here. My sister mentioned a scandal, but I'll be damned if I know what she's talking about." He stabbed at the screen, his movements agitated as he muttered, "This thing must be new."

Did the scandal have anything to do with the secret she knew? Her skin prickled, a guilty feeling pinching her conscience that she might know more about Brock's family than he did. But had he forgotten the truth only because of the amnesia? Or had his family carefully hidden their connection to the Venturas?

The road grew narrower as Hannah drove deeper into

the woods. Lost in more ways than one, Hannah wondered how she'd gotten herself so deeply embroiled in Brock's life so quickly.

"Am I still going the right way?" she asked.

He glanced up just as his phone chimed. "Yes. My father's place is up here on the right. Just around that bend."

When he glanced back down at his screen, he asked her for her phone number in case he needed to contact her later. She gave it to him, wondering if he would be in touch with her again, or if it was just a formality. Moments later, he sucked in a sharp breath.

"What is it?" She slowed down as she guided the car around the corner.

Brock's attention remained on the phone. His voice—when he spoke—sounded hollow. "A Hollywood tabloid just put my stepmother's name in the headlines."

Foreboding squeezed her belly. She took her eyes off the road long enough to see his expression.

The shock in his voice sounded genuine when he spoke again.

"Apparently my father's wife is Hollywood royalty." He peered over at her and Hannah hurried to return her focus to the road, afraid her face might reveal her lack of surprise.

She swallowed hard, pretending a confusion she didn't feel. "What do you mean?"

"If this report can be believed, Paige Samara McNeill is actually Eden Harris, the daughter of Emilio Ventura and B-movie actress Barbara Harris."

Hannah waited the space of a heartbeat. And then another.

"That means your stepmother is my director Antonio's stepsister." She hated even saying the bastard's name. But she needed to ask Brock the question that mattered the most to her. "Did you know about that?"

Brock shook his head. "You mean half sister," he said absently, his gaze on the log cabin home ahead of them with several vehicles parked out front. "If this is true, Paige would be Antonio Ventura's half sister."

"Not in a biological sense. Antonio is Emilio's adopted son." Hannah pulled over, parking behind a pickup. She had researched her sister's tormentor thoroughly, but the fact that Antonio was adopted was common knowledge. Emilio Ventura had already been a famous director in his own right before he married Antonio's mother, and he'd made headlines when he adopted his wife's son.

The son had followed in his father's footsteps, acquiring millions along with the Ventura filmmaking connections once Emilio retired. Then, he'd misused the power and prestige to intimidate Hope, banking on her silence. Or that no one would believe her.

"My father's marriage to Paige was never legal since she wed under a fake name." Brock swiped a hand over his face. Rubbed his temples. "My family—my sisters— must be reeling." He held up his phone long enough for her to see the photo on the screen of a teenage Eden Harris next to a photo of Paige's daughters with Donovan McNeill. The resemblance, especially with the youngest daughter, was unmistakable. "Wyoming doesn't recognize common law marriage. So this makes them all illegitimate."

If Hannah had to guess, she would say that Brock's shock was genuine. That he hadn't known about any connection between the McNeills and the Venturas. But was that because of the amnesia? Or had he truly never known about his stepmother's identity?

Either way, for today, he was clearly stunned.

"I'm so sorry." She reached across the console to lay a hand on his arm, the need to offer comfort too strong to resist even though she knew that touching this man had a powerful effect on her. "Is there anything I can do to help?"

She wished someone from his family would come out to the car to help him inside. Was he steady enough on his feet? But there was no sign of movement in the log cabin home.

Brock's gaze dipped to where she touched him. It shouldn't have set off sparks, especially given the family crisis he was dealing with. Yet, strangely, that's exactly what happened. His blue eyes lifted, locking in on hers.

Her breath caught.

"Are you sure nothing happened last night? After I brought you home?"

Had his memories returned? Was the doctor wrong about the amnesia? Brock had been in the emergency room so briefly.

Visions of their time together spun through her mind so vividly she feared he'd somehow see them in her eyes. But she couldn't afford to get tangled up with a McNeill—especially not now that his connection to the Venturas was public knowledge. What if her unwise affair somehow compromised Hope's position to bring charges against Antonio? Or made other potential victims less inclined to confide in Hannah?

"We just talked." She scavenged a smile as she pulled her hand away from the warmth of his arm. She thumbed the silver ring on her finger, a piece that matched one she'd given to her sister. "That's all."

Her heart thudded from the lie. And the impossible attraction that wouldn't go away.

Brock nodded as he slid the hospital discharge papers off the console. "It just makes me wonder why I sought you out today on the set to tell you about the blackmail." He levered open the door and stepped out onto the lush green grass. "That doesn't seem like something I'd confide to a woman I just met."

She could see his point. But she couldn't think of an answer.

"I don't know." Shrugging, she turned the key in the ignition. "But I hope you feel better soon."

His brusque nod was his only answer before he pivoted on his boot heel and strode up the stone path toward the cabin.

Hannah couldn't help but think about how different their parting had been the night before when she'd been wrapped in nothing but an afghan, and he'd promised they'd talk more soon.

Today, she'd gotten what she wanted—distance from a McNeill. A do-over on the relationship that should have never happened in the first place.

Yet in the process, she'd made him suspicious of her.

And with a blackmailer on the loose, Hannah wondered if she'd just made a huge mistake.

Five

Scarlett McNeill sped north on Pacific Coast Highway, the car radio tuned into the same news she'd heard on a loop, over and over again, since the family scandal broke.

With an effort, she eased her foot off the accelerator as she crept too close to the car in front of her. Her whole body felt brittle with tension, her brain too stunned to think.

"...Eden Harris, daughter of troubled actress Barbara Harris and famed director Emilio Ventura, has been living under an assumed name for over twenty years." The disembodied voice on the radio reported the story using almost the same exact wording Scarlett had heard on two other stations since she'd slid into the driver's seat of her rented vehicle.

She needed to get to Logan's house. Needed his embrace to ground her when her life felt too surreal. Everything she thought she'd known about her mother was a lie. The woman she called "Mom," a seemingly simple woman who'd shunned the spotlight for Scarlett's entire life, had run away from one of Hollywood's most famous households when she'd been seventeen years old. And she'd never breathed a word of it to anyone.

Worse, Scarlett wasn't in Cheyenne with her sisters or her half brothers when the news broke, she was on her own trying to deal with the fallout. Of course, they'd all known a scandal was brewing after Scarlett had been handed the first blackmail letter by a stranger in an LA nightclub earlier in the month. But while Scarlett had been a proponent of trying to work with the blackmailer or the police to prevent the scandal from hitting the tabloids, her father and siblings had decided not to bargain with an extortionist. Scarlett had been angry and indignant on her mother's behalf, all the more so since Paige was recovering from a coma after a hiking accident and wasn't well enough to fight for herself.

Between that fundamental difference of opinion and her brother hiring a private investigator to keep tabs on her on a trip to LA, Scarlett had it with her family. She'd moved up her timetable to relocate to Hollywood and try her hand at acting. She didn't regret it, but right now, the eight hundred miles between her and Cheyenne might as well have been a million.

Thankfully, she'd arrived at Logan's. His driveway was on the left, and she pulled off Pacific Coast Highway in front of the three-bay garage. While she parked, she continued to listen to the radio broadcaster's story. "Ms. Harris, calling herself Paige Samara, married heir to the McNeill Resorts empire Donovan McNeill, and has three daughters with him. No word yet on whether that marriage would still be legal under the circumstances."

Scarlett switched off the ignition, quieting the broadcaster's voice. The sudden silence didn't stop the last words from echoing around and around her head, though.

She'd just barely renewed her relationship with actor Logan King, but he'd seemed sincere about wanting a second chance with her. About caring for her.

Today, she needed to believe in that, in him. Locking the car behind her, she shoved open the side gate that led to the outdoor stairs alongside Logan's beach house. Running down the steps, she followed the sound of the waves crashing on the rocks below until she emerged on the patio behind the house.

"Logan!" she called, not seeing him right away.

His house opened onto the patio, with a wall of glass doors that almost completely retracted so the living room could be open on one side.

Peering into the open space, she saw him emerge from the kitchen. She had a quick glimpse of his dark hair and green eyes, his strong shoulders. He was already reaching for her.

She dropped her purse on the ground and realized she was shaking as she lifted her arms to slide around him.

"Are you okay?" he asked against her hair, kissing the top of her head. "Do you want to go home and be with your family?" He stroked a hand down her spine, warm and comforting. Enticing, in spite of everything. "I planned to fly to Cheyenne later in the week to film my final scenes in *Winning the West*, but I can change my flight so we can travel together."

She breathed in the scent of his aftershave mingled with the salty air blowing off the waves hitting the beach below them. The rhythm of his heartbeat and the steady crash of the surf helped to ease some of the panic in her chest.

Logan had a prominent role in the movie shooting on the McNeill ranch. He had offered her his beach house while he was out of town since she was staying in a hotel suite in Beverly Hills until she found a place of her own. But she was trying to take it slower with Logan this time after the way she'd thrown herself into their relationship when they'd first met.

"That's kind of you." She eased back to look up at him. The sun was starting to set, bathing the sky in shades of pink and purple. "I haven't been able to think that far ahead. I'm just so…stunned."

He drew her over to one of the love seats that looked out toward the water and tugged her down onto a cushion beside him.

"I will worry about you if you're here by yourself." He held her shoulders as he looked into her eyes. "I know you were upset with your brother that he had a private investigator keeping tabs on you. But if your family is worried that the blackmailer might target you again, then I'm damned well concerned, too."

Her dark hair blew across her cheek as the wind picked up. She peeled a strand away from her lips, touched that Logan would think about her safety.

"The last blackmail note was delivered to Cheyenne, so there is more reason to believe the person threatening the McNeills is now in Wyoming, not LA." She had kept in contact with her sisters throughout the day, aware of how events were unfolding. She might be upset with her family, but she wasn't abandoning them either. "The instructions for depositing funds into an offshore account were sent by email this afternoon, although my family ignored them since they refused to deal with the black-mailer." And now, they would all be paying a different kind of price. "According to the PI firm, the email originated at an internet service provider based in Cheyenne."

Scarlett had given up apartment hunting before noon, unable to concentrate with the texts coming from her sisters.

"How's your mother doing?" Logan asked. "Has she said anything about the scandal?"

"No. I know she's still recovering from her accident, but I can't believe she hasn't said what she thinks about this story, or if it's true." Scarlett's feelings about her mother had been all over the map since learning the news. "I go back and forth between feeling betrayed and wondering if she has a really good reason for hiding the truth about her past."

"I've seen the photos the media have been posting since the story broke. The family resemblance between you and Eden Harris is strong."

"I know." She couldn't deny it. Of her mother's three daughters, Scarlett had always resembled their mother the most, a point of frustration for her since Maisie and Madeline were more traditionally beautiful. But even Scarlett had to admit the old photos of Eden Harris revealed a lovely girl. A different kind of beauty, perhaps. One more suited to the era she'd been raised in.

A random thought occurred to her, one of many racing through her brain as she stared out at the sunset over the water. "I've been worried about getting a break in Hollywood, and as it turns out, my maternal grandfather was once one of the most powerful figures in the film industry."

"And your mother's adopted brother is my director." Logan had no affection for the man in charge of *Winning the West*. He had said more than once he couldn't wait to be done working for Antonio Ventura.

"Do you think Antonio is loathsome enough to blackmail his own sister?" Scarlett knew Antonio had confiscated Logan's cell phone on a shoot in the Congo Republic earlier in the year, in a misguided attempt to help his cast "bond." So she knew he was already regarded as a difficult director.

"I wouldn't put anything past the guy," Logan muttered darkly, slumping back in the seat. "But he sure doesn't need the money. It seems unlikely he'd risk committing a serious crime for a payday when he rakes in an obscene amount for each film he directs."

Scarlett couldn't begin to imagine who was doing this to her family. She leaned back in the love seat, closer to Logan.

"You're right. And to make matters worse back home, my brother Brock went to the hospital with a concussion today. He got hit by a light fixture during a set change." Scarlett remembered the strange text from him this afternoon, asking her to pick him up at the hospital.

Almost like he'd forgotten she was in Los Angeles.

With his arm draped along the back of the love seat, Logan toyed with a lock of her hair, winding it around his finger where it lay on her shoulder.

His touch was one beautiful thing in a day from hell, and she let the joy of that touch surround her. Heat her skin.

"Your family is struggling with a lot right now," he told her gently. "Are you sure you don't want me to take you to Cheyenne? We could get a private flight and leave tonight."

She appreciated that he was looking out for her. That he cared. Her breath caught for a moment as she glanced toward him. He was incredibly good looking. And those green eyes were only for her.

Her heartbeat quickened.

"I've got a better idea." She wanted to kiss him. Was that wrong of her on a day when everything was falling apart? Maybe that's what love was supposed to be, though.

Something good you could count on even when everything else went wrong.

"You do?" He wound the curl tighter around his finger, tugging gently.

"My mother is still recovering from a coma and clearly doesn't want to talk about her past. But her father—Emilio Ventura—is right here in town." Scarlett was the only one of her mother's daughters who lived close enough to confront the man. "I'll go see him."

"Scarlett." Logan relinquished the lock of hair, already shaking his head. "The Ventura compound will be crawling with paparazzi."

"I'll go incognito." She wanted to be an actress, after all. She'd act her way in there.

"If he's anything like his son, I'm not sure you want to go alone." Logan's voice had a warning note, but she'd just broken away from her overprotective brothers.

She was making her own decisions now.

"I'll find out for myself if my mother is really the missing Hollywood heiress, Eden Harris." Even as she said it, she knew it had to be true. The photos didn't lie. "More importantly, I'll find out why she felt the need to run away from her family and go into hiding for over twenty years." It was the first time all day she'd felt like she had a sense of purpose. A role to play in the family drama exploding all over the news. "If something—or someone—hurt her, I will find out."

An hour into the family meeting, Brock knew he'd made a mistake joining the rest of the McNeills at his father's house. He sat in the recliner closest to the door and wondered when he could make his exit. He didn't want to abandon his dad, stepmother or his siblings, but the ache in his head had shifted from physical pain to a gnawing fear that this injury wasn't like others he'd experienced.

Closing his eyes, he tried to shut out the discussion with the New York–based public relations consultant flown in the day before at Brock's grandfather's request. That was Brock's first indication that something was seriously amiss. It was one thing to forget the seductive actress, Hannah, since by her admission they'd only just met. But to have forgotten that his stubborn father had mended his estrangement with Brock's grandfather, Malcolm McNeill, after a rift that had spanned most of Brock's life?

He couldn't begin to remember how that had occurred. Yet all his siblings behaved like having Malcolm—and Malcolm's girlfriend, Rose—under the same roof as Donovan was no big deal. The extended family filled the living area to capacity, with Maisie and Madeline seated at the kitchen bar so they could be a part of the conversation.

Brock pinched the bridge of his nose, willing his thoughts to realign, his brain to make some kind of order out of the chaos of information floating around him. Strangely, despite the family drama and the very real news that his father's twenty-six-year marriage couldn't be legally recognized anymore if Paige was really Eden Harris, Brock's thoughts returned most often to Hannah.

Was that because being with Hannah was less frustrating since they had very little history together, and therefore, less for him to forget? Or did he think of her more because she made a strong impact on him? She had been beside him when no one else could be today. She'd driven him home. Wished him well.

Maybe that had been all that happened between them on the surface. But he'd felt a whole other layer of things sparking when she'd touched him. She'd meant it to be consoling. Compassionate.

Yet her hand on his arm had stirred a far more elemental response. And he couldn't shake the idea that her gray eyes hid secrets he needed to unlock.

"Donovan, they *need* to know." A soft, feminine voice from the edge of the living room suddenly distinguished itself in the rumble of conversation, quieting the McNeill family instantly.

Brock's stepmother stood framed in the hallway arch, dressed in a blue floral nightgown with a matching cotton robe, her feet bare and her long brown hair unbound. His father had his arm slung around her. She looked pale and physically frail after the weeks in bed recovering from her fall and a coma—events Brock had only learned about today. But there was a glint in her brown eyes.

A fierce light Brock hadn't seen before.

Madeline moved closer to them.

"Can we get you something, Mom?" She gestured toward the kitchen. "A drink? Some tea, maybe?"

Brock leaned forward in the recliner to hear whatever Paige had to say. Was the news true? His stepmother had always been mild-mannered, almost to a fault, given the way she allowed her strong-willed husband's opinions to rule the household. It seemed hard to believe she had masterminded a scheme to assume a new identity as a teenager, moving halfway across the country and marrying a well-known man in Cheyenne without anyone questioning her past.

Then again, the so-called missing Hollywood heiress had never been formally reported as missing. She'd simply stopped appearing in public.

"No thank you, sweetheart. I just wanted you to know." She glanced from Brock's father toward everyone else in the room, sweeping the living room with her gaze. "All of you. It's true, what the tabloids are saying about me." Her voice trembled a little, and she stopped, then tried again. "I didn't use a new name with the intent to deceive anyone. I just…needed a fresh start."

When the room remained quiet, the public relations consultant—Jasmine—looked ready to ask a question. She drew in a breath and opened her mouth, but Carson was seated next to her and he clamped a firm hand on the woman's arm, effectively silencing her.

Donovan hugged Paige closer to his side. "As far as I'm concerned, her name doesn't change the kind of wife and mother she's been. And a news story about the past doesn't alter who she is on the inside." He turned from Paige to stare at the rest of them. "I know everyone else feels the same way."

A chorus of agreement and support echoed around

the room. Maisie darted around her sister to hug their mother.

Paige's eyes were bright as she nodded. "Thank you."

Donovan gently turned her around, guiding her back down the hallway, away from the living area. "Focus on getting well," he told her softly, his words dissolving before they disappeared into the room at the far end of the corridor.

"I can't believe she kept her past a secret our whole lives." Madeline, the oldest of the daughters Brock's father had with his second wife, shook her head in the hallway, looking lost.

Brock knew someone should offer comfort. Words of wisdom. But tonight, with his head throbbing and his thoughts too damn scattered, he couldn't be that guy. The last thing his family needed was to discover he'd lost his memories for at least—as far as he could tell—the last six months. He could recall delivering two fillies to a neighbor with twin girls just after the New Year, but couldn't come up with a memory after that.

Until he woke up with Hannah Ryder staring down at him with concern and secrets in her eyes.

He was pulled out of his thoughts about Hannah when Jasmine tapped a manicured fingernail on the maple dining table to get everyone's attention. "If we're going to get on top of this, we need to issue a statement from the family as quickly as possible."

"Agreed, my dear," Malcolm announced in a weary-sounding voice from his spot beside his girlfriend on one of the sofas. "But as you can see, it's not easy for us to focus on where to go next when we're still reeling with what this means for all of us."

"We could try a diversion tactic until we've come

up with a statement," Jasmine suggested. The woman was apparently a friend of Malcom's grandson, Quinn, and his ballerina wife, Sofia Koslov McNeill. Jasmine had done some PR for the dancer before her marriage to Quinn, helping to boost the woman's profile in the dance world.

That news was, perhaps, fresher in Brock's mind than everyone else's. To him, it felt like the Manhattan branch of the family had been making headlines just last week.

Cody, the older of the twins, rose from his chair at the table and stared out the front window toward the driveway and the darkened fields beyond. "Are you suggesting we manufacture a story to take the spotlight off us?"

"Not manufacture." Jasmine sounded offended. "It has to be a real story, but something big enough to change the narrative. Maybe news about a land deal, or some kind of update about the film?"

Brock wasn't cut out for this kind of thing on a good day. And today had sucked the will—and the memories—right out of him. He needed to get out of the house where all the talk of the blackmail scheme and the film confused him. Figure out how in the hell he was going to combat amnesia.

And coax Hannah Ryder into helping him remember what had happened between them, since that memory promised to be more enticing than any other.

"I can't do this now," he announced to the room at large, regretting that he couldn't be a better family member on a day when his siblings needed him. "My head is throbbing and I can't think straight, so I'm not going to be any help to the cause tonight."

It wouldn't be the first time he'd been a disappointment to his father. The youngest son who flew under the radar was also the one who contributed the least to the ranching operations. Brock's quarter horse program wasn't about raising cattle or increasing herd production.

But it was what he knew best.

Pivoting on his heel, he headed for the exit, already making plans to text Hannah. He'd take a good horse from his father's stable to ride home, unconcerned about the doctor's orders since he was practically born in a saddle. He'd ride past the cabin where Hannah said she was staying since she was practically on the way.

As he was turning the handle, a knock sounded from the other side of the door. He opened it to find a slender brunette in running shorts and a sweatshirt. Her cheeks were pink, her forehead glistening like she'd been sweating. Her eyes were a little bloodshot, like maybe she'd been crying.

"Hey, Brock," she said softly, edging past him into the room.

He had no idea who she was.

But the way Carson charged toward her, concern etched on his features, told Brock it was someone important to the younger of the twins.

"Emma, what's wrong?"

Brock hesitated to leave when everyone else's eyes were glued on the newcomer as Carson wrapped her in his arms.

"It's my mother," she said, glancing around the room at the rest of the family, her gaze finally settling on him. "Brock, you weren't here three days ago when I was sitting with your mother and recognized the picture in her locket—it's of the woman we now know is her mother, Barbara Harris."

Brock knew the locket his stepmother had always

worn. But how the hell could one of Carson's girlfriends identify the face of an actress who hadn't made a film in decades? He nodded, though, unwilling to give away how lost he was, how thoroughly his memories had been stolen by the blow to his head. Although he had to admit, all of this news would be hard to follow even on a normal day.

"I called Mom to talk to her about it since she worked as a maid in the Venturas' home for years." Emma used her long sleeve to swipe at her eyes. "And it turns out Mom is in town. She flew here—to Cheyenne—the day before the second blackmail note was delivered to Paige."

A silence followed. And when no more explanation seemed forthcoming, Maisie stepped closer to Emma.

"I don't understand." Maisie's uncomprehending gaze went from Emma to Carson and back again. "Your mom missed you? She came to see the filming?"

"It's not that." Sniffling, Emma shook her head and straightened. "My mother had an affair with her boss— Emilio Ventura—long ago. She's always been a little obsessed with him, and she's fought manic depressive disorder my whole life," she clarified. "The fact that my mother is here, in Cheyenne, when the demand for money was sent to Paige from this town, makes me very concerned that my mother could be the blackmailer."

Six

As he left his father's house, Brock gave up trying to put the pieces of the blackmail drama together. He wouldn't be any help tonight when he couldn't even identify some of the people in the room.

Maisie made a half-hearted effort to call him back to the house, asking if he was okay or if he needed a ride home. But his father's stable would have a horse that could get him home. The animals raised on-site made the trek between the Black Creek Ranch and the Creek Spill with regularity, and Brock's house was in between, right on the river.

Not to mention, he'd trained most of the quarter horses personally for the past six years. His successful breeding and training program had given him his own domain within the ranching operation, allowing him autonomy despite all the ways the McNeill businesses intersected and overlapped.

Even concussed and suffering amnesia, he understood horses far better than his family.

He saddled a buckskin mare, Aurora, in the closest stall, taking pleasure from the details he remembered about the animal's heritage, facts that came to mind easily. She was five years old, and one of the offspring of the ranch's most prolific sire. Smart and athletic, Aurora was everything Brock enjoyed about the breed.

When he led her outside into the cool summer night, he had only to nudge her in the direction of the path to his house—a finished home now, according to the photos he'd seen in his phone. The last Brock recalled, he had been framing in the walls, so to see the thing finished had been jarring. He was anxious to see it in person, to see if those photos were real.

The mare responded with a brisk pace and soft snort. Brock straightened in the saddle, the pain in his head receding for the first time in hours as the scent of meadow grasses and wildflowers drifted on the night breeze. He could hear the babble of the creek as they neared the shallow water, and some of the tightness in his chest eased.

As they reached the turnoff that would lead to the cabin where he knew Hannah must be staying, Brock leaned back in the saddle, slowing Aurora to a walk. He hadn't texted her, so she wouldn't be expecting him.

But he could ride past to see if her lights were on. He owed her a thank-you at the very least. Their parting had been strained after he'd been blindsided by the news of his stepmother's identity. He hadn't been at his best.

Now, veering away from the water, Brock guided Aurora through a dense thicket. Big box elders gave way to elm trees and then a few scrubby pines before the land flattened and grazing meadows appeared in the moonlight. Lamps glowed from within the cabin and a hurricane lantern flickered on the patio table of the narrow porch.

Anticipation fired through him. The remnants of the day's headache dissipated at the thought of seeing Hannah.

"Hello?" she called out through the dark as he discerned the figure seated in one of the Adirondack chairs. "Who's there?"

He could hear the tension in her voice. Worry.

"It's Brock." He regretted surprising her, and lifted a hand in greeting as Aurora neared the cabin. "I didn't mean to startle you. I'm just on my way home."

To see the house he'd built himself, but for the most part couldn't remember building.

Hannah gave a soft laugh as she rose to her feet and stepped down onto the grass. "I'm not used to hearing big animals heading toward me in the dark."

She stopped short of the horse. Hannah wore a pale, hooded sweatshirt that said I Read Past My Bedtime in bright pink letters. She reached up to stroke the animal's nose as Brock swung down to the ground.

With her face scrubbed clean and her hair pulled back in a low ponytail that rested on her shoulder, she looked relaxed. Maybe ready for bed. His brain ran wild, his thoughts unchecked for a moment before he reined himself in. He stood close to her in the tall grass, the clean scent of her hair close enough for him to breathe in.

He forgot what he'd come here to say. His attention was focused solely on her. Being here felt right. Familiar.

Being with her would feel even better.

She glanced up at him suddenly, gray eyes zeroing in on his. "I wasn't expecting to see you again today."

How come the most ordinary interactions with Brock McNeill felt hotter—sexier—than blatant kisses she'd shared with other men?

Hannah tried to get ahold of her wayward libido by reminding herself why she'd lied to Brock about being with him the night before. She could not afford to be in a relationship with a man whose family had a kinship with her enemy.

It wasn't easy to keep that in mind given how different the two men seemed. But she wasn't in Cheyenne to indulge herself. She was only here to save her sister Hope from falling any further into a dark pit of unhappiness.

Brock sidestepped her, taking the horse's reins and dropping them to the ground.

"I realized I didn't thank you for all you did for me." He was still in the same clothes he'd worn earlier that day at the hospital. He had to be exhausted after the time in the emergency room and the scandal breaking with his family.

"You're welcome. It was no trouble since they canceled shooting to work on the lights." She knew the filming in Cheyenne was going to run over budget and over schedule. Which was just as well since it gave her more time to speak privately with members of the cast to find other victims of Antonio Ventura's predatory behavior. "I don't know how you're still functioning after the day you've had."

Brock lifted a hand to touch the back of his head, muscles flexing in a way that stirred something in the pit of her belly.

"I feel better," he admitted. "Actually, getting out of my father's house and away from the drama helped air out some of the cobwebs in my brain."

A sliver of panic froze her.

"Are you—" Her voice cracked. "I mean, is your memory returning?" What would she say if he asked her why she lied to him about what happened the night before?

A McNeill was a powerful enemy to make. A word in the director's ear could get her fired.

He studied her for a long moment before shaking his head. "I'm struggling to remember anything that's happened after January."

Relieved, she all but sagged onto the porch's wooden stair railing. Still, she couldn't deny a pang of empathy for him. She couldn't imagine losing a whole chunk of your life that way.

"I'm sorry." She hugged her arms around herself; the wind off the mountains was surprisingly cold once the sun went down. "And I'm sure your family couldn't be much help tonight with all the news about your stepmom."

"Are you cold?" he asked, his gaze dipping to her body as she shivered. "There's gas in the fire pit, you know." He pointed to the small stone ring with a slate mantel. "Unless you'd be more comfortable indoors."

Ever since she'd practically dragged him over the threshold into the cabin last night, the place was full of memories starring him. So indoors was not a good idea.

"A fire sounds great," she told him. "But the remote for it might be inside. I didn't read any of the instructions on operating things like that."

Brock was up the stairs and beside the fire pit a moment later. "You can switch it on manually." He reached under the slate mantel and must have found the button because there was a whoosh of orange-and-blue flame from the center of the ring.

Hannah followed him onto the porch, which was just big enough for two chairs, a love seat and the fire pit. There was a ground level patio area where she did yoga in the mornings. The views were incredible.

"This is perfect." She held her hands out to the open flame, warming them. "Thank you."

"No problem." He stood on the opposite side of the fire pit, watching her. "And as for my family not being much help with my memories—you're right. Today, the focus was very much on my stepmother."

"How is she doing?" She wanted to know if the rest of his family had been surprised by the news, or if they'd been well aware of her relationship to the Ventura family.

"I'm honestly not sure how much I'm supposed to say outside the family." He stepped around the fire pit to stand closer to her, the heat and strength of him near enough to touch. "My grandfather brought in a public relations consultant to help us figure out our next move."

"That makes sense." She shivered again, but this time it had nothing to do with the chill in the air and everything to do with his proximity. "The McNeill name is highly recognizable. You'll want to protect the brand."

He shrugged, his gaze moving over her. "It's more of a worry for the resort business than the ranching operations, I would think. And for my part, I can't imagine why anyone looking for a good horse would suddenly decide they shouldn't buy from me because my stepmother is a runaway Hollywood heiress."

"People want to know they're dealing with someone honest. Forthright." She wondered if he really believed his business would be unaffected or if he was trying to look at the bright side. There was no doubt in her mind the scandal would have an impact. "And an association with the Venturas is a dubious distinction. The family might carry industry clout, but they aren't well liked."

"You're right, of course." His lips curved in a humorless smile. "There's bound to be a business impact. I had hoped my head had cleared with some fresh air, but I'm still not thinking straight." He turned more fully toward her. "Can I ask one more favor of you, Hannah?"

Hearing him speak her name tripped pleasantly over her nerve endings. Her throat dried up.

"Sure." She peered up at him, keeping her body facing the fire and not him.

"Maybe it's because we haven't known each other long and we don't have a history. But I find it easier to talk to you than anyone in my family right now."

"You do?" His words shot arrows of guilt into her since they absolutely had a history. She tucked her hands into the pocket of her hoodie, afraid he'd see them shaking.

"Definitely." His blue eyes simmered with the same fire that had scorched her the night before. "It's less pressure to talk to you, and you don't make my head hurt."

"Oh." She knew what was coming and wanted to cut him off, since the less time she spent with him, the better. But how could she tell him that? How could she say that being with him was a constant battle not to touch him? Kiss him? Think about the times he'd touched and kissed her?

"Have dinner with me this week. When you're off, or else after you're done working for the day."

"I. Um—" She tried to think of a compelling reason why she couldn't. But as he reached to graze a touch along her cheek, it was all she could do not to close her eyes and sway into him.

His eyes turned serious. "I know I wouldn't have confided in you about someone blackmailing my family if I didn't trust you. If I didn't want…something more with you."

She straightened, needing to do damage control. Fast.

"I didn't get that impression at all," she protested. "You were just being kind to bring me home last night."

"Hannah." His voice was softly chiding, his knuckle lingering on her cheek in the barest of touches. "Even now, I feel more than that between us. Having amnesia doesn't keep me from knowing I would have been every bit as attracted to you yesterday, too."

How could she argue with that logic? Denying it felt like swimming against a riptide. She didn't have a chance.

"Attracted or not, I'm not sure it's wise." She wanted to follow that up with a compelling argument. She had none she could share with him.

"Don't say yes to dinner with me because it's *wise*. Say yes because you want to get to know me." He leaned closer, his gaze falling to her mouth. "Or because you don't want to go your whole life without kissing a cowboy." For a moment, they breathed the same air. Her eyelids fluttered. "Or hell, say yes because we both need to eat, and I can promise you better food than you'll get from the film's dining services."

He let his hand fall away from her, giving her space to decide.

And how could she refuse? He was right about the attraction, of course. But the main reason she wanted to see him again was to keep an eye on the situation. To know if he recovered his memories. To find out why his stepmother had run from the Ventura household at a young age.

It wasn't about kissing a cowboy, damn it.

Because she already knew exactly how good that felt.

"You make a convincing argument," she told him finally. "I'm done filming most days by seven."

Hannah was still thinking about that impending date late the next morning as she walked the short distance from her cabin to the day's filming location.

She wore a simple sundress and a hat wide enough to keep the freckles at bay in the intense Wyoming sun. Brock had told her he'd message her today once he'd made reservations for dinner. Considering his thoughtfulness, it was too bad her relationship with him was destined for an unhappy end. Most of the guys Hannah had dated in the past were content to go out with a pack of friends rather than make special plans for a one-on-one evening out.

So the fact that Brock wanted to do something nice for her slid right under her defenses. That, coupled with the way he'd put Antonio in his place that first day they'd met, set him apart from most men. In particular, men of wealth and privilege. In her experience, men born with that kind of advantage in life rarely saw past their own comfort.

Witness her father, a prestigious attorney who'd gladly

cut off his daughters from the family fortune when he'd walked out on their mother. Not that Hannah cared for herself. But for Hope's sake? It still made her furious a decade after he'd left. Her father had made mincemeat of his ex-wife's divorce lawyer, his precious money well protected from the family he no longer wanted.

Hannah's phone chimed, and she dug in her bag for it, glad for the distraction from the dark thoughts. She glanced at the caller ID, feeling a charge of anticipation as she wondered if it would be Brock. Her sister's number flashed on the screen instead. Instantly worried, she hurried to answer.

"Hi, Hope." She injected a brightness into her voice she didn't feel before carefully asking, "How are you doing?"

Her sister had moved in with her when she'd turned eighteen, after graduating high school, when their mother announced her plan to go "live her own life" and travel. But Hannah had loved having Hope around. She'd bought them matching rings and told Hope it was them against the world—the Ryder team. Hope attended community college for two years before switching to taking classes at UCLA—classes she'd once been so excited about. Lately, Hannah had to remind her to get out the door to attend them.

"Honestly? I'm not great, Hannah." Hope sounded wound up. More upset than usual. The last few months she'd retreated into days of near-silence, so hearing her voice so animated now put Hannah on alert. "*Winning the West* is all over the news. His face—it's everywhere."

Hannah's brain raced to fill in the blanks. She stopped in the middle of the grassy trail that led to the day's shooting location—a rocky gully where a secret meet-

ing was taking place among three of the film's charac-
ters. She still had time before she needed to be in the
makeup chair.

"Why? Because of the Eden Harris story?" She
guessed it had something to do with the scandal. "I
mean, has there been any more news today?"

"I don't know!" Hope spoke in a loud whisper, as if
she was trying to be quiet and failing. In the background,
shrill pop music blared. She must be at the mall where
she had a job in a teen clothing shop. "But all the girls at
work keep showing me videos of the ranch where you're
shooting because they know you're in the film. And his
stupid face is always there."

A new fear crawled up her spine. Tension pulled at
her shoulders. Did Brock know about this?

"There's footage of the ranch?" Hannah charged in
the direction of the shoot, worried what she might find.
"As in, the tabloids are up here now?"

She hadn't checked her media feeds this morning.
She'd been too busy enjoying the Zen-like atmosphere
of waking up in a country cabin, sipping her coffee in
the quiet as she watched the sun come up over the field.

"They keep showing clips of...*him* outside a cowboy
bar. Someone asks him if he knew Mrs. McNeill was really Eden Harris when he decided to film in Cheyenne."
Hope lowered her voice more as she rushed on, "I don't
know why you had to do this, Hannah. I never wanted
you to have anything to do with him."

Hannah hated that she was hurting her sister more.
But she had to believe she was doing the right thing in
the long run.

"Honey, I would have been an extra in this movie to
work with him. You know that." She strained to see the

film set in the distance, wondering if she should be looking for drone cameras or photographers in the bushes.
"I'm going to find evidence of the kind of person he is.
Once he's publicly exposed as a predator, he won't be
able to hurt anyone else again."

She thought about texting the wardrobe assistant, Callie, to see if there was any news about paparazzi near
the ranch, but it was hard to see her screen in direct sun.
And if she messaged anyone, maybe it should be Brock.
His family would want to know about this if they weren't
already aware.

Then again, Brock said they'd hired a public relations
manager. So they must know. For that matter, maybe the
McNeills were leveraging the notoriety for business reasons. The thought of Brock having a connection to Antonio Ventura—of possibly profiting from it—made her ill.

"And in the meantime, the man who hurt me is your
boss. Whenever I think about you working for him—"

Hannah couldn't hear the rest.

Because as the filming location came into view, so
did a crowd outside the wardrobe tent. A ring of people
standing and watching something in their midst. Something Hannah couldn't see.

"Hope, I promise I'll be careful." She picked up her
pace, jogging through the grass as the trail flattened out.
"But I really need to go. I'm due on set right now, okay?"

Disconnecting the call, she raced toward the throng
of people—production assistants, wardrobe and makeup
staffers, writers, transportation crew, animal handlers.
Everyone seemed to be gathered around something. A
fight? A member of the media?

But as she skidded to a halt behind the pack, Hannah could hear a man speaking. It was Antonio Ventura.

"—and if that's what it takes to get everyone on this production on the same page, I will do it," he was saying, his voice taking on a vaguely threatening tone. "I've done it on other film sets."

A murmur went through the group and Hannah wondered exactly what he was proposing to get them "on the same page." She sidled closer to Callie and tried to get a better view of the man she despised.

Callie, seeing her, covered one side of her mouth to whisper, "Says he's holding our cell phones hostage if we're not good girls and boys."

The director took his time glaring around at every member of the assembled group. "The added media attention is only a problem if we make it one. I will view anyone who posts updates from this set, or who publicly speculates about the Ventura family, as someone who has no interest in working with me—or this production company—again."

He stormed off toward a production trailer, one of his assistants scrambling to catch up.

He's reaching, Hannah wanted to shout to the younger crewmembers, to let the newbies know that a director didn't have that kind of hold over a production company. Ventura couldn't dictate whom that company hired for future projects. But, selfishly, Hannah appreciated that the unrest on set might result in her overhearing something damning about Antonio sooner rather than later. An unhappy cast and crew would create a better environment for one of Ventura's victims to let her guard down about the man's behavior.

So Hannah said nothing, listening as the crowd broke up. Some people seemed to think it was all grandstanding to get cooperation, but Hannah also heard someone start to recount the reports from one of Antonio's overseas productions where he did indeed collect the cast's phones, holding on to them for weeks.

As the group thinned out and people began returning to their work, Callie walked with Hannah to the makeup trailer, then held the door for her as they stepped inside the mobile unit.

"So what prompted the tirade?" Hannah asked as she dropped into the makeup chair, settling her bag under the mirrored table in front of her.

They were the only ones in the vintage Airstream. The hair and makeup people must have been lingering to talk after the director's mini-meltdown. Hannah wanted to open her media feeds and catch up on the news from the set since Hope had mentioned a lot of media focus on the film. But sometimes scrolling through a feed sent the message that you didn't want to talk, and Hannah couldn't afford to have people shut her out. She needed confidences if she was ever going to collect damning evidence against Antonio.

"One of the extras posted a photo of Antonio side by side with a photo of Paige McNeill, both of them standing in front of the Creek Spill Ranch welcome sign," Callie explained, reaching to straighten the collar on the shirt that Hannah would be wearing in the day's scene. "The extra added a caption that said, 'Separated at birth?' because they were both wearing jeans and a Stetson."

"Doesn't sound like a big deal to me."

"It shouldn't have been, except that Antonio looks like a sloppy, lewd old man in his photo, with his T-shirt barely covering his gut, while Eden Harris is still as lovely as ever. Since the two of them are close in age, it's my guess Antonio's ego took a hit."

Lewd? The word caught Hannah's attention more than anything else the wardrobe assistant said. Had Callie seen inappropriate behavior from the director? She promised herself that she would circle back to the subject.

"I thought he was angry because there are tabloid reporters in Cheyenne." She debated grabbing her phone now to see what else she could unearth online. Also, she wondered if Brock had messaged her, because he was never far from her thoughts today. "My sister said there's a lot of talk about the filming since the news broke yesterday about Eden Harris."

Callie nodded, dropping onto a bench seat across from Hannah, her long ponytail draping down her arm. "Everyone in Hollywood wants to find out if the Ventura family knew where Eden was all this time since no one ever formally reported her missing. She just sort of disappeared."

Hannah's phone vibrated. She could hear the soft buzz even with the device in her bag. But her attention went to the door of the trailer as one of the production assistants stuck his head in.

"Filming is canceled today, ladies. Security breach at the front gate of the ranch. The McNeill family has recommended we wait a day to film until they get the ranch borders secured."

A second later, the man was gone, no doubt off to spread the news.

Callie clapped her hands together. "Free day!" she shouted, doing a dance on the trailer floor before hopping out the door, too fast for Hannah to stop her or ask about the "lewd" comment. Darn it.

She reached for her bag instead, pulling out the phone to see that a text message had arrived from her date tomorrow.

Security issues mean we can't readily go to a five-star location. I'm importing a five-star chef to my home instead. I'll pick you up tomorrow night at seven thirty.

Hannah read the message twice, her heart pounding. Dinner at Brock's home sounded intimate. Decadent.

She'd have to be very, very careful that she used the time to learn more about him, and not fall further under his seductive spell.

Seven

Brock hadn't wanted to pick up his date with a security detail trailing him. But considering the swarm of paparazzi looking for a way onto McNeill lands since yesterday, he'd finally agreed to have one of the extra guards follow him over to Hannah's cabin. Brock had enough on his mind tonight without running interference with the media if reporters managed to infiltrate the Creek Spill Ranch.

And to the guard's credit, Brock didn't even see anyone else around when he halted in front of the cabin in his pickup truck. Switching off the headlights and the engine, he left the keys on the seat before striding toward the cabin.

Music drifted from the windows, a sweetly haunting aria sung in a foreign language, and not at all what he would have expected from Hannah's playlist. Not that he knew much about her outside the compelling draw between them. Still, he looked forward to learning more about this woman who felt strangely like a calm center in the storm of amnesia, blackmail and scandal.

He'd spent most of the previous day with his neurologist, discussing the results of the CT scan and trying to get answers about his memories. The consultation hadn't given him anything more concrete than he'd learned in the ER, but at least his headache had eased. He'd met with his family again the night before, and the publicist had announced a new family story for redirecting public interest. Malcolm McNeill had proposed to his girlfriend, Rose Hanson, and the pair had revealed a Manhattan wedding planned for the end of the month.

Brock might not remember anything about his grandfather before the last two days, but he had to admit the patriarch of the McNeill clan knew how to put family first. The announcement of the billionaire's late-in-life remarriage had eased some of the intense interest in Paige's Hollywood past.

Now, before Brock could knock on Hannah's door, it opened with a sudden flood of lamplight and a faint hint of orange blossoms. His date appeared on the threshold.

A silky dress swirled around her, strapless and floor length in color blocks of bright purple, fuchsia and pink. A gold lamé belt wrapped the slimmest part of her, while gold shoes peeked out from the pink hem. Her long blond waves were curled in neat coils.

"Brock." Her smile seemed genuine, her tone relieved. "After filming was canceled, I've been worried there would be a rush of photographers if I so much as cracked the door open." Her gaze skittered past him to peer out into the dark. "But there's no one out there?"

"There's a security detail at the tree line." He couldn't peel his attention away from her. "You look beautiful."

"Thank you." Her hands fluttered nervously as she hurried to pick up a remote from the coffee table. Stabbing at it, she silenced the swelling violins of the opera music. "I packed only so much for the trip, but luckily, I had a dress."

She retrieved a small gold clutch and slid her keycard inside before she switched off the wrought iron chandelier in the living area. Brock scanned the room to make sure the place looked secure before they left. Now that the ranch had become a point of interest for the tabloids, he regretted that she was staying in the cabin alone. Vulnerable.

His gaze snagged on the door to the bedroom toward the back. He had a sudden vision of them there, kissing at the threshold of that door, before falling into the bed that awaited—

"...Brock?" Hannah asked, staring at him intently. She worried her lower lip, nibbling one side for a moment before speaking again. "Is everything okay?"

How long had he been standing there, fantasizing about a moment that felt all too real? He shook off the sensation of being caught in a memory that wouldn't come. No doubt he had daydreamed about that scenario when he accompanied Hannah to this cabin before, the way she'd described. His desire for her was sharp, but that didn't mean he would act on it too fast. He looked forward to spending time with her first. Getting to know her.

"Better than okay." He had gone to considerable effort to arrange this evening with her. He refused to make a mess of it before they even set foot in his house. "I've been looking forward to this all day."

Offering her his arm, he guided her out of the cabin and into the summer night. The breeze stirred the silky layers of her dress, blowing it against him as he helped her into the truck, stirring awareness all over again.

Resolutely, he trained his focus on the grassy road that led to his place, needing to stay alert. He saw no one on the way, not even the security guard. His home was more remote than either of his brothers' since he'd chosen a tract of land near the Black Creek between the two main ranches, so perhaps that accounted for the quiet. But his brother Carson had also assured him the security team was top-notch when they messaged earlier in the day. Apparently, Carson had invested in a private security firm before he'd allowed the production company to film up here in the first place. Then, after Carson's girlfriend's shocking announcement the night before about her mother potentially being the blackmailer, Carson had hired even more guards to make sure Emma's mother, Jane Layton, didn't come near McNeill property.

When Brock cleared the final bend before his house, Hannah gasped.

"What's wrong?" He turned to look at her, but she was staring out the front windshield.

"That's your house?" She glanced toward him and raised her eyebrows. "Brock, it's gorgeous."

He wasn't sure that he'd describe it quite that way, but still, her words were flattering. "Thank you. I worked on this place for years, and I'm finding it frustrating that now I can't recall finishing the building."

Parking the truck close to the front entrance so she wouldn't have far to walk, he got out, pocketed the keys and went around to help her from the vehicle.

"You built this?" she asked as she stepped carefully down from the running board onto the flagstones beneath.

He held one of her hands, feeling the softness of her creamy skin, curbing the impulse to stroke his thumb over her palm. Letting her go, he shut the door behind her and stood beside her to stare up at the house.

At almost eight thousand square feet, there was plenty of room. Much of the first level had a river stone facade, the gray rocks blending with the retaining walls and footpaths that led up from the Black Creek. The porch posts on the first level were stone, but the wide porches of the second level were wooden, the two materials blending in a proportion that felt right for a house set against the woods and overlooking a wide creek. Now, with all of the outdoor and landscaping lights on, the house was reflected in the calm water.

"I did most of it. I contracted out the plumbing and electrical. And I had a professional excavator help me with the site's foundation. But the rest was all me." He had, at least, painstakingly preserved the effort in photos. If he never recovered the missing gap in his memories, he had the photo history. "For years, this was my second job after I finished working with the horses."

The scents of smoked pancetta and roasted hen drifted from the kitchen, a reminder that appetizers would be served shortly. Brock led her into the house, explaining a few of the features she asked about on the way, like the beams in the cathedral ceiling of the foyer and the hand-cut logs used as supports in the main archway that led to the kitchen.

They avoided the kitchen, however, since he'd given over the gourmet facility to the chef and her staff for the night. Brock had asked for the meal to be served upstairs on the covered balcony overlooking the Black Creek, a vaulted veranda with an outdoor fireplace already lit to ensure they were comfortable even in the night chill.

"This is incredible." Hannah spun in a slow circle to take in the balcony with its round dining table already set for two. Three white candles burned under a hurricane globe surrounded by sunflowers, roses and orange lilies.

Brock was satisfied that his preparations were to her liking. He only wished he'd hired musicians for the night since he would have liked the opportunity to dance with her. It would have given him a reason to wrap her in his arms.

"I'm sorry we couldn't go out tonight." He hadn't ever met a woman he wanted to romance to this degree. Not that he remembered, anyhow.

His phone hadn't revealed any liaisons in the past six months. He would guess he'd poured all his free time into finishing the house.

Hannah set her gold clutch on an end table by the fireplace. "Who wants to go out when you have this sort of luxury at home?"

"Maybe." Brock strode over to the champagne bucket on a silver stand beside the dining table. "Can I pour you champagne?" He turned the label of the bottle toward him. "The wines are the only elements of the meal I chose tonight. The chef picked everything else."

"In that case, yes." Hannah strode closer, her pink-and-purple gown fluttering around her and brushing against him. "Just a little, though, since I have to work tomorrow."

"I wouldn't be so sure." Brock used a towel to hold the cork as he opened the bottle. "Your director threatened to pack up the whole shoot and return to LA to film on a studio lot if we can't do more to ensure privacy here."

He poured the champagne into two glasses as a waiter entered with a tray of appetizers and discreetly left it on the table. Brock had ordered a tasting menu that would ensure new dishes were brought often, in small portions, since he hadn't been certain of her preferences.

"You've spoken with Antonio?" Hannah asked, her soft fingers grazing his as she accepted a crystal champagne flute. Was that worry he detected in her voice? Perhaps she was concerned about her job, or the quality of the film if the director abandoned the location.

"No, I haven't." Settling the bottle back into the ice, he picked up his glass and led her toward the screened stone hearth where a fire crackled and popped. "Antonio sent a message to my brother Carson, which he shared with the family. The director of *Winning the West* hasn't made a good impression with the McNeills, and we will be glad when he leaves." Brock leaned closer to Hannah, tipping his forehead near hers. "The same can't be said of you."

She glanced up, firelight playing over her delicate features as she gazed into his eyes. He wanted to pluck her glass from her fingers and kiss her. Taste her lips instead of champagne. He gave himself a moment to contemplate that kiss before he continued.

"I'm in no hurry for you to leave, Hannah," he told her, burning to touch her. Instead, he clinked his glass to hers. "Cheers to us, and whatever time we have together."

Two hours later, seated across the table from Brock McNeill in the loveliest outdoor living space she could have imagined, Hannah thought that if she met him now, she would have never mistaken him for a cowboy.

And not just because of the custom-tailored tuxedo that fit him as comfortably as the denim he'd worn the first time she'd seen him. Though she would have to be blind not to notice the way the rich black fabric of the jacket made his eyes even bluer. There was also something about his whole manner tonight that seemed different.

When he'd given her a ride home on his horse that first night, she'd been the aggressor, falling into his arms and kissing him after the ride because the heat had been so intense, and the stress of the shoot had shredded her defenses. Tonight, she couldn't afford to give in to temptation, so she waited. Watched. This time, Brock made the seductive overtures, and he was far more patient. Thoughtful. While she'd simply thrown herself in his arms, Brock tempted her senses with fine foods and wines, tantalized her intellect with insightful discussion about everything from acting to horses, opera to ranches.

He'd been considerate of her comfort and responsive to her smallest request, taking her on an impromptu tour of the grounds between dinner and dessert when she'd asked about the flowering trees she could see thanks to the landscape lighting. Now, pushing aside the final plate of the evening—a personal fruit sampler with one perfect berry of every kind imaginable—Hannah reminded herself she wasn't here to fall for Brock McNeill.

She had accepted his dinner invitation to learn more about his family's connection to the Venturas, and she couldn't leave until she gleaned something that could help her sister.

"So your grandfather is getting married?" she asked, leaning back in her chair while Brock poured them both more sparkling water from the bottle their waiter had left on the table.

"He is." Brock gestured toward the hearth where a blaze still burned bright. "Would you like to sit by the fire?"

"Sure." She brought her water glass with her, setting it on the wrought iron table in front of the love seat. She made herself comfortable in the deep navy cushions, sitting sideways to converse with him better. Or maybe to face him head-on so his allure didn't catch her by surprise. Slipping off her shoes, she tucked her feet under her. "Malcolm's timing must have been a welcome relief for your family. It seems like talk of a McNeill wedding has shifted a little of the tabloid attention away from your stepmother."

"My grandfather did the family a real kindness," Brock agreed, staring into the flames as he took the seat beside her, his broad shoulder almost close enough that she could have tipped her chin forward to lean on him. "His proposal came at an opportune time. But after seeing him with Rose, I believe he would have married her either way."

"You could tell just by looking at them?" she teased.

He took the question seriously, mulling it over for a minute before he nodded. "There was something in the way they looked at each other. Like they would gravitate toward each other even in a crowded room."

"Oh." The idea stole her breath. Especially coming from this man, who drew her toward him in spite of her best efforts. "That's very romantic."

Suddenly too warm, she leaned forward to retrieve

her water, craving a cool drink. Brock's gaze followed her. She could feel it, even if she didn't look his way, focusing instead on the fire.

"I suppose it is," he agreed. "I haven't seen many couples look at each other that way."

"Not even your father and stepmother? They've been together a long time. Or your brothers? I've heard rumors that both Carson and Cody have found the women of their dreams recently."

"You probably know more about my family than I do since I don't remember the last six months." He tipped his head back against the headrest, frustration lacing his voice. "Carson's girlfriend showed up at my father's house the other night and I would have sworn I'd never seen her before."

"I can't imagine how maddening that feels," Hannah admitted, returning her drink to the table. "The only reason I know about your brothers is because of gossip on the set. The McNeill men have been an ongoing source of feminine interest and speculation since I arrived in Cheyenne."

"No one was more surprised than me to learn the twins have settled down." He shifted on the love seat to face her, his knee grazing hers. "And as for my father and stepmother, I always viewed their marriage as one of convenience until I saw them together the other night. My father seemed almost…tender with her. Maybe because of her accident and the coma that she's still recovering from, or maybe he feels bad for her about the scandal."

The warmth of his leg heated her skin right through her dress, the memory of where they'd touched enough to elicit tingly sensations up her thigh. She finally had the conversation directed in a way that might yield useful information about Antonio Ventura, but all she could think about was the awareness pooling inside her. The magnetic draw every time their eyes met.

She had to do better than this. She needed to put Hope first.

"Do you think your father knows why Paige turned her back on her birth family? Or why she left home in the first place? Over twenty years is a long time to stay away."

Hannah had asked herself those questions many times since the scandal broke. Did the McNeill family hide the connection on purpose? Had they even known about it?

Brock shook his head. "I couldn't say. Paige told us she never meant to deceive us. That she just needed a fresh start. And my father supported her, saying her name didn't change who she is on the inside, which I respect."

Hannah searched his eyes, hungry to know more. Perhaps he simply didn't know. Or maybe the amnesia had compromised his ability to remember the details of the scandal in the days leading up to the breaking news. But no matter how the incident had unfolded, she believed him now. She trusted that Brock hadn't known his stepmother was a relation to Antonio Ventura. Trusted that he wasn't helping Ventura hide behind his famous name and Hollywood power.

Brock's sole concern was for his family. And it hurt to think she'd lost out on a chance to have something more with him—to follow this heat where it led for a second time—when he was an honorable man. A simple rancher who also just happened to be a member of one of the wealthiest families in the country.

"Your father sounds like a good man." With an effort, she blinked away the haze of attraction, needing to leave before she did something foolish, like kiss him again. "You're lucky to have grown up with that kind of role model."

"You're not close with your father?"

"Not at all." She shook her head, sitting forward on the love seat and sliding her feet back into her shoes. "He walked out on my mother when we were young. He's always been more interested in his career than his family."

"You said 'we.'" Brock fingered a purple silk ruffle where it rested on the love seat, smoothing his thumb along the fabric. "Do you have siblings?"

"Just one sister. Hope." She regretted that the filming, and her absence from LA, was hurting her sister so much. But she couldn't just pack up and go home when someone on this set might know Antonio's secrets. "She's lived with me in LA for the past two years. I'd do anything in the world for her."

Brock's smile was quick and genuine. Understanding. "I'd slay dragons for my sisters, too. So it kills me to think how much this scandal is turning their world upside down." He shook his head, a sadness making his eyes turn a shade bluer. "The legal battles they'll have to fight to maintain their portion of the family lands and inheritance."

The knowledge of how much they shared in common, despite the surface differences, helped Hannah to better understand why she'd been so drawn to him that first night. She might not have known all those layers of his character, but she had sensed a connection immediately. What would have happened if she'd trusted that instinct? If she hadn't lied to him after he'd awoken with amnesia, and instead admitted that they had started a relationship?

Would things be any different now?

"I'm sorry they will have to fight those battles." She reached for him, unable to stop herself from laying her hand on his knee. "I know how much it hurts when you can't fix things for the people you love most."

She'd only meant to empathize. But as she stared into his eyes in the firelight, she felt the current between them strengthen. Deepen.

Flare hotter.

Tugging her hand away, she straightened before things got even more complicated between them.

"I should go," she announced, not surprised that her voice was a throaty rasp. She'd used all her restraint to prevent herself from touching him more. She didn't have anything left to hide the hunger in her tone. "That is, I have an early call tomorrow."

"Of course." Standing, he extended his hand to her and deftly helped her to her feet. "It's been a pleasure having dinner with you."

Was it her imagination, or did he linger over that word *pleasure* a fraction longer than the others? Memories tumbled through her. Touches. Tastes. Whispers.

She remembered all of it so thoroughly she couldn't imagine how he'd forgotten.

Her throat was so dry she couldn't answer. Settling for a nod, she knew she needed to get outside, away from the romantic firelight and the allure of Brock's undivided attention.

Ten minutes later, as the truck pulled up to her cabin, she all but sprinted out, not waiting for him to help her down.

"Thank you for everything," she called over her shoulder, her whole body still on fire from that briefest of touches back at his place. The night air hadn't done anything to cool things down. "Dinner was lovely. I had a nice time."

Brock was beside her a moment later, his long legs and loafers covering ground faster than she could in her open-toe stilettos.

"If the evening was so lovely and nice, Hannah Ryder, I'm not sure why you're racing away like the hounds of hell are at your heels."

He opened the screen door for her, pinning it with his body while she fumbled for her keycard.

"I'm not sprinting." Although if she'd had her running shoes on, she would have definitely moved faster. "I'm just…not in a good position to take things any further."

"And have I done anything to give you the impression I'm the kind of man who would press the issue?" Even in the dark, his eyes flashed with a hint of anger. Hurt.

She'd offended him without intending to.

"Absolutely not." She backed up a step, leaning on one side of the doorjamb while he bracketed the other side with his broad shoulders and brooding looks. She'd tried hiding her feelings and clearly that hadn't worked out well. There was nothing left but to be honest. "My speed has to do with me trying to outrun my own desires, Brock. Not you."

Some of the tension slid from him. "And if you've already explained that to me, keep in mind, I can't remember. Just like everything else that happened between us that first night—my memory of it is gone."

The scents of meadow grasses and wildflowers wafted across the fields, the breeze catching the silk of her dress. She didn't know what to say, but she couldn't talk about that night anymore. Her conscience wouldn't let her misrepresent the truth more than she already had.

"We didn't discuss it that night." She squeezed the metallic gold clutch harder to keep herself from touching him. "But I'm very involved in my sister's life right now, helping her deal with the fallout of a…traumatic experience. This probably wasn't a good time for me to take a movie role, but I'm committed to getting home as soon as I can."

"My sister is in LA, too." He frowned slightly, looking thoughtful. "Scarlett is frustrated with the family for not protecting her mother more, and I worry about her making major life decisions about her future when she's angry."

Hannah was grateful he understood. That he didn't dig deeper into her reasons for not indulging the attraction between them.

"That gives me an idea," Brock said suddenly, straightening from where he'd been leaning against the doorframe opposite her and stepping closer. "If you end up with more days off in the shooting schedule, let me know. We could fly to the West Coast for the day. Check on our siblings." His eyes glittered with unspoken possibilities. "Share another dinner."

The thought of spending more time with him tantalized her even as she knew he needed to be off-limits that way. Licking her lips, she readied an automatic "no." But then, feeling herself sway on knees weak with want, she wondered how foolish she was being to deny herself the pleasure of his touch when he could wake up tomorrow and remember everything that happened that first night anyhow.

One day Brock McNeill would resent her for lying to him. Deservedly so. It wasn't like he would think any more kindly of her if she refused every kiss until then.

Or was she rationalizing wildly for the chance to be with him again?

"Maybe," she said finally, the word scarcely a whisper between them since they were standing far closer than she'd realized.

Drawn together. *Gravitating* toward each other.

He didn't touch her. And wouldn't, she knew, after how she'd pulled away from him earlier. If she wanted more, she would have to make the next move.

One kiss wouldn't hurt.

She wondered if she'd spoken the thought aloud because his eyes darkened with desire, his gaze moving to her lips. Staying there.

Her heart pounded harder. Faster. Propelling her to take just one taste…

Fingers landing on the bristle of his jaw, she traced the hard edge toward his chin. Swaying closer, she skimmed her hand down the warmth of his neck, curving around the back to where his hair curled against his collar.

And then, she was kissing him. Gently. Sweetly. She nipped and tasted, remembering the feel of his mouth even as the kiss was completely different from that first, no-holds-barred night together. He let her feel and explore, get wrapped up in the taste and textures of their lips brushing. Only when she sighed with pleasure did he give her more. His hand splayed on the base of her spine, a welcome, seductive weight that anchored her against him. Sensations bombarded her, from the warm strength of his chest under his jacket, to the taut muscle of his thigh where it pressed lightly against the inside of her hip.

She clutched at his lapels, straining closer, losing herself in the kiss. His tongue stroked over hers in a way that made her shudder with need. In a way that reminded her how quickly he could take her to the brink, and push her over…

He pulled away then. Slowly. It took her a moment to even register what had happened. Her gaze was fuzzy and unfocused. Her fingers still clenched the silk of his tuxedo as if he was the answer to everything she wanted. Needed. As her senses returned to her, she spied the regret in his eyes that echoed the sentiment tightening in her chest.

With an effort, she disentangled herself from the fabric, easing away from the scent of his aftershave and the taste of his lips. Her skin tingled, and her body hummed with thwarted anticipation.

"I would never press the issue," he reminded her, his fingers lightly combing through her hair before he stepped back, breaking the spell. "But the offer to go to LA is open." He lifted her hand to his mouth and kissed the palm before closing her fingers over the tender place he'd just touched. "Think about it, Hannah."

He settled her forgotten keycard in the door lock and opened it for her before he turned and strode down the steps and back to his truck. Hannah could almost swear she'd forgotten how to breathe until then. Finally, dragging in a gulp of night air, she forced herself to step inside the cabin. Closing the door behind her, she leaned against the barrier for a long moment, knowing she wasn't going to be able to get that kiss out of her mind.

Brock had told her to think about a trip to LA.

Tonight, she'd be lucky if she could think of anything else.

Eight

Gaining access to the Ventura family estate hadn't been as difficult as Scarlett feared.

She'd watched the Beverly Hills home for a day, to acquaint herself with the various entrances and to watch who went in and out of the property. There was a guard at the gate that led to a handful of exclusive homes, but getting past him was the easy part since she'd noticed he didn't ring through to the owners for service deliveries. So she'd bought a box of organic produce and claimed she was delivering it to a house at one end of the street. Sure enough, the guard waved her through the gate, and she went to the Ventura home instead.

There, she only had to wheedle her way past an elderly gardener, who gladly opened another gate for her when he saw her fake delivery. She might have regretted taking advantage of the older man's kindness if she wasn't so thoroughly convinced her mission was just. The Ventura family had done something to alienate Scarlett's mother when Paige—Eden—was just a teen.

Scarlett wasn't leaving until she discovered the truth.

Now, as she lugged two hemp bags full of apples, peaches and Valencia oranges toward the delivery entrance of the expansive French chateau–style home, she wished she had a hand free to text Logan and let him know she'd made it this far. He hadn't wanted her to enter the property alone, but as a rising star in Hollywood, Logan was too well known to sneak in anywhere.

Besides, she didn't want him to compromise his standing with the director of *Winning the West*. Not that he seemed to care what Antonio Ventura thought of him. Ever since the director had held Logan's phone captive on a movie set in the Congo, preventing Logan from messaging Scarlett for weeks, he had no use for the critically acclaimed film guru, even though he was the director of Logan's current movie.

Which, she had to admit, she really liked. She'd been so hurt when she thought Logan had ghosted her. But ever since they'd reconnected, things were looking up. At least, with her relationship. But now her family—her family *name*—was in jeopardy.

Before she could step up to ring the bell on the delivery entrance—which consisted of ornate double doors slightly hidden by a magnolia tree—Scarlett heard a tuneful whistle from the side yard. Curious, she peered through a gap in the boxwood hedge into the European gardens full of paths, statues and fountains. At the far end of the property, a raised gazebo housed a well-dressed older man with his back turned to her.

The gray-haired occupant of the garden pavilion stood

at an easel, a paintbrush in hand as he carefully shaded purple flowers with dark smudges on the canvas. Something about his bearing, or maybe it was the perfectly tailored blue shirt with cuffs perfectly turned up, announced his wealth and status. This was no servant. She'd bet her last dollar that the serene painter in the manicured gardens was the owner of the house.

Emilio Ventura, Antonio's adopted father.

Scarlett's biological grandfather.

Emotions sideswiped her like a rogue wave. Anger and resentment topped the list, total indignation that this man had done nothing to reach out to his daughter in a quarter of a decade.

"Excuse me," she called, marching toward him with a sense of righteous purpose. "Mr. Ventura?"

She was halfway across the central courtyard of the elaborate gardens, a wood nymph fountain blowing water through a shell beside her, when the man stopped painting. He slowly turned toward her.

He didn't seem surprised, or worried. He seemed to silently take her measure before he settled his brush in a clear glass container on the tray in front of the easel. Then, as she continued to charge toward him, he picked up a piece of white linen and wiped his hands on it, taking extra time to clean around his nails.

The action only served to provoke her more. Surely she wasn't related to this fastidious old bon vivant living in an ostentatious mansion, too full of himself to care about anyone else? She strode faster, ready to give him a piece of her mind.

"Do you know who I am?" she asked, arriving in his shaded gazebo at last, only to realize she'd brought her organic grocery bags with her for the confrontation.

She set them down a little too quickly, spilling a few Valencia oranges. They rolled along the cool marble floor, one of them landing right in front of his Italian leather loafer.

He stared down at it in bemusement, his bushy eyebrows lifted in surprise.

"I have a general idea," he answered as he bent to retrieve the orange, inspecting it as he straightened again.

Before she could reply, he peered behind her, giving an angry flick of his wrist, seeming to gesture to someone else. Turning, she saw the security guard from the front gate in a golf cart. He was parked on the lawn, speaking to a young woman dressed in a sharp red business suit, her hair piled on her head in an efficient chignon. The woman apparently knew how to interpret Ventura's wrist flick, and she returned to her conversation with the guard.

Scarlett wasn't sure if Emilio had saved her from being thrown off the grounds, or if he'd merely granted her a window of time to speak before they arrested her for trespassing. Either way, she couldn't afford to waste this opportunity to find out why her mother had moved away from home, changed her name and never gone back.

"You have an *idea*." Scarlett crossed her arms and stared him down. "It strikes me as a sad commentary on your parenting when you only have a general idea of your grandchild. In fact, it makes me question why someone like you should have children in the first place if your only role in their lives is donating genetic material."

He flinched just the smallest bit at those last words. He set the orange on his easel and lifted sad, dark eyes toward her. "Did she say that?"

"Who? Did who say that?" Scarlett still didn't regret the tirade, especially as she couldn't detect the least hint of remorse in his expression.

"Your mother," he ventured, shoving his hands in the pockets of his neatly pressed khaki trousers. "My daughter. Because even though you're taking me to task for not knowing my own grandchild, I certainly see my daughter's face reborn in yours."

There was something kind in the way he said it. Something that, for a moment, made her regret all the times she'd silently wished she looked more like her siblings, who favored the McNeills.

Quickly, she brushed aside any softening of her feelings toward him.

"I can't help but think a man who had treated his daughter with any kindness wouldn't need to guess at her grown child's identity." Scarlett glanced over her shoulder again, wondering if the security guard was on his way over. But the golf cart was nowhere in sight now. "But maybe you plan to have me thrown off the grounds. Is that what you did to my mom all those years ago? Is that why she's never mentioned you? Never visited? Changed her name and hid from you on a Wyoming ranch?"

The older man shook his head, the lines in his face deepening as he frowned. "Never. Eden's mother… Barbara Harris. Have you met her?"

Scarlett shook her head, curious.

"She was a mixed-up girl long before your mother was born," he explained, steepling his fingers together as he walked a slow circle behind the easel. "I loved her deeply, but she wanted no part of a traditional relationship. She was a flower child, I suppose. Full of idealistic dreams that I loved, but she fell into drug use soon after Eden was born. We broke up and I should have taken legal custody of our daughter, but at the time—men didn't do that." He glanced up from his pensive pacing, stopping as if to gauge Scarlett's reaction. "I thought I was doing the right thing to support her decision to live with her mother. I thought she would have extra help. And that worked out okay for a while, until Eden was in middle school and Barbara ran away for months."

Scarlett was drawn in by the family history she never knew, and never even imagined until the scandal broke. She didn't know what to make of her reception, and she still wasn't sure if she was about to be kicked off the property, but she wanted to hear more about her mother's mysterious past.

And as much as she dreaded cutting Emilio any slack, she couldn't deny a strange fascination with watching him as he paced. Seeing him in person and not just in pictures online revealed the likeness to her mother even more. In the way he tilted his head. The turn of a phrase.

"By then, I had married Stella, and I had adopted her son, Antonio. But I told Stella we needed to take Eden in, give her a stable home since her grandmother couldn't watch her all the time. For a few years, it was wonderful having my daughter under my roof. We were a real family." He started pacing again, tipping his chin down to the tips of his fingers. Around them, birds chirped and the fountain babbled musically in the idyllic garden.

Scarlett's stomach knotted, knowing this story didn't have a happy ending. "So what happened?"

"I came home from a long location shoot and Stella said Barbara had returned to take Eden to live with her. I wasn't surprised that it was sudden, or that Eden didn't come back to visit for the first year or so—that's the way Barbara is. I assumed they were traveling. By the time I saw Barbara again, two years after that, she was back to using, worse off than ever, and couldn't tell me anything about Eden."

Scarlett waited for more. When he said nothing, continuing to walk in circles, a fresh surge of frustration simmered.

"And that's it? You figured your daughter was gone so why bother looking for her? It's fine if she never wants to see you again after you—supposedly—did nothing wrong?" It made no sense to her, and she could see in his face that he fully appreciated that it was illogical.

"I did look for her," he protested. "A little. I asked some journalist friends to use their sources." He quit pacing. "But you're right. I always feared she had a reason for leaving."

"Like?" She gestured with her hands, making a speed-it-up motion, tired of him circling the truth the way he was pacing the gazebo. "You've obviously worked hard to give the world the impression you're living in paradise. Is life in Chateau Ventura not all you've painted it to be?"

Emilio heaved a gusty sigh, his gaze moving toward the easel where his canvas rested. The half-finished painting was of green creeping vines and bougainvillea, with the house in the distance.

"Your mother didn't care for Antonio. I wondered if he had... I don't know. Bullied her in some way." Emilio continued to speak, saying something about his wife being defensive of the boy, but Scarlett couldn't focus on what he was saying.

The pieces shifted in her brain, forming a new picture.

Had her mother run from the son, not the father?

And who was keeping Paige McNeill safe from him now that Antonio was shooting a movie in her mother's backyard? Fear for her mother coiled in her belly.

"I have to leave." She withdrew her cell phone from her pocket, dialing Logan's number. "I need to go home."

Grateful to be back at work, Brock stood outside the training yard, watching his top trainer work with a new two-year-old.

The trainer had messaged him about three of the new horses slated as prospects for competition cutting—a sport designed to show a horse's ability to handle cattle. Brock appreciated the guy's input, especially since the evaluation process was far from scientific, even for the most veteran of equestrian judges. The Creek Spill was gaining a reputation for producing winners, with a core group of elite broodmares. Their breeding program had given Brock the financial security to expand their on-site training, something he personally enjoyed.

Here, at the rail watching an afternoon workout, Brock felt almost like himself. He could forget about the amnesia for a few minutes at a time. Pretend things were normal.

He couldn't say the same for Hannah, however. The woman was firmly on his mind every moment, distracting him with thoughts of the kiss they'd shared the night before. She had surprised the hell out of him when she'd wrapped herself around him. Especially after the way she'd tried to run into the house on her own, without so much as a good-night.

My speed has to do with me trying to outrun my own desires, Brock. Not you...

Her words had floated around in his brain all night, giving him red-hot dreams starring her. Them.

He wouldn't press her about another date, let alone a trip to the West Coast with him. But he couldn't deny that he wanted her. It didn't make sense that he hungered for her this way when he still had the feeling that she was hiding something. His amnesia might leave him cloudy on the last six months, but he had a crystal-clear memory of waking up after the head injury and seeing those shadows in her eyes. Hesitation.

Almost as if she were weighing how much to share.

Pulling out his phone, he typed in a few notes about the two-year-old before he forgot what he wanted to say. He had to agree with the trainer on this one. The horse didn't show enough interest in the cow, while the best cutters usually started with a strong reaction—fear or aggression. Either end of the spectrum could be trained well for cutting, but the horses who were more blasé about the cow required more training and might never have the necessary instincts to make a competitive cutting horse.

The notes helped take his mind off his concerns about Hannah. He'd been with a deceptive woman once before. A woman who'd fed him small lies that might have been forgivable in themselves. Like the time she told him that they shared a mutual acquaintance and later he found out his friend had never met her. Or when she said she loved horses, and it became clear she'd never been around the animals in her life. One of his friends had suggested he should be flattered that Clarice had tried so hard to get close to him. But she hadn't been trying to get close to *him*.

She'd simply wanted to be a McNeill.

The truth had been agonizingly clear when he confronted her on the inconsistencies in the things she said. Brock had realized he had no idea who she really was at all since she'd shown him only a fictional side of herself, a made-up facade intended to appeal to him. It unnerved him to think how well that had worked—and what it said about him.

"Brock," a man called to him from the barn.

Turning, he saw his father ambling over, dressed in worn denim and a T-shirt with the ranch logo. Donovan McNeill had taught his kids that hard work and loyalty earned respect. Not a bank account. He walked the walk, too. Because although he'd been born into wealth and privilege, he'd cut himself off from his father after a dispute over land, and had gone on to become a self-made rancher through relentless work and sheer will.

"Everything okay at home?" Brock asked, instantly on alert. He hadn't seen his dad outside the house since the scandal broke. "How's Paige?"

"She's doing better." Donovan's gaze moved to the training rink where the two-year-old was doing his best to follow the rider's commands. The animal would make a good ranch horse, displaying a willingness to work. "How's the training coming?"

It occurred to Brock that his dad probably appreciated the distraction of ranch duties today as much as him.

Briefly, Brock outlined the trainer's concerns. Donovan had never taken much interest in the quarter horse breeding program until it began turning a profit, letting Brock run with the idea. But in the last year—at least, in the time he remembered—his dad had asked more questions. He'd pushed Brock to develop the training side to grow the business even more.

"You're doing well," his father acknowledged after Brock's explanation, words that counted as glowing praise considering the source. "I left Paige with Madeline for a little while so I could touch base with you and your brothers."

"We would have come to the house—"

Donovan waved off his concern. "Of course. But I got the impression Paige needed a break from all the family living room meetings." Squinting into the sun, his father tipped his head back, lifting the brim of his Stetson to feel the breeze. "I think she feels responsible for the recent spate of news stories, even though I told her it's not her fault."

Brock watched the handler release the cow close to the horse again. "Scarlett puts the blame on us for not trying to work with the blackmailer."

"And she has a damn good point." Donovan jammed his hat back on his head and settled a foot on the rail of the training fence. "Did you hear she waltzed right onto the Ventura estate and confronted Paige's father? Asked the old man what he did to scare off her mother?"

"She's lucky he didn't have her arrested."

Donovan laughed. "How could he? She's his family." His expression turned serious again. "Scarlett seems to think it wasn't Paige's father who made her run, but the son. That damned director we have living right under our roof at the Creek Spill."

"Antonio?" Brock tensed. He couldn't remember meeting the guy personally, but the picture Hannah had painted for him about that encounter told him enough. "We need to get that film crew out of here."

"Except that would be another PR nightmare, according to that publicist we hired. She's recommending we allow the filming to continue so we don't attract even more of a media circus." Donovan scowled. "In the meantime, our investigator has added an extra security detail around my house so Paige is protected."

"And what about the blackmailer?" Brock hadn't heard any more about that since the day of his accident when Carson's girlfriend had shared her fears that her unstable mother was behind the whole thing. "Has the investigator looked into that angle?"

"He says he's got multiple people working on it. He doesn't have enough evidence to contact the police for an arrest, but apparently Jane Layton had a lot of access to the Ventura family in her years as their maid."

Brock listened, but his brain was still stuck on Antonio Ventura possibly being the reason his stepmother had left home as a teen. He didn't like the idea of Hannah working for someone like that. Brock wondered if he approached Paige himself and shared his fears for Hannah whether he might have better luck getting his stepmother to share something concrete about her past.

"In the meantime," his father continued, "Maisie said Scarlett is coming home. At least for the duration of the filming since her new boyfriend is an actor in the thing."

"That's good." He didn't hold out hope they could convince his half sister to stick around the ranch afterward, though. "I think we'd all feel better if we could part on better terms with her. At least help her see the family's side of the decision not to negotiate with the blackmailer."

Donovan nodded. "That girl has more grit than anyone I know. I hoped if I kept her on the ranch long enough, she'd find a role for herself. Decide to stay here after all."

"She always wanted to be an actress," Brock pointed out, gesturing to the trainer that he'd seen enough with the two-year-old in the pen. As long as he was here, he might as well view the other animals.·

"And I hoped it was a phase." Donovan shrugged, then pounded his fist on the top rail. "But maybe she's going to need that acting career if she's not even a legal McNeill."

Brock noted the set to his father's jaw. The cold anger in his eyes. "Dad, you know we'd never deny the girls their inheritance."

"I'm telling you what the lawyers explained to me. There's no fast way to sort out all the paperwork that details what they're entitled to." His voice had a dry, rough tone, hinting at emotions that Brock almost never saw in him. "Without the McNeill name to protect them, they could lose out on more than just the ranches." He shot Brock a level gaze. "If Malcolm died tomorrow, they'd get nothing from his estate. And I have blamed my father for a lot, but that wouldn't be any fault of his. It's on me for not knowing my marriage wasn't legal."

"How do we fix it?" Brock asked, understanding better now. McNeill Resorts was a global corporation with a net worth that far outstripped the ranches. But even then, it wasn't about the money. It was about the name. Family. Legacy. Future generations.

Because even when Donovan had cut himself off from his father, he'd kept the name, and he'd placed value on it.

"For starters, I've got to marry Paige again." Straightening from the rail, Donovan squared his shoulders. "She has been through too much already to give her just some quickie date with a judge to make us legal. As soon as I can pull the pieces together to make it special, there's going to be a wedding at the Black Creek Ranch."

A wedding.

Brock could tell by the tone of his father's voice that he was counting the hours until he could make it happen. Did that mean tomorrow? The next day?

As his father turned on his heel, Brock guessed that Donovan was on his way to deliver the news to the rest of the family. Or maybe to shop for a new ring. Brock was seeing a more sentimental side of his dad this week, that was for sure.

For his own part, Brock already knew who he was going to ask to be his date. The trip to the West Coast might not be happening with Hannah anytime soon, but he couldn't think of anyone else he'd want at his side when his father said his vows.

Nine

"He invited you to go to a *wedding* with him?" Callie asked Hannah as they stood together in one of the wardrobe trailers.

"Shh." Hannah didn't want the word to get around the set that Paige and Donovan were getting married for a second time. She peered over her shoulder through the open door where she could see an animal handler walking past with one of the horses that specialized in tricks. "It's got to stay between you and me, okay?"

Brock had phoned the night before to ask her if she could be ready within a few hours' notice to attend a secret family wedding, tonight or tomorrow. She had tried to tell herself it would give her a perfect pretext to speak privately with Callie—she could ask to borrow a dress and then try to find out more about why she'd used the word "lewd" to describe Antonio. But instead of coming up with ways to convince Callie to confide in her, Hannah had fallen asleep thinking about how a dance at a wedding reception would put her in Brock's arms again.

As much as she'd like to think the attraction was all just sensual chemistry, she knew better. Every moment spent with Brock McNeill made her like him more. And made her regret the barrier she'd put between them that would ensure he would regret this relationship when his memory returned. She'd done it to keep herself from falling for a man like her father, like the sailor who lashed himself to the mast to keep from following the siren's song. It seemed so smart at the time, but when temptation called…

"Why the secrecy?" Callie asked, glancing up from the rolling rack where she was tucking a lace sleeve back into a garment bag.

"They won't want any media attention." Hannah hoped she hadn't made a mistake trusting her friend. "I don't want to be the one to ruin their wedding after all they've been through."

"Right." Straightening, Callie thumbed through more hangers, looking over the options for Hannah. "I forget this isn't Hollywood where everyone *says* they don't want media attention, when they actually crave it like their next hit." She pulled out a blue lace skirt. "What about this? I brought it by mistake. You could wear it with a silk tank and dress it up."

"Maybe." Hannah could already feel Brock's hands on her waist where the two fabrics might meet. Where a thumb might accidentally brush along bare skin. Shaking off the imaginings, she focused on why she really came to the wardrobe trailer after her time on set. "Callie, I have a question. About… Antonio."

She lowered her voice when she said his name. Then for good measure, she turned and closed the trailer door. They were the only ones inside. Callie stared at her curiously.

"What is it?"

"Do you remember when you told me about the photo someone posted with the 'separated at birth' caption?" At her nod, Hannah pressed on, hoping she hadn't misunderstood the woman's previous comment. "You used the word 'lewd' to describe him."

Callie's face flushed. She looked confused. Betrayed, even. "Did I?" Her hands slid away from the hangers and she folded her arms across her chest. "I'm not sure what you're getting at."

Flustered, Hannah rushed to reassure her. "I'm not getting at anything. And I don't mean to be nosy, I just… I've heard things about him. And I wondered—"

"I haven't heard anything." Callie shook her head, her eyes bright with emotion, her shoulders tense. "And I think you made a mistake about what I said. Everyone is so quick to judge."

"I'm not judging—"

"Hannah, I think you'd better go, okay? I won't tell anyone about the wedding, but this is a conversation I'm not comfortable having." She thrust the blue lace skirt into Hannah's hands and stalked into the trailer's tiny bathroom, locking the door with a *click* behind her.

Did that seem like the response of a woman who didn't know anything about Antonio's behavior? Unsure how to proceed without alienating a potential ally for Hope, Hannah walked toward the closed door. She paused outside, and said softly, "I'm leaving, but I want you to know you can talk to me if you change your mind. I didn't mean to upset you."

When there was no reply, Hannah walked out of the trailer, leaving the lace skirt behind. She didn't want Callie to think she was trying to take advantage of her. Maybe she shouldn't have used the pretense of borrowing a dress as a reason to come here at an off time.

But far from being discouraged about what she'd discovered, Hannah hoped she was on to something. Maybe after Callie had time to think it over, she would decide to confide in Hannah.

Until then, she had a secret wedding to prepare for.

Brock rode home late that night, urging Aurora faster after a long evening working with his brothers to turn an empty barn on the Black Creek Ranch into a wedding venue. The barn they'd cleaned was old and unused, but it was structurally sound with plenty of picturesque appeal. His father didn't want to hire too many outsiders to help prepare for the wedding in an effort to keep the ceremony out of the media, so Brock had pitched in with Carson and Cody to get the space in shape.

Working with his brothers had felt like old times. Especially since the barn dated from the days when the Calderon family had owned the land, before Donovan had married Kara Calderon, Brock's mother. Brock had mixed memories growing up on the Black Creek Ranch, some happy, some—like his mother's death— gut-wrenching. He'd been only three at the time, but his earliest memories were from that day. Flashes of ambulance lights. His father falling to his knees.

But life had gone on at the main house after his mother's death. Paige had joined their lives, becoming a nanny and then, Donovan's new wife. Yet somehow, she'd never really been "Mom." She'd always been quiet. Unassuming. A steady presence in their home while their father charged in and out, his bigger personality the driving force of the McNeills.

It occurred to Brock that while Scarlett favored their mother in looks, she was more like Donovan in personality—someone you noticed immediately. Whereas Madeline, the oldest of the girls, took after Paige, quietly attending to business while running the White Canyon Ranch, a guest ranch where many of the cast members of *Winning the West* were staying.

Guiding Aurora toward home, Brock slowed the mare as he neared Hannah's cabin. He had planned to drop off some things she might need for the wedding earlier, but missed an opportunity when his father asked for help at the barn. He'd had one of the ranch hands deliver the packages instead. Now, it was almost midnight, but the cabin lamps blazed and another opera aria floated on the breeze through an open window. Clearly she was still awake. Besides, the Perseid meteor shower was peaking this week, lighting up the sky with streaking stars.

How could he let her miss it?

Reining in, he dropped down to the ground and then climbed the steps onto the porch. Before he knocked, however, he pulled out his phone to text her so she'd know who was at the door. Through the open window, he could hear her phone chime and, a moment later, a soft laugh.

Then, footsteps.

Anticipation speared straight through him.

When the door opened, Hannah was dressed in a worn purple T-shirt that said But First... Coffee, and a pair of cotton pajama pants in bright blue. Her hair was woven in a messy braid, her face scrubbed clean. With no makeup, she was even prettier. There was nothing to detract from her wise gray eyes and expressive mouth.

"This is getting to be a habit, Cowboy," she drawled, stepping out onto the welcome mat to look over his shoulder. "What will the neighbors say?"

He caught a hint of her shampoo as she stood by him. He battled a fierce urge to lean down and breathe in the scent of her.

"Since there's no one around for almost a mile, I think we're okay." He gestured to his horse. "And Aurora doesn't judge."

"No?" A smile curved her lips. "Then no wonder you chose a career where you're surrounded by horses."

He heard the edge in her voice and wondered if he'd struck a nerve.

"You're in a notoriously competitive field," he said carefully, waving her outside. "And I won't stay long. I only came to show you something out here."

"Outside in the dark?" she asked, her voice full of skepticism.

"Yes, ma'am. Grab a sweater if you want. Or shoes. But you can see it from the deck."

"It's the least I can do, since I owe you a thank-you for the surprise packages you had sent over here today." She leaned to one side, pulling a gray cardigan sweater off a hat rack made of elk antlers by the door. "I was stunned to find a few options for dresses to wear to the wedding."

"It was my pleasure since you were kind enough to be my date on short notice." He tugged the lightweight cashmere from her hands. "Allow me."

He held the shoulders wide so she could slide one arm in, and then the other.

Releasing the collar, he let the fabric fall against her neck. Then, unable to resist, he slipped his hand beneath the braid trapped by the material, tugging it free. Her hair was soft as silk on his skin.

His hand faltered in midair, his brain reeling at how much he wanted to keep on touching her.

"It was very thoughtful of you. Thank you." She edged away quickly, stepping out the door and onto the welcome mat after sliding sandals on her feet. He noticed that her toenails were painted bright pink. "I'm ready."

He took her hand, telling himself it was for practical purposes since he didn't want her to trip in the dark. "Be careful."

Brock wanted to get closer to her. To learn more about her. See if he could unlock the secrets in her eyes.

Failing that, he just wanted to spend time with her. To lose himself in the warmth of her smile. The ease of being with someone who didn't want to talk about blackmail and PR strategies. Hell, he just wanted to enjoy the simple pleasure of stargazing with her.

The opera that was playing ended, giving way to a more haunting melody, the sound growing quieter as he led her to the darker back corner of the deck for the best view.

"Close your eyes." He spoke the words softly, against her hair, his jaw against her temple.

"You're being very mysterious," she accused softly. "I can hardly see in front of me as it is."

"Just trust me." He let go of her hand to cover her eyes with one hand, his arm around her. She felt so right against him, like she belonged there.

But he didn't let himself get distracted by that now. He tipped her head back.

"You can open now." He moved his hand away, staring up into the night sky with her as a streak of light grazed the heavens above their heads.

She gasped with delight, her face full of wonder in the pale glow of the waning moon. "How did you know that would happen?"

"I didn't. That was just good timing." He pulled over a cushioned patio bench for her. "It's the peak of the Perseid meteor shower this week. I thought maybe you'd enjoy one of the benefits of living far from city lights. Our views are usually really good out here."

"That's amazing." Her eyes continued to scan the skies even as she took a seat. "Should I turn off the light inside?"

"I can get it." He jogged around to the front of the house again, reaching inside the front door long enough to flip the main switch before rejoining her.

He dropped onto the bench next to her, tossing aside an extra pillow to make more room for himself. He slid off his hat and set it on the planked floor while the opera ladies sang back and forth on the music still playing inside.

"Look!" Hannah pointed overhead to a streak of green, white and red. "I don't think I've ever seen a shooting star before."

"It's comet rubble, I think. Earth passes through the orbital path of a comet this time of year, so the streaks are bits of cosmic debris hitting the atmosphere."

"'Shooting star' has a more poetic ring to it." She kept her gaze fixed on the sky. "I hope your father and stepmother are watching. It seems like a good omen for the night before their wedding."

"They've got a lock on all things romantic for tomorrow," he assured her. "I just finished clearing out the barn with my brothers, and my sisters were starting to decorate when we left. Madeline showed me a photo of what they're going for and it should look really nice."

"They're decorating now? At almost midnight?" She glanced over at him. "I'm surprised the McNeill family doesn't have a fleet of workers to do things like that for them."

"Dad has always stressed the value of hard work. But even if he wanted to hire out the jobs, his hands are tied this week since he doesn't want to attract any extra attention to the ranch or invite media speculation."

"So this will be a low-key event?"

"Not in the slightest." He spotted the start of another meteor and pointed toward the arc of white light. Here in the shadow of the house with a wide-open view of the night sky, they had the best possible seat for the event. "My father is determined that Paige feel the full love and support of the family tomorrow, so he's doing everything in his power to make it memorable."

"Such as?" Hannah slid off a shoe and tucked one foot under her. Her knee brushed against his thigh and rogue visions swamped him. Passionate visions that he needed to lock down fast.

He dragged in a deep, cooling breath of night air and kept his eyes on the stars.

"I don't want to ruin any of the surprises. But he's having services like the catering truck come through the gates at three in the morning in an effort to elude media interest." Brock had to hand it to the old man. He'd planned carefully.

"Very smart of him." Hannah clutched his knee as

another meteor streaked past in a blue blaze. "The colors are so pretty."

Brock's pulse slugged harder as he began to doubt the wisdom of inviting her out here. He wanted to get to know her better, but it wasn't easy to make friendly chitchat when the attraction rocketed between them hotter than any fiery cosmic debris.

He closed his eyes for a second, trying to stay in the moment and the conversation. Trying to remember he was here to get to know her better, not test the heat of their chemistry.

"I'm happily surprised at the level of effort Dad has made. My stepmother has been the unsung rock of our family for as long as they've been married, and I'm glad he's recognizing that."

Hannah gave a bitter laugh. "Some men go a lifetime without noticing the good people in their lives. My father walked out on Mom, Hope and me the moment he found a woman whose ambitions matched his own."

"I'm sorry you went through that." He plucked up the end of her braid where it sat on her shoulder, testing the ends against his finger. "And even though that was extremely wrong of him, I wonder if it wasn't easier on your mother than if she had stayed another fifteen years with a man who didn't appreciate her enough."

Had Paige stayed with his father only because she felt trapped? Because she was hiding from her real family, using the protection of the McNeill name?

"Maybe it was," Hannah admitted. "But he sure didn't do Hope any favors by writing her off."

"What about you, Hannah?" Brock set down her braid, easing forward on the bench to see her expression now that his eyes were accustomed to the dark. "It had to be equally difficult for you."

"No." She shook her head, vehemence in her voice. "I don't need someone who puts more value on material things than people. But my sister was young enough when he left that I think it made her more…susceptible to the promise of love and acceptance."

"Susceptible?" He wanted to learn more about her, and he'd sure latched on to something tonight, but he couldn't quite identify what it was. Resentment, yes. But Brock felt like he was only getting half the story. "You make love and acceptance sound like an illness."

"It can be when you seek it too desperately because you weren't given enough as a child." Anger tightened her voice. "It makes you a target for people to take advantage of you."

He turned that over for a long moment, thinking through the implications of the little she'd shared. The night sky gave them something to focus on so the silence didn't feel awkward. Finally, he broke the quiet.

"It sounds like Hope has been through a lot." He slid his palm over to where Hannah's rested on the cushion between them. Slipping his fingers between each of hers, he squeezed her hand. "But she obviously has a fierce protector in you, Hannah. You were probably better for her than any inattentive father could have been."

For a long moment, he simply felt her pulse gently drumming in the heel of her hand beneath her thumb. But eventually, she turned her gaze toward him.

"I would gladly trade my own happiness for hers." She spoke with a conviction that made it sound like she'd already made that devil's bargain. "But I'm not sure that it will do her any good."

Brock couldn't add up the pieces of her cryptic confidences. Maybe it was because of the amnesia, and his brain was only working at half speed. Or maybe it was because the attraction thwarted his more noble intentions. But selfishly, he wished he could ease that hurt in her eyes.

"You can't live your life for someone else. Or give away your happiness to save another person's." His free hand found the soft curve of her cheek, his thumb stroking her there. "It doesn't work like that."

Her eyes fluttered as he touched her. Out here, under the natural fireworks of the night sky, it felt like they were all alone on the edge of the world, with no witnesses except the night breeze to hear them.

He caught himself moving toward her. Knew he needed to hold back.

"I haven't given *all* my happiness away," she admitted, opening her eyes wide again, her pupils dilated so that there was only the slimmest gray ring around the edges. "I could still have one taste."

Her gaze dipped to his mouth, torching his restraint.

"One kiss. That's all," he swore…to himself? To her? To the universe?

He didn't know.

Gently, he angled her chin up and captured her lips with his. Heat spiked in his spine, tightening his shoulders and tensing everything else. She melted into him, her lips parting, back arching, molding delectable feminine curves against him.

He untwined their fingers because he needed both hands on her to steady her hips. To still her for a moment. Ensure she didn't end up in his lap. Because if that happened…

"Brock." She breathed his name against his damp mouth as her fingers raked down his back and up again.

She wriggled closer, the heat of her skin warming his palms right through the thick fabric of the pajama bottoms.

Ah, damn.

He hauled her across his thighs, knowing they couldn't take this any further outside under the stars. She straddled him, her knees locked against his waist, the heat of her sex evident right through the denim of his fly.

Things could go off the rails so fast if he wasn't careful.

Especially since he could feel her heart pounding, and the soft moans she made when she kissed him were the sweetest sounds he'd ever heard.

But there was something fragile inside Hannah Ryder. Some secret or some hurt, he didn't know which anymore, that kept her from him. So he was going to honor that "one kiss" vow if it killed him.

And pulling away from her, his breathing more ragged than if he'd run the perimeter of the ranch, he thought it just might.

"I want you," he told her simply, their breathing slowing as they stared at each other in the moonlight. Stars winked behind her, meteors streaking the sky like the world was about to end. "But only when you're sure." He slid her to the bench seat beside him, knowing he needed to leave before he broke the promise he wanted to keep. He pressed a kiss to her temple before standing. "Only when you're ready."

Walking away wasn't easy with her sigh of regret whispering on the wind, even knowing she'd be on his arm tomorrow at the wedding.

Ten

Hannah picked a stray piece of straw from the hem of her silk organza dress. She never would have guessed the first surprise of the wedding day would be arriving at the ceremony in a hay wagon pulled by a big green John Deere.

She'd heard the tractor rumbling closer late in the afternoon when she had been expecting to see Brock. Instead of her date, a boy dressed in a cowboy hat and overalls—boutonniere pinned to the denim strap—knocked on her door and invited her into the wagon. One of the ranch hands had rolled out a carpet for her so she didn't ruin her shoes, and when she'd stepped up into the unlikely conveyance, she'd been greeted by a handful of other guests, including Carson McNeill's girlfriend, the stuntwoman Emma Layton, and Cody's pregnant fiancée, Jillian Ross, the woman who'd been the location scout for *Winning the West*. Jillian, a gorgeous redhead dressed in a bright green-and-yellow tulle dress, explained that the men were helping their father get ready for the wedding, but that Brock had wanted to make sure Hannah had family to keep her company until he could join her at the ceremony.

Now, as the wagon bumped over a ravine close to the Black Creek Ranch, Hannah held on to one of the hay bales strapped to the sides. They were piled high on the exterior of the wagon to help shield wedding guests from long lens cameras and drones since the McNeills were trying to keep the tabloids from ruining their day.

Hannah feared she was going to end up ruining the day for Brock in the end anyhow. She couldn't sleep after he left the night before, regretting that she hadn't come clean with him about what they'd shared that first night together. She couldn't deny that she had feelings for him, a fact pounded home by the way his kiss had dominated her dreams in the fitful hours when she had finally closed her eyes.

She hadn't been honest about their heated first encounter because she'd been consumed with worry about her sister and hatred for Antonio. And when she'd first learned Brock was a McNeill, she'd been floored by the idea that she'd slept with a man related to Antonio Ventura—if only on paper.

Now that she knew Brock better, understood him for the kind of man he was inside, she owed him the truth. After the wedding festivities tonight, she would tell him. He'd been through so much with his family this week it didn't seem fair to ruin his day. She wanted him to celebrate his father's wedding. But her conscience wouldn't let her enjoy another one of those toe-curling kisses without telling him the truth.

And then, it would be over.

So she planned to savor this day as much as she could before she offered her heart up for Brock to break.

"Your dress is beautiful, Hannah," Emma was saying to her. A brunette with wide, dark eyes and delicate features, she wore a simply cut navy sheath. "And you look so familiar to me, I feel like we've met before."

Tensing, Hannah knew her time of reckoning would come with this family. She just hadn't wanted it to be today. At least, not yet.

Hannah forced a smile, reminding herself all the subterfuge had been for a good cause. "Now that you mention it, you look familiar to me, too. I think we worked for the same temp agency last spring."

Emma frowned for a moment, then snapped her fingers. "Yes! I remember. We shared a house cleaning assignment one day in Beverly Hills, didn't we?"

Thankfully, it hadn't been the Ventura house when they'd worked together, which would have been a little too close for comfort.

The tractor downshifted, the engine noise quieting a bit as they slowed their progress. Around them, a few of the other guests took group selfies, posing with wildflowers that one of them had picked on a stop to load more guests.

"We do what we need to in order to make ends meet between jobs," Hannah replied before redirecting the conversation. "How have you enjoyed the stunt work on this film?"

"I've grown really attached to the horses," she admitted, graciously taking the bait. "And I don't know how

I would have gotten through the shoot without Carson, and now, his whole family." She lowered her voice so that only Jillian and Hannah could hear. "I know in my gut now that my mother has been the one behind the blackmail. But we have to wait for the private investigator to have enough evidence before they will—" Emma blinked fast and whispered "—*arrest* her."

Jillian slipped a supportive arm around the woman, quietly murmuring something to her.

"I'm so sorry," Hannah said, meaning every word. She stood up enough to drag her hay bale seat in front of Emma, shielding her from view of the rest of the wagon to hide the other woman's tears. "I had no idea."

Jillian dug in her purse for a tissue and passed it to her friend while focusing on Hannah. "We know Brock has been dealing with a lot, with losing some of his memory. How is he feeling?"

Guilt gnawed at Hannah. She'd been so focused on her own family problems while Brock's had been going through hell this week. "His head doesn't ache anymore, but I know it frustrates him that he can't remember the last several months."

Emma halted in the middle of wiping her eyes. "I don't think he even recognized me when he saw me at Donovan's earlier this week."

Hannah nodded. "I know the dynamics of the scandal have been confusing for him since he doesn't remember everything leading up to it." She bit her lip, wondering if she should ask them the question that Brock couldn't help her with now that he had amnesia. The question that had kept her from telling Brock the truth when he woke up with no memory. "Do you think the

McNeill family knew about Paige's real identity before the scandal broke?"

The wagon rolled to a stop. Violin music played nearby.

Emma shook her head. Jillian blurted, "Cody was blindsided. Completely stunned."

Hannah stood with the other women, unable to enjoy the swell of excitement through the rest of the group as they caught sight of the decorated barn where Donovan and Paige would exchange their vows and host a reception.

She had hidden the truth of that first night from Brock fearing that he could have a loyalty to the Ventura family. She hadn't expected to fall for the rancher in the meantime. She hadn't thought the omission would ever come back to bite her.

As she stepped down onto the lawn outside the barn, glimpsing Brock in his black tuxedo, his blue eyes locking on her, Hannah could already feel the ache of all she was about to lose.

Scarlett felt like an alien on a foreign planet as the wedding music began.

The people filling the barn were familiar enough, of course. She'd grown up on the Black Creek Ranch, and then after college, she'd moved into a remodeled bunkhouse on the property. She'd played hide-and-seek in this barn with her sisters, and she had once rescued a scared kitten from one of the rafters.

But the barn looked nothing like it had back then, when it was full of rusty old farm equipment. With the highest windows opened to let fresh air in, the barn's gray stone walls were a beautiful backdrop to six-foot-tall candelabra spaced every few feet and decorated with cream-colored ribbons and white flowers. The heavy rafters were polished to gleaming, the wood glowing in the reflection of white fairy lights raining down from the ceiling. White tulle was hung tent-like between the beams.

The whole place smelled like lemon wax and roses. The linen-draped tables were decorated with white freesia and snapdragons in clear glass jars filled with bright yellow lemon slices.

And even the people seemed different. Her brother Brock, who normally never left the horse barn, suddenly couldn't take his eyes off the beautiful actress he was with. And their surly father had developed a solicitousness where his wife was concerned, a tender affection that Scarlett hadn't seen in all her twenty-five years.

She squeezed Logan's hand beside her as they took their seats in the front row on the bride's side. Madeline and her boyfriend, Sawyer, sat in the row with them, Maisie was sandwiched between the two couples and decidedly alone.

"I hardly recognize this place," Scarlett whispered to Maisie. "And am I to really believe Dad went to all of this trouble on his own for Mom?"

Maisie poked her with her elbow, more from sisterly habit than anything. A love poke. Scarlett jabbed her in the arm in return. She'd missed her.

"Do you see these bags under my eyes?" Maisie whispered as the wedding music began. "I was up half the night decorating, thank you very much. But yes, it was all Dad's idea."

"Unbelievable. I'm gone for a week and the whole world turns upside down. Suddenly Dad is a romantic?" She was going to have a hard time staying angry with her father after this. She hadn't seen him since her flight had landed late the night before, but her mother had seemed stronger and surprisingly happy when she'd visited with her this afternoon to help her dress.

Scarlett hadn't had the heart to quiz her mother about Antonio Ventura on the day of her second wedding to their father, but she would. Soon.

"Believe me, it's freaking me out," Maisie whispered behind her hand as they stood for the bride's entrance. "I'll be the only cynic in the family at this rate."

All the McNeill relatives in attendance were paired off, too. Ian and Lydia McNeill had made the flight with patriarch Malcolm and his fiancée, Rose. Lydia was pregnant with their first child and positively glowing. Damon and Caroline McNeill were there, too, taking a break from Transparent, the software company Damon headed in Silicon Valley.

"Even Brock is dating again." Scarlett had seen one of Hannah Ryder's films and thought she was talented but didn't know much about her personally. "I asked Logan if he's ever worked with Hannah before, but he said no."

"Brock has amnesia," Maisie reminded her. "I'm worried about him."

"I'll talk to him," Scarlett said before all eyes turned to her mother at the entrance of the barn.

Paige looked beautiful in a slim ivory gown with a lace shrug that covered her shoulders. Her brown hair fell in glossy curls that Scarlett had talked her into. Normally, her mother favored a ponytail, her part a razor-straight line down the center of her head. But Scarlett had begged for curls and a bow, and her mother had agreed that it was "time for some changes."

Behind Scarlett, Logan leaned close to speak into her ear, sending a delicious shiver down her spine just from his nearness.

"Look at your dad," he said.

Scarlett glanced around Maisie's shoulder where she could see her father's face. The naked emotion there caught her off-guard. Love. Tenderness. A shining pride in the woman who walked toward him. Scarlett gulped back a tear at the same time Maisie dug in her handbag for tissues. She passed two over her shoulder.

As the vows began, Scarlett knew she'd been mistaken when she'd accused her father of being unfeeling about her mother's welfare. Of course, she'd been right about her brothers being too protective when they'd sent a private investigator to LA to keep tabs on her. But she was going to forgive them because they were older brothers, and that was their thing.

Besides, she was empathizing a little too well now that she knew someone from her mother's past had hurt her. All her own protective instincts were roaring.

For now, she was going to enjoy the wedding. Afterward, she would talk to her mother about what had happened in Emilio Ventura's home to make Paige a fugitive from her own family. Because Scarlett wasn't interested in simply weathering a scandal and protecting the McNeill name.

She planned to find out who was responsible for hurting her mom. And then hold them accountable.

Hannah stepped outside the barn just as the dancing started, needing a breath of fresh air.

The chamber musicians who had played earlier were packing up their instruments and loading them into the back of a pickup truck nearby. Inside, a country-western band had started to play, bringing the crowd onto a makeshift dance floor in one corner of the barn. The white lights and candelabra made the whole building glow, illuminating patches of the meadow around it through the open windows and doors.

The summer night had brought a cool breeze with it, and Hannah let the wind blow her silk organza dress, the guilty knot of feelings tightening in her belly the longer this night went on.

Behind her, she heard a familiar male voice. "I've been looking forward to a dance all day."

Heat rushed through her, that jolt of reaction Brock could always elicit. With a word. A look. A touch.

She couldn't deny him this dance. Not when the bride and groom were still celebrating inside.

"Me, too," she told him honestly, taking his hand and letting him lead her back inside.

The band had swapped to a sultry slow song, the singer crooning romantic words that amplified all of the things she was feeling. The longing. The hunger. The fear that things wouldn't last. As they reached the dance floor crowded with couples, Brock spun her easily into his arms, a protective hand at her waist, holding her close.

"I'm happy for my father," he confided, nodding toward the bride and groom in the middle of the dance floor.

Donovan McNeill had eyes only for his wife as they swayed together. Paige glowed in his attention, her diamond wedding ring glittering in the reflection of a thousand fairy lights as she rested her hand on her husband's shoulder.

"He pulled off an incredible event on very little notice," she agreed. "And I haven't seen any sign of paparazzi lurking."

"So far, so good." Brock's hand shifted on her waist as he stared down at her, his touch making her breath catch. "You look beautiful tonight."

She felt herself falling for him, her defenses crumbling fast. If only this could be real.

"I owe it to you for sending me the gown." The silk organza hem teased against her calf, the delicate material fluttering around her as they moved.

Pale pink and dotted with tiny flowers, the dress was romantic without being too sweet. The cold shoulder treatment of the sleeves gave it a dose of sexy.

"I'm not talking about the gown," he assured her, leaning closer. "It's all you. Thank you for being my date tonight."

She bit her lip, not sure what to say. She just knew she needed to redirect the conversation before she dug them both in deeper.

"It's a testament to your family that you've come together this way, to celebrate a marriage and focus on the positive after all you've been through."

The slow song came to an end, but Brock didn't let go of her.

"I'm going to try to take a page from Dad's playbook and put the past behind me. Not worry about the memories I've lost. Just enjoy the present with you."

All around them, the couples on the dance floor clapped for the band. Hannah could only think about how thoroughly she'd screwed things up with Brock. Before she could say anything, he whispered in her ear.

"I want to go on a real date with you. Away from the

family and the ranch. Get to know you." He stared into her eyes, even while the singer announced the bride and groom were getting ready to take their leave.

The movement all around them, the rush to share hugs and good wishes with the couple, saved Hannah from having to answer right away.

Brock took her hand and led her toward the doors so they could see off Donovan and Paige. Hannah knew her time with Brock would come to an end once the couple made their exit. She couldn't accept his offer, not when she hadn't been truthful.

And then after she told him, she knew, he wouldn't be asking for another date.

Turning, she faced Brock. He looked far too tempting in his dark tuxedo, his handsome face bathed in moonlight.

She needed to speak fast before she weakened. Inhaling a bracing breath, she blurted, "Once we're finished here, there's something we need to talk about."

Eleven

Half an hour later, back at her cabin for the night, Hannah invited Brock inside so they could talk.

Nerves wound tight, she knew there was no other way to move forward. She needed to tell Brock the truth about that first night they spent together. Even so, it worried her that she wasn't free to tell him everything. Hope's secret was not Hannah's to share, and her sister's emotional health and well-being had to come before everything else.

No matter how much she wanted to unburden herself fully.

"You look so serious." Brock took her hands in his as they stood in the cabin's tiny foyer. "Let's sit and we'll talk."

He pressed the button on the remote that made the gas fireplace blaze to life. The orange flames leaped silently with no logs to crackle or pop. The warm light cast a romantic glow in the living area as Brock tugged her down to sit beside him on the leather sofa.

She shifted to see his face, knowing there was no easy way to say this.

"I haven't been honest with you." She stared down at her hands, her nails free of any polish because of the time period of the film she was shooting. She toyed with the eternity knot ring she wore, a simple sterling silver piece that matched the one she'd given to her sister for her high school graduation.

Even then, Hannah had known they were each other's best support system.

Brock tensed beside her. She didn't have to see him to know. She could feel it. They were so in tune with each other physically. Would she be losing that with her admission? God, she hoped not.

"How so?"

"It's about that first time we met," she answered. "The night you don't remember because of the amnesia. I didn't tell you everything that happened." She glanced up to see him watching her, his expression neutral.

Was he reserving judgment? She wasn't certain.

"What happened?" he asked, his voice remote and lacking its usual warmth. "What did you leave out?"

Her pulse sped faster.

"I made a split-second decision about not sharing the details when you woke up with no memory. It seemed like the right choice then," she said quickly, needing to explain.

"What have you omitted?" he pressed, and she could hear his patience fracturing. There was a tense frustration threaded through the words.

"We were together that night," she blurted, glancing up to see his reaction. "Intimately."

His eyebrows shot up. But other than that, he showed no reaction, saying nothing for the space of three painfully long heartbeats. She held her breath, waiting.

Then his mouth went tight for a moment and she knew. This wasn't going to go well.

"You took advantage of the amnesia to tell me your own version of events." His voice was level, but there was a flash of emotion in his blue eyes. Anger. Frustration.

Both well deserved.

"I did, and I'm not proud of it." She twisted the ring around her finger, again and again. "That night was my fault. I instigated what happened, and we hadn't even—I didn't even know your name at the time." She still couldn't believe it had happened at all. "I never do things like that. It had been a stressful night, and then we shared a horseback ride over here—that part of what I told you was true."

His jaw flexed as he listened. He did not interrupt. Instead, he waited. Shadows from the fire danced across his face.

She pulled in a shaky breath, her emotions all over the place. "The closeness and the touching... I don't know how to describe what it did to me. But the shoot had been so hellish that day, and then when we touched—"

"Why?" he demanded, cutting through her confusion and guilt with one simple question.

"Why did things ignite so fast? I don't know, we just—"

"No. Why was the shoot hellish?" he asked more gently. "Because of the director? Because of the long hours in the hay that day?"

She'd told him those details. Had shared everything right up until he'd taken her back to the cabin.

Her thumb traced the silver loops in the eternity knot. She couldn't share the impotent fury she felt every time she looked at Antonio Ventura, let alone took direction from him. She couldn't confide her sister's pain when Hope wanted more than anything to keep her ordeal private.

It tore Hannah up inside, because the secret hurt her, too. But it was a pain she could never share when Hope's was a thousand times greater.

"Yes," Hannah lied, blinking fast and hating herself. "Ventura is mercurial, and the churlishness of his demands make this business far harder than it has to be."

That much was true. But it certainly didn't give a glimpse of the real torment of her time on location in Cheyenne, the burden of it lightened only by Brock's presence. Her time with him had given her something good to savor in spite of everything ugly around her.

Still, her throat burned, the weight of what she couldn't say weighing down her conscience even as she shared.

"Hannah, look at me." Brock's voice wound around her, his hand sliding over hers in an unexpected touch.

"I didn't tell you about what happened between us because it felt like a second chance for me to...not get so carried away again." Her pulse thrummed faster, nerves knotting with agitation. "I thought if you forgot it, I would, too, and we'd both move on."

"But here we are. Right back where we started that night." His thumb brushed back and forth over her palm.

The tenderness of his touch caught her off guard.

"You should be raging at me for deceiving you all this time." She willed away the flare of heat that came with his caress. "I should have told you the truth."

"Yes. But I can think of a few times in my life that I would have grabbed the chance to rewrite history." The warmth in his voice soothed her soul. "That's forgivable, Hannah."

Not daring to believe her ears, she searched for some sign she may have misunderstood him. But the expression on his face appeared open and honest, his body language open and relaxed.

And hot.

With his bow tie loosened and the top button unfastened on his shirt, he looked enticingly disheveled. His broad shoulders filled out his jacket, the fabric stretching around his biceps as he leaned forward to touch her. His intent was unmistakable.

"Is it truly forgivable?" Her heart skipped a beat.

She hadn't even considered a scenario where Brock would want to pick up where they'd left off. She melted inside a little to think there might still be a way for them to be together.

A future that included a second chance.

"It is. The question I want you to consider is, now that you have a chance to rewrite history, do you still want to forget what we shared ever happened?" He lifted his hand to her face, grazing the back of one knuckle along her jaw. "Or do you want to relive that memory?"

Brock breathed in the scent of her, relishing the way her pupils dilated at his touch. The firelight gave her pale hair a burnished glow, her cheeks even more flushed color.

He could tell she was surprised that he wasn't more upset with her. But he searched inside himself and found only…relief. Now, he knew what she'd been keeping from him. He understood the shadows in her eyes sometimes, the nagging sense that she'd been holding something back.

Hearing what that secret had been, that she'd second-guessed herself after being with him, was a weight off his shoulders. A worry off his mind. That, he could deal with. He could still see a way forward with her. And hell yes, he still wanted her.

"Are you…sure?" She placed a hand over his where he touched her cheek, holding his fingers captive while her eyes tracked his, searching for answers. "That is, yes, I would relive the memory with you. But it's still not fair to you since you don't remember us together."

Her "yes" rang through him, igniting a primal, chest-thumping roar inside. It felt like he'd been waiting for her forever. He'd hardly slept after the dinner at his house. After the meteor shower and the kiss under the stars. She'd invaded his every thought. Dominated his dreams.

"I've imagined it so many times, it's almost real." He tugged her hand to his lips and kissed the backs of her fingers. Lingered on the base of her thumb where he could feel her pulse race. "Besides, how many people get to have a 'first time' all over again?"

She tipped her head to one side, her hair falling away to reveal the vulnerable skin of her neck. More places he wanted to taste her.

"I'm not sure if we can top the *first* first time." Her

fingers walked up his chest, slipping under the tuxedo jacket.

"I love a good challenge." His blood surged hot as he envisioned how things might have happened that night after he'd brought her home. "But tonight is going to have a whole different feel to it since we know each other better now. I've had a lot of time to think about us. To plot the best approach."

He brushed a kiss over the base of her throat and down to her shoulder, sweeping aside the strap of her silky gown for a better taste. She edged closer to him, her knee bumping his, her thigh pressing against him.

Heat seared him. He wrapped her in his arms, dragging her into his lap. She was so soft and fragrant, her hair and her dress tickling and teasing when he wanted to strip everything away and sink inside her.

Already, her fingers were at the fastenings on his shirt. He shrugged out of his jacket for her and realized they'd never pull this off here, on the couch. At least, not the way he wanted.

Lifting her in his arms, he carried her toward the only bedroom in the place. He knew the layout. But there was also something familiar about stepping into the darkened bedroom with her. Almost as if the memory wanted to surface.

For a moment, he chased it. But then, what did it matter compared to the here and now?

Gently, he set her on her feet. She'd kicked off her shoes at some point, her bare toes visible in the moonlight slanting through the blinds. He wanted to see her better, and he reached back to flick the wall switch that worked the fireplace here.

Another action that felt familiar.

"Brock?" Hannah's hand stilled on his chest; his shirt was already half off. "Are you okay?"

He fought off the déjà vu that wasn't real since he didn't remember that first night with her. Instead, he focused on her lips swollen from his kiss. Her dress already sliding off one shoulder where the strap had fallen, a hint of pink lace visible along with the curve of her breast.

Hannah waited, breathing in the scent of Brock's aftershave, a woodsy spice that she knew would make her knees weak for the rest of her days. He seemed on board with being together, but it worried her that his hand had gone to his temple. A pain? It hadn't been that long ago that he took a blow to the head.

"I'm better than okay," he assured her, lifting both her hands and twining his fingers through hers as he kissed his way down her neck. "I'm so damned good I might die from it."

His words vibrated along her neck, sending ribbons of pleasure down her back and making her skin tingle. Her breasts pebbled, the heat between her thighs impossible to ignore.

Just like the first time. Things were getting out of hand so fast she couldn't even keep track of all the ways he made her feel delicious. Feminine. Wanted.

Before she could ask for more, he was unfastening the other strap on her dress, lowering the bodice and feasting on one taut nipple right through the lace bra she wore. Sensation coiled tighter. Hotter. She gripped his shoulders, nails digging in lightly before she caught herself and eased up.

With a growl, he shrugged the rest of the way out of

his shirt, his chest a pure pleasure to see and touch. Her hands roamed all over him, feeling every inch while he unzipped the rest of her dress. When the silk pooled at her feet, she tipped him back on the white duvet, falling on top of him and pinning him to the mattress.

For a moment, he watched her in the firelight, his blue gaze tracking her every move as she kissed her way down his chest to trace the muscles of his abs.

Hannah hadn't expected their new first time together to be even more intense. But it was. Mind-blowingly so. And she intended to savor every second of it.

She worked the clasp of his belt with anxious fingers while he unhooked her bra with a clever flick. She took all new pleasure from the feel of his hot skin against her bare breasts as she slid off his pants. His boxers.

But then, a new light flared in his eyes, his shoulders tensing as sweat rose along his back. He flipped her so that she was beneath him, pinning her there while he kissed her. And kissed her.

When both of their breathing had turned ragged, he pulled himself away long enough to find a condom in a pocket of his jacket. She didn't wait for him to undress her. She eased the lace panties down with a swivel of her hips and a little help from one hand, savoring the way he watched.

Desperately hungry to have him.

He sheathed himself, and she was so incredibly ready. He kneed apart her thighs, positioning himself between them, driving himself…home.

The cry she made was a sound she didn't recognize, a throaty moan of completion when they were only just beginning. She wrapped her legs around him, losing herself in him. In this moment.

In a "first time" that, yes, was even better than the first time.

She stroked her fingers through his hair, whispering in his ear how much she liked every single thing he did to her, asking for more, giving him everything in return.

The sensations heightened even when she thought they couldn't possibly go higher. Her heels dug into his hips, her arms wrapping around him to hold him close. When he reached between them to stroke the juncture of her thighs, right where she needed him most, she went utterly still. A riot of sensation crashed through her, waves of pleasure coursing so hard she could only close her eyes and hold on.

Before she could even think how to give him that incredible sensual gift in return, he found his own peak. His thighs tensed, his shoulders and arms going rigid with the same bliss that had rolled over her.

She kissed his neck and chest, clinging to him. Lost with him.

She hadn't imagined he would possibly give her a second chance after the secret she'd kept from him, but the real possibility of more with him tantalized her now. Defenses nonexistent, she let herself feel all the delicious aftermath of being with him. The secret, joyful hope that this could be...everything.

When he rolled to her side, taking her with him to lie next to him, she tucked into his chest as if they'd been sleeping together for a lifetime. The rightness of the moment surrounding her, she savored the first sense of total well-being since the night her sister came home in tears.

The memory struck a painful note, but she pushed it to the side, promising herself she was going to find a way to avenge Hope. If anything, she felt stronger than ever in the shelter of Brock's arms.

Surely Hope would understand how much Brock meant to Hannah, and give her blessing to share the last of the secret Hannah had kept from him.

She was everything he ever wanted.

Even in his dreams, Brock relived the night with Hannah. The haze of slumber and sensation drew him deeper in, immersing him in her with an intensity that made him loath to wake up…

He lifted her in his arms, skimming off the scrap of blue lace around her hips before he pulled her down to the white duvet with him.

She made soft, sexy sounds of approval in his ear as she speared her fingers into his hair and drew him down to kiss her. Shadows flickered across the bed beside them in the firelight, the need for her—for this—ratcheting higher.

He'd never bedded a woman so fast. Never imagined a night like this where desire smoked away reason and sensual hunger roared with predatory demand. But Hannah was right there with him, her hands shifting lower to smooth down his chest, back up his arms. All the while she urged him faster, whispering soft commands to touch her. Taste her.

He couldn't get enough of her…

Waking with a start, Brock glanced down to see Hannah asleep by him, her blond hair covering her shoulder like a blanket. He eased aside the strands to stare down at her in sleep, the remnants of his dream still clinging to the edges of his memory.

Their night together had been incredible. But as his

gaze snagged on her pink lace panties on the end of the bed, he thought back to his dream. He'd been so sure they were blue.

He could picture them perfectly. Bright, peacock blue.

Even her bra had been blue.

Not pink.

Head aching, a rush of images assailed him. Of a horseback ride with Hannah. She was wearing a dark T-shirt, a black ball cap and a pair of leggings that helped him to feel every nuance of her curves when they'd been on the horse.

It wasn't a dream. It was reality. A memory.

He remembered.

The realization was so welcome, such a relief, he nearly woke her up to share the good news. Except that, with his memory came a sucker punch that landed squarely in his chest.

He'd gone to see her on set the morning after their first time, specifically to ask her about her guarded reaction to learning his name. He recalled vividly that Hannah had been upset to learn he was a McNeill. Why?

He'd asked her point-blank.

She hadn't been honest with him then. And she sure as hell hadn't told him the whole truth now. As much as he wanted it not to matter—it did.

Shifting away from her, he needed to get to the bottom of it. Before he could wake her, however, his cell phone vibrated on the nightstand. Lifting it, he saw a text from his oldest brother, Cody.

The words on the screen couldn't have shocked him more. The private investigator the family had hired wanted to talk to Hannah.

Twelve

"Hannah." Brock heard the ice in his voice but was powerless to fix it. Soften it. The realizations about Hannah were too damning. "We need to get dressed."

Already stepping out of bed, he had no choice but to slide on his tuxedo pants and shirt from the wedding.

"What's going on?" she asked sleepily, sitting up in bed, the sheet clutched to her.

"Two things." He buttoned the tuxedo shirt with impatient fingers, needing to get outside into the fresh air. Clear his head. "First, Cody asked us to come to the Black Creek Ranch main house. There have been some developments in the blackmail case, and apparently the private investigator has asked to speak to you."

He watched as she came fully awake, her face draining of color. "Me?"

"Yes." He grabbed his shoes and headed for the door. "And in other news, I've got my memory back."

He didn't wait to hear her reaction or her explanations. He couldn't process what was happening or why she was doing this to him, drawing him back into her life when she had purposely tried to distance herself from him after he'd gotten amnesia. Right now, all he could think about was getting to his brother's house fast and finally getting to the bottom of the scandal, the blackmail and—most painful of all to him personally—Hannah Ryder's deceit.

An hour later, the whole family had gathered in Cody's great room. It had cathedral ceilings and a stone fireplace that went up to the second floor, the room's tall windows letting the morning sun in on three sides.

Brock stood at the window while his brothers spoke in low voices with Dax, the private investigator who'd taken over the legwork on the blackmail investigation for the family. Hannah had attached herself to Emma and Jillian as soon as they'd arrived, which was just as well since Brock couldn't think of a single thing to say to her until he knew what was going on with the investigation.

She still hadn't been honest with him. Even after the performance she'd given the night before—the insistence that she had come clean with him. Why had she even bothered when she was still withholding information?

She'd pulled on black leggings and a long gray T-shirt and tucked her hair in a ponytail before they'd left. She was sharing a cushioned ottoman with Emma near the fireplace. Madeline and Maisie put out some of the food they'd planned to serve at today's post-wedding breakfast for out-of-towners—pastries and sweet rolls—along with coffee and fruit. Not that Brock was hungry. But the scent of cinnamon and dark roast hung in the air from the kitchen island that lined one side of the great room. His father helped himself to a plate while they waited for Scarlett and Logan, the last to arrive. As the pair walked in the door, Dax—an Ironman competitor who used his digital forensics background in his work as an investigator—strode to the middle of the room.

"Thank you all for coming." The guy looked like he hadn't slept. There were shadows under his eyes, and his gray T-shirt and jeans were both wrinkled. "To bring you up to speed, the police arrested Emma's mother, Jane Layton, last night for trespassing on the Black Creek Ranch property."

Brock turned to look at Carson's girlfriend where the stuntwoman sat beside Hannah. Hannah squeezed Emma's hand while Carson stood behind her, his hands on her shoulders. Judging by her calm expression, Emma already knew about her mother's arrest. And now that Brock's memory had returned, he recalled meeting her, as well as her announcement that she feared her mother was the blackmailer. He had no idea why she believed that, however. He'd left his father's house early that night, unable to make sense of anything with his amnesia.

The investigator flipped pages in a notepad, his eyes scanning the small pages as he continued. "Jane is being held in custody as a person of interest in the blackmail case, and I'm close to having some additional evidence to share with police. But before I delve into that, Paige and Donovan have asked me to reveal a few things about Paige's past to help orient you."

Behind Dax, Cody was ushering his pregnant girlfriend into a chair at the kitchen counter and sliding a plate of fruit in front of her.

Seeing his brothers both so damned happy and in love only underscored the hole burning in Brock's chest this morning.

"Eden Harris voluntarily left home at age seventeen with the help of her stepmother, Stella Ventura." Dax nodded at Paige before turning back to the rest of the family. "Stella covered for her absence by assuring Eden's father, Emilio, that she'd left with her mother, Barbara. Stella also helped Eden disappear by putting her in touch with someone who gave her new identification papers and Social Security number so that she could become Paige Samara."

Brock was glad to learn of the logistics. He'd wondered how it was possible for a seventeen-year-old heiress to vanish, but clearly, his stepmother had help. His gaze drifted to Hannah, wondering if any of this was a surprise to her, or if she'd already known. Resentment simmered at the thought she may have used him to get close to his family.

Cody spoke up from his place near Jillian. "Paige has asked that we respect her privacy about why she left, and we're going to do that. Dad's lawyers are already working with a government agency to help her avoid any legal trouble since she used the false name and Social Security number under duress. But we thought it was important that we all understand who helped her to leave, and who was aware of her new identity, since that narrowed the field of possible blackmailers."

Close to where he stood, Brock noticed Scarlett's thinly veiled impatience. She shuffled from one foot to another and looked ready to speak until Logan King slid an arm around her waist. She seemed to settle down then, tucking close while the investigator took over the story.

Dax paced in front of the fireplace, his leather loafers creaking softly in the quiet as he tugged a pencil out from the wire ring of his notebook. "No one knew about Eden's new identity but Stella and, Stella realized afterward, her maid Jane Layton, who had overheard some of what transpired the day Eden left home."

Brock's focus shifted to Hannah in time to see her bite her lip. Did she know something? But just then, Emma squared her shoulders and sat forward on the ottoman.

"My mother has battled bipolar disorder since I was very young," Emma explained. "I've always known she had an affair with Emilio Ventura, Paige's father, but I wasn't aware until recently that she tried to tell Mr. Ventura that I was his daughter. That's definitely not the case, by the way. I bear a strong resemblance to my father, who passed away a long time ago. But I think my mother might have tried to taunt Mrs. Ventura with the affair and with the idea that I could be Emilio's biological child."

Behind Emma, Carson shook his head. "None of that gives Jane a motive for blackmailing the McNeills, though." He cast a thoughtful glance over toward Paige. "Unless she thought Paige would pay to keep her secret quiet?"

Paige appeared unruffled. Relaxed even. Brock wondered if having her secret finally out had given her a new sense of peace. Certainly, she seemed happier than he could ever remember seeing her.

She finally weighed into the discussion. "Carson, I'll tell you what I already explained to Dax. I have no memory of Jane, either by sight or even by name. You have to remember, I was only a teen at the time, and I didn't grow up in my father's house. I simply stayed there for a few years when my mother was unwell."

"I met him, Mom," Scarlett blurted, straightening from her spot beside her actor boyfriend. "Your father, that is. And for what it's worth, I think he really misses you."

The two of them stared at one another, a silent conversation going on between them that Brock didn't begin to understand. Frustration built inside him; his shoulders pulled tight as he ground his teeth. He was tired of waiting for answers.

"So where does that leave us? Is Jane the blackmailer or not?" He was being abrupt, maybe, but his family had been dealing with too much these last weeks. Hell, *he'd* been dealing with too much trying to recover from amnesia while his family publicly fell apart at the seams. "And what does Hannah have to do with any of it?"

He heard her quick intake of breath, even from the other side of the room. No doubt he was still far too in tune with her, too aware of her every move. Breaking that bond was going to hurt, but it would be critical to moving forward.

Dax gave him a level look, a hint of displeasure on his face. Perhaps Brock had upset the guy's flow. Or maybe he'd wanted to speak to Hannah privately. But whatever it was, Dax recovered quickly enough.

"Much of what we have to tie Jane to the blackmail scheme is circumstantial, but it will be stronger once we eliminate any other possible connections between *Winning the West* and the Ventura family." Dax pointed to Scarlett's boyfriend with the chewed end of his yellow pencil. "Logan King has already spoken with me at length about his experiences with Antonio Ventura, and he has a firm alibi to clear him. The only other person with access to both the Venturas and the McNeills, as well as an interest in the movie, is Hannah Ryder."

All eyes turned toward her.

For a moment, Hannah wondered if the investigator would have tried questioning her in front of the whole group if Brock hadn't practically encouraged him to do just that. Not that it mattered. Helping her sister had somehow connected her to a blackmail investigation, and she couldn't impede a criminal case because of Hope's need for privacy.

She just wished she didn't have to speak about it in front of the whole family.

It hurt even more knowing that she was in this position because a man she'd trusted with her heart didn't trust her at all. But if she allowed herself to think about that now, she wouldn't be able to keep her composure through the questions. She was keeping herself together now by only sheer force of will.

"I can explain." Hannah stood, nervous energy making her want to pace. Or fidget. Her acting training wouldn't allow her to give in to that impulse. She understood the nuances of body language. "I was actively researching the Ventura family two months ago, and I briefly worked with a temp agency cleaning their home. I saw photos of Eden Harris and her mother in Emilio Ventura's study, and Jane Layton made an unusual remark about them that helped me link Eden with Mrs. McNeill."

"Why would you research the Ventura family?" Brock asked tightly. "You never mentioned that last night."

Hannah heard the disdain in his voice. Brock thought

she was deceitful. A liar. And that hurt after what they'd shared.

Swallowing back the pain, she focused on the investigator instead. "I can explain why I did that, but since my story involves someone else, someone who wouldn't want her name mentioned, I would ask that you let me share the rest of it privately."

She waited for Dax's reply, prepared to answer his questions to the best of her ability. Maybe it would even be a relief to share with someone. The stress of what Hope had gone through had eaten away at both of them this year.

When the investigator nodded his approval, Brock crossed his arms over his chest.

"How convenient."

His cold words froze her feet to the hardwood floor, preventing her from following Dax into the dining area.

Mute with hurt and an anger of her own, she stared him down in front of his family. Willing her jaw to unclench, she said, "Excuse me?"

"You don't think I deserve to know what else you've been hiding from me?"

Before she could answer, Paige McNeill stood. "Brock, please. Has it ever occurred to you she might need to protect someone?"

Gratitude filled Hannah's chest, a soothing balm, even if it would never fully ease the hurt of Brock's mistrust. Blinking away the sudden threat of tears, Hannah looked over at Paige. Really looked at her.

And something in the set of the older woman's chin, the tone of her voice, even the wringing of her hands, made Hannah think of her sister. It was a flash. An instinct. But in that moment, she knew without question why Eden Harris had run from the Ventura home. Why Eden had become Paige Samara McNeill and never looked back.

She'd been hurt once, too. By the same bastard who had hurt Hope.

"Thank you, Mrs. McNeill," Hannah murmured, hurrying past them to follow the PI into the dining room on the other side of the huge foyer. At the threshold, she paused, her heart thumping. She glanced back at the room full of Brock's family. And at Brock himself.

He stared out the front window, his expression inscrutable. He hadn't followed her, giving her the space that his stepmother had wanted him to. Hannah understood she'd hurt him. That in protecting her sister, she'd done deep damage to her fledgling relationship with someone she really cared for.

And maybe she'd done all she could to protect Hope now. She'd protected her sister's privacy as much as she could, even when it cost her a chance at something that could have been…so much more. Later, she would call Hope and ask for her forgiveness. Her understanding. But now, Hannah called back to the man she'd given her heart to, offering him the answers he craved. Already knowing it was too late for them.

"Brock?" She watched as his head came up. Their gazes locked, and his detached expression killed her a little inside. The hurt of what they'd lost left her breathless as she called back to him, "You're welcome to join us."

Maybe a better man would have simply trusted her, taking it on faith that her secrets were her own and didn't have any bearing on their relationship.

But Brock had been burned before. Not just by his ex-girlfriend, but by Hannah herself. Just yesterday she'd admitted she'd been lying to him. How was he supposed to take today's revelation that there were even more holes in her story? That she had some kind of connection to the Ventura family that she'd never mentioned.

So hell yes, Brock followed Hannah into the dining room, taking a seat near her as she began talking to the PI.

The story that came out made him half wish he'd never heard it. Not because the truth implicated Hannah. Far from it. His stepmother had understood the subtext of all that Hannah hadn't said, and as Hannah spelled out Antonio Ventura's crimes against her younger sister, the shattering facts made Brock fear what his stepmother had gone through living in the same household as Antonio.

It became all too clear that Antonio's sister—related only through adoption—had probably been his first sexual assault victim. And over twenty-five years later, the bastard was still getting away with taking advantage of young women who didn't have the resources or support system to take on a powerful man.

His first instinct, before Hannah had even finished giving her account, was to rally his brothers and inflict as much damage on Ventura as possible. But he knew that wasn't the way to stop a serial predator. Furthermore, he'd implied a level of discretion and respect for Hope Ryder's privacy by even setting foot in the room with Hannah as she spoke to the PI.

Now, like Hannah before him, he carried the weight of an ugly truth that wasn't his to share. But he would do everything in his power to leverage his resources and influence in a way that would help convince women to come forward. Perhaps even starting with his step-mother.

But first? He needed to find a way to talk to Hannah. To make some kind of amends for his lack of trust. Judging by the way she fled the dining room as soon as the private investigator assured her he had enough information, Brock didn't think she was going to give him that chance willingly.

Damn it.

He stood up fast, following her out into the living area. His father pointed wordlessly to the front door. And, out the huge windows, Brock could see her blond ponytail bouncing as she hurried away from the house with determined steps.

He needed to follow her. To apologize for not having faith in her. But first, he needed his whole family to understand one thing.

"Carson." Brock slid out of his dress loafers from the wedding, and grabbed a pair of boots by the door, not much caring who they belonged to. "I know you signed a contract with that movie production company. And it's fine if the movie films here, but not as long as Antonio Ventura is attached to the project. If he remains the director, we're going to shut the whole thing down, whatever the cost."

Donovan nodded tersely from his spot on the couch beside Paige, his arm tightening around his wife. "I will pay for the lawyers. Hell, I'll finance a whole army of them if that's what it takes."

Brock wondered how much his father knew about the director of *Winning the West*. He guessed Donovan didn't know the full story either, or Antonio would have met with a mysterious hunting accident a week ago.

"Thanks, Dad." He spared a quick glance at Paige, and a spear of guilt cleaved him in half for all the time she'd spent leading a quiet life, out of the spotlight, when she'd been an heiress in her own right. She'd been in hiding from a monster for too long, and it was going to end now.

He stepped over to the couch long enough to lean down and press a kiss to his stepmother's cheek. "You were right about Hannah. I love you, Mom."

Then, turning on the heel of his borrowed boots, he headed out the door, determined to find Hannah—and find a way to make things right between them.

Thirteen

Hannah had ridden over to the Black Creek Ranch with Brock, so she had no choice but to walk back to her cabin.

Not that she minded. She welcomed the fresh air after the intense family meeting with the investigator and then, the more private discussion with Dax while Brock listened. Telling Hope's story had taken a lot out of her, but she was glad to have shared the truth. Now, she planned to pack her things and fly home as soon as possible.

Her sister didn't want her here anyhow, and she was worried about leaving Hope alone for much longer. If quitting the film ruined her career in acting, she truly didn't care. She would rather go broke fighting a legal battle to break her contract than spend another day taking orders from her sister's molester. Being in Wyoming this week had given her a taste for the life she'd rather be living anyhow. One that involved midnight stargazing and walks in the country. Horseback rides.

Her heart ached at the thought of that. She knew she'd never have a ride quite like the one she'd had with Brock.

"Hannah, wait."

The voice behind her was unexpected. And feminine.

Not that she planned to see Brock before she left, but she certainly hadn't cultivated personal ties with anyone else in his family.

Hannah shielded her eyes to see Brock's youngest sister, Scarlett, hurrying toward her. They had spoken briefly at the wedding the day before, just enough for Hannah to learn that Scarlett was excited about her move to Los Angeles and starting her own career in acting. Hannah had invited the younger woman to stay in touch after the filming ended in case she needed any advice. They'd do a lunch date.

And while the offer had been heartfelt, Hannah didn't think she could make small talk with her heart breaking. As Scarlett reached her side, Hannah turned to keep walking.

"I'm sorry, Scarlett, but I need to get back home." She stared down at the worn tire tracks she was following, grass encroaching on both sides. Cicadas made a high-pitched buzz while the sun beat down. "This morning has left me wrung out. Empty."

"My brother was out of line back there." Scarlett doubled her pace in order to keep time with Hannah's determined march.

"He's entitled to his opinion." She blinked at the burning in her eyes. Beneath her feet, the grass got blurry and she cursed herself for crying over something she couldn't change.

"Not when it's so wrongheaded." Scarlett took her hand and gripped it tight, forcing Hannah to stop unless she wanted to drag Brock's sister with her. "Men aren't always on our wavelength. At least, my brothers aren't. Brock can tell you the kind of mood a horse is in the moment he walks in the barn. But a woman? Not so much."

Hannah laughed. It was a watery yelp without much humor, but she appreciated Scarlett's attempt to defuse the tension. "He's great, actually. I screwed up by trying to hide things from him."

"I get it." Scarlett dug in her bag for a tissue and passed it to her. "And my mom obviously understood what was going on back there, too, which scares me."

"I think she ran away from home because of him."

"Antonio," Scarlett clarified. "His father even admitted to me that he's always worried his adopted son was a 'bully' and that's why Eden never returned home."

"I'd call him far worse than a bully, but I really can't share any more—" There was a vibration under her feet that surprised her. Then a horse and rider came into view from around a bend.

Brock sat tall in the saddle on Aurora's back, his tuxedo shirt open at the neck, the sleeves rolled up to his forearms, his black dress trousers tucked into dark leather boots. Her thoughts, and her gaze, stayed glued to him.

"Hannah." Scarlett squeezed her hand to get her attention. "I just wanted you to know that I'll talk to my mother. She's not a scared seventeen-year-old anymore. She's a woman of considerable power if she'll step up and own it. And I feel sure she will."

Hannah tore her eyes away from Brock. "What are you saying?"

Scarlett gave her a level look. She had a feminine flair in her dress, and an almost girlish beauty with her curls and wide blue eyes. But there was an absolute certainty about her, a grit and pride that only a fool would mistake.

"I'm saying Paige McNeill is an heiress two times over, and her word will carry weight in the court of public opinion. If we can get her to condemn Antonio, it's going to be vindication for whoever you're trying to protect."

Hannah thought about what she was saying. If Paige spoke out against Antonio, shared her own story, it could be career-ending for the director. Hope would see some justice served even if she never brought charges.

But maybe, if she saw others speak out against him, she would, too.

In her peripheral vision, Hannah saw Brock dismount the horse and begin walking their way.

"That would be...amazing," Hannah admitted, nerves jangling at the thought of talking to Brock. "Thank you."

It would make her trip to Cheyenne well worth it if she accomplished what she'd set out to—to let the world know that Antonio Ventura was a sorry excuse for a human being who did not deserve his vaunted place in the film industry.

Scarlett gave her an encouraging smile before backing up a step. "I'm going to start my campaign with Mom right now."

Brock's sister stalked off in the direction she'd come from, toward the ranch house that was now out of sight. That left Hannah very much alone with the man who'd condemned her in front of his whole family.

"I'm leaving," she told him, stuffing the tissue that

Scarlett had given her into the pocket of the drapey, gray yoga shirt she'd thrown on this morning with her leggings. "I think that will be best for both of us."

She had fresh clothes on while Brock wore his recycled tuxedo shirt and pants, yet he still managed to look like a brooding lord out of a Jane Austen novel.

"That won't be good for me at all, Hannah, and I'm sorry that I've put you in a position where you feel like that would be best for you."

He sounded so sincere. And maybe he was. But it didn't change the things that had happened between them. It didn't mean he would ever trust her.

She dragged the toe of her running shoe through the grass, thinking she was going to miss the wide-open spaces here. The never-ending blue sky. She wished Hope could have seen it.

"In the end, we had different loyalties. My family had to come first for me. They—she—always will." She felt teary again and she needed to keep walking. Keep moving. "I'm in a hurry to get back now that I've made the decision. Do you mind if we continue walking?"

Brock whistled for the horse and the mare followed at an easy pace, nosing in the grass now and then.

"I know I overreacted today," he told her as they strode deeper into the wooded area along the creek. "Everything has been so intense this week. Ever since we met, I've had a scandal hanging over my head, and a blackmailer to catch. Then, the amnesia made it ten times harder to be any help to my family when they needed me most. So when my memory came back this morning and it still felt like you'd left things out, I didn't handle it well."

"You're protective of your family. I'm protective of

mine. It put us at odds today." And that broke her heart as she thought of what could have been between them if things had been different.

"It wouldn't always." He snapped a dead branch from a nearby tree and tossed it deeper into the woods, away from the trail. "That is, it doesn't have to."

She weighed the words as she allowed them to sink in, wondering if she was understanding him correctly, unable to squelch a flash of hope. Hope was scary, too, because she wanted to be a part of his life, to have more of those horseback rides and nights under the stars with him.

"I don't know what you mean." She picked up her speed, wishing she could outrun the hurt of losing him.

"I admire that you put your family first, even at the cost of you and me." He bent sideways to pick a tall Indian paintbrush, never slowing his step. "But how many times in a life does something like this come up? How often would family put us on opposite sides?"

Hannah shook her head. "Maybe never. But what does it matter when we've already broken this fragile thing we were building? When you've already shown me how quick you are to not believe me? You threw me under the bus back there, Brock."

"Like an idiot," he agreed, his boots following the worn path of one tire track while she remained on the other, a strip of high grass between them. "But just so you understand, I was thinking of my family, too. I assumed you were an enemy to the McNeills when the investigator wanted to ask you about the blackmail scheme. I didn't believe that for long. And if I'd had more time to think about it, I would have known you'd never hurt my family."

She thought about that, trying to see things from his perspective. Wondering where all of this was leading.

"So you want to call a truce? Shake hands before I leave and part on amiable terms?" She stopped walking, needing answers. "Please tell me what you hoped to accomplish by following me out here, Brock, because—in spite of what you think—I have no love for secrets. I'd prefer we speak plainly. Put our cards on the table."

Behind them, Aurora stopped to nuzzle through some grass. Hannah watched her because it was easier than looking at Brock, with his dark whiskers shadowing his jaw. She had too many memories of last night every time their eyes met.

"You want it plainly," he said. "Here it is."

She felt the soft brush of flower petals against her cheek as he encouraged her gaze. When she turned to see him, he tucked the stalk of Indian paintbrush in her pocket.

"I let one bad relationship color the way that I saw you, Hannah, and I'm sorry." He stepped closer as they faced off across the tall grass. "I pride myself on never making the same mistake twice, though, so if you could ever find it in your heart to forgive me and give me another chance, I promise I'd never hurt you that way again."

A bird chirped an optimistic song overhead, urging her to take a chance. To feel hope, and maybe even happiness.

The pull was so damn strong. Brock looked at her like she was the only woman in the world who mattered to him. The temptation to believe him, believe in the two of them together, was heady stuff.

"Let's suppose for a second that I did that. I said,

okay, we'll try again." Her chest filled with too many feelings just saying the words aloud. Talking to him about this was like lifting the lid on Pandora's box and she was afraid she'd never be able to leave once the conversation started. She shook her head, willing her voice to stay strong. "What would that even look like? Hope lives in Los Angeles and she needs me there. You're a successful rancher with livestock and family who need you here. I just don't see a way to try."

And even as she said it, she found herself hoping he had the answer to make it all work. She couldn't deny that she wanted him in her life.

Brock lifted her hands, taking one in each of his. "Those are logistics. We can work around those. And if it came down to you and Hope wanting to be on the West Coast, I will gladly find a way to be there with you. The quarter horse program won't end if I leave the ranch."

"You would do that for me?" She thought about it for a moment, trying to picture that.

"Without a second thought."

"I never really thought about moving Hope here, though. She might actually be open to a fresh start."

The months of therapy hadn't helped. Maybe a move would give her sister a chance to heal.

"We don't need to decide today. I can fly back and forth until you're sure. But, Hannah, I promise, we could make it work." He squeezed her hands gently in his. "Maybe you could start by calling your sister. See if she wants to visit Cheyenne, just as soon as we get that bastard Ventura off McNeill lands forever."

"I'd like that. And I think Hope would, too." Hannah wanted to close her eyes and hold that vision tight. Hope here with her, finding peace in this beautiful land while she grew strong again. Except if Hannah closed her eyes, then she wouldn't be looking up into the eyes of the man she loved, and she wanted to keep that vision, too.

"Like I said, those are things we can figure out as we go. What matters is if we want to—that is, if *you* want to—try. I already know how badly I want to." He kissed the back of one hand. Then the other. "I'm in love with you, Hannah."

His words shot through her confusion with the precision of Cupid's arrow. The intensity in his blue eyes made her breathless.

"I'm in love with you, too," she admitted, shaking her head, the worries sliding away in light of that one simple fact. "That's why this all was hurting so much."

Relinquishing her hands, Brock wrapped his arms around her and pulled her against him. The tightness in her chest eased, giving away to the warmth of a happiness so full and sweet she thought she might overflow with it.

"I don't want to ever hurt you again," he promised, kissing her hair, her forehead and then, tilting her chin up, her lips. "I'll do whatever it takes to make you happy, and to help keep your sister safe."

She smiled against him, her teeth nudging his as a happy laugh bubbled up. "I trust you to keep that promise."

She wound her arms around his neck, pressing herself fully to him, giving herself over to the kiss.

They lost themselves in it, mouths moving together, until they were both breathless, the promise of a future together stoking passion higher inside her. She gripped his shirt, certain of what she wanted.

A forever with Brock McNeill.

He eased away slowly, tipping his forehead to hers.

"So we are in agreement." He stroked her shoulders, warming her all over with one simple touch.

"Perfectly. I'm going to call Hope just as soon as we get home." She wanted to phone Scarlett, too. She had the feeling Brock's sister was going to be an amazing champion for Hope's cause. "Maybe we can go on horseback?"

Her gaze slid to Aurora, remembering that first night with Brock.

His wicked chuckle told her that he remembered every delicious detail, too.

Epilogue

Nine months later

Hannah's bags were packed. She finished zipping one of the designer suitcases that Brock had given her for Christmas, her brain full of lists and preparations for her first week away from Hope since her sister had moved to Cheyenne with her last fall.

"Are you sure you have everything?" Hope asked from her seat at Hannah's dressing table, where she'd plopped herself with her tablet to oversee the packing. Hope had been working on a screenplay for the past two months, her thirst for writing returning in what her therapist called a good sign of her emotional recovery. "That doesn't look like enough luggage for a Hollywood movie premiere and a vacation in wine country. You're living the McNeill lifestyle now, Hannah. You deserve some extra luxuries," she teased.

Hannah looked into her sister's eyes, grateful every day she saw the spark of happiness flaming brighter and brighter there. Of course, Hannah had a lot to be grateful for lately. Antonio Ventura was facing prison on harassment and molestation charges. To date, over fifty women—including Hannah's friend Callie—had come forward to add their voices to the case after Brock's stepmother had shared her story with the police.

Hope hadn't wanted to share hers publicly yet, and the therapist said they needed to respect her journey. Hope told Hannah she felt vindicated enough that he was behind bars, and she seemed to be thriving in Cheyenne, taking a part-time job exercising horses at the Creek Spill while she completed college classes online. She'd talked about returning to campus next fall, but for now, she had her own suite in Brock and Hannah's home.

"I just don't have the diva instinct, I guess." Hannah had found a joy in the simpler rhythm of the days on the ranch, developing a special affinity for the cowboy boots that had been Brock's "housewarming" present for her when she agreed to move in.

Like Hope, she found plenty to keep her busy helping out with Brock's quarter horses, especially keeping the website updated with photos of the animals in training, and tracking each animal's progress for interested buyers. Brock had said those stories had led to more and better sales for the ranch, so she was contributing. But like her sister, she was contemplating a second act. For Hannah, it might be in producing. She had a strong interest in bringing female-driven stories to the big screen, and it was a job that would give her flexibility, too. Something she'd need for the family she and Brock had talked about.

Hope shut off the screen on her tablet and set it on

the dressing table, folding one foot underneath her. "It's funny that you—a former Hollywood actress—moved to Cheyenne and forgot how to be a diva. While Scarlett—a rancher's daughter—moved to Hollywood and has made a name for herself as the Diva Cowgirl."

Hope was referencing Scarlett's popular social media account that had attracted followers around the globe. Scarlett and Logan King were still a hot item, and Scarlett's date nights always made great photo ops. If Brock wanted to know what his youngest sister was up to, he asked Hope, who could show him up-to-the-minute photos from Scarlett's account.

But there was far more to the Diva Cowgirl than great clothes and glitter makeup. Scarlett had been instrumental in Antonio Ventura's downfall, leading the charge against him in the media. Hannah loved her dearly.

"Diva or not, you'll notice she still comes home most weekends," Hannah reminded her, wanting to plant it in Hope's head that she could return to Cheyenne as often as she liked if she decided to move back to Los Angeles.

"That's mostly because of Charlotte," Hope added, sniffing one of Hannah's perfume bottles. "She's gaga over Cody and Jillian's new baby girl."

Their child was a double blessing since Jillian was a breast cancer survivor who had thought she'd never have children. Mother and baby were both thriving, and shortly after Charlotte had been born, Emma and Carson announced they were expecting, too. Emma had been glowing with happiness when they'd revealed the news over a Sunday dinner with most of the Cheyenne branch of the McNeill family.

Sadly, Emma's mother had turned out to be Paige's blackmailer, but Jane Layton had been found unfit to stand trial and, according to Emma, seemed more at peace now that she was receiving additional care for previously undiagnosed mental health issues.

"Of course she's thrilled. We're all excited for the baby," Hannah agreed just as Brock stepped into her bedroom.

"Who's having a baby?" Brock asked, dressed in a blue suit and white shirt with no tie, more handsome than any Hollywood leading actor, in her opinion.

But then, this was the man who made her heart beat faster with just a look. Like the one he was giving her now. The one that said they shared a secret. Hannah felt warm all over and was grateful when Hope answered for her.

"We're talking about your brother's new baby. Charlotte is too adorable for words, and I think I'll go visit her if you two can ever get out the door to catch your flight." Hope hopped to her feet, heading for Hannah's luggage. "Want me to carry a bag down?"

Laughing, Brock strode past her, gently taking the bag from her hands. "Not a chance. One of the stable workers is going to load the car for me and drive us to the airfield."

"Really?" Hope looked interested and headed for the door. "I hope it's Chad. He's the cutest." She was already hurrying down the hall to look out the front window.

"Are you ready, Hannah, my love?" Brock asked, taking both her hands in his and helping her to her feet. "Are you prepared to go see the premiere of *Winning the West*?"

The production company had done extensive reshooting of the film after Antonio was fired as the director. Hannah had to admire that they hadn't wanted their name—or the film—tainted by association, so she'd stuck it out and reshot her scenes with the new director.

"Now that I'm officially proud to have my name attached to it, yes." She stood in front of him, letting her body graze his, tempting them both with what they would share tonight. "Mostly, I'm looking forward to having you all to myself for a few days."

"How am I going to keep my hands off you in the car ride to the airstrip?" he whispered in her ear, releasing her hand so he could splay one of his along her back.

"Not to mention on the plane." She eased back a step, her arms looped around his neck. "Maybe I'd better behave."

"The plane won't be a problem," Brock assured her. "Didn't I mention we're taking my grandfather's private jet?"

The McNeill patriarch continued to be generous to his Wyoming relatives, flying them all to his spring wedding to Rose Hanson. Hannah had never attended a more romantic ceremony than the union of the dapper octogenarian to the feisty former Harlem torch singer. They were a perfect match.

Hannah smiled, toying with the hair at the nape of his neck. "You didn't say one word about a private jet, Brock McNeill, or I would have remembered."

"It's the first of many surprises I've got planned for you this week," he assured her, his gaze dropping to her lips before he slanted his mouth over hers and kissed her with slow, heart-melting thoroughness.

She would have forgotten about the trip if he had kept going. He still did that to her.

"Do you want to see another one of the surprises?" he asked.

Intrigued, she angled away from him to see his expression. His blue eyes were full of warmth. Love.

He'd kept his promise to make her happy, that's for sure.

"Okay," she said. "Yes."

He reached into his jacket pocket and withdrew a small, velvet box.

Her heart did a backflip. Her gaze was glued to this unexpected gift.

"I think we've really covered the logistics of being together," he told her, his voice serious. Sincere.

"Me, too." Breathless, she remembered that conversation with him nine months ago when she'd first trusted him with her heart.

"These months with you have been the happiest of my life, Hannah. I can't imagine spending another minute without you, knowing how much I want to be with you forever. How much I want to have a family with you." He dropped to one knee in front of her and opened the box as he took her left hand. "Will you make me the happiest man ever and marry me?"

She wasn't sure if the tears in her eyes were making the round diamond look like a huge, glowing crystal ball, or if it was simply that magnificent. But it seemed to emit a light all its own, sparkling with promise in a simple platinum band.

There wasn't a single doubt in her mind.

"Brock, you've made my dreams come true." She wrapped her arms around him again, dragging him to his feet so they could hold each other. She laughed and cried and kissed him all at the same time. "Yes, I can't wait to marry you."

She felt the sigh of relief rocking through him as he

hauled her to his chest. His heart beat fast, too, letting her know just how important this was to him. Their love was a deep, incredible gift. They held each other close for a long moment.

From outside the bedroom, Hannah heard a car horn and her sister shout that their ride was here. Hannah didn't move, though. Not yet. She kissed Brock again with all the love in her heart, knowing their story together was only beginning.

* * * * *